Murder Most Celtic

Tall Tales of Irish Mayhem

Edited by
Martin H. Greenberg

Cumberland House
Nashville, Tennessee

Published by Cumberland House Publishing, Inc., 431 Harding Industrial Drive, Nashville, TN 37211

Cover design by Gore Studio, Inc.
Text design by Mike Towle

Library of Congress Cataloging-in-Publication Data
Murder most Celtic : tall tales of Irish mayhem / edited by Martin H. Greenberg.
    p. cm.
   ISBN 1-58182-161-1 (alk. paper)
   1. Detective and mystery stories, American. 2. Ireland--Fiction. I. Greenberg, Martin Harry.
  PS648.D4 M8753 2001
  813'.08720832417--dc21

                                        2001017264

1 2 3 4 5 6 7 8 9—06 05 04 03 02 01

CONTENTS

Introduction

WRITING INTRODUCTIONS IS USUALLY just a matter of research. Whether the theme is the medieval period, the Civil War, or, one of my personal favorites, food, a simple peek in an encyclopedia or a quick surf online is all that is needed to gather the necessary information.

Fate and fortune occasionally come together to produce a remarkable circumstance that is to everyone's advantage. Like this book, for example. As soon as I had returned from a week's stay on the glorious Emerald Isle, I was given the assignment to begin work on this project. At last, after writing dozens of introductions for books on subjects less familiar to me, I finally would be able to use firsthand experience to illustrate the theme of this collection. I would also have the pleasure of revisiting all that it is about Ireland that makes it so attractive to so many visitors.

Start with the landscape. Ireland is a land of amazing contrasts. From the rugged, wind-hewn majesty of the Cliffs of Mohr and the savage storms that blow on the coast to the gentle fog-shrouded hillocks and villages of the Midlands, Ireland is a study in both beauty and hostility. Peaks and mountains of slate thrust out of a starkly beautiful land to create beautiful, sun-dappled valleys. Nestled there are centuries-old towns and hamlets, where the local residents go about their lives in much the same way as did their ancestors before them. From the River Corrib winding its merry way through the city of Galway to the majestic ruins of the ancient cathedral at Cashel Rock rising over the countryside, Ireland is a land rich in tradition and a place where the people embrace their past as well as their present.

The people of Ireland are friendly, generous, and always willing to share themselves and their culture. Being among the Irish for just a few days makes it easy to understand where they get their reputation for cheerfulness and goodwill. Whether hoisting a pint in the local pub of an eighteenth-century manor house or taking up arms against enemy aggressors trying to assert their rule, the Irish are a unique people who live their lives to the fullest, no matter the circumstances.

Which brings us to the other aspect of this collection—murder. At first glance, it is hard to see how any Irishman or Irishwoman would ever bother with something so heinous. But it should also be remembered that the Irish are deeply passionate about their kinsmen, their country, their culture, and their way of life. Slow to anger and, at times, equally slow to forgive, the Irish have always been drawn to more than their fair share of, shall we say, "high-spirited activity," some of it illegal. From the revolutionaries of the Easter Rebellion to Irish mobs of the 1930s to the equally driven Irish-American policemen of the same era, the Emerald Isle's children have had plenty of experience tasting life on both sides of the law.

In this book we've assembled sixteen top mystery writers and asked them to write or contribute crime and mystery stories featuring men and women for whom being Irish is more than just a state of mind; it's a way of life. Whether it's ancient history or the modern day, the Irish prove that any time can be right for crime. Peter Tremayne's Sister Fidelma makes another welcome appearance as she gets to the bottom of a baffling case of theft and murder. Jeremiah Healy's sleuth John Cuddy investigates the disappearance of a book on Irish heritage and, along the way, discovers the close ties that bind Irish families. Brendan DuBois tells of a man whose passion for his heritage is so strong, he'll kill to protect it. From mystery master Clark Howard comes a tale of passion, revenge, and wrong choices set against the backdrop of hardscrabble Dublin. And we have Simon Clark's haunting story of a man who is forced to solve a murder to save his own life and discovers that nowhere do the waters run as deep as they do around Ireland.

The sixteen stories of Irish mystery collected here run the gamut from good men and women to bad—heroes and villains both. So raise a glass of Guinness (or any good Irish whiskey), stoke the fire, and indulge yourself in these stories of *Murder Most Celtic*.

—*John Helfers*

MURDER MOST CELTIC

Scattered Thorns

(A Sister Fidelma Mystery)

Peter Tremayne

"THE BOY IS INNOCENT."

The chief magistrate of Droim Sorn, Brehon Tuama, seemed adamant.

Sister Fidelma sat back in her chair and gazed thoughtfully at the tall man who was seated on the other side of the hearth. She had received an urgent request from Brehon Tuama to come to the small township of Droim Sorn in her capacity as *dálaigh*, advocate of the law courts. A sixteen-year-old lad named Braon had been accused of murder and theft. Brehon Tuama had suggested that Fidelma should undertake the boy's defence

In accordance with protocol, Fidelma had first made her presence in the township known to the chieftain, Odar, in whose house the boy was being held. Odar seemed to display a mixed reaction to her arrival but had offered her a few formal words of welcome before suggesting that she seek out Brehon Tuama to discuss the details of the case. She had decided, on this brief acquaintance, that Odar was not a man particularly concerned with details. She had noticed that the chieftain

1

had an impressive array of hunting weapons on his walls and two sleek wolfhounds basking in front of his hearth. She deduced that Odar's concerns were more of the hunt than pursuit of justice.

Brehon Tuama had invited her inside his house and offered her refreshment before making his opening remark about the accused's guilt.

"Are you saying that the boy is not to be tried?" asked Fidelma. "If you have already dismissed the case against him, why was I summoned . . .?"

Brehon Tuama quickly shook his head.

"I cannot dismiss the matter yet. Odar is adamant that the boy has to go through due process. In fact . . ." The Brehon hesitated. "The victim's husband is his cousin."

Fidelma sighed softly. She disliked nepotism.

"Perhaps you should explain to me the basic facts as you know them."

Brehon Tuama stretched uneasily in his chair.

"Findach the Smith is reputed to be one of the most able craftsmen in this township. His work is apparently widely admired and has graced abbeys, chieftains' raths, and kings' fortresses. He has been able to refuse such mundane tasks as shoeing horses, making harnesses, ploughs, and weapons, to pursue more artistic work."

"It sounds as though you do not share others' appreciation of his work?" interposed Fidelma, catching the inflection in his tone.

"I don't," agreed the Brehon. "But that is by the way. Findach was commissioned to make a silver cross for the high altar of the Abbey of Cluain. He had completed the commission only a few days ago.

"The cross was extremely valuable. Findach had polished it and taken it to his house ready for collection by one of the religious from the abbey. Yesterday morning, Findach had gone to his workshop, which is a hundred yards beyond his house, to commence work. The silver cross was left in his house. His wife, Muirenn, was there.

"It was that morning that Brother Caisín had been sent by the Abbot of Cluain to collect the cross. I have questioned Brother Caisín who says that he arrived at Findach's house early in the morning. He noticed that the door was open and he went in. Muirenn lay on the floor with blood on her head. He tried to render assistance but found that she was dead, apparently killed by a sharp blow to the head.

"Brother Caisín then said that he heard a noise from a side room and found the boy, Braon, hiding there. There was blood on his clothes.

"It was then that Findach arrived back at his house and found Brother Caisín and Braon standing by the body of his wife. His cry of anguish was heard by a passerby who, ascertaining the situation, came in search of me as Brehon of Droim Sorn."

Fidelma was thoughtful.

"At what point was it discovered the silver cross was missing?" she asked.

Brehon Tuama looked surprised.

"How did you know that it was the silver cross that had been stolen? The object of the theft was not specified when I sent for you."

Fidelma made an impatient gesture with her hand.

"I did not think that you would spend so much time and detail telling me about Findach's commission from Cluain if it had no relevance to this matter."

Brehon Tuama looked crestfallen.

"What did the boy have to say?" Fidelma continued. "I presume the boy's father was sent for before you questioned him?"

Brehon Tuama looked pained.

"Of course. I know the law. As he was under the 'age of choice,' his father is deemed responsible for him in law."

"So the father was summoned and the boy was questioned?" pressed Fidelma impatiently.

"The boy said that he had been asked to go to Findach's house by Muirenn, who often used to employ him to look after a small herd of cattle they kept in the upper pastures behind the house. Braon said he found the door open. He saw the body and went inside in order to help, but Muirenn was already dead."

"And bending by the body accounted for blood on his clothes?"

"Precisely. He said that he was about to go for help when he heard someone approaching. Fearing the return of the killer, he hid in the room where Brother Caisín discovered him."

"And those are all the facts, so far as you know them?"

"Exactly. It is all circumstantial evidence. I would be inclined to dismiss the charge for lack of evidence. However, Odar insists that the boy should be prosecuted. A chieftain's orders are sometimes difficult to disregard," he added apologetically.

"What about the cross?"

Brehon Tuama was baffled for a moment.

"I mean," went on Fidelma, "where was it found? You have not mentioned that fact."

The Brehon shifted his weight.

"It has not been found," he confessed.

Fidelma made her surprise apparent.

"We made a thorough search for the cross and found no sign of it," confirmed Brehon Tuama.

"Surely, that further weakens the case against the boy? When could he have the time to hide the cross before being discovered by Brother Caisín?"

"Odar argues that he must have had an accomplice. He favours the boy's father. He suggests the boy passed the cross to his accomplice just as Brother Caisín arrived."

"A rather weak argument." Fidelma was dismissive. "What I find more interesting is the motivation for your chieftain's apparent determination to pursue the boy and his father. You tell me that it is because the dead woman's husband is his cousin? That does not seem sufficient justification. I would agree with your first conclusion, Tuama. The whole affair is based on circumstantial evidence. By the way, how big was this silver cross?"

"I do not know. We would have to ask Findach. Findach said it was valuable enough. The silver alone being worth . . ."

"I am more interested in its size, not value. Presumably, a high altar cross would be of large size and therefore of great weight?"

"Presumably," agreed the Brehon.

"Also too heavy, surely, for the boy, Braon, to have hidden it by himself?"

Brehon Tuama did not reply.

"You say that Findach's forge was a hundred yards from his house. Isn't it unusual for a smith to have a workshop at such a distance from his house?"

Brehon Tuama shook his head.

"Not in this case. Findach was a careful man. Do you know how often smiths' forges burn down because a spark from the furnace ignites them?"

"I have known of some cases," admitted Fidelma. "So Findach and his wife Muirenn lived in the house. Did they have children?"

"No. There was just the two of them . . ."

There was a sudden noise outside and the door burst open.

A wild-looking, broad-shouldered man stood on the threshold. He was dressed in the manner of a man who worked long hours in the fields. His eyes were stormy.

Brehon Tuama sprang up from his seat in annoyance.

"What is the meaning of this, Brocc?" he demanded.

The man stood breathing heavily a moment.

"You know well enough, Brehon. I heard that the *dálaigh* had arrived. She's been to see Odar and now you. Yet you told me that she was coming to defend my boy. Defend? How can she defend him when she consorts only with his persecutors?"

Fidelma examined the man coolly.

"Come forward! So you are the father of Braon?"

The burly man took a hesitant step toward her.

"My son is innocent! You must clear his name. They are trying to lay the blame on my son and on me because they hate us."

"I am here to listen to the evidence and form my opinion. Why would people hate you and your son?"

"Because I am a *bothach*!"

In the social system of the five kingdoms of Éireann, the *bothach* was one of the lowest classes in society, being a crofter or cowherder. Bethachs had no political or clan rights, but they were capable of acquiring their own plots of land by contract. While there were no restrictions placed on whom they could work for, they were not allowed to leave the clan territory except by special permission. If they worked well, they could eventually expect to acquire full citizen's rights.

"Aye," Brocc was bitter. "It is always the lower orders who are blamed when a crime is committed. Always the bottom end of the social scale who get the blame. That is why Odar is trying to make out that my boy and I were in league to rob Findach."

Fidelma was beginning to understand what Brehon Tuama had been trying to tell her about Odar's insistence that Braon stand trial.

"You and your son have nothing to fear so long as you tell the truth," she said, trying not to let it sound like a platitude. "If I believe your son is innocent then I will defend him." Fidelma paused for a moment. "You realise that under the law it will be your responsibility to pay the compensation and fines if your son is found guilty? Are you more concerned about that or whether your son is innocent?"

Brocc scowled, his features reddening.

"That is unjust. I will pay you seven séds if you simply defend him. That is a token of my faith in my son."

The sum was the value of seven milch cows.

Fidelma's face showed that she was not impressed.

"Brehon Tuama should have informed you that my fees, which are payable directly to my community and not to me, do not vary but stand at two séds and only change when they are remitted because of exceptional circumstances such as the poverty of those who seek my assistance."

Brocc stood uncertainly with lips compressed. Fidelma went on:

"Since you are here, Brocc, you may tell me a little about your son, Braon. Did he frequently work for Findach?"

"Not for Findach, that mean . . . !" Brocc caught himself. "No, my boy worked for his wife Muirenn. Muirenn was a kindly soul, a good soul. My boy would never have harmed her."

"How often did he work for Muirenn and in what capacity?"

"My boy and I are cowherds. We hire our labour to those who need an expert hand."

"So you knew Braon was going to work for Muirenn that morning?"

"I did. She had asked him to tend her cows in the pasture above the house."

"And that was a usual task for him?"

"Usual? It was."

"Did anyone else know he was going to Muirenn's house this morning?"

"The boy's mother knew and doubtless Muirenn told that mean husband of hers."

Fidelma was interested.

"Why do you call Findach mean?"

"The man was tightfisted. It was well known. He behaved as if he was as poor as a church mouse."

Fidelma glanced to Brehon Tuama for confirmation. The tall magistrate shrugged.

"It is true that Findach was not renowned for his generosity, Sister. He always claimed he had little money. The truth was he spent a lot on gambling. In fact, only the other day Odar told me that Findach owed him a large sum. Ten *séds*, as I recall. Yet Findach would not even employ an assistant or an apprentice at his forge."

"Yet he did pay for help with his cow herd."

Brocc laughed harshly.

"The herd was his wife's property and she paid my son."

A wife, under law, remained the owner of all the property and wealth that she brought into a marriage. Fidelma appreciated the point.

"So, as far as you knew, your son went off to work as usual. You noticed nothing unusual at all?"

"I did not."

"And during that day, you never went near Findach's house nor his forge?"

"Nowhere near."

"You can prove it?"

Brocc glowered for a moment.

"I can prove it. I was in Lonán's pastures helping him thresh hay. I was there until someone came with the news of Braon's arrest."

"Very well." Fidelma rose abruptly. "I think I would like to see Findach's house and speak with this renowned smith."

The house of Findach the Smith stood on the edge of the township. It was isolated among a small copse of hazel and oak.

Findach was a stocky, muscular man of indiscernible age. He had a short neck and a build that one associated with a smith. He gazed distastefully at Fidelma.

"If you seek to defend my wife's killer, *dálaigh*, you are not welcome in this house." His voice was a low growl of anger.

Fidelma was not perturbed.

"Inform Findach of the law and my rights as a *dálaigh*, Tuama," she instructed, her eyes not leaving those of the smith's.

"You are obliged by law to answer all the *dálaigh's* questions and allow free access to all . . ."

Findach cut the Brehon short with a scowl and turned abruptly inside the house, leaving them to follow.

Fidelma addressed herself to Brehon Tuama.

"Show me where the body was lying."

Tuama pointed to the floor inside the first room, which was the kitchen.

"And where was the boy found?"

Findach answered this time, turning and pushing open a door sharply.

"The killer was hiding in here," he grunted.

"I understand that you knew that Brother Caisín would be arriving to collect the silver cross you had made for his abbey?"

Findach glanced at Brehon Tuama who stood stony faced. Then he shrugged. His voice was ungracious.

"I expected someone from the abbey to come to collect the piece. It was the agreed day."

"You brought the cross from your forge to the house. Wasn't that unusual?"

"I brought it here for safekeeping. There is no one at my forge at night and so I do not leave valuable items there."

"How valuable was this cross?"

"My commission price was twenty-one *séds*."

"Describe the cross, its weight and size."

"It was of silver mined at Magh Meine. Just over a metre in height and half of that across the arms. It was heavy. The only way I could carry it was by means of a rope slung across my back."

"Brother Caisín was to carry it in the same fashion?"

"I believe he arrived on an ass, realising the weight to be transported."

"And where did you leave the cross?"

"It was standing in that corner of the room."

Fidelma went and looked at the corner that he indicated.

"You believe that the boy, Braon, came into your house, saw this cross, killed your wife, and took it, as heavy as it was, and then—presumably having hidden it—returned to this house? Having done that, hearing the arrival of Brother Caisín, he then hid himself in that room, where he was discovered."

Findach scowled at her smile of skepticism.

"How else do you explain it?"

"I don't have to, as yet. What time did you leave that morning to go to your forge?"

Findach shrugged.

"Just after dawn."

"Did you know that boy was coming to help with your wife's herd?"

"I knew. I never trusted him. His father was a *bothach*, always cadging money from the better off."

"I understand that you were not one of them." Fidelma's riposte caused Findach's face to go red.

"I don't know what you mean," he said defensively.

"I heard that you were regarded as poor."

"Silver and gold costs money. When I get a commission, I have to find the metals and don't get paid until the commission is complete."

"Braon had worked for your wife often before, hadn't he?" Fidelma changed the subject.

"He had."

"And you had no cause to complain about him before? Surely you have left valuable items in your house on other occasions?"

"My wife is murdered. The silver cross is gone. The boy was a *bothach*."

"So you imply that you were always suspicious of him? As you say, he was a *bothach*. Yet you left the silver cross in your house and went to the forge. Isn't that strange?"

Findach flushed in annoyance.

"I did not suspect that he would be tempted . . ."

"Quite so," snapped Fidelma. She turned to Brehon Tuama. "I suppose that you have asked Brother Caisín to remain in Droim Sorn until the case is concluded?"

"Indeed, I have. Much to his annoyance. But I have sent a message to his abbot to explain the circumstances."

"Excellent." Fidelma swung round to Findach. "Now, I would like to see your forge."

Findach was astonished.

"I do not understand what relevance . . . ?"

Fidelma smiled mischievously.

"You do not have to understand, only to respond to my questions. I understand the forge is a hundred yards from here?"

Findach bit his lip and turned silently to lead the way.

The forge lay one hundred yards through the trees in a small clearing.

"The furnace is out," observed Fidelma as they entered.

"Of course. I have not worked here since yesterday morning."

"Obviously," Fidelma agreed easily. Then, surprising both Findach and Brehon Tuama, she thrust her right hand into the grey charcoal of the brazier. After a moment, she withdrew her hand and without any comment went to the *umar* or water trough to wash the dirt off. As she did so, she surveyed the *cartha*, the term used for a forge. It was unusual for a forge to be so isolated from the rest of the township. Smiths and their forges were usually one of the important centres of a district, often well frequented. Findach seemed to read her mind.

"I am a craftsman only in silver and gold these days. I do not make harnesses, shoe horses, nor fix farm implements. I make works of art."

His voice possessed arrogance, a boastfulness.

She did not answer.

The great anvil stood in the centre of the forge, near the blackened wood-charcoal-filled brazier and next to the water trough. A box containing the supply of wood charcoal stood nearby ready for fueling the fire. There was a bellows next to the brazier.

"Do you have examples of your work here?" she asked, peering round.

Findach shook his head.

"I have closed down my forge out of respect to my wife. Once this matter is cleared up . . ."

"But you must have moulds, casts . . . pieces you have made?"

Findach shook his head.

"I was just curious to see the work of a smith who is so renowned for his fine work. However, to the task at hand. I think, Brehon Tuama, I shall see the boy now."

They retraced their steps to Odar's house. The chieftain was out hunting, but his tanist, his heir apparent, led them to the room where the accused boy was held.

Braon was tall for his sixteen years. A thin, pale boy, fair of skin and freckled. There was no sign that he had yet begun to shave. He stood up nervously before Fidelma.

Fidelma entered the room while Brehon Tuama, by agreement, stayed outside as, under law, if she were to defend the boy, it was her privilege to see him alone. She waved him to be seated again on the small wooden bed while she herself sat on a stool before him.

"You know who I am?" she asked.

The boy nodded.

"I want you to tell me your story in your own words."

"I have already told the Brehon."

"The Brehon is to sit in judgment on you. I am a *dálaigh* who will defend you. So tell me."

The young boy seemed nervous.

"What will happen to me?"

"That depends if you are guilty or innocent."

"No one cares if a *bothach* is innocent when there is a crime to be answered for."

"That is not what the law says, Braon. The law is there to protect the innocent whoever they are and to punish the guilty whoever they may be. Do you understand?"

"That is not how Odar sees it," replied the boy.

"Tell me the events of that morning when you went to work for Muirenn," Fidelma said, thinking it best not to pursue the matter of Odar's prejudice.

"I did not kill her. She was always kind to me. She was not like her husband, Findach. He was mean, and I heard her reprimanding him often about that. He claimed that he did not have money but everyone knows that smiths have money."

"Tell me what happened that morning."

"I arrived at the house and went inside . . ."

"One moment. Was there anything out of the usual? Was there anyone about, so far as you saw?"

The boy shook his head thoughtfully.

"Nothing out of the usual. I saw no one, except for Odar's hunting dogs . . . he has two big wolfhounds. I saw them bounding into the woods by Findach's forge. But there was no one about. So I went to the house and found the door ajar. I called out and, receiving no answer, I pushed it open."

"What did you see?"

"From the open door I could see a body on the floor of the kitchen beyond. It was Muirenn. I thought she had fallen, perhaps struck her head. I bent down and felt her pulse, but the moment my hand touched her flesh I could feel a chill on it. I knew that she was dead."

"The flesh felt chilled?"

"It did."

"What then?" she prompted.

"I stood up and . . ."

"A moment. Did you see any sign of the silver cross in the room?"

"It was not there. Something as unusual as that I would have noticed even in such circumstances. In fact, I was looking round when I heard a noise. Someone was approaching. I panicked and hid myself in an adjoining room." He hesitated. "The rest you must know. Brother Caisín came in and discovered me. There was blood on my clothes where I had touched Muirenn. No one listened, and hence I am accused of theft and murder. Sister, I swear to you that I never saw such a cross nor would I have killed Muirenn. She was one of the few people here who did not treat me as if I were beneath contempt!"

Fidelma found it difficult to question the sincerity in the boy's voice.

She joined Brehon Tuama outside.

"Well?" asked the Brehon morosely. "Do you see the difficulty of this case?"

"I have seen the difficulty ever since you explained it to me," she replied shortly. "However, let us now find this Brother Caisín and see what he has to say."

"He has accommodation in the hostel."

They went to the town's *bruighean*, which was situated in the centre of Droim Sorn and provided accommodation and hospitality to whoever sought it there.

Brother Caisín was well built and, in spite of his robes, Fidelma noticed that he was muscular and more of a build associated with a warrior than that of a religieux. It was when she examined his features that she found herself distrusting the man. His eyes were close set in the narrow face, shifty and not focusing on his questioner. The lips were too thin, the nose narrow and hooked. He spoke with a soft, lisping voice that seemed at odds with his build. The line from *Juvenal* came to her mind: *fronti nulla fides*—no reliance can be placed on appearance.

"Brother Caisín?"

Caisín glanced quickly at her and then at Brehon Tuama before dropping his gaze to focus on a point midway between them.

"I suppose you are the *dálaigh* from Cashel?"

"You suppose correctly. I am Fidelma of Cashel."

The man seemed to sigh and shiver slightly.

"I have heard of your reputation, Sister. You have a way of ferreting out information."

Fidelma smiled broadly.

"I am not sure whether you mean that as a compliment, Brother. I will accept it as such."

"I must tell you something before you discover it for yourself and place a wrong interpretation on it." The monk seemed anxious. "Have you heard of Caisín of Inis Geimhleach?"

Fidelma frowned and shook her head.

"I know Inis Geimhleach, the imprisoned island, a small settlement in Loch Allua, a wild and beautiful spot."

At her side, Brehon Tuama suddenly snapped his fingers with a triumphant exclamation.

"Caisín . . . I have heard the story. Caisín was a warrior turned thief! It was ten years ago that he was found guilty of stealing from the church there. He claimed that he had repented and went into the service of the church and disappeared . . ."

Brehon Tuama's voice trailed off. His eyes narrowed on the religieux before him.

"Caisín of Inis Geimhleach? Are you saying that you are that man?" Fidelma articulated the conclusion of his thoughts.

The monk bowed his head and nodded.

Brehon Tuama turned to Fidelma with a glance of satisfaction: "Then, Sister, we . . ."

Fidelma stilled him with a warning glance.

"So, Caisín, why do you confess this now?"

"I have paid penance for my crime and have continued to serve in the abbey of Cluain. You might discover this and leap to the wrong conclusion."

"So why did you not reveal this before when the Brehon questioned you?" she demanded.

Caisín flushed.

"One does not always do the correct thing at the correct time. This last day, I have had a chance to think more carefully. I realised it was foolish not to be completely honest even though it has nothing to do with the current matter."

Fidelma sighed.

"Well, your honesty does you credit in the circumstances. Tell me, in your own words, what happened when you discovered the body of Muirenn, the wife of the smith."

Caisín spread his arms in a sort of helpless gesture.

"There is nothing complicated about it. My abbot told me that some time ago he had commissioned a new silver cross for our high altar from Findach the Smith. I was instructed to come to Droim Sorn to collect it."

"How was payment to be made to Findach?" asked Fidelma.

Caisín looked bewildered.

"The abbot made no reference to payment. He simply asked me to come and collect the cross. As it was for the high altar, I understood it to be heavy, and so I asked permission to take one of the mules from the abbey. I had been to Droim Sorn before and so I knew where to find Findach's forge."

Fidelma glanced quickly at him.

"You went to the forge directly?"

"Oh yes. Where else would I go to collect the cross?"

"Where, indeed? What then?"

"Findach was at the forge, and when I arrived he told me that the cross was at his house and I should precede him there. He would join me once he had doused his furnace."

"Was anyone else at the forge when you arrived?"

"No . . . well, I did see a man riding away."

"I don't suppose you knew who it was?"

Brother Caisín surprised her by an affirmative nod.

"I recognised him later as Odar, the chieftain. He had his hunting dogs with him. I left Findach and went to the house. I arrived at the door. It was slightly ajar. I caught sight of clothing on the floor. I pushed the door open and then I realised the clothing was a body. It was a woman. I was standing there when I heard a noise beyond an interior door. I opened it and found the youth, Braon, hiding there. He had blood on his clothes and instinct made me grasp hold of him.

A moment later, Findach, who followed me from the forge, entered and cried out when he recognised the body of his wife. His cry brought someone else who ran to fetch Brehon Tuama. That is all I know."

Outside Brehon Tuama looked worried.

"Do you think he is being honest? Once a thief . . . ? Isn't it said that opportunity makes the thief, and this man had opportunity."

"Publilius Syrus once wrote that the stolen ox sometimes puts his head out of the stall," smiled Fidelma, mysteriously.

Brehon Tuama looked bewildered. Fidelma went on without enlightening him: "I am going to ride to Cluain to see the abbot. When I return I hope to have resolved this mystery."

Brehon Tuama's eyes lightened.

"Then you think that Caisín is responsible?"

"I did not say that."

Cluain, the meadow, was the site of an abbey and community founded by Colmán Mac Léníne some sixty years before. It was evening when she reached the abbey and demanded to be announced to the abbot immediately. The abbot received her without demur for he knew that Fidelma was also the sister of the young king of Cashel.

"You have come from Droim Sorn, lady?" asked the elderly abbot when they were seated. "I suppose that you wish to speak with me of Brother Caisín?"

"Why do you suppose that?"

"His background and the circumstances make him suspect in the murder and theft there. I have had word of the event from Brehon Tuama. Caisín is a good man in spite of his history. He came to this abbey ten years ago as a penitent thief. Like the penitent thief of the Bible, he was received with rejoicing and forgiveness and never once has he given us cause to question his redemption."

"You trusted him to go to Droim Sorn to bring back a valuable cross of silver."

"It was the new cross for our high altar."

"But you did not trust him with the money to pay for it, I understand."

The old man blinked rapidly.

"There was no payment to be made."

"You mean that Findach undertook to make this cross out of charity for the abbey?" Fidelma was puzzled.

The old abbot laughed, a slightly high-pitched laugh.

"Findach never gave anything out of charity. I should know for I was uncle to his wife Muirenn. He is an impecunious man. He made the cross for us in repayment for his indebtedness to the abbey."

Fidelma raised an eyebrow in query.

"Findach spent money like water. His wife owned the house in which he dwells and kept her own money as the law allows. In fact, all Findach owns is his forge and tools."

Fidelma leant forward quickly.

"You mean that Findach will benefit from his wife's wealth now that she is dead?"

The abbot smiled sadly and shook his head.

"He does not benefit at all. Half of her money is returned to her own family in accordance with the law. She was an *aire-echta* in her own right."

Fidelma was surprised, for it was not often that a smith's wife held an equal honour price to that of her husband.

The abbot continued: "She has bequeathed the residue of her property to this abbey in my name, for she knew how I had helped her husband over the years."

Fidelma hid her disappointment at being first presented and then deprived of another motive for the murder of Muirenn.

"Findach had been asked to make some artifact for Imleach; and rather than admit to the abbot of Imleach that he had no money to purchase the silver needed to make it, he asked me for a loan. When he later confessed he could not repay it, I offered to provide him with enough silver so that he could construct a cross for our high altar. His craftsmanship was to be the repayment."

"I am beginning to understand. I am told that Caisín had been to Droim Sorn before?"

"I sent him myself," agreed the abbot. "Last month I sent him to see Findach to remind him that the time to deliver the cross was approaching. He returned and told me that Findach had assured him that the cross would be ready at the appropriate time."

Fidelma, fretting at the delay, had to spend the night at Cluain, and rode back to Droim Sorn the following morning.

She was met by Brehon Tuama whose face mirrored some degree of excitement.

"It seems that we were both wrong, Sister. The boy, Braon, announced his guilt by attempting to escape."

Fidelma exhaled sharply in her annoyance.

"The stupid boy! What happened?"

"He climbed out of a window and fled into the forest. He was recaptured early this morning. Odar let loose his hunting dogs after him and it was a wonder that the boy was not ripped apart. We caught him just in time. Odar has now demanded the imprisonment of his father as an accomplice."

Fidelma stared at the Brehon.

"And you have agreed to this?"

Brehon Tuama spread his hands in resignation.

"What is there to be done? Whatever doubts I had before are now dispelled by the boy's own admission of guilt . . . his attempt to escape."

"Does it not occur to you that the boy attempted to escape out of fear rather than out of guilt?"

"Fear? What had he to fear if he was innocent?"

"He and his father seemed to fear that, as they are of the class of *bothach*, looked down on and despised by many of the free clansmen of this place, they would not be treated fairly," she snapped. "The law is there so that no one should fear any unjust action. I regret that Odar does not appreciate that fact."

Brehon Tuama sighed.

"Sadly, the law is merely that which is written on paper. It is human beings who interpret and govern the law, and often human beings are frail creatures full of the seven deadly sins that govern their little lives."

"Are you telling me the boy is again imprisoned at Odar's rath and is unhurt?"

"Bruised a little, but unhurt."

"*Deo gratias!* And the father?"

"He has been imprisoned in the barn behind the chief's house."

"Then let us go to the chief's house and have all those involved in this matter summoned. If, after hearing what I have to say, you feel that there is a necessity for a formal trial, so be it. But the boy is not guilty."

Half an hour later they were gathered in Odar's hall. Along with Odar and his tanist were Brehon Tuama, the boy, Braon, and his father, Brocc, with Findach and Brother Caisín.

Fidelma turned to Brocc first. Her voice was brusque.

"Although you are a *bothach*, you have worked hard and gathered enough valuables to soon be able to purchase your place as a full and free clansman here. Is that correct?"

Brocc was bewildered by her question, but gave an affirmative jerk of his head.

"You would be able to pay the honour price for the death of Muirenn, the compensation due for her unlawful killing?"

"If my son were judged guilty, yes."

"Indeed. For everyone knows that your son is under age. The payment of compensation and fines incurred by his action, if found guilty, falls to you."

"I understand that."

"Indeed you do. The law is well known." Fidelma turned to Findach. "Am I right in believing that your wife Muirenn was of the social rank of *aire echta*, and her honour price was ten *séds*—that is the worth of ten milch cows?"

"That is no secret," snapped Findach belligerently.

Fidelma swung round to Odar.

"And isn't that the very sum of money that Findach owed you?"

Odar coloured a little.

"What of it? I can lend money to my own kinsman if I wish to."

"You know that Findach is penniless. If Braon was found guilty, Findach would receive the very sum of money in compensation that he owed to you, perhaps more if the claim of theft to the value of twenty-one *séds* is proved as well. Would that have any influence on your insisting on the boy's prosecution?"

Odar rose to his feet, opening his mouth to protest, but Fidelma silenced him before he could speak.

"Sit down!" Fidelma's voice was sharp. "I speak here as *dálaigh* and will not be interrupted."

There was a tense silence before she continued.

"This is a sad case. There never was a cross of silver that was stolen, was there, Findach?"

The smith turned abruptly white.

"You are known to be a gambler, often in debt to people such as Odar . . . and to your wife's uncle, the abbot of Cluain. You are also lazy. Instead of pursuing the work you have a talent for, you prefer to borrow or steal so that you may gamble. You were in debt to your wife's uncle, and when he gave you silver to fashion a cross as a means of repaying him you doubtless sold that silver.

"Having sold the silver, you had no cross to give to the abbey of Cluain. You have not used your forge in days, perhaps weeks. Your furnace was as cold as the grave. And speaking of coldness . . . when Braon touched the body of Muirenn to see if he could help, he remarked the body was cold. Muirenn could not have been killed that morning after you left. She had been dead many hours."

Findach collapsed suddenly on his chair. He slumped forward, head held in his hands.

"Muirenn . . ." The word was a piteous groan.

"Why did you kill Muirenn?" pressed Fidelma. "Did she try to stop you from faking the theft of the cross?"

Findach raised his eyes. His expression was pathetic.

"I did not mean to kill her, just silence her nagging. Faking the theft was the only way I could avoid the debts . . . I hit her. I sat in the kitchen all night by her body wondering what I should do."

"And the idea came that you could claim that the silver cross, which you had never made, was stolen by the same person who murdered your wife? You knew that Braon was coming that morning and he was a suitable scapegoat." She turned to Brehon Tuama. "*Res ipsa loquitur*," she muttered, using the Latin to indicate that the facts spoke for themselves.

When Findach had been taken away and Braon and his father released, Brehon Tuama accompanied Fidelma as she led her horse to the start of the Cashel road.

"A bad business," muttered the Brehon. "We are all at fault here."

"I think that Odar's chiefship is worthy of challenge," agreed Fidelma. "He is not fit to hold that office."

"Was it luck that made you suspicious of Findach?" queried Tuama, nodding absently.

Sister Fidelma swung up into the saddle of her horse and glanced down at the Brehon with a smile.

"A good judge must never rely on luck in deduction. Findach tried to scatter thorns across the path of our investigation, hoping that the boy or Caisín would pierce their feet on them and be adjudged guilty. He should have remembered the old proverb: He that scatters thorns must not go barefooted."

The Wearing

of the Green

Brendan DuBois

I T WAS A COLD, wet morning in late September at Tyler Beach,
New Hampshire, and Sean P. Dumont stood by the picture window of his tiny home, looking out over the seawall and to the
great gray waters of the Atlantic. He stood still, strong hands behind
his back, like he was standing post again, like he had done for decades
as a security officer up at the Porter Naval Shipyard. He looked at the
waves, at the mist pooling and dripping down the picture window, and
sighed, wondering if this is what it looked like, on Galway Bay, over
there, thousands of miles away.

He had on worn khaki pants and a thick natural wool sweater,
sent over two years ago as a Christmas gift to himself from the great
O'Greery Sweater Company of Donnegal. He loved the sweater, imagined each time he wore it that he could smell the scents of the old sod,
the peat moss, the smell of the pub, the soft Irish sunshine on the
green hills. Tyler Beach was a summer resort, but he loved the fall and

21

winter the most, for that's when he imagined he could be back where his soul called to him, to Ireland.

He shifted from one foot to another, winced as his right knee twinged at him. The place was warm, and he was fortunate that even as small as the place was, it had a tiny gas fireplace in the living room. He usually didn't start a fire this early into fall, but the Atlantic was playing her usual tricks on the seacoast, and the fire felt so warm and nice. He tapped his fingers against each other, listening to the music that was playing on the CD player, just to the right of the fireplace. Tommy Makem and the Clancy Brothers were singing those old rollicking tunes, tunes that would usually make him tap his feet and whistle along as he bustled through another day of retirement.

But not today. Not today.

Traffic was fairly light on this afternoon, but he kept a close eye, a close eye indeed, and sure enough, there it was. A dark blue Ford Crown Victoria with a whip antenna on the trunk slowed down and parked across the street and was followed by a green and white Tyler police cruiser. Sean sighed. *So it begins*, he thought. The driver's door to the Crown Victoria swung open and a woman in a green parka came out and talked to a uniformed male police officer, who had emerged from the cruiser. He was wearing a bright orange raincoat that said TYLER POLICE in black letters on the rear. They conferred for a minute or two, looked right over at his home, and then crossed the road, one delivery truck going by close and spraying them with water as they made it to the sidewalk.

He rubbed his hands together, looked over at the door, and listened for the chime, which came just a few seconds after the two cops had made it to this side of the road. Sean shook his head and went to the door, opened it up.

"Mister Dumont?" the woman asked. She seemed to be in her mid-thirties, had short brown hair and a white scar on her chin. Over her shoulder she had a small black leather bag. "Mister Sean Dumont?"

"That's right," he said. "What can I do for you?"

She held out her hand, displayed a little black leather wallet with a gold shield in the center. "I'm Detective Diane Woods, with the Tyler Police Department. This is Officer Wrenn. We're working on a matter, and I was wondering if we could talk to you for a bit."

She seemed polite enough and the weather was miserable, so Sean backed away and said, "Certainly, come right in. Let me take your coats."

Within another minute, the green parka and the orange raincoat were on a wooden coatrack near the entranceway, and he seated them both on a couch that had a good view through the picture window of the beach, and where the fireplace could warm their feet. He took a simple wooden chair off to the side, after putting on a pot of water for a morning cup of tea.

"One of the few vices I have remaining," he said, crossing his legs, hearing the slight pop as a knee joint made its regular protest. "My morning and afternoon cups of tea. Are you sure I can't get you both anything?"

He noticed that the detective answered for them both, when she said, "No, we're just fine." While the detective had on blue jeans and a black turtleneck sweater, her companion was more formally dressed, with green uniform slacks and blouse, and heavy black boots. Officer Wrenn's blond hair was cut short and he had pale blue eyes, and Sean said, "Officer Wrenn, if I may?"

The officer looked over to the detective and received a slight nod in return. "Yes, what is it?"

"Your last name, it's quite Irish. Do you know where your ancestors came from?"

"Excuse me?" the cop said, and Sean immediately felt sorry for the lad. He smiled at the young man and said, "Your ancestors. Your great-grandparents. Which county in Ireland did they come from? Do you know?"

The cop smiled. "Not a clue."

"A pity," Sean said.

The detective spoke up. "If you don't mind, Mister Dumont. We're looking into something that happened in Tyler last night, and we're looking for your help. If that's all right."

Sean shrugged. "Go right ahead."

She crossed her legs, leaned forward a bit. At her feet was her small black leather bag. "The Black Rose. You're familiar with it, aren't you?"

"Of course," Sean said. "It's an Irish pub, down on M Street. I practically have my own stool down there."

Detective Woods smiled. "That's what we've been told. You go down there a lot, don't you?"

"Sure," he said. "They have imported Irish beers, good Celtic music on the jukebox, and most weekends, live music. There's no rock and roll, no youngsters looking for dates or for some action or whatever else they call it. It's just a good Irish pub, a few thousand miles away from home."

"A nice, friendly tavern, right?"

Sean nodded. "Sure, but it's more than just that. It's also a gathering place."

"A gathering place?"

"Absolutely," Sean said. "Those of us of Irish extraction, and some Irish expatriates working in the area, they like to go to the Black Rose. It either reminds them of home, or reminds them of where their ancestors came from. It's a wonderful place."

She kept her smile. "Truth be told, I have been there a couple of times. For lunch. You're right, it is a nice place."

The teakettle started whistling and Sean said, "If you'll excuse me."

"Go right ahead," the detective said, and Sean got up and went past the couch, into the small kitchen. From the cupboard he took out a white mug that said "Kiss Me I'm Irish" on the side and prepared his tea makings. There was no tea in tea bags in this household, and he let the boiling water pass through the little metal globe that held real Irish tea, bought at a specialty shop up in Porter. He called out from the kitchen, "Are you sure I can't get you anything?"

Again, the woman detective answered for them both. "No, we're fine."

When he was done, he started back into the living room and noticed that the young man was watching him with every step. He felt like sighing out loud. *Oh, what will be done?* he thought. *What will be done?* But he sat back in his chair and listened to Tommy Makem and the Clancy Brothers keep on singing, and he took a sip and enjoyed it, and felt calm.

"Well," Sean said. "I'm sorry for interrupting you. We were talking about the Black Rose."

"Yes, we were," she said. "Excuse me, do you mind if I take some notes here? My memory is awful."

Sean laughed. "If you think it's awful now, Miss, wait until you get to be my age."

She managed a smile in reply, as she pulled a notebook out of her bag. "I'm sure you're right, Mister Dumont. Now, I just want to make sure I've got all the facts clear. Your name is Sean P. Dumont, right?"

"That's right," he said.

"And what does the *P* stand for?"

"Patrick, what else."

"Unh-hunh," she said. "And you're retired?"

"Yes, I am," he said. "Spent some time in the merchant marine, and then got a job working security at the Porter Naval Shipyard."

"And what did you do at the shipyard?"

"Security."

Her smile now seemed forced. "Besides that, Mister Dumont."

He took another sip from his tea. "I'm sorry, Detective Woods. The nice people up at the shipyard, they work for the Department of Defense and work on nuclear-powered and nuclear-armed submarines. When I left their employ, I had to sign a nondisclosure form. The only way I'll say anything more than that is if you get a lawyer in here from the shipyard."

"Really?" the detective said, and Sean noticed that the white scar on her chin was getting more pronounced.

"Really, and I'm sorry I can't be more gentlemanly about that, detective, but that's the way it is."

"All right," she said. "I guess we can move on. So you worked all these years up in Porter. Why did you come to Tyler?"

"This was my parents' place," he said. "Why should I buy anything else? And besides, there was the pub."

The detective looked up from her notebook. "The pub? You would decide where to live because of a pub?"

Sean looked at her youthful and attractive face and felt a flash of envy for the number of years ahead for her. He put his teacup down in his saucer and said, "Miss, look at me, will you? I'm nearing my seventh decade. I've never married. Except for the merchant marine and the shipyard, I've done nothing else with my life. I have no siblings, my parents and uncles and aunts have long passed on. I'll be damned if I'll sit here and watch the soaps and the daytime nonsense on television, and slip away until I'm wearing adult diapers and eating oatmeal three times a day. I like to go out, I like to go to a place that's homey and that welcomes me, and that reminds me of my heritage. So be it. I've had a good life and I have nothing to apologize for. Nothing."

Officer Wrenn's look was blank, and Detective Woods went back to her notebook. "You said something about your heritage. I find that interesting."

"And why's that?"

Another scribble in her notebook. "Because of your last name, Mister Dumont. That's not very Irish, is it?"

Sean said flatly, "No, it's not. It's French-Canadian."

Detective Woods looked about the living room, and Sean knew what she was looking at. The framed prints of Irish castles. The books on Ireland in the bookshelf. The little statuettes and knickknacks of leprechauns and Saint Patrick in the little glass case in the corner of the room. She had a half-smile on her face. "So, why the Irish first name and the French last name?"

Now, he sighed. The old story, once again. "My paternal grandfather's real last name was Lindsay. He was adopted as a boy by a French-Canadian family named Dumont. But he was Irish, through and through. As were my other grandparents, and my parents. Names like Callaghan, Hanratty, Mullen, and O'Neil. We're quite Irish."

"But with a French last name . . ."

He shrugged. "My family history. I can't do much about it."

"And where did your family come from?"

"County Armagh, in the northern part of Ireland. Almost all of my ancestors came from that one place."

"And what's it like?"

"Excuse me?"

She turned over a page in her notebook. "Ireland. What's it like? I'm sure you've been there, haven't you?"

He said nothing. She looked up. "You mean . . . you've never been to Ireland?"

"No," he said, feeling a flush of shame.

"Really?"

"Look," he said, his voice rising. "When I was working, I was working hard, trying to support elderly parents. So that's where a lot of my paycheck went. And then I had to help pay for them in a nursing home. And when they were gone, I was broke, Miss, quite broke. And it didn't take long after that I was retired myself, and every time I saved enough or thought enough about doing it, then something would happen. A new roof for the house. A new furnace. My prescription pill prices going up. No, I've never been to Ireland. Not yet. But I will. You can count on that."

Officer Wrenn was beginning to look like a breathing statue, for he had hardly moved since sitting down on the couch. Sean had a very good idea of what the man was doing here with the detective. He was the muscle, the backup. *How sweet,* he thought, though it sure looked like the woman detective could take care of herself.

"I see," Detective Woods said. "So you've never been to Ireland, but you've been to the Black Rose Pub, am I right?"

"Yes," he said.

"How often?"

"Three or four times a week," he said.

"Really? Wouldn't you get bored after a while?"

"No, not at all. There's always good music, good talk, good things going on. And there's always new faces there. May I ask you something, Detective Woods?"

She shifted in her seat. "Sure. Go ahead."

"You said you're here because of something that happened last night at the beach. Am I right in thinking that whatever happened is connected to the Black Rose Pub?"

Now the male officer seemed even more attentive. Detective Woods slowly nodded. "Yes. You're right. Something happened at the Black Rose Pub last night. You were there, right?"

Sean held his teacup carefully in his hands. "I was."

"And who else was there?"

"The usuals," he said. "I'm sure if you talk to Pat Boyle, the owner, he'll give you a list of the regulars who go there all the time. Just like me. Plus the few tourists and the expats."

"The expats?"

Sean said, "The expatriates. The Irish who are here working in the States. You know, don't you, that's one of the many things Ireland has given to the world—its people."

"Really," Detective Woods said.

"Really," Sean said firmly. "The young have always left the country, to seek their fortunes elsewhere. They've also gone to help the less fortunate, the ones who need help. You read any story or see any television program about a famine or a civil war, the Irish are there. Either they are there as doctors and nurses, or as UN peacekeepers. The Irish are first to volunteer, to help out."

"I see, but—"

Sean interrupted, his voice rising some. "Ever since the 1840s, when the potato famine struck and millions died and millions left to live somewhere else, the Irish have been a wandering, helpful people. That's where the term comes from, you know. The Wild Geese. The young Irish men who traveled the world, seeking their fortune. And they're still doing it, spreading their culture about and contributing to dozens of other countries. There you go, Detective Woods. Even today, there are expats here in the United States. The newest generation of the Wild Geese. Both men and women."

Detective Woods looked quickly to her side, and then said, "All right. Expatriates still go to the Black Rose Pub, am I correct?"

"Yes," he said.

"And what kind of Irish people go to a pub like the one here in Tyler Beach?" she asked.

He sipped from the last of his tea. "Sometimes it's college students. They get visas where they can work here for the summer, at the hotels or restaurants. They make good American money, lots of tips, and if the weather is warm all summer long, they get better weather than they would at home. Other times it's specialists, whether computer or finance. There was a time, Detective Woods, when the only kind of labor that the Irish could export was physical labor. Those times are changing. You have very bright men and women, coming out from Dublin and Belfast and Cork and other places."

"And some of them come to New Hampshire, and some come to Tyler, and even a few make it to the Black Rose Pub."

"Yes," he said, "but I'm sure you already knew that."

Detective Woods again made another glance to the officer at her side. "That's right. We do."

"And something happened last night."

"Yes, something did. At the Black Rose Pub. Were you there last night, Mister Dumont?"

"If I said no, you'd know I was lying, so I won't do that. So yes, Detective Woods, I was there. I arrived at 6:00 P.M., had a meat pie and two glasses of Guinness stout. Mister Boyle, he had a tape delay running of a European football final, Ireland versus France. Soccer, as we call it over here. The place was fairly crowded, and I left by 10:00 P.M."

"Did anybody see you leave?"

"Sure," he said. "Pat Boyle did, right when I left."

"And where did you go when you left the pub?"

"I came right home."

"Did you drive?"

"No, I walked."

Detective Woods looked skeptical. "All the way from the main beach to here? That's quite a walk."

"It surely is, but I enjoy it. Especially after a couple of Guinnesses. It clears my head and gets me ready for sleep."

"I'm sure it does," she said. "Tell me, when you were at the pub, who did you talk to?"

"Talk to? I'm sure I talked to a lot of fellows there."

"Yes, but did you talk to anybody in particular?"

Sean hesitated, then said, "I think you already have an idea of who I talked with, Miss. Am I right?"

"Perhaps," she said. "Let me try it this way. Did you talk to any, as you say, expats from Ireland when you were at the pub last night?"

In his lap the teacup began to shake just a little bit, as if a heavy truck had driven by the house and had caused the foundation to vibrate. But no traffic was going by. Sean looked at the detective and her officer companion, knew what was going on behind those polite looks.

"Yes," Sean said, "yes, I did."

"Do you know who they were? What their names were?"

"There were two of them, two young men. Brian and Neil, I think, that's what their names were. Both were in their mid-twenties."

"Both from Ireland?"

"Yes, Dublin," he said. "They told me that they were over here at a trade show up in Porter, a computer trade show. They work for a software company in Dublin and were in the States for a week."

"Unh-hunh," the detective said. "And what did you three talk about?"

"The usual," he said.

She looked at him, pen held firmly in her hand. "Humor me, Mister Dumont. What's considered the usual?"

"What most Irish men talk about in a pub," he said. "Sports, beer, women, politics. All that and more. But, as an aside, Miss Woods, the Irish are more than just good talkers, you know. Did you know that the Irish saved civilization?"

Officer Wrenn brought a hand up to his face, perhaps to hide a tiny smile. Detective Woods's face looked just a bit irritated, Sean thought. She said, "Really? And how did they do that?"

Sean said, "During the Dark Ages, the monasteries in Ireland kept the old books and records. Irish monks kept reading and writing alive, and Irish monks also traveled to Europe and other places, spreading the gospel. They kept civilization alive while the rest of Europe descended into barbarism. And that's how the Irish saved civilization, Miss Woods."

"Thanks for the lesson," she said quietly. "These two men, Brian and Neil, did you get their last names?"

"Perhaps, but I don't remember," he said.

"And your conversation with them, it was polite, wasn't it?"

Sean felt the teacup begin to rattle again. "Define polite, Miss Woods."

She crossed her legs, kept her notebook in plain view. "I think it's like pornography. I can't define it, but I know it if I see it."

"All right," Sean said.

"And if I had been at the Black Rose Pub last night, I think I would have been able to see conversation that wasn't polite."

"Really."

"Truly," Detective Woods said. "A conversation among an older American and two young Irishmen. A conversation that started out polite enough, and then got louder and louder. With angry words. With curses. And with the American storming out of the pub, his face red with anger. That would be an example to me, at least, of a conversation that wasn't polite. Wouldn't you agree, Mister Dumont?"

"Perhaps," he said, finding it odd that he was now almost enjoying this little give and take with the woman detective. "But we Irish tend to argue hard, especially if we've had a few. It's part of our nature.

We argue hard and respond to any slight, however real or imaginary. I mean, look at some of the bombers over there, still working in Northern Ireland. They're working on slights and grudges and defeats that happened hundreds of years ago. And it's still as new to them as if it had happened yesterday."

"Or perhaps last night," Detective Woods responded, and Sean admired how deftly she had steered the conversation back to her turf. "Perhaps something happened last night with you and those two men that resulted in a grudge on your behalf. A sense of wrong, of something that needed to be righted. Would that be possible?"

"As my mother would say, anything's possible under the sun," Sean said, "and let me tell you, my mother was one for not forgetting a slight. A number of years back, I don't rightly remember when, some banker had given her a hard time over a late deposit. Oh, the language she used, and I don't mean vulgarities. My mother would never let such a word slip through her lips. No, she told the banker— a Mister Wilson—that if he didn't straighten the matter out, that she would tell all of her friends and acquaintances and women at the parish and at the social clubs what he did. She went on and on, almost cursing him and his family for generations to come. It was quite the performance."

"And last night, at the pub," Detective Woods said, "was that a performance? Is that what you're saying? Because the people I've spoken to, who were in that pub last night, said they had never seen you so angry. Correct?"

Now it came back to him and Sean nodded, keeping his lips firm. "Yes, I was angry with them. Quite angry."

"Over your conversation, true?"

"True."

"And what did you talk about, the three of you?"

He waited, the cold cup in his hands. On the CD player, Tommy Makem and the Clancy Brothers were singing again of heartbreak and loneliness. He looked down at the cup for a moment and then looked up at the two members of the Tyler Police Department.

"Are . . . are you sure I can't get you a cup of tea?" he asked, realizing how soft his voice now sounded.

"No," she said. "We're fine."

"But perhaps your friend there—"

"No," she repeated, a bit more strongly. "We're fine, Mister Dumont. Please, could you tell me what the three of you talked about?"

He shook his head, wiped at his cheek, and then said, "It started out just grand, that's all. I struck up a conversation with them about Ireland, about their families, about their jobs. Just friendly stuff, and then we watched the football on the big-screen TV. That's all."

She said, "You mentioned it started out grand. What happened then?"

He sighed. "That's the problem with the Irish. We drink our liquor and then voices get raised, and then the harshness starts. Miss Woods, I—"

"Mister Dumont, please," she said firmly. "I appreciate your knowledge and love of all things Irish, but can we concentrate on what happened last night? You said everything started out grand. Then what happened?"

He rubbed at his cheek again. "One of the two boy-os, I'm not sure if it was Brian or Neil, he started making fun of the pub. That's what he did. He started saying something under his breath to his friend, about the silly Americans. I mean, why did he have to start insulting everything like that? We were just trying to show them a good time, that's all."

Detective Woods scribbled something in her notebook, said nothing. Sean cleared his throat and continued. "At first, I thought they were just joking with me. I mean, I had bought them a round of beers and we had cheered on the Irish football team and that, but they started making fun of the pub and its decorations. The pictures of Ireland and Saint Patrick. The green bunting. The old walking sticks. The statues of Brian Boru and the other old Irish kings. The little model of Blarney Castle."

Sean felt his throat tighten up and bowed his head for a moment, then went on. "They said . . . they said everything was so fake and unreal, not Irish at all. They laughed and said it was typical of us silly Americans. The fake Irish, the Saint Patrick's Day Irish they called us."

"What does that mean, the Saint Patrick's Day Irish?" Detective Woods asked.

Now his throat was quite tight, and he was finding it hard to continue, but the story was now tumbling out of him. "Saint Patrick's Day Irish, that's what they called us. We're just regular Americans, 364 days out of the year. But every March 17, we put on green sweaters or green neckties, drink green beer, and have drunken parades down the middle of our cities. While in Ireland, the real Ireland as they pointed out, Saint Patrick's Day is just a religious holiday, that's all. And to think of dressing up in green and drinking green beer and stumbling drunk down a parade route wouldn't even be considered. Then they laughed some more."

"And what did you say?"

He found that the teacup and saucer in his lap was getting heavier, like it was slowly transmuting into lead, but he didn't dare move it from his lap. He was afraid that it would fall to the floor and shatter.

"I . . . I played along with them at first, thinking it was just a big joke, that they were having fun with me, but no, they were cutting loose. They went on about how fake everything in the pub was, how unreal it was, and that they were tired of being from a place that so many thought was a theme park, like Euro Disney. So I said back to them, if the place was so fake and so silly, why were they there, and they said because it was the only place they knew in the area that would be showing the football match. And that's why they were there. And besides, the place had a rotten selection of beers. Oh, they were going on for a while, they were."

Detective Woods said, "Is that when your voice started to get loud?"

Sean didn't answer the question, decided just to keep going. "Ireland's different now, they said. It was prosperous and working toward a real peace up north, and its economy was so strong that it was nicknamed the 'Celtic Tiger.' And that instead of people leaving the country each year, like the Wild Geese of old, that refugees and immigrants from Bosnia and Croatia and Bulgaria were trying to get in. They laughed and called me a silly old man, that I didn't even know one thing about modern Ireland, and . . . um . . ."

Detective Woods was now gazing straight at him, as was Officer Wrenn. "Go on, Mister Dumont, what else did the two men say to you?"

"They looked at the way I was dressed and the way I talked, and the way I rooted for the Irish football team to win, and they laughed and said I should be rooting for the French team, since I had a froggie last name," Sean said.

"I take it you explained to them what you told me, about your grandfather, didn't you?"

Sean felt himself sit up straighter in the chair. "They didn't believe me! Not for a moment. They thought I was faking it, that I was a typical American mongrel, a mix of everything European, and that I was trying to hook up with the Irish because they had the better beer and better music and prettier girls and . . . I . . . I even showed them my driver's license, showed them that my first and middle names were Irish, and by then, they had turned their backs on me. They called me a silly old froggie, and that was that."

The teacup and saucer were trembling again. "I even asked Pat Boyle, the owner, to help me out, but they wouldn't listen to him either. They just laughed and went back to watching the football match. Then I left."

Detective Woods glanced again at the officer next to her. "I see. That's when you walked home, correct?"

Sean nodded. Detective Woods made another mark in her notebook and said, "Tell me, Mister Dumont, and this is very important."

"All right."

"How long did you stay home when you got here?"

Sean said nothing.

"When you got home, was there anybody who saw you come in? Did anybody see you go to bed for the night? A neighbor? Somebody walking by? Anybody?"

Sean said nothing.

"You see, Mister Dumont, we have a problem here. We truly do. And I think you might know what I'm talking about."

Sean cleared his throat again. "Perhaps you could make it clearer."

"All right, I will," she said, flipping through the pages of her notebook. "This is the problem we have. After you left, about an hour later, the two gentlemen—Brian O'Halloran and Neil Glynn, both from Brass Cannon Software Limited of Dublin—they left the pub. But they didn't return to their hotel room in Porter. In fact, their rental car was found parked near the pub, where it had spent the night. Are you with me so far, Mister Dumont?"

"Yes, Miss, I am."

"Good. Because a number of hours ago, both Mister O'Halloran and Mister Glynn were located, right on the sands of Tyler Beach, across from M Street. They were found by a state park cleaning crew, cleaning up the beach sands. They're both dead, Mister Dumont, both shot in the head."

"I see," Sean said.

"Well, I don't think you see the trouble here, Mister Dumont," she said gently. "Two young men from Ireland, shot dead at Tyler Beach, just a while after you've been seen, arguing with them at the Black Rose Pub. Can you see the problem, Mister Dumont?"

"I surely can," Sean said.

"Right now, you're the person we're talking to, the only person we're talking to. Their rental car was still there, as were their wallets and watches and rings. So robbery wasn't a motive, not at all."

"Yes, I see what you're driving at."

"I'm glad you do. You're the only person who had an argument with these two, the only person who might be considered a suspect. Do you understand that, Mister Dumont?"

"I do," Sean said.

"I mean, prison can be hard for a man of your age, and perhaps if we knew about what was going on, what was happening in your mind—"

"Don't threaten me with prison," he said sharply. "Some of the best and brightest from Ireland have spent time in prison, for their beliefs and their actions. So don't threaten me with prison. It won't work."

"All right, I won't then," she said. "You've told us plenty about your beliefs, Mister Dumont. Don't you think it's time to talk about your actions?"

By now the CD player had stopped, the soothing voices of Tommy Makem and the Clancy Brothers had been stilled. Sean looked around his snug little house and the memories and memorabilia for a homeland he had never been to, and then gingerly moved the teacup and saucer off his lap and placed it on a nearby coffee table.

Sean said, "I came home, just like I said, but I was pacing. I was wound up. I could not sleep. I felt like I could not leave those boys back in the bar thinking that they had bested me. So I walked back, walked back as fast as I could. And as luck would have it, they were both walking out from the bar, heading down to the beach. Maybe they were going to look at the stars. Maybe they were going to drain their bladders. Who knows. All I know is that I followed them, and I started talking to them."

"And what did you say?"

"I said they should be more considerate. That their descendants here and other places around the world still loved the old Ireland, loved the old stories. That they should be gracious to the descendants of their ancestors, descendants who had supported them and sent them money and arms during their wars, descendants who had kept the stories and memories alive of Ireland. Saint Patrick, Saint Brigit, Saint Kevin, Brian Boru, Yeats, all the great names, all the great tales . . . I asked them to be more considerate, that's what I asked them. I said the Irish who lived here looked out for each other and so should the Irish from back home."

Detective Woods said, "And what did they say in return?"

"They told me to piss off, froggie."

"I see. And then what?"

Sean shrugged. "I shot them both."

"Okay," she said. "What kind of weapon did you use, and where did you get it from?"

"My old .38 revolver, from when I was a security officer. I brought it back with me when I went back to the pub. I thought they'd pay me better attention if they saw I had a gun with me, that they would take me seriously."

"I guess they didn't," Detective Woods said.

"No, they didn't," he said.

"Where's the revolver now, Mister Dumont?"

"Upstairs, bedroom closet, in a shoe box in the rear."

Officer Wrenn spoke up for the first time in a long time. "Detective?"

"Yes, please."

Officer Wrenn got up and took the staircase by the kitchen, and when Sean looked back at Detective Woods, she was sitting such that a part of her sweater had ridden up, revealing a holstered pistol. She noted his look and said, "Just so there's no misunderstanding, Mister Dumont, I want you to stay nice and still in your chair. All right?"

"Of course," he said. "You've treated me politely, Miss, and I'm glad to return the favor."

There came a clumping sound as the officer descended the stairs and handed a tan shoe box over to the detective. She lifted the lid, nodded, and looked over. Sean sat there, hands clasped.

"A word of advice, Mister Dumont?"

"Certainly," he said.

"Get yourself a good attorney. There might be a diminished capacity defense for you, though I'm not sure."

"Thank you," he said.

"Now, Mister Dumont, will you please stand up? Officer Wrenn is going to put handcuffs on you. I'm afraid you're under arrest."

Sean felt his throat tighten up, and then stood up and held his arms behind him, hoping to help the officer along, for he had seen such matters before on the television. He thought of the patriots of the Easter 1916 rebellion and the troubles they went through, and he was heartened, just for a moment, at the thought of ending up in prison. So many great Irish had ended up in a prison. Why not him?

And when the handcuffs snapped about his wrists, Sean thought of something else. "Do you suppose," he said, "that I might be getting a judge that's Irish?"

Detective Woods shrugged. "I couldn't say. All the judges I know are American."

The World Is Mine; Or, Deeds That Make Heaven Weep

P. M. Carlson

W E'D ALL SCRUBBED OFF our greasepaint and changed from our rags and finery into street clothes when Jimmy O'Neill asked me, "Bridget, you speak beautifully for a child of ould Ireland. How did you train your voice?"

Jimmy was, as Shakespeare has it, a young man of excellent growth and presence. I replied, "I had the kind offer of a letter of introduction from a relative of the illustrious actress Mrs. Fanny Kemble, who deigned to give me lessons." Well yes, I must admit the letter had been more coerced than kindly offered—but that's another story. Besides, my Aunt Mollie always said a girl was foolish to tell every detail of her life to handsome new acquaintances. I went on,

"One could make the same observation about your voice, Jimmy. Who tutored you?"

Jimmy laughed and shifted to brogue. "I tutored meself, colleen! But didn't a pair o' great Edwins give me hope? Edwin Forrest said—"

"But Jimmy, you're too young to have met Mr. Forrest!"

"'Twas his last tour, and I was little more than a boy. He said—" Here Jimmy's voice suddenly became gruff and bombastic and terribly British—"Harrumph! If that young man manages to forget his brogue, he is going to make a capital actor."

I laughed and quoted, "'May the brogue of ould Ireland niver forsake your tongue—may her music niver lave your voice!'"

He beamed at me—and didn't he have lovely white teeth and manly, chiseled features! "A mustached Adonis," the papers called him. He said, "Bridget, have you too played in *The Colleen Bawn*? It was my first venture onstage!"

"And mine also!"

I soon learned that Jimmy O'Neill and I had much in common. Like Papa, Jimmy's father had immigrated with high hopes for the future but then had drunk up his money in barrooms. So Jimmy and I had both been raised hungry as little birds, subsisting on the few coins earned by the women and children in our families. Both of us had scrambled from one desperate job of work to another. Both of us dreamed that the theatre might allow us to escape poverty, despite being Irish, if we persevered.

And both of us had worked our way up to Mr. Palmer's lovely production of *The Two Orphans* in the fashionable Union Square Theatre. My role was small but Jimmy, a few years older and recently triumphant in San Francisco and Chicago theatres, was one of the two leading gentlemen—not the Chevalier, but the crippled Pierre, even though Jimmy's strong voice and magnetic stage presence made him perhaps overly powerful in the role.

Ever eager to learn, I said, "But Jimmy, please tell me about the other Edwin, for Mr. Booth is the finest Shakespearean actor alive today."

"Indeed he is. And at McVicker's theatre in Chicago, I had the good fortune to be cast as Othello to his Iago, with an ancient scimitar to punctuate my speeches." He swept an imaginary sword through the air. "'Do deeds that make heaven weep!' And Mr. Booth was kind enough to say—"

He trailed off, and I realized that something behind me had distracted his luminous gaze. I turned to see a lovely young lady of nineteen or twenty years, taller than I and expensively gowned. I was not surprised—Jimmy's manly vigor and good looks attracted young ladies and schoolgirls in droves, to say nothing of actresses like Adelaide Nielson, said to be the loveliest Juliet on two continents, and Nettie Walsh, who claimed to be his wife though he denied it, and Louise Hawthorne, who had thrown herself from a Chicago hotel window for Jimmy's sake, though he denied that, too. The thought of adding myself to his list had great appeal, yes indeed; but I prefer prosperous gentlemen.

Tonight's pretty visitor had a sweet face and a rich cascade of curls that glinted bronze and copper in the gaslight. Her eyes, big and brown and as lustrous as Jimmy's, locked on his for an instant, then looked away in fluttery confusion. Jimmy said, "Miss Quinlan? Can it be?"

She took courage and said, "Uncle, may I present Mr. James O'Neill? Mr. O'Neill, my uncle Mr. Brennan, who kindly brought me to see your wonderful play."

"I'm happy to meet you, sir," said Jimmy. He introduced us all and added, "I'm very glad Miss Quinlan enjoyed tonight's performance."

Mr. Brennan smiled. "Ella gave me no peace until I agreed to bring her! She remembered you as a friend of her late father's."

"My mother and I appreciated your note of sympathy, Mr. O'Neill. Though I can hardly believe that he's gone—" A shadow flitted across Ella's childlike face. "Well! I mustn't think of that! And now my mother and I can live here in New York."

"Why, I thought you were going to stay in South Bend and become a nun!" Jimmy teased.

Her hand patted her curls nervously. "For now I want a home in New York, just like my father's. And you are here, too! My friends in South Bend will be so envious!"

Her innocent smile combined with her roguish glances was having a devastating effect on the worldly Jimmy. He said, "Dear Miss Quinlan, the hour is late now, but perhaps you would allow me to call on you and your esteemed mother tomorrow."

"Oh, that would be lovely!" she exclaimed, pulling a card from her sleeve and pressing it into Jimmy's hand. He smiled at her, which threw her into confusion again, and she slipped her hand into her uncle's elbow as they bade us good-bye.

I murmured, "A pretty child. Who is she?"

He was gazing after her, memories in his eyes. "Miss Ella Quinlan is the daughter of my friend Thomas Quinlan, who crossed from Ireland the same time we did. Thomas always welcomed actors to his liquor store in Cleveland, especially fellow Irishmen. He worked hard, invested wisely in property, and became quite prosperous. He sent Ella to Saint Mary's Academy in South Bend for a first-rate education."

I was thinking that Shakespeare had it right when he said, "foolish over-careful fathers Have broke their sleep with thoughts, their brains with care, Their bones with industry." Foolish over-careful Thomas Quinlan's hard work had left behind a lovely daughter with much education and so little knowledge of the world that she treated Jimmy as though he were truly as rich and eligible as the characters he played, instead of that doubly disreputable creature, an Irish immigrant and an actor. But I didn't want to cast aspersions on Jimmy's old friends, so I said, "How pleasant for her!"

Jimmy said seriously, "I admire Thomas for creating such a lovely world for her. I dream of doing the same someday," and I realized that Jimmy had a deep gnawing hunger to be rich and respectable. Well, I knew that hunger, too. And I knew that if Ella Quinlan represented that ideal to him, she'd best beware. In a moment Jimmy came back to himself and smiled at me. "But what's an Irish lad without his dream? Pay me no heed, Bridget! Let's go to supper at O'Riley's, for we Irish must stick together and help each other prosper, right?"

I was happy to go to supper, though thoughtful, because Jimmy's remark about the Irish sticking together had put me in mind of Mora Corrigan.

I'd met Mora a few weeks before, when I was still looking for work. Mora was approaching her middle years, still slender but with a few silvery streaks in the raven-black hair around her honest blue-eyed Irish face. A red burn scar on her right forearm attested to her profession of cook and housekeeper. She had come to the corner of Union Square where actors hoping for work gathered each day. My training with Mrs. Kemble was exactly what she was looking for, she told me, if I was willing to take on a job paying good money. Well, of course I was, as I'd had little to eat for a month.

Still, it was disappointing to learn that I had to hire on as an English chambermaid in the rich Pritchard house where Mora worked. "But Mora, that's just what I'm trying to avoid!" I complained. "Everyone knows that servant girls are soon ruined by the man of the house!"

"And aren't you a silly goose to be worrying about that!" Mora scolded, sounding exactly like my dear departed Aunt Mollie. "Old Mrs. Pritchard is a widow and can't abide her son's wife, so he doesn't visit often, even though the old lady's on her deathbed. And you should see the lovely jewels she has! And generous—she gave Sadie a silver necklace when she married."

Well, that made the position seem more attractive, yes indeed. But I was disheartened to learn that the last chambermaid had been let go when she'd been caught attempting to steal a brooch. "And didn't old Mrs. P raise a ruckus! That girl was Irish, so her son told me this time I must find an English chambermaid." Mora snorted. "As though I'd ever trust those sneaking English vermin! No, we Irish must stick together."

So I agreed. Oh, I know, it's not proper to mislead a rich dying lady, but what's a poor girl to do when hunger gnaws and an honest fellow Irishwoman offers her plenty of good food, wages steadier than a theatrical living, and the possibility of some lovely jewels?

Almost everything at Mrs. Pritchard's was as Mora had described it—a richly furnished house, a mistress who was pleased to have an English chambermaid, a handsome jewel case filled with lovely emerald brooches and ruby necklaces in a drawer close by Mrs. Pritchard's bed. I had changed my red hair to blonde so as to appear more English, and wore a plain black frock and white apron, and ran up and down the steep back stairs dozens of times every day to dust Mrs. P's camphor-scented rooms, or bring her tea, or help her with unmentionable tasks involving the chamberpot, or listen to her stories.

One thing did not fit Mora's description, for Mrs. P was hardly on her deathbed. She was bedridden, but still sharp as could be, with a prominent beaky nose, quick hazel eyes, skimpy white hair, and a hearty appetite. One day, as she took another big bite of Mora's chestnut-stuffed chicken, she mumbled, "You seem a good lass, who has had a little schooling."

"Only a little, mum," I replied, bobbing a curtsey.

"Well, you're much better than those Irish wenches. I hope you will remain with me many years, and then marry an industrious young fellow of English extraction. I'll see to it that you receive a nice emerald brooch for your wedding. Dear Mr. Pritchard would have approved," and she was off again with yet another story about the dear departed.

Kind as Mrs. P meant to be in the future, I saw little likelihood that she would soon fulfill Mora's dream of bestowing gifts on us. I had now eaten well for nearly two weeks and secretly hidden away enough apples and potatoes from Mora's stores to see me through a lean winter if necessary. But I would wait a few days before giving notice, for I wished to repay the kindness Mora had shown me, and besides, I couldn't collect the week's wages until Friday.

On Wednesday, Mora handed me a supper tray as usual, straightened my apron and cap, and sent me up with Mrs. P's meal of roast beef, potatoes, and boiled greens with bacon. Mrs. P thanked me warmly and attacked the food and, simultaneously, a tale about a roast-beef meal she'd had with the dear departed Mr. P. After a few minutes she began to look rather queasy and said, "I have quite lost my appetite, lass. Please take it away!"

I obliged, though she'd left half the beef and potatoes. As I reached the door she called weakly, "And do return soon!"

"Yes, mum." I carried the tray down the two flights to the scullery, then climbed wearily back up again. When I pushed open her chamber door I was greeted by the pungent odor of someone who has been very ill and saw Mrs. P curled up in pain and mumbling incoherently.

"Mrs. Pritchard, mum! What is it?" I cried, running to the bedside. But she only coughed and slipped into a faint.

I looked about the room. I found some smelling salts, but they failed to revive her. I ran to the door and called the housemaid, who tried to help but was no more successful than I. A boot boy, wide-eyed, peered into the room, and I asked him to run for a doctor. To the housemaid I said, "Wait with her a moment, and I'll go fetch some rum. It helped my uncle."

Halfway down the back stairs I put my hand in my apron pocket and realized something was there. I pulled out an empty packet of Paris green, so useful for killing ants and other pests.

Lordie, it gave me a turn! I stared at the dreadful little packet and in a flash saw how I'd been betrayed.

I continued down the stairs to the kitchen, where Mora was laying the table for the servants' supper, and cried, "Oh, Mora, the most dreadful thing has happened!"

"Why, what is it?" There was concern in her honest blue eyes.

I threw myself into her arms. "It's dear Mrs. P! We tried to revive her but I fear—oh, Mora, you can help her, you know more than I! I'll go fetch help." I snatched my cloak from the peg. "Please go up to her. Maybe some rum will help?" I ran out the door and up the steps to the street.

At the corner of the avenue I found a policeman. "Oh, please, sir, poor dear Mrs. Pritchard has been poisoned by her cook!"

"Mrs. Pritchard?" he said, looking down the block.

"Just there, where the doctor is entering," I said. He bustled off after the doctor, and I after him. We all ascended the front stairs to Mrs. P's room. The doctor looked carefully at her poor little body and said, "She has been poisoned."

Mora cried, "Poisoned? That's impossible, sir, begging your pardon! Haven't I prepared wholesome meals for these three months now?" The other servants were nodding agreement and she added, "Unless—the only other to touch the tray was the new chambermaid!"

"The chambermaid? There she is!" cried the housemaid, pointing at me.

The policeman approached, scowling. "Now, me girl, did you poison the old lady's victuals?"

"Of course not!" I exclaimed.

"Perhaps you should look in her pockets!" Mora suggested.

Hang it, isn't that about as low-down as you've ever heard? I reckon when Saint Patrick drove the serpents out of Ireland, he left one behind and it was Mora's great-grandfather!

The officer searched my pockets, but, of course, there was nothing there. I said to him, "Sir, perhaps you should be looking in the cook's pockets instead!"

He did, and to Mora's astonishment he discovered the empty packet of Paris green, together with some necklaces and brooches that the housemaid—and later Mrs. P's son—identified as coming from the jewel case by the bedside. Oh, 'twas sad indeed, having to part with the jewels I'd scooped up before I'd called for the housemaid! But of course I couldn't allow a policeman to find jewels in my apron, so I had nobly sacrificed them to make certain that a poisoner and cruel betrayer of her fellow Irishwoman was discovered with the evidence in her pockets. Sometimes the law needs a little help.

Mora was taken away to the Tombs. Well fed now, but not much richer, I returned to Union Square and soon had the good fortune to be chosen by Mr. Palmer for the role in *The Two Orphans*, where I met Jimmy O'Neill.

Alas, life in the theatrical profession is not predictable, and at the end of the year Jimmy's path diverged from mine. Mr. Palmer decided to send *The Two Orphans* to the Brooklyn Theatre across the river and off we went, all except for Jimmy, who stayed behind to play the lead in Mr. Palmer's next Union Square show. You may have heard of the dreadful fire at the Brooklyn Theatre—but that's another story. I remind you of it here only because one of the actors who died in that horrid conflagration was dear Mr. Murdoch, who had replaced Jimmy as the crippled Pierre.

Everyone was amazed by Jimmy's good luck. And he was lucky again, we all believed, in persuading the rich Miss Ella Quinlan to become his wife the next year, and lucky again in finding a splendid play to make him rich and famous.

And now, as in that play, we must jump a dozen years to our second act, and—You don't know the play? You don't know *The Count of Monte Cristo*? Poor thing, you were born too late! 'Twas a grand play, the most popular in the nation for the thirty years before the Great War, and it was all because of Jimmy O'Neill. Playing the hero, Edmond Dantes, demonstrated his great versatility. In the first act Edmond is a frisky, handsome young seaman with a new bride, about to be promoted to captain. But jealous, corrupt rivals conspire to have him arrested on trumped-up charges at the end of Act I. Next comes that jump of a dozen years. The second act finds a dirty, bearded Edmond Dantes still in prison. A fellow prisoner, on his deathbed, reveals to him where the treasures of Monte Cristo are hidden. Edmond puts his friend's dead body in his own bed, then crawls into the corpse's bag. Guards fling the bag out of the prison into the sea, and soon, in a great storm—oh, it makes my spine tingle just thinking about the moment, Jimmy did it so well!—a ragged, sodden figure pulls himself from the sea, raises his arm to heaven amid the crashing waves and salt spray, and cries in that great melodious voice, "The world is mine!"

Matrons wept, schoolgirls swooned, and all were delighted after intermission when Jimmy—now shaven, combed, and ravishingly handsome as the rich Count of Monte Cristo—revenged himself on one after another of the scalawags who had plotted against him.

So, that chilly January of 1889, a dozen years after meeting Jimmy, I was looking for work in Chicago and feeling low because I would have preferred to stay longer with my dear little six-year-old niece in Saint Louis. But I brightened when I saw a young advance man, red-nosed in the bitter wind, supervising the posting of bills for *Monte Cristo* with James O'Neill, coming soon to the Columbia Theatre. "Oh, good, Jimmy O'Neill is coming!" I exclaimed. "We have been friends ever since we shared the stage in Union Square."

The young man smiled at my red hair and freckles. "If you are as Irish as you look, I'm sure Mr. O'Neill will be happy to see you again when he arrives. He says to me, 'George, if you ever need a favor, find someone whose name begins with O'. We stick together, we O's.'"

I laughed. "It's true, he's proud to be Irish. Are you?"

"I fear I am a mere Tyler. George Tyler, his advance man."

"A pleasure. I am Bridget Mooney. No O', but just as Irish, and an actress. I've acted with Edwin Booth and Tommaso Salvini, as well as Jimmy O'Neill."

"Oh, that's capital! Miss Mooney, I am so eager to learn about theatrical matters. I'm nearly finished here—would you be kind enough to join me at supper, and tell me about Mr. Booth and Mr. Salvini?"

Well, he was a polite and pleasant young fellow, and I happily agreed to sup with him at his hotel. "I would take you to Rector's Restaurant if I could," George explained, "but part of my duties as advance man are to settle Mrs. O'Neill and the baby into a comfortable hotel while Mr. O'Neill plays those dreaded one-night stands.

This week he's in Columbus and Dayton, Lima and Fort Wayne—not suitable for an infant. So I must stay nearby in the hotel to run errands until he arrives."

"Oh, is there another baby? I was abroad for a while and hadn't heard. A friend told me that Mrs. O'Neill was so heartbroken when the second baby died of the measles that she could hardly move."

"Yes, poor lady. She is so frail. The older boy was a solace to her, but they've just left him at his school in South Bend. Mr. O'Neill says we mustn't let her dwell on her child's death. His hope is that the new baby will draw her mind away from morbid thoughts. But now, tell me of Mr. Booth!" So young George Tyler and I had a pleasant supper and quite a lengthy discussion, so engrossing that I was still with him at 4:00 A.M. Oh, I know, but what do you expect a poor girl to do when the wind is bitter and she hasn't yet found work? Sleep in the snow?

Suddenly, there was an urgent knock on the door of his room. He cracked it open, and I had a glimpse of a plump arm and a heap of silvery hair. George said, "Mrs. O'Hara! What is it?"

"Oh, Mr. Tyler, sir, it's the baby! He's colicky, and Mrs. O'Neill is beside herself! Please, come help!"

"Yes, of course, just a moment." George closed the door and reached for some clothes. "Bridget, come with me, please do! You say you have a little niece, so I'm sure you know more about babies than I do! Oh, this is dreadful, if the little fellow is ill—poor Mrs. O'Neill!"

I refastened my bustle, pulled my hair into a hasty swirl atop my head, and followed George down the rose-carpeted hall. The heartfelt yowls of the infant were evident from some distance, despite the thick walls. Mrs. O'Hara opened the door to us, glanced at me in surprise, then ducked her head deferentially.

Ella Quinlan O'Neill was still beautiful, and wore a rich blue break-fast jacket, but her eyes were huge and shadowed with grief. She clutched the screaming child to her breast and cried, "Oh, George, George, my baby is dying! And I didn't leave him this time, I didn't, I'm right here!"

"Of course you are, Mrs. O'Neill," said George uncomfortably. "Here is Miss Mooney to help. She is good with infants."

"Oh, Miss Mooney, I haven't arranged my hair, I must look dreadful—" Ella O'Neill's hand fluttered to her beautiful coppery-bronze tresses. "But please, can you help my baby? He's inconsolable! George, please, you must go for the doctor!"

"Yes, of course!" George ran hotfoot out of the room, relieved to have a task that did not require remaining with the squalling infant. The little fellow was perhaps three months old and had certainly worked himself into a pet, gasping and hiccupping between bellows, his little face purple with fury. I said as reassuringly as I could, "He's probably just got colic."

Ella O'Neill said doubtfully, "That's what Mrs. O'Hara thinks too, isn't it?"

"Yes, mum." Mrs. O'Hara was in the corner, arranging blankets in the little crib.

Ella continued, "But my first boy, Jamie, was never like this, and neither was—but no, I mustn't think about—oh, my baby is dying, I just know it!"

I said, "Mrs. O'Neill, please, calm yourself. If you are upset the baby will be, too."

"Oh, I know I mustn't—but my nerves—When I married James, you know, he said we would have a home in New York. A lovely home like my father's. How can I be a good mother without a home?"

What a silly creature she'd been, to believe an actor's promise to stay in one place! I said, "With *Monte Cristo*, your husband has achieved every actor's dream of large profits and a vast adoring public. But success requires travel."

"Yes, Miss Mooney, that is what James says, too. And we both find it painful to be apart for long. But hotels are not homes!"

She was certainly right about that. I said, "I leave my dear little niece with a reliable woman in Saint Louis while I travel."

Ella's eyes brimmed. "Once I left my babies behind in the care of my mother. And they caught measles and the little one—but no, I mustn't think of that!"

Hang it, my heart quite went out to her. If anything happened to my precious niece while I was away earning money for her, I might never recover. Ella continued miserably, "Miss Mooney, do you think God is punishing me? You see, I was going to be a nun—but then I fell in love with James O'Neill—oh, it's my fault! My nerves— Mrs. O'Hara, are you quite certain there is no more nerve tonic?"

Mrs. O'Hara's blue eyes glanced up from where she was working in the corner. "Sorry, mum, there's none."

Ella cried, "If only I had a home, I could—but he's dying!"

Well, I was made a bit uneasy by the baby's purple color and by plump Mrs. O'Hara lurking in the corner, but I thought it best to calm the mother. I said, "Mrs. O'Neill, the boy is obviously healthy. He's strong, and his lungs are certainly powerful. He's nursing still, isn't he? He gets no other food?"

"None at all! Sometimes Mrs. O'Hara gives him a sweet to quiet him, that's all."

A dreadful suspicion was forming in my mind. "Perhaps I can help Mrs. O'Hara find a more suitable sweet. Yes! Here come Mr. Tyler and the doctor now."

The doctor, unshaven and as hastily garbed as young George, entered. Ella wailed, "Oh, doctor, my baby is dying!"

He took one look at the angry, gasping infant and said, "Colic, madam. He's not dying. You must calm yourself, for your distress is disturbing him."

"Oh, I know, it's my fault! Please, doctor, may I have something for my nerves?"

The doctor obligingly pulled something from his bag and Ella held out her arm to him. I took advantage of the diversion to seize the nanny's plump elbow and march her from the room, saying, "Mrs. O'Hara and I will return in a few moments." She came along willingly enough, though when I reached the gaslight and pushed up her right sleeve she jerked her arm back. But I had already seen the red burn scar on her arm. Mora Corrigan, silver-haired now and grown plump as butter on Jimmy O'Neill's generosity. "I thought you'd been hung, Mora!" I exclaimed. "How did you escape the Tombs?"

"In a laundry bag."

Well, Jimmy O'Neill's wonderful play gave ideas to all the wrong people. I said, "And just what are you doing here?"

"Working hard! I've reformed, Bridget, and Mr. O'Neill likes to hire the Irish."

"You deny that you've been feeding Paris green or worse to that poor little baby?"

"I've done no such thing! I swear it, Bridget! I would never hurt Mr. O'Neill's child, and him as Irish as I am!"

Well, I thought Mora was low before, poisoning an old lady, but only the rottenest skunk would do in a little baby, don't you agree? I said, "I shall tell them immediately about the nanny they have hired!"

I saw the long glint of the kitchen knife in her hand before she could raise it, so I skedaddled down the hall to the stairs. Mora ran after. My skin shivered at the thought of that knife, and I galloped down the stairs and out the door into the bitter wind. There was nary a policeman to be seen, and she was only a few steps behind. I raced down the street and turned a corner. At a construction site I paused to pick up a brick, but before I could throw it, Mora and the knife were almost upon me. I felt the fabric of my skirt rip as the blade sliced through it, so I ran again.

The icy wind blew, and no one was about to help, and I could hear her panting close behind me.

In moments we had reached the inky Chicago River. In the faint light from a streetlamp a block away, I could see a few boats rocking on the frigid ripples.

I hoisted my skirts, leaped sideways, and kicked out my foot to trip Mora as she came plunging past me. As she fell, she dropped the knife and it skittered across the cobblestones. She began to get up, so I lifted the brick high and cracked it down twice on her silvery head.

I know, I know, the Irish should stick together, and perhaps Mora should have had her day in court. But we'd tried that already, when all she'd poisoned was an old lady, and the law had failed us. And did you really believe her when she said she had reformed? I thought Jimmy's poor wee miserable son would have a happier, longer life in a world without Mora.

I rolled her into the river and returned shivering to the warmth of the hotel.

A few days later Jimmy O'Neill came to town and had his usual grand success playing *Monte Cristo* and making heaps of money. He was annoyed that the Irish nanny he'd been so pleased to find had suddenly left without a trace. "But Bridget, what a joy to see you! I'd hire you for my company, but I've signed these pesky contracts," he said ruefully. I took work instead in a spectacle called *A Dark Secret*, which featured scenes on the River Thames, with real water in the river, real dories and racing shells in the water, and a real dog circus on the shore. But the river stirred up unpleasant memories for me, so I gave notice, deciding to try my hand in New York again. My last night in Chicago I accepted Jimmy's invitation to sit backstage with Ella while he enacted the Count.

The O'Neill baby was still colicky and nervous, though his color was better. In the greenroom Ella, as lovely and expensively dressed as when I first saw her, held him out to me and said, "Please hold little Eugene for a moment. It's my nerves. I know I must be calm, and not think of sad things. I love James dearly—but it's so difficult to be calm in theatres and trains and hotels. And I can't keep good servants; they know it's not a real home. Like Mrs. O'Hara—" Her back to me, she was rustling through a valise. From the stage we heard the roar of the fake storm, the rumbling of the metal thunder sheets. Ella turned back to me with a happy smile.

I looked at that smile, and then at the fussy baby I was handing back to his mother, and remembered how eagerly she'd held out her arm to the doctor. I stepped around her to peek into the valise. Inside were several little ampoules and a hypodermic.

The baby whimpered, and from the stage, the storm raged on.

Hang it, I owed an apology to Mora Corrigan, who poisoned old ladies but perhaps not babies as well. If I'd known I would have cracked her head only once. I said gently, "Mrs. O'Neill, I have heard that it is best not to take morphine when you are nursing a baby, for it sometimes makes them colicky and irritable."

She smiled at me sunnily. "Oh, he's not colicky! He's a fine healthy baby, and we couldn't be happier!"

From the stage Jimmy's voice cried, "The world is mine!"

Yes, indeed.

A roar of applause filled the house. They were still cheering a moment later when an unkempt bearded prisoner's head smelling of spirit gum poked into the room. "And how's our little one, dear?" asked Jimmy's lovely voice.

Ella gave him a melting smile. "Doing well. Miss Mooney is so helpful!"

Jimmy said to me, "Thank you! And isn't Ella a beautiful mother? Fairer than the dawn!" Even through the scruffy beard his smile dazzled and his eyes were luminous and happy, and I decided I didn't want to be the one who told him. He added, "I'm sorry we can't spend much time with you after the show, because we must pack to go on to Michigan."

"I too am traveling, to New York on the first train."

Jimmy O'Neill kissed my hand, and Ella O'Neill smiled vaguely, and baby Eugene O'Neill clasped my finger in his angry little fist, and we said our good-byes, for ahead of us all lay a long day's journey.

BLACK IRISH

Doug Allyn

BITTER MORNING. NOVEMBER. WIND off the Detroit River chasing scraps of newsprint and Big Mac boxes down the alleys. Chasing Irish Mick Shannon down the Cass Corridor on his morning run.

Mick was used to the cold, liked it, in fact. Icy wind in his teeth, overcast skies painting Motown a monotone, grimy gray. On sunny days, training was a downer. Who the hell wanted to run five miles, work weights, then spar or pound the bags when you could be catching some rays on Belle Isle or a Detroit Tigers home game?

But on grim, gray days? Might as well be boxing or working out. Or running. And thinking.

Couldn't get the woman out of his mind. Theresa Garcia. Schoolteacher. Spotted her the day she moved into the Alamo Apartments with her nine-year-old daughter. Took Mick weeks to meet her accidentally on purpose so he could introduce himself. Irish Mickey Shannon. The fighter.

She wasn't impressed. Only curious.

"Isn't calling yourself Irish Mickey Shannon . . . redundant?" she asked. "I mean, isn't someone named Mick Shannon automatically Irish?" That was Theresa. Direct as a right cross.

"In Dublin, any Mick Shannon would probably be Irish," he conceded. "In Detroit, *Irish* is a code word for *white*."

"I don't understand."

"Most Motown boxers are black or Hispanic. They put Irish in front of my name on fight cards to show I'm white. Saves the promoters the price of printing my picture, that's all."

"But not all Irishmen are white," she countered. "Aren't some of them called Black Irish?"

And like a moron, he started to explain the whole deal of shipwrecked sailors from the Spanish Armada swimming ashore in Ireland. To a history teacher, for chrissake. She listened politely, never cracked a smile. He hadn't realized she was joking until much later.

They'd had a half-dozen dates over the past month, but he still couldn't be sure she was joking unless she smiled. He didn't mind. Her smile was worth it—damn! A wind gust rocketed out of an alley, nearly blew him into the street.

Definitely a Michigan November. Up north, in Tawas, Alpena, Onaway, hunting season would open in a few days. In Motown it never closed. Open season on chumps, year 'round.

He'd spotted the car a few blocks earlier. Big car, black four-door sedan. Noticed when it whipped around, making a quick U-turn. Coming for him? Didn't wait to find out. Ducking into the alley, Mick broke into a flat-out sprint, pounding down the narrow drive. If he could make it to the loading area in the middle of the block he could lose anything on wheels.

Halfway down the alley he glanced over his shoulder. Nothing. No car, nobody following. False alarm. Probably getting paranoid—suddenly the car screeched across the alley ahead of him, blocking it off. Mick whirled—too late! A black guy was strolling casually toward him from the alley mouth, an automatic in his hand. Not aimed at anything, just showing it. No point in running now. Nowhere to go.

Ahead of him, the driver stepped out of the car, tall guy, Latin, maybe. Also with a gun. And showing a badge in his free hand. Cops? Sweet Jesus. Now what?

Raising his hands to show he was unarmed, Mick continued down the alley toward the car. The driver was well dressed, dark suit, tailored from the look of it. Loden London Fog raincoat.

"Mick Shannon?"

"Yeah."

"Face the wall and assume the position. Now."

Mick did as he was told, leaning against the wall, ankles spread, while the black cop patted him down. He was bigger, solid as a linebacker, wearing a navy peacoat and black watch cap.

"He's clean," he said, stepping back.

"Turn around, Shannon. I'm Lieutenant Menendez. This is Detective Bennett. Do you know why we stopped you?"

"Speeding?" Mick asked.

"We could have. Why did you take off?"

"Thought you might be somebody else."

"Like who? Is somebody looking for you, Shannon?"

"Anybody who bet on my last fight. Besides, this is a rough part of town."

"The whole town's rough. What are you doing out here?"

"Running. I run to the gym every other day. Why?"

"Where were you last night?" the black cop put in. "From dark until now."

"Ummm . . . had dinner with a friend from about seven to eight-thirty, Papa Doc's in Greektown."

"You eat at Doc's?" Bennett asked, surprised. "You're a little light for the color scheme in there, ain'tcha?"

"The owner was a pretty good light-heavy once. Lets fighters run a tab."

"He's an ex-con, too. Did you know that?"

"Nope. He's just Papa Doc to me. After dinner I went for a walk with my date, just talking, you know. Got home about . . . nine-thirty, I guess. Hit the rack, watched the news on Channel 50, zonked about halfway through. Up at seven, did isometrics, two hundred marine push-ups, three hundred crunches, stretched out some, suited up, headed out, and here we are. And now it's your turn. What's this about?"

"Can anybody besides your girlfriend confirm your story?" Menendez asked.

"It's not a story, it's what happened. And the *lady* can only vouch for the dinner-and-walk part. I spent the night alone."

"Tough luck for you on both counts. You know a guy named Brooks? Tony Brooks? Runs a karate dojo on Dequinder?"

Damn. "I've met him," Mick said warily.

"Met him?" Bennett snorted. "We hear you two mixed it up."

"It wasn't like that."

"No? Then what was it like?"

"A . . . misunderstanding, that's all. A guy I know asked me to talk to Brooks, straighten him out. Said Brooks was bothering his sister."

The two detectives exchanged a glance. "You'll have to do better than that," Menendez said. "Brooks was gay."

"I know but—what do you mean *was?*"

"He's dead," Bennett said. "Somebody whacked him last night."

"I'm sorry to hear that, he seemed like a nice guy. But I sure didn't do it, and I don't know anything about it."

"Maybe you do," Menendez said. "Tell us more about how you straightened him out."

"I didn't. I went to his studio, dojo, whatever you call it, but before I laid a hand on him he pulled some karate move, kicked my feet out from under me. So there I sat feelin' dumber than a coal bucket while Brooks explained the situation. The girl was one of his personal training clients. She hit on him, he turned her down, she went crying to her brother. End of story."

"She didn't know Brooks was gay?"

"Nah. I've known this girl a long time. She's . . . nice, but she ain't the brightest crayon in the box, you know? She's kinda plain, takes care of her mom and her grandfather, doesn't get out much. I doubt she had a clue about Brooks."

"So what happened after your conversation with Brooks? What did you tell the girl's brother?"

"The truth. That I talked to Brooks and he'd never bother Ma— the girl—again. And that was the end of it."

"Really? And if we talk to this brother he'll confirm all this?"

Mick hesitated. "Maybe. Maybe not."

"Why not?"

Mick took a deep breath. "This guy . . . doesn't talk to cops much. It's a religious thing, I think. He's Sicilian. His family made a lot of money in Prohibition. Get the picture?"

"He's mobbed up?"

"I wouldn't know. It's not the kind of thing you ask a guy like him, you know?"

"Who is he?"

"What's the difference? He won't talk to you."

"And that's supposed to explain why we can't check out your story?" Menendez said, shaking his head. "Jesus, Irish, who do you think you're playin' with? I gotta tell you, you're real high on our hit list for this. You tangled with Brooks, he told people about it, you were seen in the neighborhood. And any brain-dead doper could come up with a better alibi than yours. I thought Irishmen were supposed to be mighty storytellers."

"We are. And there's your proof."

"What proof?"

"The Irish are a race of poets, Lieutenant. If I was lyin' to ya, I'd make a better job of it. Maybe work in a leprechaun and a pot o' gold. The truth isn't as interesting, but it's all I've got. So. You gonna bust me for this?"

Menendez eyed him for a moment, thinking. Then he shook his head slowly. "No. Not today. Maybe later. You sure you won't give me the brother's name?"

"Not today. Maybe later."

"Later may be too late for you, Irish," Bennett put in. "I saw you fight Killer Kroffut a few weeks back. Tough luck."

"Better than no luck at all," Mick said. "Are we done, fellas? I still got roadwork to do."

"Yeah, go ahead on, Shannon. We'll be in touch."

"Right," Mick sighed, trotting back toward the mouth of the alley. "I expect so."

THE SIGN OVER PAPA DOC'S said Best Barbequed Baby Backs in East Detroit. It was half right. The city changed its name to Eastpointe back in the eighties but Doc's sign remained as it was. The rest of the diner dated from the fifties. Or before. Formica counter with chrome stools, dark booths upholstered in naugahyde, ribs revolving over an open barbecue pit in the front window, filling the air with an aroma that could convert Gandhi to a carnivore.

Ordinarily, Papa slid a Diet Coke across the counter whenever Mick walked in. Not today. Instead he casually carried it down to the end of the counter, away from the other customers.

"You in trouble?" Papa asked as Mick eased down on the stool. Papa was crowding sixty but was as hard and scarred as an ebony fist.

"Could be. Why?"

"Two guys in earlier, lookin' for ya."

"Cops? They found me."

"Not cops, Easties, that Irish bunch. Dolan and Doyle. Know 'em?"

"I've seen 'em around," Mick said. "Mutt and Jeff, right?"

"Both mutts, you ask me. Legbreakers. Mostly do collections for Eastside bookies. What'd the cops want?"

"Me. Or thought they did. A guy I know got whacked last night."

"Tony Brooks?"

"Yeah," Mick said, surprised. "You know him?"

"Know about him," Papa nodded. "The one they call Black Irish?"

"What do you mean, Irish? Brooks was a black guy."

"Half black, and definitely half Irish. His mama was Dinah Brooks, the soul singer? Had some hit records for Motown in the sixties. Send me your looooove . . ." Papa crooned in a gravelly baritone, drawing a few stares from his customers. "His daddy is Big Danny Guinn, the Wayne County Drain Commissioner."

"The guy they call the Irish pope?" Mick whistled.

"The Man himself. Controls all them city jobs and contracts. Guinn's got more juice than the mayor of Detroit."

"And Tony Brooks was his son?"

"Guinn never admitted to it, had a wife and kids in Grosse Pointe. But everybody on our side of town knew about him and Dinah. Not so many knew on yours, I expect."

"What do you mean *my* side of town? I live in the same neighborhood you do."

"Same 'hood, maybe," Papa nodded. "But you ain't never lived on the black side of Detroit. Irish."

Papa stalked off to wait on other customers, leaving Mick puzzled. He'd known Papa Doc for years, now all of a sudden they were back to basic black and white? What the hell was up with him?

He was still mulling over Papa's mood when two guys in dark overcoats and silk scarves walked in, spotted him, and sauntered over, standing behind him, one on each side.

"I know you," the smaller one said. "Irish Mickey Shannon, right? The fighter?"

"Guilty," Mick said, swiveling to face them. Smaller was a relative term. Dolan was probably six foot, two hundred pounds, with reddish hair and a permanent Irish grin. Doyle topped him by six inches and a hundred pounds, darker hair, darker outlook. Mick doubted he ever smiled at all. "Something I can do for you boys?"

"Actually, there is," Dolan said. "We'd like you to come along with us to meet a fella. Big fan of yours. *Big* fan."

"Nice to know I have one, but I'm afraid I can't, guys. I'm meeting my manager in a few minutes. Business. Some other time, maybe."

"You know who we are," Dolan said quietly. It wasn't a question. "You probably even know who we work for. So you know I'm not kiddin' when I say you're comin' along. Easy or hard, Shannon. But you're comin'."

Mick didn't answer for a moment, eyeing the smaller man. Dolan's smile was still in place. But his eyes had gone stone cold. Fifteen years in the ring, Mick was good at reading eyes.

"I know what you're thinkin'," Dolan murmured, leaning down, his voice barely a whisper. "You're thinkin' you're a pro fighter, maybe you can take us both. Well, maybe you could. In a fair fight." He opened his coat just enough to show the gun. "But it wouldn't be a fair fight, boyo. And we wouldn't leave any witnesses. So we're just gonna walk outa here, three friends goin' for a drive. Okay?"

"Since you put it that way," Mick sighed, rising.

"Mick?" Papa said, strolling over, a meat cleaver in his scarred fist. "Everything all right?"

"No problem, Papa," Mick said. "They're fans. From my side of town."

Maybe they were. Their maroon Lincoln Town Car had all the comforts of home: telephone, color TV, even a wet bar. Dolan offered him a drink but Mick passed. In training, he said. Dolan didn't drink either. Instead he kept up a cheery banter about the weather and the eternally lousy Lions while Doyle drove them through the noon-hour crush down along Jefferson Avenue. Doyle still hadn't said a word. Mick was beginning to wonder if the big guy could talk.

Tuning out Dolan's blather, Mick tried to guess where they were taking him. Waterfront district. Only a few years ago the area was an eyesore, abandoned warehouses with eyeless windows, empty factories. Now it was booming. Spurred by the success of the Renaissance Center and the Ojibwa casinos, the waterfront was a fever of construction.

Parking the Town Car in one of the casino lots, the three men walked a few blocks away from the river to a spanking new high rise, still under construction, its skeletal frame soaring twenty-five stories above its neighbors.

"It'll be called the Golden Shamrock," Dolan explained, as he led them beneath a catwalk to a freight elevator. Tools and wheelbarrows were scattered about, but no workmen were in sight.

Mick glanced the question at Dolan.

"Temporary labor problems," Dolan shrugged. "That's why the Man's here. To fix things. It's what he does. This way."

Mick followed Dolan onto the elevator as Doyle pulled the lift-gate shut then cranked the toggle over. Shuddering, the lift clattered its way upward. Five stories, ten. At the twelfth floor they left the masonry walls behind, nothing around them now but naked steel girders, pulleys, chains, and overhead cranes. And still they climbed, finally rattling to a halt on the twentieth floor.

Half a floor, actually. It was really just a platform, plywood sheets scattered over half-inch steel mesh. No real barriers. Nylon safety lines that were strictly decorative. A clear view for ten miles in any direction. And a twenty-story drop to the concrete below. The only furnishings were a couple of work tables covered with architectural drawings.

And the Man. Sitting on a tall drawing stool, Daniel Guinn looked larger than life. Round-faced and rosy-cheeked with a comfortable paunch he didn't bother to camouflage, the Man looked sleek as a TV preacher, a pussycat in a five-thousand-dollar cashmere overcoat and felt Homberg. He eyed Mick in silence a moment, wind whistling through the iron H-beams framing the floor, nothing around them but scaffolding and a dull November sky.

"Irish Mickey Shannon," Guinn said at last, keeping his hands in his overcoat pockets. "I've seen you fight a time or two over the years. Weren't always victorious but you gave your best. Can't ask for more than that. Still fightin', are ya?"

"Now and again."

"But in the twilight of it all, I'd guess. Must be hard for a man like yourself, when the cheers start to fade."

"It's not as much fun as it was," Mick acknowledged. "Is that why I'm here? To talk about my crummy career?"

"A direct man," Guinn smiled. "A rare thing amongst the Gaels. Most Micks greet the world with a smile. Makes it easier to catch the bastards off-guard. Personally, I prefer the direct approach. Saves time. The police believe you're involved in the death of Tony Brooks."

"I'm not. I only met him once. Liked him, in fact."

"He liked you as well. He told me what happened, that somebody rented you to scare Tony away from some girl. Is that how it was?"

"Something like that," Mick nodded warily.

"He also said he dumped you on your arse."

"Sad but true. He used a karate move. It was embarrassing, but if you've followed my career at all, you know it wasn't the first time I've been dumped on the deck. Or even the tenth."

"So you bore the lad no hard feelings? Is that what you're tellin' me?"

"It's the truth."

"Maybe. Tony thought you took it well, but he could have been mistaken. He was a sweet boy. I doubt he thought he had an enemy in the world. And now he's dead. Somebody blew his head off last night. Maybe someone who bore him a grudge. Someone who already knew he couldn't take him on the square. Someone like you, Shannon?"

"No way. I had no beef with him and I've never owned a gun in my life."

"You were in the marines, boyo. I expect you know one end of a weapon from the other. And Tony was killed with a shotgun anyway. Any moron can pull a trigger. Do you know what a plea bargain is, Shannon?"

"More or less."

"Well, that's what I'm givin' you. A chance to save your life. Tony Brooks was my son, Shannon. I want Tony's killer, but I want the man who hired it done even more. Give me his name and you can walk away from this. Hell, I'll even double what he paid you."

Mick said nothing.

"Unless you think you can fly, I'd answer the man," Dolan put in.

"Don't know if I can fly or not," Mick said with a shrug. "Never tried. But it still won't get you anything, Mr. Guinn. I talked to Tony as a favor to a friend. It was a misunderstanding that came to nothing. I didn't kill him, and my friend had no reason to either."

"Then give me his name."

"No. You offered me a plea bargain a minute ago, suppose I offer you one? I'll ask my friend about this. If I think there's even an outside chance he knows anything about it, I'll give him to you. No charge."

"And I'm supposed to take your word for that? Sorry, Shannon, the stakes are too high. I've lost too much already. Come here a minute, let me show you something." Rising, Guinn sauntered over to the edge of the platform, standing at the rim of the abyss with the city spread out below and the November wind whipping his slacks around his ankles.

Mick joined him warily, keeping an eye on Dolan and Doyle. But if they meant him harm, they gave no sign.

"Do you know where we are?" Guinn shouted over the wind.

"I'm not sure what you mean—"

"Corktown," Guinn said, cutting him off. "In my granddad's day and even when my father was a boy, this whole district was Irish. From Lafayette to Myrtle, east to First Street, west to Brooklyn, all Irish. We controlled the police, the courts, the Detroit mayor's office, half the legislature. Even won the governorship, most years."

"And your point is . . . ?"

"In those days, no man would have dared to harm any friend of mine, to say nothing of my son. Then the Greeks came, and the Dagos and the blacks. And they got good jobs at Ford and G.M. and they think Detroit is their town now. That they can do as they please. Even kill one of us. I intend to prove they're wrong. To send them a message. Like the old days. You want to talk to your friend? Go ahead. I'll give you one day to find where the guilt lies. But if you can't give me a name by tomorrow, then you'll be the message I send. Right or wrong. Do we understand each other, Mr. Shannon? Or are you one of those dumb Micks they tell all the jokes about?"

"No sir, I'm not. But understanding's a two-way street, Mr. Guinn. If you figure on teaching me to fly, you'd better buy a set of wings for anybody you send after me. I won't be flying solo."

IT WAS LATE AFTERNOON when Mick finally tracked down Tommy Ducatti at his dealership. New Millenium Motors occupied a whole city block in Hamtramck. Premium, Pre-owned Vehicles, Fleet Leases, and Repossessions. A used-car lot, but a classy one.

Tommy Duke's office was equally classy. Thick green carpet, a massively carved desk, and a brag wall covered with awards and photographs. Tommy Ducatti with Muhammad Ali and with Evander Holyfield. At Kronk's gym with Emmanuel Lewis, at banquets with Mayors Archer and Coleman Young. And even one with Irish Mickey Shannon, back when he was winning. When Mick was somebody.

Time hadn't been kind to either of them. Mick had scar tissue around his eyes now, and his nose was wider.

Tommy looked like the picture Dorian Gray had hidden in the attic. Tall, fleshy, and forty, his eyes were red-rimmed, hands trembling, skin patchy. Mick guessed he was in rehab mode from another hard night on the town.

Fidel Ramos, Tommy's bodyguard, was leaning against one of the narrow windows, looking out over the lot. Cool, slender as a stiletto, impeccably turned out in a gray sharkskin suit, Fidel scarcely gave Mick a glance when Tommy's secretary showed him in.

"Hey, Irish," Tommy said absently, scanning some paperwork, "how's it going?"

"Not good, Tommy. We've got a problem."

"I don't do problems," Tommy sighed without looking up. "Problems are Fidel's department."

"Not this time. Remember that guy you asked me to talk to a few weeks back? Tony Brooks?"

"Brooks?" Tommy echoed blankly.

"That black guy who was giving Maria a bad time," Ramos prompted.

"Oh, yeah, right," Tommy nodded, wincing at the movement. "I forgot. What about him?"

"He's dead, Tommy. Somebody blew him away last night. The cops heard I had a beef with Brooks, tracked me down this morning to ask me about it."

"Cops?" Mick had their attention now. Tommy's father and grandfather were hard-core mobsters, gunsels for the Purple gang, both of them. His father died in a gangland shoot-out when Tommy was away at college. Tommy supposedly went legit afterward, but he hustled used cars, owned fighters, and promoted bouts. Which meant on any given day he was probably guilty of something.

"I kept you out of it, Tommy. So far. Wanted to talk to you first. Do you know anything about this?"

"About what? Brooks? Hell no! You straightened him out, that was the end of it far as I was concerned. Maria was off my back and . . . that was all I cared about."

Mick caught the hesitation, but let it pass. "And that was it? I talked to Brooks; you forgot about it?"

"I just said so," Tommy said sullenly. Avoiding Mick's eyes.

"How about you, Fidel? You ever meet Brooks?"

"Wouldn't know him if he walked in the door. Guess that ain't likely, though. How'd he buy it?"

"Shotgun, the cops said."

"Amateur night," Ramos snorted. "Noisy, splatters blood all over everything, hard to carry concealed. Besides, they mess up the cut of my suit. Never use one."

"Look, we don't know squat about this, Irish," Tommy said. "You've got my word. But I don't want to talk to the cops about it or have 'em bugging Maria, getting her all upset. Can you keep me out of it? It's worth a c-note to me."

"Yeah, I guess I can do that. Can't promise they won't turn something up on their own, though."

"I don't see how," Tommy said, opening his desk drawer, peeling two fifties off a roll he kept there. Next to a gun. "We're the only ones who know about this, right?"

"Brooks could have told somebody."

"If he had, I'd be talkin' to the cops already. This finishes it, Irish. We're done. Paid in full." He slid the bills across to Mick.

"Right," Mick said, eyeing him warily as he picked up the fifties. "Paid in full."

NOT QUITE. MICK HAD planned to head for the gym after talking to Tommy. He didn't. Walked along Woodward Avenue instead, thinking. Fighting for a living, you get good at reading faces, especially a man's eyes.

Maybe Tommy wasn't involved in Brooks's killing, but he knew something about it. For one thing, he'd given Mick his word. In the fight game, deals up to a hundred grand are often done over the phone, no contracts, no lawyers. Word alone. Welshing on a deal isn't an option. You don't get sued, you get busted up or killed. Tommy was a serious player so his word had to be rock solid. That was a given. And yet he swore to Mick he wasn't involved. And that was overkill. Obviously, he wanted Mick to believe him.

Why? To keep the cops away? Maybe. But Mick had a hunch something else was going on. It was in his eyes when . . . he said Maria was off his back and that was all he cared about. And again when he said he didn't want the cops bothering her. Why not? Could Maria be involved somehow?

Not a chance. He'd known Maria Ducatti since she was a gawky teenager mooning around the gym, plain as a crowbar and not much brighter. She thought boxers were romantic, like knights or something. Yeah, right.

Hadn't seen as much of Maria in recent years. She'd grown out of her crush on boxing, disliked the violence. But not much else had changed for her.

The ugly duckling grew into an awkward horse of a woman, as tall as Tommy and with a similar build. But with a good heart. She'd never worked or had much of a life of her own. She'd stayed home to tend her ailing mother and grandfather instead.

He could see Maria falling for Brooks. Could even see her whining to Tommy after Brooks politely gave her the brush. But blowing his head off? Hardly.

Still, there'd been something in Tommy's eyes . . . Unfortunately, Mick had no idea what it could be. Something to do with Maria, perhaps? It seemed unlikely but . . . maybe. And he wondered if Maria had heard the bad news about Tony Brooks yet. The kid they called Black Irish.

THE DUCATTI PLACE WAS in a real neighborhood, an all-Italian enclave cut off by the freeway back in the sixties. Tall, ornate older homes of brick or stucco standing shoulder-to-shoulder, largely unchanged since the days of Prohibition, when illegal booze had paid for a good many of them.

Maria had definitely heard about Tony. Mick knew it the moment she opened the door. Her pudgy face was tear-streaked and she was still in her bathrobe and pajamas.

"Mick? What are you doing here?"

"Hi, Maria, sorry to bother you. I was in the neighborhood and I wondered, well, if you'd heard about Tony."

"I . . . heard earlier," she said swallowing. "What an awful thing."

Maria looked equally awful. Haggard and hurting. But what struck Mick most strongly was an emotion he recognized instantly from the ring. Fear. Maria Ducatti was as terrified as she was grief-stricken. Why?

"Can I come in for a minute?"

"I, um, of course," she said reluctantly. "Come to the kitchen, I was just making a little snack for my mom."

He followed her through the beautifully furnished home, richly carpeted, with comfortable, overstuffed furniture, a decorator's mix of maroon and gray.

But dark. The day was overcast, a standard sunless November afternoon, yet the living room blinds were drawn. Permanent twilight.

Brighter in the kitchen, a sprawling affair with brick ovens, dozens of copper pots suspended from a rotating rack that probably dated from the days the Ducattis had servants. Hell, maybe they still did.

"Sit down," Maria sniffled, waving him to the small enameled kitchen table against the wall. "Coffee?"

"Please," Mick said, easing down in the ladder-back chair, watching her. "Black is fine."

"How did you . . . hear about Tony?" she asked, filling a mug from a percolator.

"The police told me. They thought I might know something about it."

"You?" she said, puzzled. "I don't understand."

"Maria, I'm the one Tommy sent to talk to Brooks when he was . . . bothering you."

She winced as though he'd slapped her. But when she handed him the mug of steaming Italian coffee, her face was a blank. A Sicilian mask. "I knew Tommy . . . straightened things out, but . . ." Her voice faded away, as though she'd forgotten she was speaking. She shook her head, swallowing hard.

Mick didn't get it. She was clearly overwrought, only a word away from breaking down completely. Could she have cared about Brooks that much? Or was something else—

"Maria!" The old man's voice cracked like a whip as he strode angrily into the kitchen. "Are you deaf? Angelina calls you—who is this man? Why is he here?"

"A friend of Tommy's, Grandfather. *Un pugile Irlandese*, the Irish boxer. Please tell Mama I'll just be a moment, Nonno."

"I know you," the old man said, eyeing Mick suspiciously, ignoring Maria. Taller than Tommy and gaunt as Death, he was carefully dressed, white shirt, old-fashioned string tie, black vest, silver watch fob.

"Irish Mickey Shannon, Mr. Ducatti." Mick rose, offering his hand. Salvatore Ducatti was eighty if he was a day, but his grip was like iron.

"No," he said, frowning. "Not Shannon . . . I remember now. You're the one is going to fight Barrow, no?"

"Barrow?"

"Louis Barrow, the black champion. Joe Louis he calls himself now. An *infamia*, a curse, this black champion of America. He was nothing when we brought him up from Saint Louis. Now he thinks he's a big shot, a *pezzonovante*. But any white man can beat him. They have no heart for a real fight, the blacks."

"I, um, won't be fighting Louis, sir," Mick stammered, his mind reeling. "Joe's a heavy, I'm a middleweight. I think . . . Marciano's scheduled to fight him."

"Yeah, that's right, Marciano. I forgot. Maria! Angelina calls you. She's hungry." He started to turn away, but stopped when he noticed Mick. "Who are you?" he asked.

Mick met Maria's pleading eyes, and in that moment he understood. All of it.

"I'm a friend of Tommy's, Mr. Ducatti," Mick said carefully. "And I was just leaving."

HE HURRIED AWAY FROM the house, not slowing his pace for a good six blocks, trying to assemble the pieces of what he'd seen. When had Joe Louis died? The eighties? Earlier? But he was an old man then. He fought Marciano for the championship back in . . . Mick couldn't remember the year. But he knew the fight had taken place long before he was born.

"HAVE AN OYSTER," DANIEL GUINN said, waving Mick to a seat. Guinn was in the middle of supper at the Top of the Ponch, the exclusive restaurant atop the Ponchartrain Hotel, downtown Motown. His reserved table was piled high with the wreckage of a lobster, prime rib, french fries smothered in gravy, cherries swimming in brandy, and two slices of pecan pie, one topped with cheddar, one with ice cream. The meal could have fed a stable of fighters for a week. Guinn was dining alone.

"No thank you, Mr. Guinn. I only have a few minutes."

"You may have less than that," Guinn observed, glancing pointedly at Dolan and Doyle, who were seated two tables away, sipping coffee. And watching Mick like bird dogs on point. "What do you have for me, Shannon?"

"A theory," Mick said, and quickly outlined what he thought had happened. That when Maria had confided her unhappiness to her brother, her grandfather overheard. Or perhaps she poured out her heart to the old man as well, never dreaming that in his confusion he'd actually act on it.

"You're saying that old man killed Tony?" Guinn interrupted. "Not a chance. Tony was a karate teacher, forgodsake."

"Which is probably why he let Mr. Ducatti in without a qualm. But physically, the old man's fine. He's got a grip like a vise, and how strong do you have to be to pull a trigger? Years back he was a hit man. And in what's left of his mind, it's still 1950. He thought he was defending his granddaughter's honor. With a shotgun. The way they did in those 'good old days' you're so fond of. When a guy like Ducatti could kill a black man in this town and expect to get away with it."

"But he's not going to get away with it! I don't give a damn how old he is or whose kin he is—"

"What are you going to do, Mr. Guinn? Have your goons throw him off a building? What would that prove? He won't understand what's happening or why. And killing him won't be the end of it. You'll have Tommy and his crew to deal with afterward. And maybe more people will die. For what? Vengeance against a crazy old man?"

"Then what would you suggest I do? Go to the police?"

"No," Mick sighed. "I have no real proof and Tommy's got top-notch lawyers on his payroll. Needs 'em in his line of work. The law can't touch the old man. And you don't want the cops sniffing around your business any more than Tommy does."

"What then?" Guinn continued his meal as he talked, wolfing his food as though he hadn't eaten in a month.

"A plea bargain. You offered me one this morning. Do the same for Tommy. He's guessed what happened, I saw it in his eyes when I told him about Tony. Suppose Tommy puts his grandfather away in a place where he can't hurt anyone else? That's all the courts would do anyway."

"It's not enough. Not for a life."

"Maybe not, but we're not talking about what's right, we're talking about what's possible. Do you really think Tony would want more killing over this? Do you?"

Guinn stopped chewing, a forkful of lobster poised in mid-air. Then he lowered it to the plate. "No," he said quietly. "I suppose he wouldn't. But it's not that simple. I can't just . . . let this go. As though Tony's life didn't matter."

"No, of course not. But nothing can bring your son back, Mr. Guinn. All you can do is see that he's not forgotten."

"How do you mean?"

"A memorial. Right downtown. A big one. In honor of the Corktown Irish who helped build this great city. Something made of stone that'll last a thousand years. In your son's name."

Guinn didn't answer for a moment, thinking. "Perhaps you're right," he said at last. "Perhaps that would be best, but . . . Tony was only half Irish."

"The first Black Irishmen were Spaniards. But their children were Irish. How could a son of Daniel Guinn be anything but Irish at heart?"

"You've the devil's own tongue, Shannon," Guinn nodded, showing the faintest trace of a smile. "Black Irish. I like it. I like it a lot."

Murder in Kilcurry

Mary Ryan

THE MARCH WIND WHISTLED down Sliabh Rua and swept across the townland of Kilcurry. Mary O'Farrell felt it as soon as she left the fire. Her cough was still bothering her. Her chestiness was exacerbated by the turf smoke that scented the room, but she blamed it on the east wind that sneaked under the door. Poor Hannah's efforts to draught-proof the door with canvas bought in Bandon had not been successful.

Hannah was Mary's daughter. The latter observed her now through the window as she fed the hens, throwing out handfuls of mash. The birds squawked and bobbed for the food; the boldest of them flapped awkwardly to land on the edge of the basin.

"Get down out of that, you *oinseach*!" Hannah cried crossly, "before I wring your impudent neck!" Hannah did not know about the visitors who had called earlier; Mary did not want to worry her.

MARY'S EYES SEARCHED THE yard. It was a square farmyard, puddled from last night's squall, with a fuschia hedge along the side that bordered the road. To the left was the old iron pump, painted a long-faded green, from which the family obtained their drinking water; behind it were the outhouses where the cows were milked and the pony had its quarters. Above the stable was the hayloft in which Mary's elder son, Paddy, had his bedroom. They had not seen sign nor light of him for nearly two weeks. He had gone to the fair in Bandon and had not returned.

It could be over yet another woman, Mary acknowledged. You wouldn't know with Paddy. But he obviously didn't give two straws for the worry he caused his family. When did he ever think of anyone but himself?

For years his mother and siblings had endured his overbearing ways. They had no other option; since his father Patrick's death, the farm belonged to him. It was he who held the purse strings.

"Sure maybe he'll grow into a decent man yet!" Mary consoled herself. And then she remembered that Paddy was already in his forties and the chances of a sea change in temperament were not enormous.

SHE SCANNED THE GATEWAY and the road beyond, looking for any sign of Con, or of Billy, his dog, whose panting arrival would mean that her second son was not far behind. She often wondered why Con was so different than his brother; there wasn't a mean bone in *his* body. She remembered his rueful grin of that morning when she had advised him to wrap up against the wind:

"*Sure I don't take one bit of heed of the cold, Mam! Don't be worrying your head.*"

She had heard the bravado. It was a shame, she thought, that Con had not even a warm coat to show for all his work on the farm.

What would he say when she told him her news? Or maybe he already knew? Maybe he had met the two *gardaí*; they might have seen him crossing the fields.

THE TWO POLICEMEN MARY was thinking of had called a little earlier. Hannah had been in the village at the time, shopping for tea and flour. Con had been out on the farm. He had returned from the Travers place where he worked most mornings, eaten a quick bite before rushing off again, muttering that a farmer's work was never done. A couple of hours later the *gardaí* had arrived on bicycles. She heard the voices and the rattle of their machines.

"Lift the latch, let ye," Mary called from her seat by the fire when she heard their knock. She thought it was some of the neighbours and was astonished when the door opened and two uniformed policemen stood on the threshold. She gasped and put her hand to her heart.

"Would Con be about, Mrs. O'Farrell?" the sergeant asked politely.

"Musha he's around somewhere all right . . ."

"We'll look for him so, ma'am . . ." he replied, and both had moved back to take their bicycles from where they had propped them against the stable wall.

Mary got up with difficulty and went to the door.

"What is it ye want him for?" she called after them. "He's not in some kind of trouble?"

The younger of the pair, who had blue eyes and an important little moustache, opened his mouth to say something. But the sergeant silenced him with a look.

"No, ma'am," he said gently, coming back a few paces to answer her question. "We just thought he might be able to help with a few inquiries . . ."

As they went out the gate she saw the sergeant look meaningfully at his younger colleague. The latter said something, but the wind carried away his words and she could not catch them.

Mary narrowed her eyes and muttered aloud, "Now what would they be after . . . ?"

Maybe it was that Con had been out on his bicycle after dark without a light?

She shut the door, wondering at the weight on her heart. It had been there these two last weeks, a nameless dread. She knew it was because Paddy had not come home. But it did not occur to her that the visit from the police had anything to do with him. She knew in her bones that he would turn up sooner or later.

Her eyes wandered to the grey clouds. The rain would be back later, maybe turn to sleet. She glanced up uneasily at the thatch that could be seen through the rafters. They would have to renew it in summer; it would not see them through another storm. The last thatching had been done in that glorious June four years ago, just before Patrick had died. His yellowing photograph was on the mantleshelf under the framed picture of the Sacred Heart. He was holding himself stiffly for the camera.

Mary's heart quickened with memory as she looked up at the portrait of her late husband.

Oh, Patrick, a chroí, *do you watch out for us at all?*

PATRICK HAD FOLLOWED RURAL tradition in leaving the farm to his firstborn son. He had also bequeathed a right of residence for the rest of the family—Mary as his widow, and Con and Hannah for as long as they might need a place to reside.

What would he have made of Paddy's absence? Mary wondered. Would he agree that it was as likely as not to do with another wild filly with red hair? Like Nora O'Keefe, the publican's daughter, the girl he had had such a great notion of some months ago, even though she had been more or less engaged to Dan Riley the blacksmith? Mary was glad that had ended before there was trouble. The girl had gone off to England and there had been no word of her since.

But the *gardaí's* visit had sharpened her anxiety. She searched in her pocket for her rosary beads and eased herself back into the settle by the fire. Gráinne, the tabby cat, looked up from the hearth and jumped into her lap.

"Sure you're nothing but an ashy pet!" Mary told her, looking with dismay at the marks on her black dress. "And the four feet of you covered! And you thinking only of cat affairs and knowing no more than myself about what's happening in the parish . . ."

What Mary did not know was that a ten-year-old local boy, on his way home from school, had discovered a potato sack in the hedge bordering the O'Farrell land and, on inspecting the contents, had flung it back into the brambles and raced for home. His father had listened to his story and alerted the police.

IN A FIELD BY the road bordering the O'Farrell farm, the two *gardaí* who had earlier spoken to Mary O'Farrell—Sergeant Touhy and Garda McHugh—were examining the hedgerow.

Con O'Farrell was standing beside the officers of the law in an old gaberdine coat with missing buttons. The coat was open at his chest and disclosed a grimy V-neck jumper. Under it a striped collarless shirt was held at the neck by a single stud. Con's cheeks were wind-flayed and had red thread veins, but his face was strong and kind.

The light was almost gone now, but the *gardaí* had bicycle lamps. They shone them around the edge of the field and into the hedgerow where Billy was nosing with increasing excitement.

"There's something there!" the sergeant announced suddenly, pointing his lamp at a spot in the hedge where a bundle was partially concealed by the brambles.

Young Garda McHugh leant down and pulled at the bundle. It emerged into the torchlight, a jute sack of the kind commonly used for carrying potatoes.

"There's something in it right enough!" he said doubtfully, holding it up and shaking it a little. He turned to Con and asked.

"What's in it?"

"Wisha, how would I know?"

"It's your land!"

"Faith 'tis not!" Con said with a short laugh. "It belongs to my brother. And divil a one of us patrols the road!"

An unpleasant sweetish smell rose from the sack. The *garda* gently tipped its contents onto the wet grass. They rolled a foot or so, and came to rest against the sergeant's boot, stared up at him. In the torchlight they saw half-open eyes, a mouth agape. They were looking at a crude-ly decapitated human head.

The *garda* exclaimed in horror. The sergeant started back. The beam of his lamp wavered, then found the dead countenance once more. He turned grimly to Con.

"Is this your brother Paddy?"

Con stared at the head for several seconds without moving.

"If you could move it so that I might see the temples better . . ."

The sergeant nodded, and the garda gingerly held up the grisly find by the hair while the sergeant played the beam of his torch over it. The nose was smashed, a deep indentation marked the side of the skull; the dead flesh was mottled, blue and ghastly white, already beginning to slough from the skull.

Con showed no emotion.

"Yes," he said eventually. "That is Paddy sure enough."

"Where is the rest of him?"

"How would I know?"

It was March 7, 1925.

AT FIRST LIGHT THE search began again and, as the day wore on, the farm began to disgorge its secrets. In a field adjoining the one where the head had been discovered was another potato sack, concealed like the first. It contained a human arm, still wearing its shirtsleeve. It had been severed at the shoulder.

In the afternoon fresh discoveries were made; a human leg was found, then a torso, then the second leg. They were all concealed in the same manner. Toward evening Billy came trotting from the wood. In his mouth was a human arm. The body parts were assembled. Only the genitalia were still missing.

THE GARDAÍ ASKED CON to accompany them. They brought the remains to the nearby village and placed them, still wrapped in sacking, on a table in a room at the back of O'Keefe's public house, which had been shut temporarily at their request. The superintendant now took charge of the case. He sent for the local doctor and for Hannah, watched as she came cycling up the village street, a well-built woman pushing forty, with a handsome face that was closed and tense. When she entered the pub she looked around for Con, saw him seated in the corner, and made to speak to him, but Con shook his head. He had said nothing about what had been found on the farm in the last twenty-four hours, dreading the effect it would have on his womenfolk. Now he evaded his sister's interrogative glance.

"Do you know where your brother Paddy is?" the superintendant asked the woman.

"I do not. He went to Bandon fair to buy a colt two weeks ago."

"Why didn't you make inquiries about him when he failed to return?"

"Paddy was his own master. He wouldn't have taken kindly to inquiries. We were expecting him back any day!"

"Would you be surprised if I told you he was dead?"

Hannah's eyes widened, but the superintendant detected no sign of grief.

"I wouldn't believe you. He was a fine stout man."

"Would you be frightened if I told you someone had killed him?"

Hannah paled. "Sure who would do a thing like that?"

The superintendant looked at the doctor.

"Would you come in here, please," he said to Hannah, opening the door to the back room. Con made to follow, but the sergeant barred his path.

Hannah entered the little room, followed by the doctor. Her nose twitched at the unpleasant smell; her gorge rose. *'Tis like rotting meat,* she thought with disgust.

The superintendant took the head out of the sack and placed it on the table.

Hannah glanced at it without flinching, and then directed her gaze around the room as though desperately seeking any other object on which to rest her eyes.

"Will you look at the head again, ma'am," the superintendant said, "and try to identify it for us."

Hannah glanced at it sideways. She shook her head.

"I don't know him."

The superintendant, who had already recognised Paddy O'Farrell from his own acquaintance with him, stared at the dead man's sister with disbelief.

"Are you sure?"

"Paddy was not so thin in the poll," Hannah added after a moment, glancing at the head again.

"Your brother Con has already identified it for us!" Hannah redirected her eyes to the evidence. After a moment she said in a calm, toneless voice:

"I am beginning to think it is Paddy! Yes, it is him, right enough!"

IN THE THATCHED FARMHOUSE at Kilcurry, Mary O'Farrell sat propped up with pillows in the fireside settle. Hannah had fussed over her today, for her cough was worse and she croaked occasionally, trying to shift the mucus from her lungs. Above the mantleshelf the Sacred Heart looked down on the flagged kitchen, the old woman in the settle, the young cat that lay curled by the embers. The deal table had been scrubbed by Hannah that morning; the dresser with willow pattern cups and plates had been dusted. The old clock with weights and chains, bought years before by Patrick, struck a sudden, melodious 4:00 P.M.

Mary's arthritic hands moved over her rosary beads. She was praying for Paddy. Her anxiety over him had escalated during the night when she had woken from a nightmare unable to breathe, and now she was besieging heaven for him. Why hadn't he come home? Had he followed the O'Keefe hussy to England? Was Hannah keeping something from her?

She called "Hannah," but there was no reply.

She finished the Rosary, put the beads back in her pocket.

It was strange to have the house so empty. Hannah was generally around all day, cleaning and cooking, washing and ironing, preparing mash for the hens. She was a great housekeeper and would have made someone a grand wife, some children a devoted mother. But it had not worked out like that and the waste of a passionate life weighed on her mother. Mary longed for grandchildren; she could also remember the yearnings of her own heart when it was young.

She sighed. It was hard for a woman not to have her own man. Only a year ago things had looked good for Hannah. Denis Donnelly from the next parish—a man who had inherited ninety good acres—had taken to visiting regularly, and it was clear that he was set on Hannah. It was a great chance for her daughter, and she had never seen her so happy.

"Do you mean to have him?" she had whispered conspiratorially to Hannah one evening after the men had retired—Paddy to his room in the hayloft, Con to his bed in the small bedroom. "Are you for marrying Denis?"

"Oh, Mam, the truth is that I'd marry him in the morning. He's decent and kind and we'd rub along grand together. But I'd need some class of a dowry, for Denis has to think of his sister . . ."

"I've no money, *a stór* . . ."

"I know, but Paddy has."

Hannah drew her chair closer to her mother and continued eagerly. "Do you think he'd let me have something, a hundred pounds, even fifty . . . I'll give up my right of residence here, so it's not as though I'd be asking something for nothing."

"Sure all you can do is put the question to him."

Mary did not divulge her misgivings. She knew that not only was her firstborn miserly, but he was arrogant and brutal as well. He had attacked Con for taking a job in the Travers place—a neighbouring farm of some two hundred acres—telling him he was a disgrace to abandon his home place to work for strangers. The row had taken place in the yard one moonlit night. Mary had woken, gone to the window, heard Con's voice and his attempt at reason.

"I can't live without a shilling in my pocket. There are things a man needs besides work . . ."

Then Mary saw Paddy lift the stout blackthorn stick he carried around with him and deliver a blow to his brother's chest that made the latter gasp and double over.

"God damn you to hell!" Con cried when he got his wind back, lifting his fists and approaching his brother, "for there's five devils in you—one for every season of the year and one for yourself . . ."

Mary had opened the kitchen door and screeched:

"Stop that . . . stop it now!"

"Stay out of this, old Mother O'Farrell," Paddy shouted back. "Mind your own business, woman . . ."

But it had been Con who had hurried to help her back to the settle bed, soothing her. "It's all right, Mam . . . Just a tiff . . ."

"It's not lucky!" Mary whispered. "For brothers to behave so . . ."

This happened around the time that Con had taken to staying out late of an evening, but was always noncommittal about where he went.

Is it the drink? his mother had wondered. Is my poor Con down there in O'Keefe's propping up that bar with the rest of the *amadáns*, spending the few bob he gets from Dick Travers?

But apparently not. Con always returned at midnight with no sign of liquor on him, but with a glow that told his mother more than he realised.

Who was it? she wondered with a sinking heart. If he wanted to marry, he could not bring a wife into his brother's house.

Next day Paddy went to the Travers' and made a scene, his chest shoved out, his blackthorn stick thumping the ground.

"*Mr. Travers . . . It's one thing to have Con over here, working like a slave for youself, but his home place needs him . . . It's neither right nor decent to have him spending himself here . . .*"

WHEN MARY EVENTUALLY FOUND out from Hannah that Con was walking out with little Minnie Dwyer who kept house for her half brother, Séamus, near the main road, a lot of things fell into place for her. She had heard that Séamus was about to be married and knew that Minnie must be desperate to escape. "Minnie says that if she can't have Con, it's the boat to America . . ." Hannah confided. "And he's dead set on her, Mam . . ."

Mary's heart ached for Con. He was a trapped, landless man. Even if he went to Dublin there would be nothing for him. Many a one had tried it, but had ended up in the slums—dreadful places where a body would sicken for the breezes from the hills and the clean, wild sky.

And he was too old to emigrate. When he had mooted it years before, his brother had persuaded him to stay, with vague promises, never honoured, of putting the farm into joint names.

And now his job at Travers was about to disappear. Dick Travers, fed up with Paddy's loud-mouthed interference, had given Con notice. And Minnie, too, had been as good as her word. A cousin in New York had sent her a steamship ticket and she was due to sail from Cobh within the month.

MARY'S THOUGHTS RETURNED TO Hannah. She had been offered a real chance. Denis would have made a good husband and she would have wanted for nothing. But when she asked Paddy if he would let her have a small dowry, he had refused.

"No, no, no. Sure where would I get that kind of money? Anyway, we need you here. What would the house do? . . . Who would look after your mother? If Denis Donnelly wants you he'll have to take you in your shift . . ."

This had been communicated to Denis whose visits had ceased. Hannah had waited every evening for almost three weeks, her apron off, her hair coiffed, but he had not come. She had gone around white-faced, too proud to show how deep was the wound until, one night, Mary had taxed her on it:

"I know how you feel, Hannah *a croí* . . ." she had whispered when they were alone together in the kitchen. "If it's any comfort to you . . ."

Hannah burst into tears.

"Is it to be a skivvy here for all the days of my life, Mam? Is it never to have my own home, my own children? Oh, Mam, I wish I had never been born . . ."

This from the daughter whose laughter had once filled the house!

Mary surfaced, wondering if she was dreaming that Billy was whining outside the door. But it was him all right. He normally accompanied Con around the farm and his presence alarmed her. She got up and let him in.

"Where has Con got to?" she asked him. "Where's Hannah?"

The dog wagged his tail and lay down by the door. The cat, from her warm spot by the hearth, opened one eye in a cautious slit.

"Has Hannah gone to the village again . . . ?" Mary continued. But Billy was uninformative.

Mary returned to the settle and said the Hail Mary in Irish under her breath. It always comforted her:

A naomh Mhuire.

A mhátair Dé . . ."

the cadence of the old language reaching into her soul. Holy Mary, Mother of God, Pray for us sinners now and at the hour of our death.

Her mind turned to the past, the sweet, safe place in which she always found refuge.

She remembered her wedding day, Patrick beaming at her when he turned at the altar, the blue poplin dress that she had made herself crisp and cool against her young flesh, like the starched sheets when Patrick had reached for her that night, shy and urgent and so full of love. There had been a shadow on that day, because Patrick's illegitimate half brother, Liam Ward, had arrived drunk. He was the family's shameful secret, Patrick's elder by five years, a man bitter at his illegitimate status and resentful that he could never hope to inherit his father's acres. His mother had been a sultry tinker woman who had been ostracised by her tribe.

"Bad cess to ye," he had shouted at Patrick when the latter told him to leave. "Ye'll have no luck out of this land . . . nor yeer children after ye . . ."

"Don't be talking like that!" Mary cried. "On our wedding day and all . . ."

"Oh, you think you're doing well for yourself, pretty Mary McCarthy . . . marrying into this farm. But the day will come, mark my words, when you will wish you had never set eyes on your fine bridegroom here . . ."

A *tinker's curse on my wedding day?* Mary thought in disbelief and prayed silently that God would avert it.

FOR A LONG TIME there were no children. One miscarriage followed another. Novenas—prayers said over nine consecutive days—succeeded each other until Mary was desperate.

Why could she not have babies? She longed for them with a passion, could feel their gentle skin, their little bodies against her heart.

"God—if you send me children I will ask for nothing else; I will work all my days for them . . ."

Seven years to the day from her wedding, Mary went into a labour that seemed without end. Two days of torture passed and still she fought and strained, gripping the iron bedstead, while the midwife, old Molly Kerrigan, muttered between her teeth at the baby that didn't want to be born. Eventually, Patrick had sent for a doctor all the way to Bandon. He arrived in a motor car, examined the labouring woman and went into the kitchen.

"I can save only one of them, Mr. O'Farrell. . . . Which do you want, mother or child?"

Although the Church said the child must be preferred above the mother in such circumstances, Patrick replied through the tears that started in his eyes:

"Save my Mary!"

Molly, listening at the bedroom door, turned and whispered to her moaning patient:

"There's a man out there that loves ye sore! So never mind the fancy oul' doctor! Let's have that baby, girleen . . . *Let it come* . . ."

And then she had begun a stroking of Mary's abdomen, while she set up a soft crooning in Irish. Mary felt herself in a dream, slipping somewhere between this world and the next, alternately racked as though her bones and sinews were being sundered, alternately strangely comforted by the noble language her race had spoken for thousands of years. She collected the last of her strength. Even as the Bandon doctor made dismissive comments on the midwife's chant, even as he took from his black bag the instruments that would have drawn the infant from her in pieces, Mary with a last terrible effort cried aloud in triumph as she felt the child's head break from her in a gush of blood and water.

Death had been cheated. Patrick had come in to embrace her a little later, full of joy. They had named the baby after his father and almost immediately called him Paddy.

A year later Con had arrived, easily, followed in just another year by Hannah. Now, across the reach of forty years, their mother's heart remembered their little heads pressed against her breast, their small toes clenching as they nursed. All three had grown into fine, handsome children.

And she had honoured her promise to God. She had never complained, although the years had been hard. She had milked the cows, and kept the hens, and run the house, and made clothes, and cooked and cleaned until she became arthritic. She had been so proud of her beautiful family, knew that if there had only been the money for their education they could have held their own anywhere in the world.

Patrick had been a kind father. But, no matter how hard he had worked, luck seemed to have left him. Harvests had been disappointing; cows dropped their calves. Someone had suggested it was because his father had ploughed a fairy fort, a well-known cause of such ills. Someone else suggested, with a knowing inclination of his head, that if it had *only* been a *fort* that had been ploughed by his father . . .

In those long-ago days Mary had thought that their love would overcome everything. But even it had been squeezed hollow by the grinding effort to live.

MARY ROUSED HERSELF FROM her reverie. Her mouth was parched and she longed for a cup of tea. She called Hannah's name again.

She must be still at the village. Poor girl! How desperate she had been when her romance with Denis had ended, how she still had wept at night thinking no one could hear.

Sometimes, Mary mused, *I am glad God gave me no more children, for their sorrows are breaking my heart.*

There was a step in the yard. The door opened and Hannah's form filled the doorway. She was wearing her hat and coat.

"I didn't know you had gone to the village," Mary said reproachfully.

"Oh, Mam," Hannah said in a voice full of anguish, "I have something terrible to tell you . . ."

THE INQUEST WAS HELD the next day. Con gave evidence about his brother's disappearance and how he had expected to see him return any day. Hannah refused to give evidence. The coroner returned a verdict of homicide by person or persons unknown.

"Hannah has ruined us!" Con confided to Garda McHugh afterward.

"How is that, Con?"

"She should have given evidence," Con replied. "She should have told them how we thought Paddy would walk through the door any minute."

Garda McHugh turned to him.

"Will you be having the funeral tomorrow!"

"Aye."

They passed the forge. Dan Riley's bulky form could be glimpsed within as he swung the hammer onto the anvil with a mighty clang and a shower of sparks. He had become taciturn since Nora O'Keefe had gone to England. The forge was no longer the centre for badinage and *craic* as it once had been.

But everyone understood. The man, for all his size and strength, had a broken heart.

THE FOLLOWING DAY MARY O'FARRELL felt her mind was wandering. They had a coffin in the parlour. Poor Paddy was in it, they told her, for he had been killed.

But how could he be killed? There was peace in the country these days. The troubles were over.

They would not let her see the remains. They made her stay by the kitchen fire, where she closed her eyes and fingered her beads while tears crept down her face and her mind struggled to find answers to the riddle of her life.

THE NEIGHBOURS CAME TO the wake, shook hands with the family; the women knelt to say the Rosary around the coffin; the men joined them, bareheaded. When the prayers were over, they stood around uneasily, accepted whisky or stout and spoke in whispers. Con and Hannah served the drinks, accepted the condolences, lifted the coffin lid when Willie Cassidy asked to see the corpse.

"I must say," the latter blurted, "that it is a terrible state of affairs, Con, to see your brother cut up in pieces and you not a bit worried over it!"

"There is nothing I can do about it," Con replied. "And *my* hands are clean."

DAN RILEY CAME LATE to the wake. He spoke to Hannah briefly, shook Con's hand, and then he left.

Mrs. Travers and Mrs. Coonihan, the priest's housekeeper, followed him as quickly as they could. The atmosphere in the O'Farrell house was oppressive.

"Poor Dan Riley was looking very strange in himself . . ." Mrs. Travers confided, after the two women had exchanged horrified comment on the murder.

"It's the O'Keefe girl! He would have done anything for her, but she ran off to England!"

"Her mother told me she has a good job there and won't be coming home!"

"A good job?" Mrs. Coonihan remarked, pursing her lips and glancing sideways at her companion. "Between ourselves, Mrs. Travers, that girl had more in her purse when she left Killcurry than a decent girl should have . . . if you take my meaning . . ."

Mrs. Travers widened her eyes. She knew Mrs. Coonihan knew more than anyone else in the parish, except the parish priest.

ON THE DAY FOLLOWING the funeral the police investigation continued. They knew Paddy O'Farrell had died by repeated blows to the head. It was clear that he had not gone to the Bandon fair as both his siblings had claimed; the murder had been committed while he was still in bed asleep. His room in the hayloft bore the marks of the assault. The headboard of his bed showed evidence of having been wiped, but wormholes in the wood still contained dried blood. The bed frame and the floor beneath were bloodstained; the inside of the loft roof was stained rust red from arterial spouting. But the bed clothes were free of stains, and looked fresh. The mattress was missing, but pieces of bloodstained mattress were found in a field near the house.

WHEN THEY HAD COMPLETED their inspection of the loft, Garda McHugh and Sergeant Troy came to the house. Hannah was giving Con his dinner. The two policemen came in and stood uneasily.

"Will ye have a bite to eat?" Hannah asked them.

"No . . . We have something to say to you and Con . . ." the sergeant replied, glancing meaningfully at the old lady by the fire.

"Say it then, man," Con replied. "We've nothing to hide!"

The sergeant took a deep breath.

"Cornelius O'Farrell and Hannah O'Farrell, I am arresting you both for the murder of your brother Paddy. You are not obliged to say anything, but anything you do say may be taken down and used in evidence against you . . . ."

There was a cry from the old lady in the settle.

"Oh, Mam . . ." Hannah cried. "Oh, Mam . . ."

But Mary gave a deranged, keening wail. The hairs on the back of the sergeant's neck stood up.

God blast this job, he thought.

AT THE TRIAL THE state pathologist gave evidence that the dismemberment had been effected by a blunt, nonsurgical instrument. The right side of victim's face had been reduced to pulp, possibly by a hammer or the blunt end of a hatchet; the base of the skull, left cheekbone, and nose were extensively fractured.

But Con's clothes, which had been taken away for examination, showed no bloodstains of any kind. Hannah's had not been investigated.

Con and Hannah exercised their right not to give evidence, and, in his address to the jury, Mr. Justice Hanna commented unfavourably on their failure to do so. The jury returned within half an hour with a verdict of guilty for both accused.

Turning to the dock where the two O'Farrells stood like creatures turned to stone, the judge asked:

"Cornelius O'Farrell, have you anything to say as to why sentence of death should not be passed on you?" Con said in a ringing voice:

"I had not hand, act, or part in Paddy's murder."

The judge put on the black cap.

"It is the sentence of this court," he said, "that on the 28th July you be taken to a lawful place of execution and there be hanged by the neck until you are dead, and may God have mercy on your soul."

Con replied: "I am going to die an innocent man!"

Hannah cried out as the judge turned to her: "I did not kill my brother."

At the back of the court Dan Riley slipped from his seat and left, closing the heavy door carefully so that it made no sound.

CON O'FARRELL WAS HANGED on 28 July 1925. Hannah's death sentence was commuted to life imprisonment. The locals were left to ponder the fate of their neighbours; they gave the O'Farrell farm a wide berth. No one would buy it or graze it. The *mí-ádh*, the bad luck, was on it, they said, and crossed themselves when it was mentioned. And when a man by the name of Michael Casey came down from Dublin and quietly assumed possession, no one hindered him. They knew he was Liam Ward's son, blood kin from the wrong side of the blanket. But better him to have the farm, even though he was a tinker woman's son, than have it overgrown, with silent windows and mouldering thatch.

DAN RILEY RETREATED INTO himself. He worked night and day, had to be reminded to charge his customers, and eventually took so heavily to whisky that the forge became cold and Dan's eyes as red as the furnace over which he had once hammered the hot iron. Some said he grieved still for the red-haired vixen Nora O'Keefe.

* * *

THE COUNTY MENTAL HOSPITAL had high walls of limestone. Behind them were two acres of shrubbery and well-kept grounds and the old hospital itself with its barred windows. The deranged were housed according to the severity of illness—those likely to be dangerous to themselves or others in locked and padded cells, those dwelling in a cloudland of their own making, in dormitories. Despite the efforts of the well-meaning staff, there clung to the whole establishment the miasma of bewilderment and despair.

But in the midst of the tormented, one woman stood out. Everyone who looked at her felt cheered; for, although she was old, her face was luminous with serenity and peace. Mary O'Farrell had good reason for her serenity: her three beloved children—Paddy, Con, and Hannah—played happily all day at her feet.

(This story is loosely based on a murder committed in County Cork, Ireland, in 1925.)

Great Day for the Irish

Edward D. Hoch

B RENDA CONWAY HAD BEEN working her Saint Patrick's Day scam for seven years, and it seemed to grow more successful each time. Perhaps it was just that the economy was good and she was becoming a better actress. She always started the day over on Fifth Avenue, before the parade began, standing for a moment in the middle of the street looking north along that long green line that the city so generously painted down its center each year. Then she retreated to the sidelines as the rumble of the first drums reached her ears and watched the spectacle from afar.

There was a certain ritual after seven years, and Brenda was careful to abide by it. She waved to her friend Tom O'Toole when he marched by in his kilt with the Saint Bridget Bagpipers and cheered wildly as the contingent from Holy Apostles in White Plains came into view with their banner flapping in the March breeze. A decade earlier she'd been a senior at Holy Apostles herself, carrying one end of that very same banner.

After the parade passed the reviewing stand along Central Park, it was traditional for the marchers and many of the spectators to congregate at various private parties and Irish bars around midtown Manhattan. Brenda always waited till evening when the revelers were at their loudest, and she never picked the same bar twice. Last year it had been that place on Fifty-seventh Street near Lexington, and this time she made her way down Eighth Avenue to a block near Forty-second that boasted Irish pubs almost side by side. Both had live music and it made no difference that the one she wanted, the Harp & Shamrock, was actually owned by a restaurant chain that bought it from the original owners. Tonight it was as Irish as any place in New York.

Brenda, who now became Molly Malone for purposes of her scam, entered and managed to squeeze her way up to the bar at the near end. Her father always said she had the map of Ireland on her face, and it served her well at this time each year. "Here! Let this fine colleen through!" a young dark-haired man insisted, making room for her. He was dressed for the office and held a laptop computer carrier in his nondrinking hand.

"Thank you, sir," she said, trying not to lay the Irish accent on too thick.

"What'll it be? A pint of Guinness?"

"A lager. Harp will do me nicely."

"Harp it is, Rocky!" The bartender in a green hat nodded and poured a foamy pint, smoothing off its head before presenting it to her.

"How much?" she asked, fumbling for her kelly green purse with the sequin shamrock on it.

"On me," the dark-haired man said. "I'm Michael Behan." He held out his hand, and as Brenda stepped closer to grasp it she could smell the beer on his breath.

"Molly Malone, like the girl in the song."

"Wouldn't you know it? They were playing that a while ago."

She glanced at a couple of young men who were strumming guitars and singing on a low platform at the far end of the noisy barroom. "I hear it a great deal back in Ireland. It's a favorite in the pubs."

"You're a true Irish lass! I should have known from your brogue. What are you doing here in New York?"

"I live here now, but I'm flying home for a visit tomorrow."

"Great! Let's drink to a lovely trip."

They touched glasses and she glanced around, taking in the scene. The place was so crowded it was impossible to tell where the tables started, or even if there were any tables. There was green everywhere, from the ceiling banners and crepe paper to the customers' apparel. Caps and shamrocks and Kiss-Me-I'm-Irish buttons. The bartenders, wearing paper hats, were working as hard as they could to keep up with the demand.

Brenda spotted the rest room sign she'd been seeking and turned her attention back to Behan and the other men who'd clustered around. "Do you boys come here regular?"

Most of them confessed to frequenting other bars, but this one was close to the bus terminal and a good place to stop on the way to their homes in Jersey. Behan simply shrugged and said, "I'm meeting someone here later."

"Ah! A girlfriend!"

"It's business." He shifted the conversation back to her. "Where's your family live in Ireland?"

"Killarney. I'll be almost there by this time tomorrow. I'll take the bus from Shannon Airport. Just another Molly Malone coming back to the old sod."

One of the others, a jovial red-haired stockbroker named Ken, caught the name this time. "Hey," he shouted at the musicians. "We've got the real Molly Malone here!"

She hardly resisted as the crowd propelled her forward and the lead guitarist helped her onto the low bandstand. "Is it true your name is Molly Malone?" he asked into the microphone. His name was Slim and his partner was Roy. Slim & Roy, the Irish Troubadours, the banner behind them read.

"That's me," Brenda agreed, and of course they launched into the song.

"*In Dublin's fair city where girls are so pretty I first set my eyes on sweet Molly Malone . . .*"

Brenda started singing along, and the crowd at the Harp & Shamrock joined in, rocking the place with their voices until the emotion was so great it brought her close to tears. Finally, she had to run off the stage to the ladies' room.

She emerged a few minutes later, looking puzzled and just a bit distraught. "Where's my purse?" she asked around the bandstand. "Has anybody seen my purse?"

"What does it look like?" Slim asked, putting down his guitar.

"It's kelly green with a sequin shamrock on it. All the money for my trip is inside!"

Some of the men she'd been drinking with remembered the purse. "I saw it," Ken the stockbroker said. "I thought you had it with you on the bandstand."

"I thought so, too, but it's gone."

They looked all over the bar and the floor, even making an announcement that the purse was missing. She returned to the ladies' room with one of the other girls, but it was not to be found.

"Was your plane ticket in there, too, Molly?" Slim asked.

"No, just the money. I took it out of the bank this afternoon before I came here. I know I should have gotten travelers' checks, but I was in a hurry. I had almost a thousand dollars. I was planning to give some to my mother." The tears came now, rolling down her cheeks and ruining her makeup. Brenda had always been good at crying on cue.

After another five minutes' searching, Slim held up his hands. "Folks, folks, listen to me! We've got the real Molly Malone here, and she's going back to Ireland in the morning to visit her mom. The purse with her money in it is gone. I'm not saying anyone here took it, but it's gone and so is the money. Let's pass the hat for Molly Malone!"

He picked up a big cowboy hat he sometimes wore and dropped a twenty-dollar bill into it, starting it around the far side of the room. Brenda saw Ken adding a twenty. She tried to find Behan in the crowded pub but he was nowhere to be seen. While the hat was passed there were more cheers as Slim and Roy launched into another rendering of "Molly Malone."

When the hat had been passed through all corners of the room Slim made a show of dumping the collected bills into a paper bag and presenting it to Brenda. Roy had slipped off to the men's room. "There now, lass. Don't lose it this time."

"I won't!" she assured them. "Thanks to everyone! I'll never forget you!"

She would have been out the door in another minute, safely on her way, had not a strong hand gripped her shoulder as she made her way through the noisy crowd. "Hello, Brenda."

She was so startled to hear her real name that she swerved around to see who it was. "Tom! What are you—"

Tom O'Toole smiled at her. "—doing here?" he completed "Well, it's Saint Patrick's Day and this is an Irish pub. What more reason do I need? I just came in and saw them passing the hat for you." He was still in his kilt and carrying a big leather pouch with his bagpipe inside.

"I waved to you in the parade," she said, trying to cover her embarrassment.

"I saw you. What's this?" he asked, tapping the paper bag. "Don't tell me you lost your purse again this year!"

"Tom, can't we go outside? It's too noisy in here." She didn't want anyone overhearing them.

But before they could reach the door there was a commotion at the far end of the bar. "Call the cops!" a man was shouting. "There's a dead guy in the men's room!"

AFTER THAT, NO ONE left. Brenda stood there with her bag full of money, frozen in position next to Tom O'Toole. He was several inches taller, a good six feet, and he'd told her once that the kilt only came out for the annual parade. She'd met him two years earlier at a pub on Saint Patrick's night when she was working her scam, and they'd gone out drinking a few times after that. He'd remained a friend, but she'd never told him that the lost purse and passing the hat were all a scam she repeated annually.

The police arrived and it quickly became obvious that no one would be leaving the Harp & Shamrock for a while. Ken, the stockbroker who'd been standing at the bar with Brenda and Michael Behan, had worked his way through the crowd to her. "It's Behan," he said. "Someone killed him in the men's room."

"Oh no!"

"I'll want to talk to you," he told her, and suddenly his demeanor had changed. He was no longer a carefree Irishman celebrating the holiday. He showed her a badge and ID for Kenneth Wagner, Federal Bureau of Investigation. "We can use the office back here."

He led the way to a little room behind the bar, and she had time only for a quick appealing glance at Tom O'Toole. "What's this all about?" she asked the FBI agent. "What were you doing here?"

"We've been watching Behan for some time now. We suspect he was a conduit supplying American money to a violent Irish splinter group. Do you know anything about that?"

Brenda shook her head. "I only met the man a couple of hours ago. You were standing there. You saw me come in."

"He'd told me he was meeting someone here tonight on business. It could have been you. You're flying to Ireland tomorrow."

"I'm not—" she began and then decided she couldn't admit too much. "I have a mother back in Ireland. There are no ties to any splinter groups." When Wagner remained silent she added, "Look, there are over two hundred people out there. Any one of them might have killed him."

"Almost certainly it was a man. He was found in one of the men's room stalls, seated on the closed toilet and fully clothed. He'd been stabbed twice in the chest and died almost immediately. I think he went in there to meet the person who killed him. His carrying case was empty on the floor. If it held a laptop computer, the killer stole it."

"Maybe that's all he wanted. They're not cheap."

"There could be another motive. That laptop might have an address list of contributors to Irish causes."

Brenda was doubtful. "Would someone kill for that?"

"Quite possibly. There could be a great deal of money at stake. The police are out there searching for the laptop right now."

"And you suspect me because I'm going to Ireland tomorrow?"

"You said your mother lived in Killarney, didn't you?"

"That's right." Somehow she felt everything was closing in on her.

"Behan lived just long enough to start writing a word in his own blood, on the wall of the toilet stall. He wrote *kill*. Maybe he was try-ing to write *killarney*."

"How could I have gotten into the men's room unnoticed?"

"The place was crowded, noisy. Somebody got in there to stab him, why not you?"

Before she could respond, there was a knock on the office door. It was the bartender, Rocky. "Lieutenant wants to see you."

The FBI agent stepped outside but left his fingers on the door's edge, not quite closing it. She heard the police lieutenant say something about laptops, and Wagner replied, "Get everyone's name and address. Make sure they have IDs."

"Are you letting them go?" she asked when he came back inside.

He nodded. "There were only two laptops in the place, and each had an owner who could prove it was his."

"Why wouldn't the killer have taken the carrying case, too?"

"It has Behan's initials on it."

"If you're releasing the others, does that mean I can go, too?"

"As soon as you show me some ID with your New York address."

"I—it was in my purse that got stolen."

Kenneth Wagner allowed himself a slight smile that seemed more menacing than friendly. His hand dipped into the side pocket of his jacket and pulled out her little green purse. "This one?"

"Where did you find it?"

"The police just located it in the disposal bin for paper towels, in the ladies' room."

"Thank you." She reached out for it but he didn't immediately let go.

"There's nothing in it, Molly. That is your name, isn't it? Molly Malone?"

She nodded. "The thief must have cleaned it out."

He sighed and motioned for her to leave. "I'll talk to you again later."

She put her purse in the bag with the money and went back into the bar. Patrons were lined up, showing their identification to a police officer who carefully noted names and addresses before allowing them to leave. Slim and Roy were putting their guitars away and taking down their banner. She walked over to them and Slim said, "You'd better get out of here."

"I'm trying," she assured him.

But she had no identification in the name of Molly Malone, and one of the bar's patrons was sure to overhear if she gave the officer the name of Brenda Conway.

Tom O'Toole was standing in line, his bagpipe in its case over his shoulder. "Let's get out of here and go somewhere else," he suggested.

"These cops are unbelievable! I had to unzip my pouch and show them the bagpipe. It's a wonder they didn't make me play a tune."

"The dead man had a laptop that was stolen. That's what they're searching for."

"You knew this guy?"

"I just met him here tonight."

He rested his hand on her shoulder. "I don't know what you're into, Brenda, but be careful. There's lots of stuff going on here that you don't know about."

"I know enough. I know that Behan was supposed to receive money from someone that could be sent to an Irish splinter group. Only that someone killed him instead, and stole his laptop with a list of other donors."

"Stick to singing 'Molly Malone,' " he suggested. "You sounded great doing that."

"Oh, Tom!" She felt a sudden sadness, as if she'd lost a close friend. She walked away from him blindly, clutching her paper bag. Somehow the money didn't seem important any longer.

"We have to talk," Slim said as she walked past him.

"Later."

She found Kenneth Wagner with the police, standing at the entrance to the men's room. Inside, they were preparing to remove the body. "I can tell you who killed him," she said. "I can tell you where that missing laptop is."

He studied her face for a moment. "Go on."

She pointed across the room at the line of people waiting to leave. "The third man in line. The laptop is in that leather pouch under his bagpipe. His name is Tom O'Toole and he's your killer."

TOM SAW THEM COMING and tried to bolt through the door, but they had him. The laptop was in there, and also the knife that was the murder weapon. When it was over, Wagner simply looked at her and shook his head. "How did you know?"

"He thought I was great singing 'Molly Malone,' but he'd told me earlier he'd just come in while they were passing the hat. That was a good fifteen minutes after I sang. He was here all the time, but I didn't notice him in the crowd. He went to the men's room, carrying his pouch, at the agreed time, and killed Behan for that computer and its lists. Behan didn't know his name, and in his dying moment he tried to identify him with a single word."

"Killarney?"

"No, I was Molly to him. He would have written that if he'd meant me. He didn't write *kill*, he wrote *kilt*, meaning that his murderer was wearing one. He didn't live long enough to cross the *t*, and with his dying scrawl it probably looks like an *l*."

"It does," Wagner confirmed grimly. "But how did you know where the stolen laptop was hidden?"

"If Tom was the killer, where else could it be? He unzipped the pouch for the police, but probably only enough to show the bagpipes. They didn't go feeling around underneath." She thought of something else. "Actually, he'd have made his escape if he hadn't stopped to talk with me on the way out. Someone found the body and then we were all stuck here."

Kenneth Wagner nodded. "You'd better get going yourself. And take care of that money."

A while later, at a coffee shop in the Port Authority bus terminal, she met Slim and Roy. "How much did you get?" Slim asked, resting his guitar case next to the booth.

"Twenty-one hundred and thirty dollars. Better than last year. Here's the five hundred I promised you."

"They were tanked up and generous. It's always a great day for the Irish."

"Unless they get killed, like Behan."

"We'll let you know where we'll be playing next year."

Brenda shook her head. "Don't bother. I'm retiring from these scams. Tonight was too much for me."

Slim shrugged. "What are you going to do with the money?"

Brenda thought about it. "Hey, maybe I'll take a trip to Ireland."

Stealing the Dark

Jane Adams

AMONGST THOSE ITEMS RECOVERED was an album of faded photographs. Sepia-toned faces gazed out at him from foxed pages decorated with roses and twining tendrils of honeysuckle. The cream boards that formed the cover had pulled loose from their binding and flapped limply as he removed the book from the evidence bag and lay it down on the wooden table of the interview room. *It was,* he thought, *a sad little volume, filled with the faces of the long dead, stiffly posed and their eyes gazing from the book at a world so changed it made him wince to think of it.*

The young man accused of theft sat opposite him, blank-eyed and sullen. His chair had been pushed back from the table and his long legs stretched beneath it, the air of studied nonchalance designed to make him look hard, though all it did, to Colm's practised eye, was emphasize how scared this kid was.

Colm checked the tape and announced himself and the others in the room for the benefit of posterity, then, gently, careful not to dislodge any of the fragile images, he began to turn the pages of the book.

"Where'd you get this, Michael?"

The boy glanced at the book, a mere flick of his eyes sideways and down.

"Where'd I get what?"

"It's an album, Michael. Family pictures. Someone's grieving for this loss." He paused, again noted the swift sideways look, but aimed at him this time and not at the book upon the table.

"Some old book?" the boy said boldly. "You going to charge me with stealing some old book." He jerked upright and then sat forward, pushing the album back toward Colm.

"Well, no," Colm said. "I thought we'd charge you for the video recorders and the bits of jewellery that we found first, but I'd like you to tell me about the book. Call it curiosity."

The boy shifted awkwardly. He was baffled by this, Colm knew, by Colm's interest in some tatty old photo album full of people who'd most likely been dead even before the lad was born.

"It's me auntie's, ain't it?" he said at last.

"And which auntie would that be, Michael? Your auntie May that lives in Galway or your auntie Joan that married the teacher and won't have anything to do with your lot now?" Colm shook his head and allowed the creases on his ugly face to compose themselves into a look of deep sorrow at the boy's situation.

"Your mam told me you were going straight, Michael. She told me you'd even got a job. What was it Michael, couldn't earn enough honestly, you had to make a bit extra thieving from those who worked hard for the things they've got?"

"What, like that scrappy old thing? Look at it. It's filthy dirty and falling to bits." He lunged forward and gave the book a shove that sent it to the floor, the poor old covers flapping and flailing in flight and the back one breaking away as it hit the floor.

Colm crossed the room and bent to pick up the book, an anger burning in his chest that was quite out of proportion to the boy's action.

"It's people's lives you're wrecking," he almost shouted at the boy. "People like the ones here in this book. Ordinary working folk that can't afford what your thieving costs them, never mind about thinking what it's costing you, lad."

"Like you care."

"Like I care!" Colm sighed and returned to his seat, placing the book once more upon the wooden table. "To be honest with you, lad, I don't know that I do care any more," he said more softly. "Three more days I have until I'm gone from here. Retired. Three more days and I'll be away from the likes of you and all the other little thieves and tow rags and scrotes and clowns, and shall I miss it? Shall I damn, so you see, lad, you're quite right when you say I don't care. I'm leaving the caring to someone else and I'll be on my way." He paused, not looking at the boy, and was silent for such a long time that the young constable standing by the door felt compelled to record the fact on tape. Colm's fingers traced the outline of the book, the worn covers with the frayed binding and the thick cardboard showing through where the cloth had worn away. There were words embossed and inked in black. "Family Album" they said, and inside the cover, neatly scribed in a rounded old-fashioned hand, the words, "For Sarah, who steals the dark."

COLM KNEW WHAT THEY were saying, even while they slapped his back and brought him drinks and fed him the sweet iced cake someone's wife had made for him. Even while they got him drunk—or near as dammit—Colm knew what they were saying about him.

"The old man's lost it."

"Retirement coming just about the right time. Just as well, he can go with a bit of dignity."

"He's been a good officer. Straight as they come, our Colm."

"Best he go now then, he's a dying breed!"

"Away with yer. Don't you be spreading them rumours again."

"You should have seen him with that kid, Mick Brady. Thought he were going to thump him. His face! God, you should have seen it, and all over some old book or other."

He knew what they were saying as he emptied his desk for the final time and carried the taped-up box away to the pub, and he felt . . . a part of him felt . . . that they were right, that the old man *was* losing it, while the rest of his heart shouted aloud that this was a new beginning and he no longer had a thing to prove.

"No," he said out loud, knowing that everyone else was too drunk and too loud to hear. "Never anything to prove."

COLM LIVED ALONE IN a big old place his mother had left to him. Once it had been a farm but the family had long since sold the land, and the stone house, sprawling and cold in winter, was all that now remained. He got up early on his first day of freedom and went downstairs in his dressing gown to make his tea instead of dressing straight the way, feeling that he ought to make some statement, however small, that his life was changed.

Waiting for the kettle to boil, he opened up the cardboard box, spilling the assortment of pens and pads and cards from well-wishers out onto the kitchen table, then reaching down for the thing hidden in the bottom.

Colm had only stolen twice in all his life. The first time had been chocolate and a comic when he was nine years old and his mother had lambasted his backside with a wooden spoon so well that he couldn't sit for days. The second had been yesterday and now he retrieved his prize, sliding from the evidence bag the dirty, board-covered book that almost fell apart between his hands but which felt like treasure.

COLM HAD NEVER KNOWN a day pass so slowly. Used to imposed routine, finding he had none of his own was a major shock and Colm knew, even from that first day, that he could not live long like this. He tended to his garden, a job usually reserved for weekends off, and scrubbed the kitchen table, a task his mother had carried out twice daily but which he could not remember doing for himself. And then feeling idle and unwanted rather than glorying in his freedom, he made more tea and sat beside the garden window to look once again through Sarah's book.

There were thirty pages and pictures on all of them. Most were posed studio shots, many of couples or families, and he guessed that three or four must have been for weddings. A man in a uniform he did not recognise, wearing cavalry boots and epaulettes, stared proudly from a picture, a cloth backdrop of forest behind him. The date on the picture was 1915. As he touched it, the photograph fell from the page, the four little dots of glue holding it there finally giving in to age. Curiously, Colm turned it over.

"Uncle George," he read. "1892 to 1915."

He turned it about once more, looking closely into the youthful, eager face of the man who stood so proudly in his uniform, and it struck Colm how often men felt the need to dress for death as though the garments of every day were not fine enough.

Carefully, he began to detach other pictures from the frames. Most were stuck only lightly and came away almost eagerly, falling into his hands. Many were blank behind as though the images were so well known to the owner that she needed no reminder of the who or when, but some were dated and given names, and from these Colm gained vague knowledge of George and Edward, Gracie and her sister Jo. Elizabeth on her wedding day—her husband, oddly, unnamed—and Sarah herself in a high-necked blouse, the throat decorated with a simple beaded pin and her hair piled high away from a broad forehead and decided eyebrows arching over intense dark eyes. Unlike so many of the other pictures, this was no studio shot. It was taken in the open air with a line of hills behind her, faded and distant. She was seated and her skirts were spread upon the grass and one tightly buttoned boot peeped from beneath them. Sarah's name was written on the back, Sarah Connelly, 1917, and also a brief line of description beneath.

"Beautiful day," the note said, in the same rounded hand that had written Sarah's name at the front of the book. "Beautiful day. March 1917, Glendalough. Wicklow."

Gently, Colm slipped the other pictures back into the album, careful to place them in the proper order, but the picture of Sarah he kept aside and that night when he slept he placed it on his bedside table propped against the light.

"I'M SORRY TO BOTHER you, sir."

"Not sir anymore, Robbie, and it's just Colm now. You'd better come in."

The young man was out of uniform, just come off shift, and Colm knew why he was there.

He opened the drawer in the kitchen table and handed Robbie the evidence bag, the album safely back inside.

"I expect it was still on your desk," the young man said. "I mean, when you were packing stuff away ready to be gone. It was a bit mad that day." He smiled, a real affectionate smile, Colm was glad to see. "We thought that's what you'd done, just picked it up along with all your other things."

Colm nodded, relieved not to have had to make up a lie. The fact that the book had been bagged and tagged and left with the other evidence in care of the property master was not mentioned. He handed the album over and enquired as to the health of Robbie's new wife, delighted in the fact that they were expecting a child, and pretended sorrow that the young man did not have time to stay for tea or something a little stronger. The truth was, Colm was relieved when he had gone. He stood beside the door, watching the car maneuvre through the farm gate and back onto the lane. One day only but already the gulf was widening between himself and those he had called colleagues if not friends.

He closed the door and went upstairs as though needing to be certain of something. To be certain that he had not done wrong, that she would not reproach him for giving her family away so freely and keeping her there, but Sarah gazed at him from her place beside his bed and there was neither sadness nor reproach in the dark blue eyes—and he knew that they were blue—he saw only understanding and compassion in her smile.

LEAVING WAS EASY AND took little preparation. He had no one to say good-bye to and little to pack aside from a few clothes. He saw no reason to wait until the morning.

He drove north, to Wicklow, the hills when he reached them hidden by a curtain of fine grey rain that parted with the wind to give him only a fragile glimpse. Glendalough was on the farthest side and not easy to find on badly signed lanes and in a veil of rain. Finally, he pulled the car over into a farm gate and, covering himself with the car blanket he had ready in the back seat, he fell asleep and waited for the daylight.

"DID HE SAY ANYTHING, Colm, I mean, when you collected the album?"

Robbie shook his head. "Asked about Dierdre and the baby. I said to him like you told me to, that we thought he must have picked up the book by accident, like, when he packed to go."

"Good, good," Superintendent Philips nodded approvingly. "And he seemed fine aside from that?"

"Yes, sir. He seemed well enough."

"That's all right then. Best left at that." Philips frowned, "Funny, though, but when we interviewed the Brady boy again he asked about the book. Said he didn't know why he'd taken it, rambling on about some woman . . ." He shrugged, losing interest, his mind already onto other things.

COLM WOKE, STIFF AND cold, to a dawn that was more mist than daylight. His limbs were stiff and aching and he almost fell getting out of the car, stumbling about amongst the tussocks of grass and the ruts left from his tyres until his feet came back to life and the feeling in his legs was not just the pain of returning blood.

Leaving his car he walked farther up the lane, the road climbing steeply and bending about the hill until it reached the summit after a quarter mile.

The mist was thick about him, deadening his footsteps and filling his ears with the sound of water, the air so thick with it that it seemed to drip into the silence and run constantly beneath his feet. His own breath returned to him, sodden and chilled against his face, and in time he gave up, returned to his car, and drove back along the lane in search of breakfast and a place to get warm.

ROBBIE WAS NOT QUITE sure what had piqued his curiosity, but the nagging at the back of his mind had grown throughout the day and drew him to the photograph album. It was back in the evidence store, wedged between two seized video players and a box filled with car radios. He turned the pages slowly, examining the faces of those whom the camera had caught in time, exposed for the examination of future generations. A woman, the boy Michael had said. Something about a woman. There were women aplenty in the album, but Robbie had the impression he had meant a woman alone and there were none like that in the little book. All had accompaniments, a sister, a husband, a clutch of children clinging to their skirts. An old couple pictured with a single girl was the clearest he could get to a lone woman and Robbie knew instinctively that this was not the image he sought.

And there was another thing, something he was certain had changed since the album had been in Colm's possession. Every image had been eased free of its page then placed back carefully between the leaves. Robbie would have been willing to swear that when he had first seen the album on the table in the interview room the pictures had been glued down, not floating free and ready to fall from the book if you tilted it too far.

Slowly and carefully he placed each one back in its space, pausing only to read the brief inscriptions on the back identifying Uncle George or Great Aunt Rose, and when he had finished, he was sure. One image was missing, not a large picture if you went by the glue marks on the page, but one, Robbie was sure, which had been the picture of the woman.

Puzzled, he put the album carefully away and replaced it in the evidence store.

COLM HAD WAITED FOR the sun to rise fully enough to burn away the mist. He had found a place for breakfast, sitting outside until the cafe opened and ignoring the curious looks from its proprietors, Colm being neither local nor tourist and therefore something of a novelty. As he paid his bill he took Sarah's photograph from his pocket and showed it to the woman behind the counter.

"I'm looking for family," he explained. "This woman and her family . . ."

He stopped, the quizzical expression on the woman's face bringing him to his senses.

"Ay, well, like I said," he blustered, "old family . . ."

He left, feeling like a fool. The woman's gaze burning at his back. Showing a photograph as old as this to someone and expecting her to say, *Oh, yes, she lives in Dunscomb Street just down the way*, was patently ridiculous. He'd be the talk of the village by mid-morning, no doubt. Colm made a note to himself not to pass back that way.

HE RETURNED TO WHERE he had parked the night before and again walked up the hill, the narrow road becoming less than a farm track as it rounded the bend to overlook the valley. This time there was no mist and the valley of Glendalough opened out below him. Weak autumn sunshine sparkled on the surface of the two lakes from which it took its name and, at the farthest end of the steep-sided valley, stood the round tower and small squat church that he recalled they named Saint Kevin's kitchen after the saint who had made his home there.

The road to Wicklow and Kildare curved at the valley's closer end, the road back to Colm's world. Colm turned his gaze away and began to scramble down.

ROBBIE LOOKED CURIOUSLY AT the balding, round-faced man who had come into the front office enquiring for his property.

"Your belongings have been laid out in the interview room, sir, but I don't know if I can release them to you yet; you'll have to have words with the sergeant."

He led Mr. Williams through to the interview room and stood by while the man inspected his video recorder and his little portable television and the bits and pieces of cheap jewellery that the boy Michael Brady had said came from the same house.

The VCR had been postcoded and the television had a sticky label fixed to its underside with its owner's address, something Michael Brady had not thought to look for. He would never make even a good thief, thought Robbie, and he seemed to have little talent for anything else.

"Anything wrong, Mr. Williams?" Robbie asked.

"No, no." The man paused awkwardly, something clearly on his mind. "There was a little book along with the things I had taken," he said at last. "A book of pictures, photos, you know. A family thing. I wondered . . ."

"Ah, yes, the family album."

"Oh? So you have it here?"

"We have an album, yes, that might be yours. Perhaps you could describe it to me, just to be sure?"

Williams hesitated, "It's, well, it's old, very old, and with creamy covers. Rather worn and dirty like. And there's a picture inside I'm fond of. A woman in a high-necked blouse. Her name was Sarah, I believe. The book was hers."

"She was a relative of yours was she, this Sarah?"

Mr. Williams shuffled his feet uncomfortably.

"I suppose she must have been," he said. "She was a pretty woman . . ." He caught sight of Robbie's frown. "Is something wrong, officer?"

Robbie recovered himself. That woman again. "I'll get it for you to look at, sir," he said, "if you could just hang on here for a minute or two?"

Mr. Williams nodded eagerly. Too eagerly perhaps, and on impulse Robbie turned back, his hand on the handle of the door. "Mr. Williams, this isn't a family album, is it? Not from your family? Is there maybe something you'd be telling me?"

"Oh God, how did you know?" The man crumpled and sat down in the nearest chair, his plump face flushed to the roots of his balding head and then ran pale with such speed that Robbie thought that he was going to faint.

"Are you all right, sir? That's right, you sit down there." He left the door and came back across the room, perching himself on the table edge. The truth was, Robbie had known nothing until that moment. Some blend of instinct and pure mischief had led him to the question, no more than that, but now he was intrigued. "Tell me, Mr. Williams," he invited. "Maybe I can get you a cup of tea? And the two of us can have a little chat."

ROBBIE PUSHED OPEN THE door of the dusty little shop and went inside, avoiding the stacks of books piled on the windowsill and balanced precariously on the floor beside it.

Shelves stood floor to ceiling around the musty little room, a converted parlour before the big windows had been fitted and the shop sign hung outside.

Other shelves were crammed so close there was scarcely space for Robbie to slide between as he made his way to the rear of the shop and rang the counter bell. "Yes, can I help you?"

The man was younger than Robbie had expected.

"Are you the owner, sir?"

"That's my father, he's not here today." He examined Robbie thoughtfully, taking in the uniform, his eye falling upon the package tucked under Robbie's arm.

"The album!" he said. He sounded startled. "Where on earth did you find that old thing? My dad's been going mad about it these past months."

"It came from here, then?"

"Well, yes, we got it from a house clearance, somewhere out near Wicklow."

"So it's not a family thing?"

"No, but from the fuss Dad made when it was gone, you'd think it had been. He hardly spoke to me for weeks afterward, but I mean, how was I to know he wanted to keep that old thing. I just put it out in the bargain box with all the other cheap books." Robbie nodded. That fitted well with what Mr. Williams had told him.

"Did you look at the pictures inside?" he asked.

The shopkeeper shook his head. "We'd that lot arrive and three other house clearance batches all within the one weekend. My dad had to go away for a day or two and I did what I always do, look through for the odd first edition, shelve anything that seems worth the trouble of pricing, and shove the others in the box. To be truthful, I don't know why he bothers with that stuff; most times it costs us as much in diesel to collect as we'll ever make, but he won't be told."

Robbie lay the evidence bag on the counter and withdrew the album. At first glance it did indeed look like a tatty piece of rubbish, but, had he been in this man's place, Robbie knew that he would have at least looked inside and have been fascinated by the old-fashioned pictures. He found it hard to understand such lack of curiosity; though, to be fair, he supposed working in a shop as packed to the gills as this, with what to even Robbie's untrained eye was clearly unremarkable, it might become a little difficult to maintain enthusiasm.

"You have records, I suppose, of where this stuff comes from."

"Of course we do, though all they'll say is the address and how many boxes we took."

"That should do," Robbie told him. "That should do very well." He paused, then asked, "Did your father say why he liked this old book so much?"

The other man laughed. "Quite right he did, something about a woman's picture and how he wanted to frame it. He gets these odd notions from time to time." He leaned across the counter toward Robbie. "Privately, you know, I don't think he'd sell any of this stuff

unless he'd been forced. He'd keep the lot and just keep adding to it."
He frowned. "I thought it was funny though, you know. As I say, the
book was in the bargain box. Ten pence a shot we charge for that stuff.
Ten pence and some bugger still had to go and steal it."

COLM HAD REACHED THE valley floor. Breathless and hot despite the
chill of the day, he stood on the banks of the lower lake and gazed
across its ruffled surface feeling more than a little foolish and wondering what he should do.

He had hoped for revelation, for a wonderful thing about to happen that would help him to make sense of his newfound freedom.
That would help him to make sense of these feelings that he had for a
woman he had never known.

He tried to rationalise his actions, this wild-goose chase in search
of the location in a photograph. He told himself that it was the
inscription in the front of the book that had so drawn him, that it
reminded him of things long past and it was nostalgia that had drawn
him here, not the overfull, overblown feelings for some woman he had
never even seen.

"For Sarah," he said out loud. "Sarah who steals the dark." It came
close to something his mother was fond of saying in those days when
there'd been just the two of them trying to run the old farm alone.

"To let the daylight in," his mother had told him, "sometimes you
just have to steal the dark." It was like a proverb to her, words of wis-
dom to be said when life was at its worst and the debts were piling at
their door. Finally, they had been forced to sell the land and they were
left only with the garden to tend, all that was left of the rich black
earth that his mother had grieved for all the remainder of her days.

"For Sarah," he said again. "Who steals the dark." He stared hard
into the depths of the peaty waters, his eyes filling with tears.

COLM'S HOUSE LOOKED EMPTY and deserted even as Robbie turned into the lane. Colm's old red car was absent from the drive and when he tried the door it was locked up tight. Robbie could not explain the feelings of dread that gripped him when he realised that the man was gone.

He walked down the road to the nearest farm a quarter mile away and enquired after their neighbour, but they had nothing to tell. They saw Colm little enough at any time, and for them not to see him now was nothing to be wondered at. But they had heard a car go by in the early hours, last morning or the one before, it was hard to say, and noticed only because the world was so quiet in the hours before the dawn.

Robbie fetched his car and went back to work, telling himself that he was not Colm's keeper and the chances were he had gone out only to shop or visit friends, until he remembered that Colm never mentioned friends. That Colm never mentioned anyone or anything outside of work and duty and that hours went by, unbooked and unnoticed when Colm would work a case deep into the night rather than go home.

Robbie let his anxiety ride through the afternoon until he could stand no more of it.

"I may be foolish, sir," he told his superintendent, "but I can't get out of my mind that something's happened to him."

"And you think he'd be grateful to you if you go looking for him and the man most likely just taking a holiday."

"I'll risk that. I'd rather he told me to get lost and mind my own than go on being bothered by this feeling."

Superintendent Philips frowned at him disapprovingly. "I always deplored too much imagination in the young," he said. "And in this profession, lad, it can lead to nothing but grief. But go your way, see if any of our lot spot him on his travels. Tell them that you found a window insecure or some such when you went out to Colm's farm."

Robbie thanked him. "I will, sir," he said gratefully, wondering just why he should feel so relieved when it was clear that his superior officer thought he was making an idiot of himself and that, surely, could do his career not one bit of good.

"THE LAKE IS CALLED LOCH PEIST, you know. It means the lake of the water monster. I used to think he must lie very still in the peat and mud waiting for the little boats to float by."

"You still think that?" He dared hardly breathe, watching her reflection in the tea-coloured water. Afraid to turn, just knowing if he did that she would disappear.

"I'd like to think it, but my auntie reckons he moved out long ago when the tourists came and he got tired of being pointed at and of having grown men fishing for him all the summer."

"And where did he go to? Did she tell you that?"

"Oh, along the hill a little way. To the Loch na h'Onchon I've no doubt. It would be more peaceful there."

"And *Onchon* does mean monster," Colm agreed with her. "It would be a good place for a water dragon to be at home."

He took a deep, quavering breath and held it in, still afraid to turn, like Orpheus in the story fearing to lose Euridice. But he could not bear to be so close, so close that he could hear the rustle of her dress when she moved, catch the lavender hint of her perfume, and not be able to look her in the face.

"Sarah," he whispered softly, and he slowly twisted his head around and she stood still behind him, holding out her hand.

THEY HAD FOUND COLM'S car. A full day and night had passed since Robbie had spoken of his anxiety and another day would have gone by if the farmer had not complained of a car blocking the gate to his top field. They had moved the car, Robbie was told, pushing it farther up onto the grass verge, and the farmer said that he thought he had seen a man walk from it up the hill and then disappear over the crest as if he had gone down on the other side.

Robbie followed, walking more swiftly than Colm had done, breasting the hill and then almost running down the vast and variable slope to the wide valley below.

It had been too much to hope that he would see Colm there. The valley was peopled only by sheep and three skittish horses that bolted

at the suddenness of his descent and a few walkers, distant, colourful
figures set against the green. But of Colm there was no sign but for
boot marks in the mud beside the lake, half obscured by the impres-
sions of sheep pads and the hooves of horses. Desperately, Robbie
stared about him, willing the man to appear; but there was no one
close, no Colm, no hunched-shouldered man in tweeds looking as
though life bore down on him, only, as Robbie looked, a woman
standing on the far-side shore, her long skirt blowing in the brisk wind
and a white blouse fastened high against her throat.

COLM HAD DRIFTED IN deep waters, the coldness closing above his
head and the darkness surrounding him; but aside from the cold he
felt no discomfort and experienced no regrets. Sarah's hand was
clasped tightly in his own and he had never felt so much at peace or
more beloved.

THE DOCTOR CAME THROUGH the double glass doors to the waiting
room and approached Robbie.

"Your friend was lucky," he said quietly. "He was half dead when
the fishermen pulled him from the lake. Just as well, one of them knew
some first aid, and they had the good sense to wrap him warm and
bundle him into their car. Then they brought him here. He's still
shocked, but he's taken no great harm." The doctor hesitated before
he asked. "He says he's just retired?"

Robbie nodded. "Just a few days ago."

"And he's maybe been depressed? It's hard to cope sometimes
when the job's been your life."

"He'll be all right," Robbie said defensively. "Anyone can fall into
a bloody lake."

"He didn't fall . . ." the doctor began, then paused, shaking his head beneath Robbie's glare. "Yes, well, we can talk about this later on. Now, I'm sure you just want to see your friend."

Robbie nodded. "And I'd like a word with the men that pulled him out. Thank them."

"They're tourists," the doctor said, "but I've got their details ready for you. It's a funny thing, though, they said there was another helping them. A woman in a long black skirt and white blouse that waded in and grabbed your man even before they realized what was going on. She held onto him until they reached her and then they pulled the two of them into their boat and rowed ashore. She must have been local, though, because the men said when they looked up from seeing to your friend she'd taken off somewhere and neither saw the way she went."

ROBBIE SAT QUIETLY AT Colm's bedside waiting for him to open his eyes. Colm looked more peaceful and rested than Robbie could ever remember seeing him. He sat watching the older man's face, seeing the fleeting expressions pass across it like a man who dreams and the dreams are pleasant ones, until at last Colm opened his eyes.

"You found her then?" Robbie asked him softly.

"I found her," Colm answered him. "She reached out her hand for me and I have never felt so warm nor so safe before in all my life. It's a good feeling, Robbie, for a man to know that he is loved."

Robbie nodded but Colm didn't see him, he had closed his eyes again and gone back to dreaming. Dreaming of Sarah who had stolen the dark and let the daylight stream, warm and golden, back into his heart.

A Book of Kells

(A John Francis Cuddy Story)

Jeremiah Healy

T HE IRISH-AMERICAN HERITAGE CENTER was located in a red-brick building three blocks off East Broadway in South Boston. Growing up in the neighborhood, I remembered the structure as a public elementary school, but when the city fell on hard times in the seventies, the mayor and council sold a number of municipal properties to keep real-estate taxes from rocketing skyward. As I parked my old Honda at the curb, I got the impression that the Center was doing a lot better by the building than the school department ever had.

The main entrance consisted of three separate doors, the one to the left having a sign in gold calligraphy, reading TRY THIS ONE FIRST, which I thought was a nice touch. Inside the lobby area, the same ornate lettering adorned the walls, including a mural with the homily: MAY YOUR TROUBLES BE LESS/YOUR BLESSINGS BE MORE/AND NOTHING BUT HAPPINESS/COME THROUGH YOUR DOOR.

On my right was an office complex, probably where the principal used to hold court. A woman sitting behind a reception counter rose when she saw me.

"John Cuddy," I said, "here to see Hugh McGlachlin."

"Oh, yes." Her expression shifted from concerned to relieved. "Please come in."

A buzzer sounded. She opened the door nearest her counter and showed me through a second inner door. "Hugh, Mr. Cuddy," she said.

A voice with just a lick of the brogue said, "Thank you, Grace. And hold any calls, if you would, please."

Grace nodded and closed the inner door behind me.

The man rising from the other side of the carved teak desk was about five-nine and slight of build, wearing a long-sleeved dress shirt and a tie. His hair was gray and short, combed a little forward like a Roman emperor's. Despite the gray hair, his face was unlined around the blue eyes, and his smile shone brightly enough for a toothpaste commercial.

A woman occupied one of the chairs in front of McGlachlin's desk, but instead of standing as well, she turned toward me while twisting a lace handkerchief in her lap. I pegged her as middle forties, with florid skin and a rat's nest of red hair. She wore the drab, baggy clothes of someone catching up on her housework, a canvas tote bag that had seen better days at her feet.

The man came around his desk and extended his right hand. "Hugh McGlachlin, executive director of the Center here. Thanks so much for coming so quickly."

I shook hands with him, and McGlachlin turned to the seated woman. "This is Mrs. Nora Clooney."

She swallowed and shook hands with me as well, hers trembling in mine.

"Well," said McGlachlin, tapping the back of the other chair in front of his desk, "I'm not sure of the protocol, but I think I'd be most comfortable using first names."

"Fine with me."

He and I sat down at the same time, and McGlachlin studied me briefly. "I didn't tell Michael O'Dell why we needed a private investigator," he said.

O'Dell was a lawyer in Back Bay who'd fed me a lot of cases over the years. "Probably why he didn't tell me."

The toothpaste smile again. "Michael is a member of our advisory board. And he assured me you were the soul of discretion and someone to be trusted."

"I'll be sure to thank him."

McGlachlin leaned back in his chair. "I think you may be just the man for the job, John."

"Which is?"

He pursed his lips. "How much do you know about the Heritage Center?"

"Only what I've seen so far this morning."

Hugh McGlachlin rose again, picking up a manila envelope from the corner of his desk. "In that event, I think a brief tour might prove instructive. Nora?"

Clooney preceded us out the inner door.

"We incorporated as a nonprofit institution in '75," said McGlachlin, "and moved into this building four years later. I don't mind telling you, John, the city left it quite the mess." He made a sweeping gesture with the envelope. "But thanks to some Irish-American tradesmen generously donating their time and talents, we've been able to renovate the interior a bit at a time and rejuvenate the community we serve."

I sensed that the operative word for me was *donating*.

The three of us were moving down a hallway festooned with the various crests of the thirty-two counties of Ireland, that signature gold calligraphy naming each. On the left, double doors opened onto a large and beautifully rendered country-house room, sporting an exposed-beam ceiling, slate floor, and massive fieldstone fireplace on the shorter wall. In the hearth was a cauldron suspended by metal bars over an unlit fire, an iron milk jug bigger than a beer keg to the side.

I said, "Hugh, what exactly is the Center's problem?"

McGlachlin just stopped, but Clooney seemed to freeze in her tracks. He looked up at the crests over our heads. "Would you know where your forebears hailed from, John?"

"County Kerry on my father's side, Cork on my mother's."

"Ah." McGlachlin pointed first to a shield with a white castle and gold harp. "Kerry . . ." and then to a crest with a galleon sailing between two red towers, "and Cork."

He took a step into the room. "In both places, John, they would have broken their backs hoisting jugs like that one onto a pony cart to carry their cows' milk to town." He fixed me with those blue eyes.

"'Tis a marvelous thing that we who emigrated are more fortunate, don't you think?"

"Hugh," I said, "until I know why you called Michael O'Dell—and probably why Clooney seems nervous as a wet cat—I won't be able to tell you whether I can help the Center for free."

McGlachlin grinned this time, but without showing any teeth, and I had the feeling that despite my being six inches taller and fifty pounds heavier, I'd hate to meet him in an alley. He said, "Yes, I do believe you're the man for our job. This way, please."

We took an elevator to the second floor. As I followed McGlachlin down the hallway, I tried to stay abreast of Clooney. No matter how I adjusted my stride, though, she always stayed a step behind me.

McGlachlin stopped again, this time outside a large classroom where the chairs and tables were shoved against the walls. Perhaps a dozen girls and young women were moving in a circle, their hands joined but held high. "We have step-dancing classes in here," he said, "though we also host Lithuanian folk dancing for our neighbors of that extraction. The Nimble Thimbles teach needlework over there, and every Wednesday we have instruction in Gaelic."

I nodded.

Another toothy smile. "All right, then. The next floor is the one that concerns us most at the moment."

"THIS IS OUR MUSEUM, John."

McGlachlin used a key to open a heavy security door in a corridor filled with construction odds and ends, plaster dust on every surface. The area at the end of the hallway was still just undefined space, only a few wall studs in place.

The security door opened into a large viewing room, glass-faced cases along two walls displaying china in all shapes and sizes, lots of pastel green "icing" on the edges of plates and pitchers.

"Recognize it?" asked McGlachlin.

My mother had a piece she prized. "Belleek."

"Very good. The finest of Irish porcelain." He waved a hand at the third wall. "And there's the loveliest collection of lace you may ever see."

I took in the white fabric spread on trays of green velvet. "You said downstairs that—"

"—this is the floor that concerns us most right now. Yes, indeed I did." McGlachlin's voice dropped to the subdued tone of a devout man entering his church. "Over here, John."

We went through a doorway into a smaller room with soft, recessed lighting. In the center was a freestanding case about two feet square. Its top, or cover, evidently had been glass, though it was hard to judge further because it was shattered into crumbly crystals lying fairly evenly on the otherwise empty green velvet.

I said, "You've had a theft."

McGlachlin looked my way as Clooney began twisting her hankie again. After glancing at her, he turned back to me. "John, you recognized the Belleek. Would you also know about *The Book of Kells?*"

"Something the Irish monks did back in the Middle Ages?"

"Close enough. During the eighth and ninth centuries, Celtic scribes painstakingly copied each passage of the four Gospels onto 'paper' made from the stomach lining of lambs. Every page is an artist's palette of flowing script and glorious colors, with the original book carefully guarded at Trinity College in Dublin. However, in 1974 some reproductions were permitted—they called them 'facsimiles.' Only five hundred copies. But they are works of art themselves, down to the wormholes in the pages."

I looked at the smashed case. "And you had one of those."

"The Center purchased its facsimile in 1990 for twenty thousand dollars."

I thought back to my time as a claims investigator. "You've notified your insurance carrier."

McGlachlin shook his head. "On the collector's market now, the price is ten times what we paid; but the money is largely irrelevant: Nobody who has a facsimile is willing to part with it."

"Still, the policy would pay—"

"It's not a check I want, John. It's the book itself. There'll never be any more facsimiles produced, at least not in our lifetime. The Center needs its copy back as a matter of"—another sweeping gesture with the manila envelope—"heritage."

I looked at him. "Let me save you some time. The Boston police have an excellent—"

"Not yet, John." McGlachlin seemed pained. "I'm rather hoping this can be resolved without resorting to our insurance company or the police." He opened the manila envelope and slid a single piece of paper from it. "This was on top of the shards there."

I stepped sideways so I could read it without touching it. In simple block lettering on white photocopy stock, the words were TAKEN, BUT NOT STOLEN, AND WILL BE RETURNED.

"Who found this?"

"I did, sir," said Clooney, the first words I'd heard her speak.

McGlachlin cleared his throat. "Nora volunteers her time to clean for us. Given all the plaster dust from the ongoing renovation, it's no small task."

I looked at her. "Where was this piece of paper when you first saw it?"

Clooney glanced at her boss. "It was just like Mr. McGlachlin told you. The note was lying atop all the broken glass." The brogue was woven through her voice much more than her boss's.

"And the glass hasn't been disturbed since?"

McGlachlin said, "I've kept the room locked since Nora came to me this morning with the news."

I let my eyes roam around before returning to Clooney. "Do you clean this room the same time every day?"

"First thing in the morning, sir. Eight o'clock. It wouldn't do for visitors not to be able to see the book for the plaster dust covering its blessed case."

"And nothing was wrong yesterday at eight?"

"No, sir." The lace hankie was getting wrung some more.

I glanced around again. "Other than the locked door, what kind of security do you have for this room?"

"None," said McGlachlin. "We've been spending every available penny on the renovations."

I stared at him. "But what about visitors wandering in?"

"Access to these museum rooms is restricted solely to those of us with a key to that door. As anyone can plainly see, there's been no attempt to jimmy it or the windows, even assuming the bastard—

sorry, Nora—thought to bring a ladder with him to lean against the outside wall."

I thought about it. "I can see why you haven't gone to the police."

McGlachlin sighed. "Exactly so. This had to be—is it still called 'an inside job'?"

I turned back to Clooney. "So the incident must have occurred sometime between 8:00 A.M. or so yesterday—"

"More like nine, sir, the time I finished in here—"

"To eight this morning?"

"Yes, sir."

I looked at McGlachlin. "All right, how many people have keys to that door?"

"I do, as executive director. And Nora, for her cleaning and turning."

"Turning?"

She said, "Every day, sir, I go up to the book and turn a page."

McGlachlin pointed to the windows. "So the sun fades the ink only a tiny bit, and more or less evenly."

I looked at the shattered glass. "How did you open it?"

They both stared at me.

"The glass cover, or top. How did you open it to turn the pages?"

"Oh," said Clooney, and moved to a wall panel. She threw a switch, and the remaining structure of the glass top clicked upward.

McGlachlin went to demonstrate. "You can then lift this—"

"Don't touch it," I said. "Fingerprints."

"Ah, yes. Of course."

I gestured toward the paper he still held in his hand. "And please don't let anybody else touch that. As it is, the police will need elimination prints from you, and—"

"Harking back to what I said earlier, John, we hope we won't be needing the police, thanks to you."

I waited before asking, "Who else has keys to the security door?"

McGlachlin raised a finger. "The chairman of our advisory board, Conor Donnelly. He's a professor of Irish studies." He named the college. Another finger went up. "Conor's brother, Denis, was a generous contributor to the Center, so he received a key as well."

"Denis Donnelly, the venture capitalist?"

"The very one."

"The man kicks in enough, he gets his own key?"

McGlachlin cleared his throat again. "Given the amount of Denis's contribution, John, that would be an awkward request to deny."

"Anybody else?"

"Only Sean Kilpatrick. The carpenter donating his time to do our work down the hall."

I looked around one last time. "These museum rooms look pretty well completed. Why would Kilpatrick need access to them?"

"In the event anything went wrong," he said. "But, John, Sean's somebody who's completely trustworthy."

"Hugh, at least one somebody with a key obviously isn't."

We were back in the executive director's office, the door closed. "Mr. McGlachlin, will you or Mr. Cuddy be needing me anymore today?"

McGlachlin glanced at me, and I shook my head. "Go home, then, Nora," he said. "And tell Bill I'll be by to visit after work."

After Clooney picked up her tote bag and left us, I said, "Bill's her husband?"

"Just so. And a fine, generous man to boot, but suffering from the cancer. You know how that can be."

Though I figured McGlachlin meant his comment rhetorically, I still pictured my wife, Beth, asleep in her hillside less than a mile away. "I do."

He shook his head sadly. "They met each other here at one of the Center's first socials. But then, we've sparked a lot of unions from our activities."

"Who else besides Nora—and you—actually knew how the cover over your *Book of Kells* opened?"

McGlachlin grew wary. "And what difference would that make, John? The case was smashed."

"That 'ransom' note—it was lying on top of the broken glass. Being a single sheet of paper, it's pretty light."

More wary now. "Agreed, but—"

"—so the note wouldn't have disturbed the broken glass under it very much, if at all."

McGlachlin seemed to work it through.

To save time, I said, "And since the glass shards were spread almost evenly . . ."

The executive director closed his eyes. ". . . the book was probably taken out of the case before the cover was smashed."

"Somebody wanted you to think that the glass had to be broken in order to take the book. So my question still stands: Who else knew about the cover mechanism?"

McGlachlin fixed me with his blue eyes. "John, I just don't know. But I do know this. Nora wouldn't know what to do with our book. And she's honest as the day is long."

I filed that with his endorsement of the carpenter, Sean Kilpatrick. "You didn't mention if Grace, your receptionist, also had a key."

"She does not. But given where Grace sits, she's in a position to see who comes and goes."

"Assuming everyone comes through the main doors."

"The other outside doors are alarmed, John. And besides, Grace tells me she saw all three of our key holders walk by her yesterday."

"Both in and out?"

"No, but each of them had either a knapsack or briefcase or toolbox big enough to hold the book."

"You have any suggestions on where I should start?"

"More a question on *how* you should start." McGlachlin paused. "So far, only Nora, Grace, and you know about what's happened."

"And given the tenor of that ransom note, you're hoping the book will be back by the time anyone else has to know?"

"On the button, John. There's an advisory board meeting here next week—five days hence, to be exact. The members have a tradition of reading a passage from the book—as a benediction, you might say."

"Meaning the book is taken from the case?"

"No. No, we all troop up to the room, and thanks to Nora's turning the page each morning, there're always different passages to choose from."

"Anything else about this situation you haven't told me?"

"One of the reasons I'm trying to resolve things quickly." McGlachlin pursed his lips. "You see, Conor—our board chairman—was asked by his brother, Denis, a few months ago to loan out the book for a party. Denis was giving a la-di-da affair at his home, and he wanted to have our facsimile on display for his guests."

"And what did Conor say?"

"That he'd have to put it to the Center's advisory board, which he did. And they voted not to allow the book to leave its case."

"How did Denis take that?"

"Not well. He stomped in here the next day, gave me holy hell. He thought I could perhaps permit him to borrow the book anyway."

"For a small . . . stipend?"

He nodded. "I told him I couldn't do that." McGlachlin winced. "You could have heard him yelling all over the building."

"Denis believed he should have been accommodated because of that large contribution you mentioned?"

"More specific than that, I'm afraid. You see, John, 'twas Denis's money that let our Center buy the book in the first place."

After getting McGlachlin's home number—"Call, John, any time of the day or night"—I drove from the Center to another repository of memories. Irish-American also, but different. And more personal.

Leaving the Honda on the wide path, I walked through the garden of stones until I found hers. The words ELIZABETH MARY DEVLIN CUDDY never changed, but they became a little fainter, the freeze/thaw of Boston winters taking their toll even on polished granite.

"I've been asked to find a book, Beth."

A book?

I explained the problem to her.

After a pause, she said, *I remember seeing an illuminated page from it, in an art-history text, I think.*

"That would make sense."

An incredible collector's item.

As I nodded at her comment, my eye caught the plodding movement of a lobster boat down in the harbor, chugging along in the light chop of a northeast wind that smelled of rain to come. Its skipper seemed intent on collecting his pots before the storm began to . . .

John?

I came back to her stone. "Sorry?"

How are you going to approach these three men without tipping them to who you are and what you're doing?

"It took a while, but coming here has shown me the way."

I fooled myself into thinking I could hear the confusion in Beth's next, unspoken question.

PICTURE THE KIND OF campus that would bring tears of joy to a high-school guidance counselor. The classroom and dormitory buildings were a Gothic design like the lower, auxiliary structures tacked onto cathedrals—imposing mullioned windows, ivy winding from the ground nearly to the rooflines.

After stopping three students with enough earrings piercing them to fill a jewelry box, I was directed by the last to a sallow, four-story affair. Inside, red arrows with small signs beneath them directed me to the second floor, and a receptionist swamped by students picking up exams waved me toward the office on her immediate right. The stenciling on the door reminded me of my own office's pebbled glass, but instead of JOHN FRANCIS CUDDY, CONFIDENTIAL INVESTIGATIONS in black, this one read CONOR DONNELLY, IRISH STUDIES in green.

I knocked and received a "Come," repeated three times like an oft-intoned litany.

The door opened into a large office with a high ceiling and two banks of fluorescent lights suspended over the bookshelved wall. The opposite wall had five of the multipaned windows throwing as much sunshine as the day was offering onto the head and shoulders of a standing man.

Conor Donnelly scribbled in a loose-leaf notebook lying on one of those bread-box lecterns you can lift onto a table to make a podium. His shoulders were rounded under a V-neck sweater over a flannel shirt. The brown hair was thinned enough that he had resorted to one of those low-part comb-overs, the scalp showing through between the strands that were left. His bushy eyebrows made up a little for the hairline, though. As he stepped toward me, Donnelly had to shuffle around stacks of papers on the floor.

His gray eyes blinked. "You're not a student." Brooklyn instead of brogue in his voice.

"No, but I'm hoping you're Conor Donnelly."

"A fair assumption, given where you've found me." Donnelly returned to his notebook. "But these are office hours for the students, so I can't spare you much time, Mr. . . ."

"Francis, John Francis," I said, which amounted to only one-third of a lie. "I'd like to speak with you about *The Book of Kells*."

That seemed to catch Donnelly's interest, because he motioned me toward a captain's chair across from his desk, though he stayed at the lectern. "We can speak about it, but you're a good three thousand miles from the original."

"All right, *A Book of Kells*, then. I represent a collector who'd very much like to own one of those limited-edition facsimiles, and I understand you have access to such."

Donnelly cocked his head. "In a functional sense, yes. However, I'm afraid ours at the Heritage Center is not for sale."

"No matter the money involved?"

Now Donnelly frowned. "Well, as chair of the advisory board, I'd be honor-bound to entertain any serious offer—subject, of course, to board approval."

"Professor, I'm aware that the going rate for a reproduction is tenfold what the Center paid, and my client is prepared to substantially sweeten even that inflated price. Provided, of course, that you can open that glass cover over the book so she can inspect the item."

No reaction to my "cover-opening" comment, which told me Donnelly already knew of the mechanism. "Well, Mr. Francis, you're welcome to submit your offer in writing, but I must inform you, I doubt the board will approve it. We take great pride in our copy of the book, and frankly, I don't know that any owner not desperate for money would part with one of the facsimiles."

I decided to explore what might be a gambit from Donnelly. "Would it have to be the technical owner who was desperate for money?"

He looked confused. "I don't follow you."

Leaning forward in the captain's chair and lowering my voice, I said, "Or would a person even have to be desperate for money just to be interested in having himself a little—no, a lot—more of it?"

"Ah," said Donnelly, "the light dawns. A bribe, eh?"

I shrugged.

Conor Donnelly smiled and returned again to his notebook. "Mr. Francis, get the hell out of my office before I call campus security and have you thrown out."

HIS BROTHER'S RECEPTIONIST, IN a lovely office suite overlooking Faneuil Hall, told me politely, if firmly, that Denis Donnelly would not be in that day. Both of Boston's daily newspapers had run profiles on him, though, and in each story the venture capitalist's obsession with his home in Weston Hills shone through. It didn't take long to find the place—read *estate*—and once I gave the hard-eyed man at the driveway's security gate two-thirds of my name and mentioned *The Book of Kells*, I was escorted by a younger hard-eyed guard up the drive and into a mansion on a par with the gold-domed statehouse on Beacon Hill.

The second guard watched me admire—without touching—a dozen paintings, sculptures, and vases in the parlorlike anteroom before a pair of gilded doors opened and a man I recognized from his newspaper photos came out from a spectacular atrium to greet me.

The financier was a glossy version of his brother the professor. A hair weave of some kind made this Donnelly look as if a lush bush had been planted in the middle of his head and was spreading symmetrically outward. He'd colored his eyebrows to match the new do, and his gray eyes had that jump in them I associate with race-car drivers and serial killers. He wore a silk shirt over his rounded shoulders. A pair of painfully casual, stonewashed jeans ended an inch above some loafers, no benefit of socks.

After we shook hands, Donnelly glanced at his security man. "I'll be fine with Mr. Francis, Rick," he said, his brother's Brooklyn accent on his words, too. "But advise Curt no more visitors until I'm done here."

Rick nodded, gave me a look that said, *Don't make me come back for you,* and left us.

Donnelly suggested the Queen Anne love seat might hold me, while he sank into a leather, brass-studded smoking chair. "So, Mr. Francis, you mentioned to Curt *A Book of Kells.*"

"Actually, *The Book of Kells,* but I'm sure we mean the same thing."

A look of frank appraisal. "You want to buy a facsimile, or sell one?"

"Buy, as intermediary for a client of mine."

No change of expression. "I'm in and out of the art market quite a bit. I don't recall anyone with judgment I respect ever mentioning your name."

"It's an easy one to forget."

A grin that you couldn't exactly call a smile. "You, my friend, are trying to scam me. Why?"

"No scam. My client wants one of the reproductions, and I understand you have a brother with—shall we say—sway over one of them."

"Hah!" said Donnelly, though it came out more as a bray. "I haven't so much as spit in Conor's face for a good two months now."

I tried to look disappointed. "Why?"

Donnelly lazed back in his chair. "I'm guessing you already know. I'm guessing also that you're playing me for some reason I can't figure. But I also can't see how this bit of information can hurt me. Come along."

I followed him into the atrium room, even on a dark day spectacularly lit by a rotunda skylight. I couldn't describe the furnishings if I had an hour to write about them. Except for one piece. It rested on a pedestal in a corner, shielded from potential sunlight by a glass cover that was smoke-colored on top but crystal clear on the sides. Donnelly moved directly toward it, beckoning me.

As I looked down at the large and open book, Donnelly said, "You've never seen one before, have you?"

"No," I said, my voice a little clogged as I took in, up close and personal, the filigreed detail on the capital letter at the top of the left-hand page, the depictions of people and animals—some real, some fantastical—occupying the margins and trailing after the end of paragraphs, even just the calligraphy in the text—some version of Latin, I thought.

"My brother thinks I wanted to borrow his Center's copy just to show it off for a party here. And I did." Donnelly's voice wavered. "But once I got a look at it, even in that pop-top candy case in their museum room, something—a kind of tribal memory, maybe—kicked in. What Conor seemed to forget is that I could have had the Center's own copy by just buying it for myself ten years ago. And once he and his snotty board turned me down on the party idea, I went out last month and quietly—bought another one."

I tore my eyes away from the pages in front of me. "For how many times the twenty thousand you shelled out for the first?"

Donnelly moved over to twin columns extruding from his wall. He pushed a button, and I looked back at the book pedestal, expecting its glass case to open the way the one at the Center had. It was maybe five seconds before the button's purpose hit me.

I heard a noise behind my back and wheeled around. The two hard-eyed security guys were standing inside the double doors of the atrium, arms folded in front of their chests. Looking a little more critically now at each, I didn't see any evident weapons.

I said to Donnelly, "That business of 'no other visitors' was code for 'hang close,' right?"

A nod with the bad grin. "And now, since you've obviously wasted my time on some sort of false pretenses, I think I'll enjoy watching Curt and Rick bounce you around a bit."

I tilted my head toward the door, my eyes still on Donnelly. "Just the two of them?"

The venture capitalist's eyes went neon. "Oh, I might jump in at the appropriate time."

I turned to Rick and Curt. "Denis, you're one man short."

Rick, the younger one, stepped up to the plate first. He extended both his hands to push on my chest, just like a demonstration of unarmed defense back in the sawdust pit when I was an MP lieutenant. I danced to Rick's lead for two steps, then reversed my feet and sent him over with a hip throw. When he landed on the floor, the sound of his lungs purging air was a lot easier on the ears than the gagging and dry-heaving that followed.

Curt was on me before I could turn back, clamping a choke hold across my throat with one of his forearms. I smashed my left heel down hard on his left instep and he cried out, lifting the foot. I hammered back with my left elbow and found his rib cage, feeling some of his cartilage separating as I drove into it.

Curt slid off me and cradled his left side with both hands, eyes squinched shut like a little kid who really doesn't want to cry but doesn't see how to avoid it. When I looked at Rick, he was still trying to give himself mouth-to-mouth resuscitation.

Denis Donnelly said, "So much as touch me, and I'll sue you and your client for every cent you've got."

I walked up to him, Donnelly apparently forgetting that those twin columns behind him significantly limited his mobility. He tried to kick me in the groin, but I caught his ankle in my right hand, then bent upward until he began to moan.

"Denis, I lift six more inches and you lose at least a hamstring, maybe an achilles tendon as well. We communicating?"

A strangled "Yes."

"Okay. I was never here."

"Right, right."

"And I'm never going to have to worry about Rick or Curt or any of their successors trying to find me, am I?"

"No. No, of course not."

I left him then, but not before taking a last look at Denis Donnelly's *Book of Kells*. I'd found one facsimile, but Donnelly's arrogance seemed more consistent with his trumping story of buying a facsimile for himself than with stealing the copy he had in essence donated to the Center. Which left me just one last key holder to the museum rooms.

It was nearly dark by the time Sean Kilpatrick's carpentry truck pulled into the driveway across the street from where I was sitting behind the wheel of the Honda. When the pickup approached the garage of the modest ranch, security floods came on, bathing the front yard in a yellow glow. Thanks to the lights, I could see that his truck had a primered front fender and the tailgate was held in place by bungee cords.

As Kilpatrick got out of his vehicle, I got out of mine and began crossing over to him. At the sound of my footsteps, he straightened up and turned to me.

Kilpatrick stood about six feet, with broad shoulders and curly black hair. He was wearing a sweatshirt with the sleeves cut off at the armpits over jeans and work boots. By the time I reached the foot of his driveway, his right hand had a claw hammer in it.

I stopped short of his rear bumper. "Mr. Kilpatrick?"

"And you'd be?" A brogue heavy enough that if you didn't listen for the rhythm of his cadence, you might not catch the words themselves.

"John Francis. I understand you're doing some work over at the Heritage Center."

I'd expected him to tense even more at the mention of the place, but instead he visibly relaxed, tossing the hammer toward the passenger's seat of his pickup before wiping his right palm on his thigh and approaching me to shake hands. Up close, he had a pleasant face around a genuine smile with crooked front teeth.

"Mr. Francis, pleased to make your acquaintance. What can I do for you?"

Letting go of his hand, I said, "A client of mine is a collector."

Confusion on the pleasant face. "Collector? You mean of bills, now?"

"No. Art, sculpture, rare . . . books."

"And what would that be to me?" Kilpatrick gestured toward the truck. "I'm just a carpenter."

"But a carpenter with access to the Heritage Center's museum."

"Yes." He actually started to pull out a key ring from his back pocket, the ring itself anchored to his belt by a clasp and coiled cord. "I've got—" Kilpatrick reined up short. "Wait a minute, now. What are you saying?"

"I'm saying there's a particularly valuable book under a glass case in one of those museum rooms, and a considerable commission to be earned by the person who obtains it for us."

Kilpatrick lost the crooked smile, the face now anything but pleasant. "You're wanting me to steal *The Book of Kells?*"

"Let's not say 'steal.' Let's just say you flip open the thing's glass cover before knocking off one night, and you slip the book itself into a—"

"Boyo, if you're not out of my sight in ten seconds, I'll kick every fooking tooth in your head down your fooking throat."

No need to listen for the rhythm there to know what he meant. "Sorry to have troubled you," I said.

I turned, half listening for those heavy work boots to come clumping after me. But as I got back into the Honda, Sean Kilpatrick was still standing at the rear of his battered pickup, fists on hips and staring me down.

EVEN AFTER DARK, YOU can see the dome of the Massachusetts state-house from my office window on Tremont Street. It's a pretty impressive effect, the gold leaf painstakingly reapplied by artisans a few years ago for what it probably cost the Navy to buy a carrier jet. But the dome also helps me to think somehow, especially when I'm stuck.

And I was stuck fast that night.

A very valuable reproduction of *The Book of Kells* disappears from the locked room in which it's kept, the glass top of its case smashed. Most people with access to the museum know that this top opens to allow Nora Clooney to turn a page each day, but the thief smashes it anyway, maybe to deflect suspicion onto others less informed. Hugh McGlachlin as executive director of the Center has a key, though he's the one calling me into the matter, through a member of the advisory board, Michael O'Dell. On the other hand, reacting immediately and internally like that might be a good cover story for McGlachlin himself. Of the three people he "reluctantly" suspects, none acts suspiciously—or even smugly—about my suggesting the book could be pinched: Professor Conor Donnelly orders me to leave his office, brother Denis wants me beaten up for "scamming" him, and carpenter Sean Kilpatrick stops just short of mayhem himself when I imply he could steal the Center's copy for me.

Which, according to the note left on the broken glass, wasn't actually what had happened, anyway. "Taken, but not stolen, and will be returned." No apparent sarcasm in the words or even a double meaning.

If the one person who'd asked to borrow the book had now apparently acquired a copy for himself, who would need the facsimile only temporarily?

Then, staring at the statehouse dome reminded me of something else I'd seen at the Center. It was a long shot, but worth at least a call to a certain home phone.

After dialing, I got a tentative, "Hello?"

"Hugh, it's John Cuddy."

"Ah, John. You've found something, then?"

"Maybe, but I need to ask you a question first. Who did all that calligraphy work at the Center?"

THE FRONT DOOR TO the three-decker in Southie opened only about four inches on its chain inside. The one eye I could see through the crack seemed troubled. "Oh, my. Mr. Cuddy, how could I be helping you at this hour?"

"I'd like to meet with your husband," I said.

Nora Clooney tried to tough it out. "He's asleep. Perhaps in the morning?"

I shook my head.

She squeezed her lips to thin lines. "Then let me just pop up there, sir, make sure my Bill hasn't—"

"Nora, we both know what I'll see. Can we just get it over with?"

Her head dipping in defeat, she undid the chain on the door. "That'd probably be best, I suppose."

Terminal cancer has a certain aura to it. Not always a smell, though. More an edge in the air, a sense that something's very wrong but also irreparable. Bill Clooney's bedroom projected that aura.

His wife led me into the ten-by-twelve space. There were matching mahogany bureaus with brass handles and framed photos of a younger couple wearing the clothes and hairstyles of the late seventies. The bed was of mahogany too, a four-poster that I could see newlyweds buying shortly after their ceremony. A set to last a lifetime.

Bill Clooney lay under sheets and a quilt, his head nestled in a cloud of pillows. There were a few wisps of gray hair on top of his head, a patchy fringe around his ears. His eyes were closed, but the mouth was open, a snoring so faint you might lose it in the hum of the electric space heater near one corner of the room. His hands lay atop the quilt, bony and heavily veined.

Centered between Clooney's throat and waist, a bed tray straddled his torso. A very large book was open on the tray, a couch cushion propping the text at an angle toward his face.

"My Bill was a graphic artist," said Nora Clooney, her voice bare-ly louder than her husband's snoring. "He came over from Ireland five years before me, and he was ten years older to start with. The charmer told me he fell in love the moment he laid eyes on me, but I wasn't sure of him till I saw his wondrous calligraphy, after a social at the Center that very same night. Modest about it though, my Bill was, telling me that I'd not use the word 'wondrous' for his lettering once I saw *The Book of Kells*."

I kept my voice low as well. "You wanted to bring the book home so your husband could see it again."

"See it, yes sir, and touch it and even breathe it as well. But after the terrible row between Mr. McGlachlin and that Mr. Donnelly at the Center, I knew the board would never grant my Bill what it refused a rich man."

"You took the book out of its case before you broke the glass."

"Yes, sir." She made a sign of the cross. "I'd never have forgiven myself if I'd damaged so much as a page of it."

"And you carried the book out in your tote bag."

"Brazen, I was. Walked right by Grace behind the reception counter, her not suspecting a thing."

"Then why did you leave the note?"

She blew out a breath. "I thought it might keep Mr. McGlachlin from calling in the police right away, sir. Buy me the time to let my Bill pore over the book during his last days before I took it back to the Center unharmed." She turned toward her husband, and I had the sense that Nora Clooney always looked at him this way, with the same expres-sion. A loving one that went beyond duty and maybe even devotion as well.

"Every morning he was able, my Bill would come to the Center with me. Oh, his eyes would shine, sir, watching me turn that day's page, him feeling honored as though he was the first modern man to look upon the work of those long-ago scribes."

I waited a moment before saying, "Nora, I need to make a phone call."

She closed her eyes and dipped her head again. "The one in the kitchen, please. So we don't disturb my Bill."

As I followed her down the stairs, I said, "You wouldn't know whether Hugh McGlachlin has Caller ID on his home phone, would you?"

From the look on her upturned face, I could tell that Nora Clooney thought I was crazy.

I dialed and got that tentative hello.

"Hugh, John Cuddy again."

"John, are you calling from the Clooneys, then?"

"No," I lied, "a pay phone. I'm afraid Nora and Bill couldn't help me. But listen, Hugh, I've traced your *Book of Kells*."

"Traced it?" His voice was thick with hope.

"Yes," I said. "The book'll be back in the Center before your board meets next week."

A long pause on the other end. "John, is there something you're not telling me?"

"There is."

An even longer pause. "Michael O'Dell said I could trust you."

"And you can."

No pause at all now, but a considerable sigh. "Then I will. Good night, John Cuddy, and thank you."

As I hung up the phone in Nora Clooney's kitchen she blinked three times before kissing the pads of the index and middle fingers on her right hand and then touching them to my forehead.

Skiv

Wendi Lee

T HE PHONE RANG FIVE times before Maggie O'Malley picked it up. There had been a robbery last night in Kill, a tiny village ten miles from Rathcoole, and she had been called to assist the *garda* until nearly two in the morning. To be awakened at seven in the morning seemed unfair, but she propped herself up on her elbow and reached for the receiver.

"Yeah," she croaked into it, "O'Malley here."

"Maggie?" It was her boss, Detective Chief Superintendent Aidan O'Rourke. "We've got a murder down in Saint Jude's. Thought you'd like to take it." Saint Jude's, a boarding school for boys of wealthy Protestants, was located five miles outside of Rathcoole.

"Don't tell me—one of the students finally murdered one of the masters," she replied.

"No, actually, it's a missing student."

So, she thought, one of the masters finally killed one of his students and hid the body. But she didn't say it out loud. Maggie knew that the reason she was being handed this assignment—her first case— was because she had once worked at Saint Jude's as kitchen help.

143

She dropped onto her back and peered out at the weather. Gray and misty. Not unusual for Rathcoole. "Yeah. I'll be ready in fifteen minutes." Time enough to splash her face with water, brush her hair, and put on her uniform with the new shoulder tabs.

"Sergeant Leary will be ready with an auto," O'Rourke replied before hanging up.

Donal Leary had recently advanced from *garda* to sergeant. As the first woman to advance to detective within the Rathcoole police force, Maggie was often paired with the newest *garda* recruits, so she was grateful to have someone with experience by her side. Ireland had a long way to go when it came to equality for women, so she tried not to show her impatience when she was watched more closely than her male peers, or when a man with less years on the force advanced before she did.

WITHIN HALF AN HOUR, Maggie and Sergeant Leary pulled up to the main building on Saint Jude's grounds. Students and staff headed to their next class slowed down and watched Maggie and Leary, both in uniform, head for the school warden's office.

The school warden—still Mr. Jack Garvey—was waiting for them in his dark, wood-paneled office. Garvey was a tall man, in his fifties, still handsome.

Maggie stepped up and introduced herself. Garvey peered at her as if he was trying to place her. She wasn't wearing her usual kitchen scrubs, and it had been five years since she set foot on Saint Jude property as a *skiv*, the derogatory word used to describe the menial workers.

Maggie recalled the social order she'd had to endure when she left the farm eight years ago. She was just out of secondary school and in need of a job. She came to work at the school as a *skiv*. Skivs got up at five in the morning to bring in the fifty-pound cans of milk and lug the food trays up to the dining hall before serving it to the students and faculty. They cleaned up the dining hall after meals and scrubbed up the dishes, flatware, pots, pans, and serving trays. The work was hard, dirty, and the pay was embarrassing. The only advantage to the job was that room and board were provided, making it easy to save up her money—as long as she didn't spend her money at the pubs.

As a skiv, she had been at the bottom of the social order and had been treated accordingly. She had worked there for three years and had barely been able to stay on. One of the cooks, Nora, had been a nasty piece of work who spent much time standing in the doorway of the washing-up room and screaming at them like a taskmaster to "stop lagging and work until you drop." All Nora needed was a whip to complete her image.

Maggie shook her head and turned to the school warden. "Tell me the situation, Mr. Garvey. What is the name of the missing student?"

"Trent Taylor."

"How old?"

"Seventeen."

"What kind of student is he?"

"A fair student, from his grades."

"Has he ever been in trouble?"

Garvey made a show of studying the file in front of him. "No."

"Is it possible that Mr. Taylor slipped away from the school last night to go drinking?" Maggie knew that a certain percentage of the students at Saint Jude's would obtain fake ID's and slip out of school to go to the pubs.

The warden looked shocked, but it was a practiced expression. "I don't know what kind of school you think I'm running, but—"

She smiled and patted the air. "I'm not suggesting anything, Mr. Garvey. I know you don't approve, but it's common knowledge that some of the boys here can get themselves into trouble with fake ID's."

Garvey paused and studied her. "Forgive me for saying this, but you seem familiar to me. Not that I spend a lot of time at the Rathcoole police station—"

Maggie gave him her professional smile. "I attend a lot of charity dinners," she said evasively. She didn't want him to remember her as a skiv. Not that she was ashamed of the job she had once done, but it would color his view of what he would tell her. "Is there anything else you can tell me about Trent Taylor?"

"He has a younger brother here named Brad."

"Do the brothers share a room?"

"I don't believe so, but to be certain, you'll have to ask the house-keeper, Mrs. Crawford."

She turned to Sergeant Leary. "You take Mrs. Crawford and ask her where Trent Taylor's room is located. Search it for anything that might shed light on why he disappeared." She turned back to the school warden. "Thank you, Mr. Garvey," she said, snapping her note-book shut. "I'll get back to you."

There was no point asking him any more questions. He was so high up on the food chain at the school that it was doubtful that he knew much about the Taylor boy other than how much his parents forked over in tuition, room, and board.

As they left the office, Maggie saw Christopher Ferrot, one of the masters, passing by. He glanced at her and smiled in recognition.

Maggie had always liked Ferrot, the literature master, when she was a skiv. He was a vegetarian, always introducing himself as "Ferrot, which rhymes with carrot."

"Ah, a former coworker. How are you—Maggie O'Malley, isn't it?" His head always appeared too large for his body. The thinning hair and small glasses didn't help alleviate that illusion. Ferrot was bony to the point of emaciation. Maggie remembered often overhearing students making fun of the quirky master.

"Yes. How are you, Master Ferrot?" she asked.

"Christopher, please," he insisted.

Maggie smiled. She found Christopher Ferrot charming. But she was here on duty. "Sorry. It will have to be Master Ferrot for now."

"This is about Trent Taylor, isn't it?"

"'Tis," she replied. "Do you know him well?"

Ferrot nodded. "I had him in class last term."

"Good student?"

Ferrot shrugged. "It depends on what you call good. He received good grades, but there's no spark there. He's just marking time until he graduates."

"Has he ever been in trouble?"

"He fancies himself a ladies' man. I don't know for certain, but I suspect that he and his friends have slipped out of the school and gone to the pub down the road."

That would be Kavanagh's Pub, Maggie recalled. It was approximately a mile down the road. An easy enough walk.

"Can you give me the names of his friends?" she asked.

Ferrot gave her two names: Reg Fortune and Feroze Pappas.

"Do you happen to know if they were in class today?"

Ferrot thought. "I was on breakfast duty this morning, and I saw both of them. But I didn't see Trent."

"How did they seem to you?"

Ferrot shook his head. "The same as always. As if nothing happened."

Maggie found that odd, considering that their friend was missing. Wouldn't they be concerned?

"So they didn't come to anyone with their concern for their missing friend? Do you know who reported his disappearance?"

"That would be his brother, Brad. In fact, he came to me with his worry."

Leary was at her side and she excused herself, thanking Ferrot for his cooperation.

"You seem to be familiar with himself," Leary observed, slipping into the vernacular.

She smiled grimly. "I'm familiar with most of the masters here. I need a room to interview the brother and friends."

They went to the dormitory where Trent stayed and found an empty office near the common room. Leary went away to gather up the boys Maggie needed to interview. A few minutes later, he returned with Brad Taylor, a slight blond boy, large teary blue eyes, American accent, southern. Expensive designer frames perched on his narrow nose. His navy blue uniform blazer seemed to float, it was so big on him.

Maggie introduced herself and began immediately. "Tell me the last time you saw Trent."

Brad frowned. "I'm two years behind him, so we don't travel in the same circles, see?"

Maggie nodded encouragement. "What is your brother like? Is he quiet?"

Brad laughed, but there was no humor behind it. "Trent quiet? Definitely not a good description. You knew Trent was coming for miles. He was loud, and when he entered a room, you knew it five minutes before he was there. He was very athletic, playing on the soccer team, and cricket and golf for fun." A tear slipped down his pale cheek.

"I noticed that you're using the past tense with your brother," Maggie observed. "Do you think something happened to him?"

Brad looked guilty. "No," he said quickly. "No, I'm sure he's fine. I guess . . . I'm just concerned and afraid something's happened."

"Can you think of any reason why he might have disappeared? Had he appeared troubled lately?"

Brad shook his head. "No, Trent was—is—always the same—always one for the girls."

"So you think he went out last night and just might not have made it back here? Maybe he's with some girl?"

"Not that I'm aware of," Brad said wearily.

"Did he have any habits?" Maggie searched for a way to phrase the question. "Sometimes boys do things like drink or smoke or do drugs . . ."

Brad sighed heavily. "He went out drinking a couple of times."

"Do you know where?"

Brad shrugged. "The pub down the road, I imagine. Sometimes Trent and a few of his buddies would go there."

Maggie raised her eyebrows. Kavanagh's Pub again. "Trent and his friends had fake ID's?"

The boy nodded.

"Trent liked the girls?"

Brad smiled shyly. "The girls like Trent, too."

Of course. With his American accent, his designer clothes, the money he probably flashed around, what girl wouldn't be attracted to him?

"Are your parents notified?" she asked gently.

"Headmaster Garvey doesn't seem to think it's necessary for at least a day. I hope you find him, Inspector. He's going to be in trouble at the school, but I worry what kind of trouble he might be in right now."

She verified the names of the students whom Maser Ferrot had mentioned as being friends of Trent Taylor.

"Yes, both of those boys are his friends," Brad replied.

"Can you think of any other names of friends?"

Brad shook his head. "Those are his buddies."

Maggie thanked him and told him to get to class. A moment later, Sergeant Leary slipped into the office.

"Do you have the other boys ready for an interview with me?" she asked.

"I do, but we just received a call from Aidan Kavanagh."

"The pub owner down the road."

Leary nodded. "He's found a body. The body of a student from here."

FIFTEEN MINUTES LATER, THEY were in the field back of the pub. Gardai from the neighboring town had joined them—a photographer, a medical examiner, a forensic specialist, and several *gardai* to keep the curious away.

The boy was about sixteen years old and looked like an older version of Brad Taylor. There was no doubt in Maggie's mind that this was Trent Taylor. He wore jeans and a nice shirt. His jeans were unbuttoned and a red windbreaker was wadded up next to him. He had been hit in the head, and the murder weapon was one of any number of rocks scattered in the field. Three *garda* were combing the area, literally turning up rocks.

Maggie inspected the body. "Can you tell me anything I might need to know about this murder?" she asked Dr. Reagan, the medical examiner.

Dr. Reagan straightened up. "He was killed by several blows to the back of the head. He didn't die immediately, which is why he's turned up. He was also sexually active before he was murdered."

Maggie wrote it all down.

Master Ferrot was brought to the scene to make a preliminary identification. Maggie hadn't wanted the younger brother to do it and Christopher Ferrot knew Trent well enough to confirm whether it was the missing student or not. A sheet covered the body now that the photographer had taken pictures of the crime scene, and Maggie escorted Ferrot carefully up to the body and had a *garda* pull down enough of the sheet to expose the face.

The master nodded reluctantly, swallowing hard. "Yes, that's him. That's Trent Taylor."

"Thank you, Master Ferrot. I'll have one of the *garda* bring you back to the school."

"Thanks, but I think I'll walk." He looked a little green. "I need some air before I go back to teaching class."

"Master Ferrot," she called after him. He turned around, a sad look in his eyes. "I don't have to tell you to please keep the news quiet. The school warden may know, but neither of you should say anything to the students yet."

He nodded that he understood and turned his back for the long mile back to school.

"SERGEANT," SHE CALLED TO Leary, "I'll be interviewing Aidan Kavanagh now."

Leary led her into the pub to the back where Kavanagh kept his rooms. He was a beefy man, red-faced from too much of his own product, and had an unkempt beard.

"How did you find the body?" she asked.

The pub owner ran a hand over his face, clearly still upset by his discovery. "I was heading out to milk the cow. I saw something red in the field and—I found him."

"Do you recognize him?"

Kavanagh hesitated.

"Mr. Kavanagh," she said, "I know that he's a Saint Jude's boy. I used to work at the school about five years ago, and I'm aware that the boys try to get into the pub with fake ID's."

Kavanagh let out a breath. "Well, I try to keep 'em out, but I'm not always successful. Sometimes the ID's are just so good, and the pub is so busy, I don't always succeed."

"Do you happen to remember his face from last night?"

The pub owner was clearly reluctant to say, but he finally nodded. "I remember him, only because the boys with him were clearly too young, and I threw 'em all out."

"Do you remember anything else unusual about last night?"

Kavanagh paused, then said, "There were a couple of young girls who tried to get in as well, and I threw one of them out about the same time."

"They had fake ID's as well?"

He nodded. "I don't know how they thought they'd get away with it. I'm friends with their da. The older one can drink, so she stayed for a half-pint, but I turned the other girl away."

"Who are these girls?"

"It's the Herlihy girls. Both of 'em work as kitchen help at Saint Jude's."

Maggie and Leary drove back to the school. "Round up the boys for interviews. I'm going to the kitchen to talk to some of the help."

"Do you need directions?" Leary asked.

"I know where it is, sergeant. Carry on."

Both cooks, Nora and Bernie, were working for the noon meal. Three younger girls were helping. The kitchen was a large room with industrial gas ranges and ovens, whitewashed concrete walls, and a brick floor. The wonderful smells coming from the oven made Maggie's stomach growl in response.

Nora was the first to notice Maggie's appearance. "Well, if it isn't herself come to see how the little folk are doing." She was a short, big-busted woman with a homely face and dark stringy hair. She'd made Maggie's year at Saint Jude's miserable.

Maggie crossed her arms. "Is Nora seeing leprechauns again, Bernie?"

Nora glared at her and made a harrumphing sound.

Bernie, a tall rangy woman with frizzy red hair and pale freckles scattered across her friendly face, suppressed a smile. "How are ye, Maggie? I heard ye became a *garda*. The uniform looks good on ye."

"I made detective recently," she said, not being able to help boasting a bit.

Bernie looked interested. "And what would you be doin' here?"

"A disappearance."

Bernie turned to Nora. "I told you there was somethin' funny goin' on when that boy didn't show."

Nora snorted.

"What do you mean, Bernie?" Maggie asked. She noted that Bernie was making scones. She'd loved Bernie's scones when she worked here.

"We're short two today and Nora and I had to cover breakfast. One of the boys didn't show. Someone told a master that the boy was sick and in his room, but when the master went to check on the boy, he wasn't in his room."

"Do you know who it was who reported Trent Taylor as sick?"

Bernie thought. One of the kitchen workers spoke up. "I think it was his brother, the young one."

Maggie made a note to check on that bit of information. "You said you're two short today."

"Aye," Bernie said. "The sisters went back home for a visit."

"The sisters?" she asked, already knowing the answer.

"Siobhan and Nuala Herlihy. They called this morning to say their da took sick and needed tending. Siobhan said they'd be back tomorrow." She gestured to the other girls. "Now these three have to work an extra shift."

"Thanks for the help. Good to see you, Bernie," Maggie said.

"'Tis good to see yourself, Maggie. Come back on a good day and we'll have scones and tea." Before Maggie could leave, Bernie said, "I hope you find out what happened to that poor boy."

Ignoring Nora, who did likewise, Maggie left for the dorm to talk to the friends of Trent Taylor. She took up residence in the small office she'd used earlier. Maggie consulted the names Master Ferrot had given her, Reg Fortune and Feroze Pappas, and instructed the sergeant to bring in the Fortune boy.

Reg Fortune was about sixteen or seventeen, fair-haired, athletic build, light brown eyes, and a killer smile. And he knew it. When he came into the office, he looked Maggie up and down in appreciation, then sat down across from her.

She ignored his leer. "I'm Inspector O'Malley. I need to ask you a few questions about Trent Taylor's movements last night and this morning. When was the last time you saw him?"

"Last night. We went to the library to study."

Maggie doubted he was telling the truth. She raised her eyebrows. "When I worked here in the kitchens, we often went out to Kavanagh's Pub, and we often met boys from Saint Jude's there. I imagine things haven't changed that much over the past five years."

"You worked here?" he asked, a spark of interest in his eyes.

"In the kitchen."

His face closed up and a sneer replaced the interest. "A *skiv*."

"A kitchen worker," she said evenly. "Where were you last night?"

"We went to the library," he insisted.

"You didn't meet the Herlihy sisters?"

"I don't know what you're talking about," he replied.

Maggie asked him a few more questions, but felt he was lying.

"Can I go now?" He stood up.

"For now. I may want to ask you additional questions, so don't leave the grounds."

Feroze Pappas was next, a striking combination of Arabic and Greek parentage. His dark good looks and tousled black hair made him appear older than Reg. It was clear that he came from money and had the European worldliness to pull off looking older. Maggie doubted Feroze needed to show his fake ID to get into a pub. If he had gone to the pub alone, he might have passed as eighteen or older.

He sat down and looked coolly at her.

"To begin, it has been established that Trent, Reg, and yourself went to Kavanagh's last night. There was some trouble." She was taking a chance, to make a guess like this about something that happened.

Feroze's expression froze. "I don't know what you're talking about."

She gave him a severe look. "I talked to Mr. Kavanagh and he remembers all of you well."

"He's mistaken. We weren't there. We were at the library."

Neither boy was willing to admit that he was at Kavanagh's Pub. Maggie was tempted to take both boys by the scruff of the neck and haul them in front of Kavanagh, but decided to wait on that.

"You can go," she told Feroze in a severe tone, "but you are not to leave the premises until I say so."

He gave her a haughty look. "My father will hear about the way you're treating me, and it will cost you your job."

Leary popped his head in the door. "What now, Detective?"

Maggie sighed. "Take this boy out of my sight," she said in a disgusted tone. She had a good notion of what had gone on, but she needed to fit a few pieces into place before presenting her theory.

SHE GOT DIRECTIONS TO the Herlihy farm, a ten-mile drive. Men along the side of the road were cutting peat and tending sheep.

The cottage was whitewashed stone with a gaily painted red door. Laundry hung out to dry, even though it had rained a bit that morning.

Maggie knocked on the red door. She could hear movement inside and a moment later, a young girl answered the door. She looked at Maggie, then beyond to the police car. She shut the door on Maggie, who imagined there was some discussion about whether to let the *gardai* into their home.

Maggie knocked forcefully to distract the girls from concocting a story. They finally allowed Maggie and Leary inside.

Siobhan was the older of the two girls. She told Maggie she was just eighteen and had been working at the school for a little over a year. She was petite, small-boned, and had a mass of dark curls that floated around a face with sharp, not unpleasant features.

Her fifteen-year-old sister, Nuala, had just left school six months ago and taken her first job at Saint Jude's. She sat in a dark corner, and Sergeant Leary made a move toward her, reaching out to steer the younger girl toward a chair. Nuala looked at Leary with frightened eyes and shrank away from him.

Maggie eyed the younger girl—taller than her older sister, gawky, but with a certain charm. "Sergeant, will you do me the favor of going out to the auto and waiting?"

He hesitated, then nodded.

"Now girls, I think there's something you want to tell me."

"What are you talking about, Inspector?" Siobhan asked.

"Girls, there's a student who's been murdered down at Kavanagh's Pub."

Siobhan sat at the table, cool as a soft day in Ireland, her hands clasped in front of her on the kitchen table. "I don't know what you're talking about, ma'am."

Maggie turned to Nuala. "Do you know what I'm talking about, Nuala? You were down at the pub last night, you tried to get in with a fake ID, you were turned away. So were three boys from Saint Jude's—"

"She doesn't know what you're after, Inspector," Siobhan broke in. "She waited for me to come out after I had me half-pint of Guinness, and we walked home from there."

Maggie turned to the younger sister. "Is that true, Nuala?" she asked softly.

Nuala looked about to break, but Siobhan kept stonewalling, keeping Maggie from doing her job.

After half an hour of trying, Maggie stood up. "It's clear to me that you're withholding information about Trent Taylor's death. It's also clear that Nuala here has been seriously hurt, perhaps sexually attacked. Why are ye not talkin' to me?" She asked this last question plaintively.

Siobhan glanced at Nuala, who looked up at Maggie with dark, haunted eyes. "We have nothin' to tell you, Detective. We walked back to the school last night by ourselves, then received word that our da was sick."

Maggie looked around. "And where is he now?"

Siobhan thrust her chin up. "In hospital."

"I can check on that."

Nuala stood up and came toward Maggie. "Why are ye question-in' us? We're not the criminals here," she said, her voice about to break.

Maggie stood her ground, but it was difficult. Siobhan came between them. She stood nose to nose with Maggie. "We have nothin' to say. And if you continue to persecute us, we will report you to your superior."

Maggie shook her head and turned to leave. As she opened the door, she said, "I suspect Nuala has been molested. Why are you protecting them? Why are you denying it? It's clear that it was self-defense."

Siobhan looked back stonily. "I don't know what you're talking about."

Maggie said more softly, "Your sister is going to need more help than you can give her. Call me if you want some resources in Dublin."

Siobhan shut the door on Maggie, but a moment before the door closed, she saw the expression of the older sister, the desperation and vulnerability that told her that she'd hit on something important.

BACK AT THE SCHOOL, she pounded away at Reg Fortune and pushed Feroze as far as she dared. Neither boy gave an inch. She brought Kavanagh to the school and had him identify the two boys.

"What about the other boy?" he said. "Don't you want me to identify the fourth boy?"

"Oh?" she asked, feeling slightly stupid for not asking how many boys he'd turned away. She had just assumed it was the trio. "And what was he like?"

"I told you that one of the boys looked too young." Maggie had assumed it was Reg, who was the youngest-looking of the group. Kavanagh went on to describe Brad Taylor to a *T*.

MAGGIE STOOD WHEN BRAD TAYLOR was brought into her office. "Sit," she said. "You were with the other boys, with your brother last night. I know about the girl."

"I don't know what you're talking about," the boy muttered, keeping his head down, avoiding Maggie's eyes.

Maggie had always heard that silence spoke louder than words, so she remained silent. Less than a minute later, she detected Brad's shoulders shaking.

"You're carrying a heavy burden, young sir," she said gently, "and you're not the only one to bear it. Those two girls are denying everything now, as are Trent's friends. But eventually one of you will break down. Maybe not the two tough cases I've had in here previously, but—"

"I killed him, all right?" Brad looked up, his face streaked with tears. "I killed my own brother." He got up and paced. Everything came tumbling out as if he'd been holding back by the skin of his teeth.

Trent had gotten Brad a fake ID and took him along last night to go, as he put it, "trolling for girls." "He wanted easy girls. He told me it was time I had sex." Brad paused, shaking, unshed tears brimming, threatening to spill. "He told me he'd had sex for the first time at my age, and he said it was my time. I didn't want to go, Inspector, but I was bullied into it by Reg and Feroze. I knew I wouldn't pass as eighteen even with an ID, so I went along to the pub. I thought I'd be thrown out and that would be the end of it."

He sobbed. "But the pub owner threw all of us out. We saw the two girls go into the pub, and the younger one came out a few minutes later. Trent recognized them as kitchen help from Saint Jude's. He whispered to me that they were skivs and skivs were known to be easy. I told him I just wanted to go back to the school. I could tell the younger girl was scared, and I offered to walk her home." He stopped, as if he wasn't sure he could go on.

Maggie gently prompted him. "Trent wouldn't let you, would he?"

A heavy sigh. "He said we'd all walk them home and he knew a shortcut through the back of the pub. When we were away from the lighted area, Trent took hold of the girl and started ripping her clothes off. Reg and Feroze just stood and watched—"

Maggie waited, knowing this was difficult for him.

"—she fought and got away, but Reg and Feroze went after her. I just stood there, not believing that this was happening, that my brother could be this cruel. Feroze came back and dragged me to where Trent was—" it was clearly difficult for Brad to talk about this."—raping the girl. She didn't have any fight left in her, but she was crying and kept saying that he was hurting her and she kept saying no. I finally found my voice and told him to stop." Brad looked up at Maggie. "He wouldn't. I felt so sorry for her. She's probably my age."

"How did you feel about what was happening?"

"I hated my brother. I was scared and angry at the same time."

"What happened next?"

He sobbed again, a heart-ripping sound. "I tried to pull him off but I'm not very athletic and he threw me off easily. So I finally picked up a rock, only meaning to knock him out." His face was in his hands and an animal cry came from him. "I killed my brother. I killed him. It was an accident. I'm sorry, I'm sorry—"

Maggie pulled him up gently and put an arm around him. "There, there. We'll get you some help. Don't you feel better for telling?"

But she knew she was giving him empty words. He would never feel better, never be able to reconcile killing his brother, choosing a girl's dignity over his brother's life. Nothing would ever make it better for him.

So Where've You Buried the Missus Then, Paddy?

Mat Coward

WHEN I FIRST MET Polish Pat he was a single man, albeit single in a peculiarly Irish way—his wife, the lovely but enormous Charmaine, was "off visiting the family in Dublin." I was so young in those days, my barman's towel so new you could still read the print on it, that I took this time-tried euphemism entirely at face value. Luckily, I never did say to Polish Pat, "That's a long visit your wife's having, Paddy," as otherwise I suspect that Pat, sweet little feller though he was, might have punched my nose clean off my face.

(Would this be a good place to explain about the names? Polish Pat—known as Paddy to everyone who knew him, and not known at all to those who didn't—was not Polish, but Irish. However, when he first began drinking in the Old Boar, there was already a Paddy Pat amongst the regulars, and so Paddy—*our* Paddy, the Paddy of this story—became Polish Pat, on the unspoken understanding that he would succeed to the title of Paddy Pat upon the demise or departure of the incumbent. Paddy was never in the least Polish, but nobody was too bothered by that, since Paddy Pat himself was not Irish, but Californian. It must seem confusing to anyone unfamiliar with the pubs of north London. All I can say in our defence is that it makes sense to us; or at least, it doesn't make *sense*, exactly, but it keeps us busy, which is the next best thing.)

Anyway, Paddy seemed to be enjoying his long separation from his lovely but enormous wife, judging by the number of impromptu after-hours parties he hosted in his unpleasant but spacious basement flat, about five minutes' walk from the pub.

I attended several of these do's, not because I was a particular pal of Paddy's, but simply because I was a human being who looked as though he could do with a drop of friendly company. "Come on over when you've finished here, son," he'd say to me, at closing time.

One day I'm going to write a book of advice for young lads finding themselves alone in a big city for the first time. Advice like, "Don't smile at strangers in public lavatories," and "If you're offered a job by a man in a pub at three times your present salary, consider the possibility that there might be a catch." But the biggest piece of advice, printed large on the first page to make sure no one misses it, will be this: "Get yourself in with an Irish crowd." For the Irish man or woman who can bear to see a poor boy without a glass in his hand and a plate of beans-on-toast on his lap has yet to be born. I say this as an Englishman, of my own free will.

It was whilst enjoying Paddy's good hospitality one late Friday night in August that I asked a fellow guest whether Charmaine perhaps had illness in the family.

"Illness?" replied Rasta Jack. "Not that I know of. Why?"

"I was just wondering. She seems to have been away in Ireland an awful long time; ever since I've been working at the Boar, in fact."

Rasta Jack laughed. "The thing is, son, they've not been getting on so well lately, Paddy and his missus. But not to worry, I'm sure she'll turn up again sooner or later. She always does."

I looked across at Paddy, playing cards on the other side of the large, under-furnished room with a bunch of lads from the pub. He was a short, wiry man, with bow legs, thin ginger hair, and jug ears. He worked, in an informal sort of way, in the building trade, but was out of work more often than he was in, due, so he often told us, to a wickedly infirm back.

"It's hard to imagine such an easygoing bloke falling out with his wife," I said. "Or with anyone else."

Rasta Jack shrugged. "She's five times his size," he said, "and has ten times his brains. Maybe she just gets fed up with looking after him every now and then and needs to get away for a while. Now pass me that bottle, will you—what sort of barman are you, that allows a man to die of thirst sitting right next to you?"

An *off-duty one*, I thought. But I passed the bottle, anyway.

IT WASN'T UNTIL CHARMAINE had gone unseen for nearly three months that people began to think it odd. Previous occasions on which she had been "off visiting the family" had never lasted more than a month, and it was generally agreed amongst the regulars at the Old Boar that three months was significantly longer than four weeks, whichever way you looked at it.

"He's done her in," suggested Mike the Bike one evening. "That must be it."

"Can't be," countered another concerned drinker. "There's no garden to that flat of theirs, where would he bury her? And she's a big woman, you'd never get her under the floorboards."

"Besides," added a third, "it'd be more believable the other way around. She's a lovely woman, is Charmaine, but she's got a temper on her. And her the size she is, you'd need a gang of fit men to get her down."

"Poison," said Mike. "That takes no strength at all."

"Poison's a woman's weapon," declared Big Rick definitively. "And whatever Paddy is or isn't, he's certainly a man's man by anybody's standards. If he was to kill a wife, it'd be with straightforward strangulation, or a decent blow to the head—not something as dirty as poison."

"You're right, of course," said Mike, "and I apologise to all concerned for raising the matter."

Conversation then turned to someone else who hadn't been seen for a while, Jonathan Lansdowne—"Hungry Jon" as he was known, not because he was poor (he was a millionaire by anybody's standards), but because he was always hungry. He would often come in to the Boar and order a beer, half a dozen sandwiches, three bags of crisps, and a packet of peanuts. And then go off to a restaurant for lunch. The regulars used to tease him—"Does she not feed you at home, Jon?"—but nobody said that any more, since he'd recently become a widower.

Of the two mildly missing persons, I have to admit that I found Hungry Jon the more immediately interesting. No offence to Charmaine; it was just that Jon had been a pop star in the sixties, and although he now worked as a record company executive, wore a plain suit and a sensibly outdated haircut, he still carried with him a certain cachet of celebrity.

As time went on, however, with still no sign of Charmaine, my fickle attention returned to her case. If a recording executive is away for a few weeks, after all, however uncharacteristically, it is no big surprise. But an Irish housewife, whose husband continues to host post-pub parties throughout her absence . . .

"Tell me about Charmaine," I invited Rasta Jack, one night when a Siberian wind had kept most of the pub's potential customers at home with their televisions. "I always hear her described as 'lovely but enormous.'"

"So she is," said Rasta. (Picture a white man, completely bald, who worked in insurance, wore faded corduroys, and spent all his money on operatic LPs.)

"How enormous?" I asked.

"She's tall," he said. "She's taller than me, and I'm five-ten. And big, with it. She must be thirteen, fourteen stone. And if you think a two-pound bag of sugar weighs two pounds, which it does, and there's fourteen pounds to a stone, then you're talking about someone who weighs roughly the same as ninety-eight bags of sugar."

"That *is* fairly enormous, isn't it," I agreed, "by anybody's standards. Especially given that her husband is, what, five-foot-six?"

"And if he's a chocolate biscuit over nine stone, I'd be significantly surprised."

I tried to picture this woman I'd never met; this couple I'd only ever seen half of—or less than half, by the sound of it. I tried to picture a six-foot-tall pile of sugar bags walking down the aisle with a mostly eaten packet of chocolate biscuits. And as for the honeymoon—it was like that old joke about the Rottweiler and the Chihuahua.

"I'd know her if I saw her, then?"

"You would that," Rasta agreed.

"And what about 'lovely'?"

"Oh, she's lovely, all right. Charmaine is a lovely girl." He took a sip from his pint. "Just, you know, not to look at."

She sounded more fascinating than ever. I looked forward to meeting her.

THE FIRST TIME I ever heard it *seriously* suggested that I might never get a chance to meet the lovely but enormous Charmaine was when a quite large, middle-aged woman, with a southern Irish accent, arrived in the pub one Saturday lunchtime inquiring after the whereabouts of her estranged sister.

"Sure, you'd know Charmaine if you saw her," said Tessie, after introductions had been made and drinks served.

"Oh, yes," said Griff, the landlord, a Yorkshireman with a prematurely grey beard and posthumously raven sideburns. "I know who you mean, all right. It's just that—"

"Or failing that," interrupted Tessie, "I'll settle for her husband, wee Paddy. I certainly expected to find *him* in here. Don't tell me he's gone crazy and actually taken a day's work somewhere! I knocked at their flat, but there was no answer."

"Well, it's just that . . ." Griff's voice trailed off and his face showed anguish. A pub landlord's job description is notoriously infinite in its scope and most definitely includes the role of diplomat. Nonetheless, I got the impression that this particular tricky situation was a new one on him. He looked for aid to his patrons, but seemed to find it hard to catch an eye. "The thing is, Tessie," he said, "we understood, we *all* understood, that the lovely but—er, that is, the lovely Charmaine was currently staying with your family."

"With *my* family?" said the quite large but soft-spoken Tessie, plainly bewildered.

"Well, with your parents. In Dublin."

"But *I* live with my parents," said Tessie. Many eyes flicked to her left hand. "And you'd not find Charmaine there, not as long as my mother is alive." She lowered her voice and added, somewhat superfluously I thought: "They don't get on, you see." This was her first-ever visit to Britain, she explained, and she wouldn't be able to stay long; she'd come on a peace mission. Her mother was poorly, with heart trouble, and anxious to be reconciled with her other daughter.

Once Tessie had left, in a taxi operated by one of the Boar's customers, to book into a small hotel managed by another, and with the promise of an immediate news flash from Griff should either Paddy or Charmaine be sighted in the vicinity, those of us left behind gave full vent to our speculation.

The consensus view, I have to report, was that "obviously he's done her in, else why would he have lied about her trip to Ireland?"

Over that weekend, Paddy himself joined the absent-without-leave list, which did nothing to reduce the suspicions of his friends.

Until then, the parties at his flat had continued on a regular basis, though old hands had begun to complain that the gatherings lacked a certain something. They couldn't quite put their fingers on precisely what the lovely but enormous Charmaine had contributed to the scene—but whatever it was, many agreed, had been the essential element that transforms a mundane booze-up into a social occasion of note.

I MUST INTRODUCE YOU at this point to another man who was a regular of the Boar in those days. He too was an Irishman—as so many in north London are, of course; and even those who aren't tend to know at least three verses and the chorus of "Wild Rover."

O'Nuff was an interesting chap. A Protestant from the South, a man of broadly Republican-Marxist outlook, an independent speculator upon the Stock Exchange by profession, and a graduate with high honours of Dublin University, in a subject so intensely esoteric that he claimed to be unable even to pronounce it, let alone to remember what it actually meant. He was also the only person any of us had ever met who held a private eye's license, valid in the state of New York. How he came to own such a thing was one of the very few subjects on which he was known to be reticent.

On top of all that, O'Nuff was a handsome fellow, in his late thirties, strong and healthy, popular with men and women alike, erudite without ever being condescending, and kindly to a fault. Needless to say, there were those in the pub who couldn't stand the sight nor sound of him.

I am not ashamed to admit that I admired him as a kind of hero. He made me feel that, as long as there were such men in the world, it meant the rest of us could happily fritter away whatever talents and energies we might have been born with, secure in the knowledge that better people than us would always be around to take care of the difficult stuff.

Late one autumn evening, after a particularly sweaty session behind the bar, I was standing in the Old Boar's small courtyard, smoking a cigarette and enjoying the fresh air and thinking whatever thoughts I had left in my head by that time of night, when a voice spoke a few inches from my ear.

"Did I scare you?" were the first words it said to me, and the first intimation of any sort I'd had that I was not alone. I took this to be an example of the globally fabled Irish humour, rather than a sincere attempt at homicide by startlement.

"You did," I admitted. "You scared all of it right out of me. I'll be needing a dustpan and brush here."

"Oh, sure 'nuff. Sorry about that, kiddo. I just wanted a private word."

"A private word? With me?" I hoped it was nothing to do with the Theory of Relativity.

"Oh, sure 'nuff," said O'Nuff, again; thus relieving me, I trust, of the burden of explaining his nickname. "Now, the thing is, a young man in your position—polishing all those glasses, pouring all those pints—you'd be ideally placed to overhear all sorts of interesting items from the careless lips of your clientele. That's so, no?"

Was he suggesting that I was some sort of eavesdropper? It wasn't an accusation I'd take kindly. Especially since it was one I could hardly deny. "What is it you think I might have overheard, O'Nuff?"

"Well, now," he said, taking out a packet of Major and offering me one—possibly to replace the Benson I'd dropped when he'd first appeared. "You're aware, naturally, that there is some concern in the air about the current whereabouts of our friend Hungry Jon?"

"Naturally," I agreed, wondering—not for the first time—how it was that the Irish could be so good at beer and so very bad at cigarettes. "And the same goes ditto for our friend Charmaine."

"Oh, sure 'nuff. Indeed. But whereas I am quite confident that she will turn up when turning-up time comes, I am less sanguine about him. About Hungry Jon, I mean."

That was unpleasantly exciting news. "Why so?"

"Well, now. You know, of course, that I lived for a while in America."

"New York, wasn't it? I've often wondered, if you don't mind me asking, what brought you back? I should have thought that being a private eye in the Big, Bad Apple—"

"Green beer," he said, with a bitter grimace. "Green beer and shamrock hats."

The words meant nothing to me, but they clearly meant something to him, so I left it at that. "And your time amongst the diaspora is in some way connected to your worries about Hungry Jon?"

"It is, so. And what I would like to ask of you, my friend, is this: if you were to hear anything which you feel might go toward explaining why the aforementioned gent has not been seen in this pub for some time, and why there is no answer at his door or upon his telephone, I would be most grateful if you would bring that same information to me. Only to me, you see? And without unreasonable delay." He extinguished his cigarette underfoot. "I mean, finish serving the round, obviously, but don't leave it until the next Bank Holiday."

"Well . . ." I said, which meant—as it so often does—*I'm not too happy about this.*

"You needn't worry, at all. No ill will is meant toward Hungry Jon. I am merely acting for some folk back in America, who are eager for news of the evanesced popster. It's nothing heavy—you have my word as a licensed private detective."

He smiled, to show that his words were intended both humorously and seriously. It was an honest and broad smile, but even so I couldn't help remembering that his license to privately detect was valid only in a place far away from the Old Boar.

IN THE END, IT was I who found Paddy.

Pub-goers in this part of the world are naturally territorial, and in any case no loyal habitue of the Old Boar would be seen dead or alive in the King's Head, ever since an unfortunate incident during a darts match seven years earlier. I wouldn't have been there myself, but for the presence of a particular barmaid (another story; not relevant here).

Which made it, of course, a perfect place for Paddy—who had heard of the arrival on the scene of his sister-in-law—to lie low.

Acting upon my report of his location, a deputation hurried to escort Paddy back to the Boar and confront him with the accusation that he had malice aforethought'd his good wife.

Any thought of fight or flight had quite gone out of the little man, as he slumped in his usual chair at the bar, all stubble and weary eyes.

"You might as well know," he told us, "Charmaine is—"

"Is she under the floorboards, Paddy?" called out Big Rick, who I believe had been wagering on the subject with Mike the Bike. "Or should we be digging up the Heath?"

"She's left me," said Paddy, in a horribly quiet voice. "That's the truth, and I'll hide it no longer. My wife has abandoned me for another man."

This admission produced deep sighs from Paddy's audience; sighs of sympathy, of course, but also of disappointment at a mystery too easily solved.

"It's true," the self-proclaimed cuckold continued, running his bony fingers through his thin hair. "She has run off with Hungry

Jon—and who can blame her? He can offer her so much more than I ever could."

Perhaps so, the rest of us thought. But what could *she* offer *him*? (Lovely though she was.)

The meeting adjourned to Hungry Jon's doorstep, just across the street from the Boar. Paddy, "too ashamed to face that man," stayed in the pub, bravely forcing down a nourishing pint of stout.

Prolonged ringing on Hungry Jon's doorbell eventually produced the ex-pop star, looking a lot more ex than star that day, and he reluctantly admitted us to the immense, white-carpeted sitting room of his four-storey house. A fully equipped bar, fitted out in white leather, stood at one end of the room, a white piano at the other.

"I don't know what you're talking about," Jon insisted, when Paddy's allegations had been put to him by Griff, our duly elected spokesman. "I'd heard she was away in Dublin, visiting her family? As for me—well, I've been busy, that's all, no time for socialising. Big album deal on the cooker."

He seemed convincing enough. In the cold light of that white room, the idea of him eloping with poor Paddy's missus did seem a little unlikely.

"So, Jon," said Griff, uncomfortably, "let me just get this a hundred percent clear. You are not now, nor have you ever been, insanely enamoured of the lovely but enormous Charmaine?"

Jon treated us to a distinctly ungallant laugh. "Come on, guys! Can you really imagine—"

And that was when the singing started. Loud, lusty, but undeniably tuneful. An old Irish rebel song.

Coming from the cellar.

"*Ah!*" said one of the older members of our little mob, clicking his fingers in revelation. "*That's* what was missing from Paddy's parties. Of course—his dear wife's enormous but lovely voice!"

THE ANSWER, AT LAST, seemed clear. Recently widowed, and entering a difficult period of middle-age, poor Hungry Jon had, indeed, been driven mad by his love for Charmaine—so mad, that he had kept her locked in his cellar for months, an unwilling love slave.

Not a murder, then, but something which was, for those regulars privileged to witness its climactic moments, almost as enjoyable, and just as retellable.

Upon her release from her luxuriously appointed prison, however, Charmaine herself shot that one down.

"Love slave?" she gasped, restored at last to her own kitchen. "Sweet Jesus, isn't that just like a load of men, to think of sex, sex, sex, and nothing but!" It was a small kitchen, and there was barely room enough for the dozen or so men present to look suitably abashed. We did our best.

"But if not love," asked Griff, neatly summarising the question of the moment, "then what?"

"An insurance swindle," said Big Rick, authoritatively. "I always knew Paddy was in on it." He wouldn't have said that if Paddy had been around to defend himself, but Paddy wasn't. He was busy in the bedroom, sleeping off the regrettable side effects of being left alone for thirty minutes in an unattended pub.

"Nothing of the sort!" snorted Charmaine. "If you must know, Jon wanted to turn me into a recording star."

This announcement was met with a loud silence.

"He'd heard me singing here at the flat, during one of our wee soirees," she continued. "He said he could make me into the Irish Cher."

"But," said Griff eventually, "you weren't keen?"

"I was not. Though Jon wouldn't take no for an answer. I was flattered, of course. But, you see—Paddy has very strong views on married women pursuing careers outside the home." As the silence got longer and louder, she added, by way of clarification: "He's against it, I mean."

The illusions of marriage, eh? Where would we all be without them?

NO CHARGES WERE PRESSED. "The poor man wasn't himself," Charmaine ruled, displaying the innate kindness for which she was so well known. And besides, as Griff's own wife pointed out later, those weeks of well-fed captivity were probably the only ones in Charmaine's life during which she had not been required to cook, clean, or run errands. An unorthodox kind of holiday, to be sure, but sometimes a rest can be as good as a change.

A week later, she and Paddy returned to Ireland, permanently, which was bad news for the Old Boar and its patrons, but good news, no doubt, for Ireland, a country that has suffered more than most over the years from excessive emigration.

We never saw Hungry Jon in the pub again, even after he had returned from treatment in a private clinic for nervous exhaustion. Too embarrassed, I suppose; about the white piano, one can but hope, if not the kidnapping.

Paddy and the lovely but enormous Charmaine send the pub a collectively affectionate card every Christmas, but in the years since their departure they have never appeared here in person. Charmaine, so it's said, reconciled with her family, has sworn never to leave her native land again; while Paddy, I suspect, would not care to make a solo visit.

People in pubs have long memories (long *long*-term memories, at any rate), and Paddy would naturally dread the prospect of walking into the Old Boar on his own and being greeted after all these years with cheery cries of "So—*where did you bury the missus this time then, Paddy?*"

ALL OF WHICH, I am well aware, leaves one loose end; and it's not even a small one. You'll forgive me, I hope, but you see I have learned my storytelling manner, such as it is, from my Irish neighbours—and as you'll know if you've ever sat in a pub in north London (or, I daresay, in Boston, or Sydney, or Hong Kong), there is a right way and there is a wrong way to end an Irish story. Even one told by an Englishman.

The right way is to finish it just a little after your listeners think it is already finished. The wrong way is to finish it before closing time.

Following our crepuscular conversation in the Boar's courtyard, I didn't see O'Nuff again for some weeks. Which, given the givens, struck me as a little odd.

About a month after Paddy and Charmaine had left us, we held a Christmas football match one Sunday afternoon, up on the Heath. It was not a formal affair. All were invited, and all were guaranteed a game, if they wished to play; those who didn't were welcome to watch, and encouraged to barrack.

The day was fine and the turnout good. There must have been thirty or more of us gathered there, and many bottles of beer and hip flasks of whiskey were in evidence. Some people even brought sand-wiches—though the purists amongst the crowd muttered that such preparedness was evidence of an orderliness of mind that bordered on the clinically obsessive.

Men and women took part—even one or two kids—and substitu-tion was frequent and liberal. You would simply play until you got tired, or bored, at which point you would jog off the pitch and your place would be taken by whoever felt like doing so.

I was not much of a footballer and had no deep knowledge of the rules, so I confined my own active participation to one or two spells as referee. This brought me many offers of free drinks in exchange for particular interpretations of the laws of the game, all of which I hap-pily accepted, and none of which, as I remember, were subsequently honoured.

We were about twenty minutes into the match, with the score standing at six-all (or not, depending on who you asked), when I saw the skinny Greek girl who had been keeping goal at the south end trot off the field, to be replaced by O'Nuff. I surrendered my whistle to the nearest unoccupied person and took a long route round the pitch to arrive right behind the goal.

I was about to reach out and tap him on the shoulder and say, "Did I give you a scare?" when, without turning around, O'Nuff spoke.

"Now then, kiddo—I've been hoping for a chat with you."

"I'm glad to see you. It's been a while."

"Oh, sure 'nuff. I wouldn't miss this; it's a great laugh for a Sunday afternoon. Have you ever been to a pub up West, called the Irish House?"

"I have, yes."

"Good. I'll meet you there tomorrow lunchtime, if that would be convenient to yourself?"

"It would, so," I said, which made him laugh. I watched him for a short while and saw him let in two goals. (Or not, depending on who you asked). He was wearing smart clothes, and he got them dirty diving after the ball, but he didn't seem to mind.

THE IRISH HOUSE WAS famous for serving the best stout in London, and the slowest. The customer would place his order at the bar in the centre of the big room, and then go to his table. When the pint had been poured, and allowed to settle, and topped off with a palette knife, and topped up from the tap, and allowed to settle again, it would eventually be delivered to its dry-throated purchaser by a waiter.

When you wanted a refill, you did not take your empty glass with you to the bar—that would be a faux pas. It was all very different from the Old Boar.

"When people think of the Irish in Britain," said O'Nuff, as I sank my face into the black-and-white elixir, "and *pace* our cousins in the North, they think only of County Kilburn. But every city in the country has an Irish centre, or an Irish club, or at least a couple of Irish pubs. Now, do you think of London as an English city?"

I thought before answering. It was that sort of conversation. "English," I said. "And Scottish and Welsh and Irish and Bangladeshi and Jewish and Nigerian and—"

"Exactly!" said O'Nuff. He drank a slow throat-full of his beer and sighed. "That's good. My father was over here in the fifties, you know. Working on the roads, laying the tarmac. In those days, you would still see signs in boardinghouse windows: 'No Coloured, No Irish, No Dogs.'"

"Awful."

"Oh, sure 'nuff, inexcusable. But my father was a man of strong opinions, particularly where men of the cloth were concerned, and relating to the rights of the working man, and he found it easier to hold those opinions, at that time, in this country than in his own."

"Did he find lodgings?"

"He did." O'Nuff nodded. "With a Jamaican woman who bred poodles."

I had to laugh at that. So I did.

"Did you know that Irish citizens can vote in British elections?"

"I didn't."

"Oh, sure 'nuff. But, naturally, British citizens cannot vote in Irish elections. Now, does that strike you as unfair?"

I shrugged and finished my pint. O'Nuff went to order two more. "It's not unfair, obviously," he said on his return. "And I'll tell you why: because what British person would ever want to vote in an Irish election? *That's* the point."

If that was the point, then I was none the wiser. "I do know it wasn't Hungry Jon you were interested in," I said, "when you spoke to me that time outside the Boar."

"Ah, well," said O'Nuff. We sat quietly and smoked, until our beers arrived.

"You told me that Jon wasn't answering his doorbell or his phone. But when we all went over to his place from the pub, he did answer the bell eventually."

"Bet you rang it awful hard, mind." O'Nuff sipped, nodded his head, and sipped some more. "Fair enough. What was the final score in the football yesterday, do you know?"

"It depends who you ask."

"Ah well, then, I reckon we won. Let's drink to that."

We drank to that. "It wasn't really me you were hoping for a word with that night. You just said all that about Hungry Jon to stop me wondering what you were actually doing, loitering outside the pub in the dark," I said. "Were you really a private detective in America?"

"I was, so. Did night classes and everything." He offered me one of his Majors, which I declined. Politely, I hope.

"Unless there was yet another missing person, who I know nothing about, then I'd guess that it was Paddy you were watching for."

"The Boar was his local, right enough, but there were one or two other pubs where he would put in the odd guest appearance. I did the circuit that evening and ended up back at the Boar, just on the off-chance."

"And through him you were hoping to learn the whereabouts of his wife."

"The lovely but etcetera," he confirmed. "Quite so."

I set my drink to one side and thought it through. All the while, O'Nuff watched me closely. After a time, I realised that I had one more question. "So, who was it thought that Paddy had killed his wife?"

He cocked an eyebrow at me. "Apart from everyone in the pub, you mean?"

I shook my head. "That was just messing around. No one who knew Paddy could really think such a thing of him."

"I feel at home in this city," said O'Nuff, after a pause. "Britain, Ireland, America—home for me is wherever I happen to find myself when I wake up in the morning. But not everybody's like that. My client was away from home for the first time, amongst strangers— kindly strangers, but strangers nonetheless. She was confused, afraid, not sure how best to discharge her responsibilities. It's natural enough to fear the worst in such circumstances."

She? The sister: Charmaine's sister. "How did she get on to you?"

He laughed. "Ah, you'd have to be Irish. Or Romany, maybe. The short version is, she phoned a cousin in New York, who phoned a fellow member of the Grand Order of This and That in Boston, who remembered that he used to know a PI, a reliable man, Irish, too, and sure, didn't he happen to be living in London just now? The diaspora, you know."

"So the reason I didn't see you in the pub after that . . ."

"Oh, sure 'nuff. I was busy looking for Charmaine, or Paddy, or— I hoped—both. Looking in all the wrong places, as it transpired. If I really *had* been looking for Hungry Jon, I'd likely have found Charmaine a lot sooner, wouldn't I?"

"And does Paddy know that—"

"Nobody knows. You, me, and my client. No one else." He didn't ask me for my silence—obviously didn't consider it necessary to ask— which, young as I was, I found flattering.

I sat and stared at my beer. O'Nuff read my face and read it correctly. "Look, son. As we now know, no one was killed. There was no murderer. There was some foolishness, true enough, but that's supplied as standard where human beings are concerned. On the other hand, we have a family reunited and a marriage born afresh."

I said nothing. When he held his cigarettes out to me across the table, I took one absentmindedly.

"What we have here, in summation, is a happy story. Am I right? Not a sad one. So, that being the case, my friend—why the long face? As the psychiatrist said to the horse."

It seemed to me a story with a not-unhappy ending, true, but with a lump of irredeemable sadness at its core; of suspicion and fear and misjudgment. Perhaps it was because I wasn't Irish—except by adoption, so to speak. Which, it struck me then, was precisely what O'Nuff had been trying to tell me earlier.

He leant over and put a hand on my shoulder. "I'll tell you what. I see you don't accept what I've said, and that's fair enough. But as a personal favour to me, as a mark of our friendship . . ."

I looked up at him. "Yes?"

"Will you just take my bloody *word* for it?" He drained his glass. "Now, up to the bar with you, and two more of the same, please."

My glass was still three-quarters full. "I haven't finished this one, yet."

O'Nuff laughed, and shook his head. "You make me feel very Irish, kiddo, you really do. Look: you'll have finished drinking *that* one by the time they've finished pouring the *next* one!"

He was right, of course. He was, so.

GREEN LEGS AND GLAM

(A "Henry Po" Story)

Robert J. Randisi

1

I WAS NOT IN NEW ORLEANS specifically to ogle naked women, but I figured what the hell? Where was the harm?

I was actually in the Big Easy as a favor to my boss, J. Howard Biel, the Chairman of the New York State Racing Club. He had asked me if I would help out a friend of his who had a problem. Requests like these were not outside of my job description. Recently, one of them had taken me to Ireland for a few days. I figured why turn down an all-expenses-paid trip to New Orleans, the French Quarter, and the Fairgrounds Race Track.

The Fairgrounds was where Biel's friend hung his hat. Not the big magilla Biel was in New York, his friend, Andrew Cone, was still the number-two man at the Louisiana track.

Cone had handled all the travel arrangements and had booked me into a hotel right in the Quarter, on Bourbon Street, called the Bourbon Orleans. When I arrived at 2:00 P.M. there was a message

177

waiting for me at the desk, in writing. I waited until I got to my room before reading it.

"Enjoy what the Quarter has to offer," it said, "and meet me at the Blue Orleans Gentlemen's Club at 1:00 A.M."

It was signed, "With thanks, A. C."

I assumed by "Gentlemen's Club" we were referring to a strip joint. I wondered about the lateness of the meeting, but Cone was footing the bills, so I decided to keep the appointment.

Oh, did I mention it was Saint Patrick's Eve? March 17 was never a big holiday for me. I wasn't one of those people who suddenly became one-quarter Irish when Saint Paddy's Day rolled around, so it didn't bother me to be away from New York and miss the parade.

Since the meeting was for one in the morning, it would actually take place on Saint Patrick's Day. I spent the rest of Saint Paddy's Eve walking around the Quarter and—as Cone had suggested—taking advantage of what it had to offer. That meant great food and music and an interesting few hours spent in Jackson Square, getting sketched, read—tarot and palm—and fed.

I went back to my hotel after a late dinner to take a two-hour nap before meeting Cone at the Blue Orleans. I left a wake-up call, because I was pretty groggy after the flight and spending the day walking around.

Now, I had spent a short time walking down Bourbon Street because it was so famous and I had never been there before, but that had been during the day. I left my hotel at 12:30 A.M. to give myself plenty of time to find the club, but I needn't have bothered. After midnight Bourbon Street was like no street I had ever seen before, even in New York.

For one thing the street was closed to all vehicles, so people were just walking in the center of the street, as well as up and down the sidewalks. There were gentlemen's clubs everywhere, each with a unique way of advertising itself. One had a girl on a swing moving in and out of a window, apparently naked, but to be sure one had to go inside—and pay the cover charge. All you could see from outside was a pair of excellent bare legs and maybe—if she swung out too far—just the hint of a bare bottom.

Some of the clubs just had one or two girls loitering at the doors, just inside, so that as you passed you got a glimpse of a nice set of boobs or an excellent derriere.

Other clubs had girls dancing in the windows, but the windows were opaque, so that all you saw was a very shapely silhouette dancing and touching herself.

Music emanated from all these clubs, as well as the regular bars and jazz clubs along the street. There were vendors open that late still selling the traditional New Orleans hotdog called "a Lucky Dog." On almost every corner there was a daiquiri shop selling the icy drink in all flavors, and people strolled and sucked them up through straws while they stepped in and out of the gift shops. Amazingly—at least, amazing to me—each of the daiquiri shops and a lot of the gift shops had their own ATM machines. I had never seen so many bank machines on one street before; but then they were necessary, because everyone you saw on that street was either buying or selling something.

I found the Blue Orleans Gentleman's Club with no problem. It was one of the ones that had a naked girl or two right at the front door. As I entered I immediately had a nude girl on each arm, pressing a bare boob against me. I had a B-cup on one side and a D-cup on the other. Being a D-cup fan, I gave her most of my attention.

"You here to see me, honey?" she asked. "I'm Alicia."

"I'm here to see you," I said, "and to meet a friend."

"I can be very friendly," she said, rubbing her boob up and down my arm, now. It was very firm and warm and the sensation was any-thing but unpleasant. Both girls were wearing that patented "stripper scent" that most strippers seem to wear. They must all buy it from the same central location. It's very sweet and heady and stays with you a long time after you've left the place.

Okay, yeah, this wasn't my first time in a strip—excuse me—a gentlemen's club.

"Would you like me to come to your table later and show you?" she asked.

"I won't leave here until you do."

"You want to sit down in front or in the back?"

"What's the advantage of down front?"

Now she wiggled both boobs at me, the magic of silicone keeping them from jiggling uncontrollably, and said, "Well, a bird's-eye view, for one."

"And for another?"

"You never know when a naked girl will plop herself down in your lap."

"Well," I said, "my friend and I are going to be discussing some business, so I guess you better put me in the back."

She pouted at me and said, "I'll have to come find you, then."

"You do that."

She brightened and said, "I'll show you to your table and then I'll know where you are."

"Sounds like a plan."

Somewhere along the line the B-cup had disentangled herself. Guess I hadn't noticed.

What can I say? I'm a boob man.

2

By 2:30 I was starting to wonder if Cone was going to show, and I was considering moving down front. I was still working on my first five-dollar beer, which had been dyed green for Saint Patrick's Day.

"There you are!" Alicia said, running up to me.

"I saw you up there," I said. She had been up on one of the stages doing her thing a little while ago. Her thing was to be noticed, and she did it very well.

She sat down next to me and said, "Your friend stood you up?"

"Maybe," I said. "It's been an hour, but I guess I'll give him a little more time."

"How about a lap dance while you wait?" she asked. She leaned over so that her stripper smell was very strong in my nostrils and put her hand on my arm. "For twenty bucks I slide into your lap and wiggle all around!"

Having her think she had to explain a lap dance to me made me realize how young she probably was. I started to feel like a dirty old man.

"Wow," I said, "I'm tempted, but I better put it off until a little later."

I had given her a five-dollar bill just for showing me to the table, and now I slipped her another so she wouldn't forget about me.

"Gents," the announcer said into the microphone, "put your hands together and give a nice Saint Patrick's Day welcome to . . . Glam!"

The lights went down, a spotlight hit the center stage, and a girl stepped into it. She had green hair, and green legs, and her name was Glam. All of a sudden I was reminded of Dr. Seuss—but that didn't last long. Once she started moving she was nothing like the Cat in the Hat, at all!

She was different from the other girls. For one thing, as the spot hit her she was already naked, except for the green stockings, or leggings, whatever they were. The other girls all strutted on stage with little outfits on and proceeded to move around in some parody of a dance, stripping the outfit off little by little. This girl had the body and the moves of a trained dancer so she was actually more of an entertainer than a stripper, since she had nothing to strip off.

Her body was lean and muscular, her breasts small but solid. When she moved you could see the muscles in her calves and thighs rippling, when she turned the muscles in her buttocks were evident. While she danced to Joe Cocker singing "You Can Leave Your Hat On," everything else in the place stopped.

Then the music stopped and the spot went off, and when it came back on she was gone.

There was a collective sigh from the spectators, me included. We all knew we'd just seen something special.

At this point I realized Alicia had not left, but had remained seated there during "Glam's" number.

"Is she the headliner?" I asked.

"Hmph," Alicia said, "she thinks she is."

"How long has she been dancing here?"

"Only a week, and already she's got her own dressing room."

Well, I thought, somebody else thinks she's the headliner, too—like maybe the boss?

"And what about the green wig and stockings? Does she always wear that?"

"No," Alicia said, "that's for Saint Patrick's Day. Who is she kidding? She's not even Irish."

At this point I saw a man come in the front door, accosted by a B-cup and another girl, probably a C. He shook them off and spoke to a man who came walking over. Unmistakably, there was a handoff between them, but some people passed into my line of sight at the crucial moment and I couldn't tell which way it went.

"I'll be back later to see if you want that dance," Alicia said, and went stalking off, obviously upset that I had enjoyed Glam's number. She didn't know that, if she was a bit older, she'd still be more my preferred body type.

I looked for the customer involved in the handoff and was surprised to see him coming toward me.

"Henry Po?" he asked, as he reached the table.

"That's right," I said, standing up.

"Andy Cone." He extended his hand and I shook it. He was younger than I had expected, maybe because Biel—who was in his sixties—had described him as being a friend. This man was closer to my own age, somewhere in the mid to late thirties. "Sorry I'm late. I got caught up in something."

"That's okay," I said. "I've been entertained."

"I thought you might, that's why I had you meet me here," Cone said. "I come here a lot. Who showed you to your table?"

"A girl named Alicia."

"Ah," he said, his eyes lighting up, "nice."

"A little young," I said, for some reason.

"Maybe," he said. "Look, I hate to do this, but how about having another beer on me. I have to go in the back and talk to one of the girls, but then I'll come out and join you."

I shrugged and said, "It's your party, and your dime."

"Great," Cone said. "Thanks for being understanding."

Actually, I didn't understand at all, but the girls were naked and the beer was green and . . . well, none of that mattered. I was feeling pretty relaxed and mellow, at the moment. The pulse of Bourbon Street was dancing in my head and in my veins, it seemed. I'd never been anyplace like it, and I liked it; so I was quite willing to sit there and wait. Having nothing to do was a luxury for me.

Cone disappeared, somehow managing to get backstage. A waitress came over, topless and pert, and I ordered another beer.

3

THE BEER HADN'T ARRIVED when Cone reappeared, moving a lot faster than when he had disappeared. He looked at me and stopped, fidgeting, appearing to be in a quandary over whether to come over to me or head for the door. Suddenly, there was a scream from somewhere in the back and Cone froze, unable to even fidget.

Nobody seemed to know what to do. Patrons looked around, torn between the girls on the stage and the scream. Even the girl on stage seemed unsure. I sighed; Nothing was going to get done unless I did it. So much for relaxing.

I got up and rushed over to Cone, grabbed his arm.

"What happened?"

"I didn't . . ." he stammered, " . . . I didn't know . . ."

"Take me there."

"What?"

"Take me into the back!" I probably wouldn't get back there without him.

"Come on." I pushed him in the direction he had come. He led me to a curtained doorway I couldn't see from my table. A man was blocking it, obviously a bouncer.

"Hold it!" he said.

"Police," I said, not knowing the penalty in New Orleans for impersonating a cop, and not wanting to know.

"Oh," he said, "okay. What's goin' on?"

"That's what I'm gonna find out," I said, and pushed Cone ahead of me again.

We went through the curtain into a hall, and from there I didn't need Cone anymore. There was a small crowd in front of a door at the end of the hall. I didn't need him, but I pulled him along anyway, pulled this time, instead of pushing.

When we reached the door the crowd parted, probably something in my eyes or the way I was moving.

"Stay here," I said to Cone.

"But—"

"Don't make me have to find you."

He nodded, and started fidgeting. I turned and went into a small dressing room.

She was on the floor, arms and green legs askew, her green wig half on and half off, revealing red hair underneath. She wasn't naked anymore, wearing what looked like a silk dressing gown that was half on and half off. Her red pubic thatch was peeking up at me. There was blood under her head, soaked into the wig and spreading. The bullet had entered dead center in her forehead. The bloody puddle beneath her stood out in stark contrast to her pale skin.

There was a man in the room, wearing a cheap suit, a cheap hairpiece, and a frightened look.

"I don't know what to do," he said to me. I guess I looked as if I did. He was sweating so bad I could smell him.

"Who are you?" I asked.

"The manager."

"How many bouncers you got working?"

"Five"

"How many ways in and out?"

"Three."

"Block them," I said, "nobody in and nobody out."

"Okay," he said, glad to finally have something to do.

"And call nine-one-one."

"The police?" he asked, looking frightened again.

"They usually get called to the scene of a homicide."

He reached for a phone on a dressing table.

"Not from here," I shouted. "Go to your office and call them."

"But . . . I pay, I'm protected."

"Not against murder, friend."

4

UNIFORMS ARRIVED FIRST, THEN detectives. It was the same in every state, I guess.

They got the back hallway cleared out, probably putting everyone in the club. The music had been stopped a long time, and the girls had probably all covered up. There were two detectives, and they were in the dressing room with me and the dead girl.

"From what I've been told, you're the only one who knew what to do," one of them said.

"Somebody had to do something."

"Why you?" he asked. "I mean, how did you know what to do?"

I took out my wallet and handed him my ID.

"Private?"

"That's right."

"From New York."

That wasn't a question. It was on my ID. He handed it back.

"The manager says you made him call us."

"That's right. He told me he was protected. I assumed that a little protection money didn't include murder."

He impressed me by not denying anything, but simply saying, "You assumed right."

He looked at his partner, who nodded. They were the same age, forties, and had all the signs of having worked together a long time. The nod was one of the signs. They had communicated without saying a word, and had come to a decision.

"Mr. Po," the first man said, "my name's Detective LaSalle, this is my partner, Detective Batiste."

Batiste and I exchanged a nod. I had the feeling I had just gone up several notches in their estimation. With most cops, when they see your PI ticket, you go down; but I had known what to do in this situation, and that worked for me.

"Quick thinking to keep everyone inside," LaSalle said. "Now just tell me one other thing."

"What's that?"

"Who killed her?"

"I wish I knew," I said. "She was . . . special."

"How do you know that?" he snapped.

"I saw her dance," I said. "She was different from all the others."

"You don't know how different," LaSalle said, looking down at her. No one from the Medical Examiner's office had arrived, so they hadn't moved her. "She was one of ours."

"A snitch?"

He shook his head and looked at me with tremendous sadness in his eyes.

"A cop," I said.

He nodded. "She was working undercover."

"One of the girls said she came in a week ago."

"That's right," LaSalle said.

"And she already had her own dressing room."

"She has—had—dance background. That was why they sent her in here."

"Too bad."

"About what?"

"If she hadn't had the dance background, hadn't distinguished herself from the others, she might have shared a dressing room and not been alone."

He nodded. "I see what you mean."

"What was she working on?" I asked.

"Somebody is selling drugs from inside the club," LaSalle said. "It was thought that all that was needed was somebody on the inside who would keep their eyes on something other than the girls. That's why they sent in a woman."

I frowned, thinking back to what I had seen in the club.

"You didn't hear a shot?" LaSalle asked.

"No," I said, "just the scream of the girl who found her."

"Must have been suppressed, then," LaSalle said.

"The murder was planned," Batiste said.

"Somebody sniffed her out," LaSalle said. "She was a good cop, but somebody spotted her."

"One of the other girls, maybe," I said. "Even if she had her own dressing room they still saw more of her than anyone else."

"This is not the way a woman kills," LaSalle said.

I shrugged. "A woman may have fingered her."

LaSalle looked down at Glam again. Each time he did the pain in his eyes was evident. Batiste's glances at her were more dispassionate.

"I want this guy," LaSalle said.

I looked at Batiste, who simply stared back at me without expression, and yet I felt as if he'd passed me something.

"Look, Detective," I said, "I'm not from here, and I don't mean to try and do your job, but . . . if I could have a minute to leave the room?"

"If you can do anything to give me the killer," LaSalle said, "you can leave the state and come back."

"No," I said, "just the room."

"Go."

As I left he was still sitting, his shoulders slumped, and I thought I saw his partner put his hand on his shoulder.

5

I WENT OUT INTO the club and looked around. There was still a bouncer standing at the front door and one that I could see at a side door. In each case a uniformed policeman had joined him. Since there were three ways out, I assumed that there was also a bouncer and a cop on that door, as well.

I found Andrew Cone seated at the table I had been sitting at, with three other people, none of whom seemed to know each other. The police had simply made everyone sit down, so that most of the seats were taken.

"Cone," I said, "come with me for a minute."

"What for?" He looked frightened.

"Just come on."

He stood up, and I walked him over into a corner where we could talk alone.

"Tell me what happened in the back." I said.

"Did you tell them—"

"I didn't tell them anything," I said, "and if you answer all my questions I might not. Why did you go into the back?"

"I—I'm having a thing with one of the girls. I went in the back to see her."

"And what happened?"

"I—I saw the new girl's dressing room door open and I . . . I saw green legs on the floor. I . . I walked over and took a look. She was on the floor . . . there was blood . . . I wanted to get out . . ."

"Why?"

"I . . ." He stopped, as if answering that question was harder than the others.

"Is it because you have drugs on you that you're afraid would be found in a search?"

His eyes widened and he looked around to see if anyone had heard me.

"No one can hear us," I said, keeping my voice low. "When you walked in I happened to be looking at the door." That was when I found out how young and dumb Alicia was, and I lost interest in her, D cups or not. If not for that I might not have seen what I did. "I saw a hand-off when you walked in, but I didn't see what was exchanged. Were you selling, or buying?"

He didn't answer right away.

"Come on, Andrew," I said, "you can answer me or the cops."

"Buying," he said, quickly in a barely audible voice. "I was buying."

"So the bouncer is the one selling drugs out of the club?"

"That's right."

"Which one?" I asked him. The sale had taken place at the door, but that didn't mean that the bouncer on that door was the one. As it turned out, it was.

"That one," Cone said, and pointed at the man.

The bouncer must have been watching us. Maybe Cone was the last person he had sold drugs to, maybe the only one in the club he had made a sale to. In any case, when Andrew Cone pointed him out the man bolted for the door.

"Stop him!" I shouted to the cop who had been standing with him. "Stop that man!"

Too late. The cop was too slow and the bouncer was out the door. I took off after him, ran out the door myself before the cop could intercept me.

Out into the combination of people and sounds and lights and music that was Bourbon Street after midnight.

6

THE BOUNCERS IN THE club all wore the same thing, black pants and a black T-shirt with the club's logo on it which—luckily—was yellow. As I ran out the door onto the street I looked both ways and spotted the yellow logo hightailing it up Bourbon Street. I took off after him, and then we were both dodging two-way traffic of people who were having a good time, moving slowly, men and women trying to stop us to throw beads on us or flash us. The bouncer literally ran over three or four people, knocking them to the ground, scattering green daiquiris onto the street, forcing me to try to avoid them and in the process knocking one or two people down. The only difference is that although neither of us stopped, I tried to toss apologies over my shoulder.

The bouncer stayed on Bourbon Street, probably figuring to lose himself in the people, rather than turning off on a side street. However, he was knocking so many people over that he was leaving a trail behind him. Neither one of us was making much progress, me in catching him or he in getting away. He risked a look over his shoulder once or twice and saw me chasing. I didn't know if there were cops running behind me or not, and I didn't take a look, not wanting to risk taking my eyes off him.

Finally, he decided he wasn't getting anywhere and turned down a side street. When I reached it I saw that it was Orleans Street. Now we were away from people and running down a darker street. I could still see him ahead of me and hear his feet pounding on the ground. With fewer people to avoid—literally only one or two of them—he was able to pick up speed, but so was I. He ran one block and turned right at the corner, trying to lose me. As I turned the corner I saw him make a quick left and duck into Pirate's Alley, a street I had been on earlier in the day. I had been to the Faulkner House bookstore and I knew that the alley would give out onto Jackson Square. In the afternoon the square was teeming with as much life as Bourbon Street was at night. At this time of the night it would be empty. I had to keep him in sight to see which way he would go when he reached the square.

As luck would have it we were now running on a cobblestoned street, something the bouncer was probably not used to. Truth be told, neither was I, but I didn't stumble and fall and he did. It happened in every movie, and it happens in real life. Sometimes you're just running too fast for your feet to keep up with, or you simply trip. He did one of those things and went down flat on his belly. I could hear him slide as he hit the cobblestones, then the sound his hands and feet made as he scrambled to get up. He had just gotten his balance when I hit him, tackling him low around the knees. He was a lot bigger than me, and I still didn't know if I had help behind me. I took him at the knees because it's easier to fight a man who is bigger than you if you take him off his feet.

We went down together. His hands and knees must have been smarting from his first fall, and I heard the wind go out of him as he hit this second time.

I scrambled this time, trying to get on top of him so I could keep him down. I got into his back and as I did he heaved himself up and me with him. He was big and strong, and if I was alone in this alley with him I was going to be in trouble.

Luckily, that was not the case.

As he tossed me off him and tried to get to his feet two uniformed NOPD cops hit him and took him down for a third and final time.

7

"SO YOU SAW AN exchange take place at the door, but you didn't see what was exchanged," LaSalle asked me, about half an hour later, "or who the exchange was made with."

"Right."

"And you figured drug buy?"

"What can I say?" I asked. "I have an extremely suspicious mind."

He stared at me, not sure whether I was telling the whole truth or not. I was trying to keep Andrew Cone out of it, because I believed what he had told me. He'd simply chosen the wrong night to make a drug buy and to have a meeting with me to discuss whatever problem it was he needed help with. I didn't know what that problem was, or if it had anything to do with drugs, but I knew I wasn't going to hang around to find out. If LaSalle would let me I was going to be on the first plane home the next day.

"So you went out into the club to see if he was still there?"

"Right."

"One of my boys said you talked to someone else."

"Right," I said. "I came here to meet someone, and I wanted to check in with him when I had the chance. Then I started toward the bouncer, and he took off."

"Why would you figure he was the killer?"

"Well, if it was a drug buy, it fit in with what you told me about, uh, the girl, Glam, and what she was doing here."

"And how did you come to see this buy?"

"I told you," I said. "I just happened to be looking at the door."

"With all these naked girls here you were looking at the door?" he asked, doubtfully.

"Like I said," I replied, "I was waiting for someone."

"Yeah," the detective said, "you did say that. I'm going to need his name by the way."

I gave it to him. I figured they'd question Cone, but not search him. What happened while they were questioning him would depend on how guilty he felt. That was his problem, not mine.

At that moment the M.E.'s men came out of the back carrying the body of the dead cop. We both waited until they had passed and gone out the front door. Batiste was gone, having taken the bouncer to wherever they'd take him to question him and book him.

LaSalle looked back at me.

"How do you figure the bouncer got back there to kill her?"

"He works here, he's got access. According to the manager there are five bouncers working and three ways out. Put one on each door, and one on the door to the dressing rooms, and you got one guy who can float. He was probably the floater when he went back and killed her. Check with the bouncer who was on that door and see if he went back there."

"We did," LaSalle said. "He says the guy went back there only for a minute and came right out again."

"Then it fits."

"There were girls going in and out, too."

"Like you said," I reminded him, "not a woman's crime."

"I wonder how he made her."

I thought about Alicia, and how jealous she seemed of "Glam."

Some of the other girls probably felt the same way. I wondered if one of them had made her for the killer, maybe even innocently.

His cell phone rang then, and he plucked it from his belt and answered it by saying his name. He listened, nodded, grunted, said, "Thanks," and hung up.

At that moment a uniformed cop came over with a gun in a plastic bag. Also in the bag was a suppressor.

"Where'd you find it?"

"In a garbage bag in the back. Had to go through a bunch. The bags had all been tied off, but whoever had the gun was able to shove the gun and suppressor through a hole without untying it."

"Good. Get it down to the lab. We should be able to get some prints off it."

"And they'll match those of the bouncer," I said, helpfully.

As the uniformed cop walked away LaSalle said, "Yeah, they will. That was my partner on the phone. The guy confessed. He did it. He killed her."

"All right," I said. "You got him."

"You got him, Mr. Po," LaSalle said, and I was surprised to see that he was close to tears. "And I'm very grateful."

"Detective . . ." I said, then decided not to ask.

"You got a right to know," he said. "She and I . . . we were . . . well, close."

"I'm sorry."

"Yeah," he said. "Listen, if you'll come down and make a statement tomorrow, I don't think we'll have to detain you in town any longer."

"Thanks. I'll be down first thing."

He handed me his card with the address of the police station I was to go to, then turned to walk away.

"Can I ask . . ." I said, and he turned around ". . . what her real name was?"

"Shannon," he said, "her name was Detective Shannon O'Brien."

"So she was Irish, after all?"

"Oh yeah," he said, "she was definitely Irish. She loved Saint Paddy's Day."

Neither one of us appreciated the irony.

One of Our Leprechauns Is Missing

Bill Crider

1

BEING ON RETAINER TO Gober Studios can be pretty strange sometimes. Once, for example, the Easter Bunny slept off a drunk in the back seat of my car.

Usually, though, I'm on the run, trying to keep Mr. Gober's stars from disgracing themselves, and incidentally the studio, by getting their names in some scandal rag because of their odd, to put it politely, behavior. You just never know what some of those fun-loving Hollywood characters will get up to. The big war with Germany and Japan had been over for a couple or three years, but maybe the stars were still celebrating the victory.

Take Monty Raines, star of a series of black-and-white oaters about a character called Dan the Drifter. For some reason no one was quite able to explain, Raines had developed a sudden affection for livestock during the making of a ranchers-versus-sheepherders movie and set off to deflower all the virgin sheep in California.

It's not easy to find sheep in California, much less virgins, so Raines crossed the state line and headed for greener pastures, so to speak. I caught up with him in West Texas and dragged him back to Tinsel Town after dealing with irate sheep owners in three states.

Raines wasn't any happier than the sheep owners, but Mr. Gober was pleased. And if he was pleased, so was I. He was the one writing the checks, which is exactly what he was doing at the moment as he sat behind his big desk with a top about the right size for landing a P-38.

"Good work, Ferrell," he said in a voice like a rock crusher at work. He tore my bonus check from the checkbook and waved it in the air to let the ink dry. "You're sure no one from *Inside Secrets* heard about Raines?"

"I can't guarantee it," I said. I was sitting across from him, and my fingers were itching to get hold of the check. "One of the sheep might have squealed."

Actually, I'm pretty sure some of them squealed when Monty got to them, though I was hoping no one had heard them except other sheep.

"Goddamnit, Ferrell, I don't want to hear any cheap jokes, I want to know if the studio is protected."

"I think so. I paid off enough sheep owners."

"All right, then."

He handed over the check, and I tried not to look too pleased as I folded it and put it in my wallet.

"Now that we have that settled," Mr. Gober said, "there's another little problem."

I didn't want to hear about it. I was tired, I smelled like sheep, and I wanted to take a bath and sleep for a week. Besides, as far as my experience went, there was no such thing as a *little* problem where the studio was concerned. But Mr. Gober was the man with the checkbook.

"Tell me about it," I said.

"One of our leprechauns is missing," he said.

I didn't laugh. A man who's hauled the Easter Bunny around in his car is ready for anything.

"I suppose there's a pot of gold involved, too," I said.

Gober sat up straight and glared at me over the top of his enormous desk.

"Goddamnit, Ferrell, who told you?"

"Let's just call it a lucky guess. How can you lose a leprechaun, anyway?"

"Lost? I didn't say lost. I said missing."

I didn't see the difference, but I said, "Okay. So what do you want me to do?"

"What the hell do you think I want you to do? I want you to find him. Now. There's another bonus in it for you when you do."

"Okay," I said.

GOBER STUDIOS WASN'T ONE of the biggest. It wasn't one of the best, either, but it made money, and now and then it even came up with a genuine hit. That's what happened with a musical called *Smilin' Irish Eyes*. It was set in Ireland (naturally) and starred Jackson Kendall (from Fort Worth, Texas) as a young lad named Sean O'Grady, who fell in love with a visiting British lass (Karen Swan, from Kansas) whose family hated all things Irish. The sly local priest, played by Basil Cooperworth (real name: Harry Melon, from Saint Louis), played cupid, and of course all was well in the end.

Kendall and Swan sang a couple of solos apiece and a humdinger of a duet on the sort-of title song, "When Irish Eyes Are Smiling," but the real success story of the movie was a group of three girls whom Gober had dubbed "The Singing Shamrocks," sort of an Irish Andrews Sisters. Their recording of "You Can Kiss the Blarney Stone, but You Can't Kiss Me" played on every jukebox and radio in the country for months. The movie was big box office for nearly as long.

With all that success, the studio naturally had to make another movie as much like the first one as possible. So *Leaping Leprechauns* was born. It would be bigger and better, of course. It would even be in color, which was unusual for a Gober project. It was getting the full treatment.

It must have seemed like a good idea at the time. But someone should have thought about the fact that less than ten years earlier, *The Wizard of Oz* hadn't done especially well with its cast of singers and dancers and little people. There was plenty of room for things to go wrong, and they did.

"We hired the wrong guy," Gober admitted to me. "He was a problem on the Oz set, but he swore to me that all that was behind him. The goddamned little liar."

The little liar was Jerry Fitzgerald, a midget with a practically authentic Irish heritage, or at least name, and the perfect man to play the leprechaun that led Jackson Kendall astray in a search for the pot of gold that leprechauns were supposed to guard.

"Or maybe he wasn't so perfect," Gober said. "Leprechauns are boozers, aren't they?" He didn't wait for me to answer. He said, "So is Fitzgerald."

"Leprechauns are supposed to disappear, too," I said. "Take your eyes off them, and they're gone."

"That's the way it happened with Fitzgerald. I had a man assigned to watch him, and he must've blinked."

"And now I have to find him. I hope they're shooting on location. I've always wanted to go to Ireland."

"Try the back lot," Gober said.

2

IT WAS A GOOD deal like Ireland, I guess, if you could ignore the thick black cables snaking around, the cameras, the Klieg lights, the crew, the scaffolding, the dollies, and all the rest of it. The grass was green (painted, of course), the sky was blue, and the air was full of the sound of bleating and the smell of sheep.

I was all too familiar with the smell. I thought immediately of Monty Raines, and I wondered if any of the sheep were friends of his. I hoped he didn't hear about this movie. He'd move heaven and earth to get a part in it. There was no way that could happen, however. I'd stashed him in a little bungalow way out near Coldwater Canyon with a hypnotist that Gober had imported from Australia. "An expert in human/sheep relations," was the way Gober had put it, though I thought the real expert on that topic was probably Raines. Not that I mentioned my thought to Gober.

The crew was swarming around setting up a scene, and I didn't see any of the stars. They were probably in their trailers getting a massage or whatever it was that they got. I did spot Lenny Jorkens, however. Lenny was a guy I knew slightly, and he was the leprechaun wrangler. He was standing in the midst of a swarm of little people. They were jumping around excitedly, and they wore green hats with giant shamrocks stuck in the bands, green shirts and pants with a leather apron over them, and gold-buckled shoes. Each one had a fringe of beard along the jawline.

I walked over to see what was going on and also to have a private word with Lenny if I could get him off to himself. I wanted to find out just how he'd managed to let Jerry Fitzgerald disappear.

As it turned out, I didn't ask. Jerry had already been found. That's what all the excitement was about.

"I tell you, he's lying behind the Blarney Stone," one of the leprechauns said. "Dead as a doornail, too."

"Dead drunk is more like it," Lenny Jorkens said.

He was a real string bean of a guy, with a prominent Adam's apple, a shock of black hair, and thick glasses. Surrounded by leprechauns, he looked even taller and skinnier than he normally did.

"Why don't we go have a look," I said, walking up to the group.

"Hey, Bill," Lenny said. "I didn't know you were on the set. Gober send you?"

"Right the first time. I'm here to check on Jerry Fitzgerald."

"He's dead," one of the leprechauns told me. "And the pot of gold's missing."

"It's not real gold," Lenny said.

"Jerry said it was real," the leprechaun said.

"We'll see what we can find out," I said. "Why don't you and Lenny come with me. The rest of you take a break."

The other leprechauns scattered, and I asked the one who remained his name.

"Michael O'Shea. You can call me Mike."

"You're pulling my leg."

"Nope, that's my name. I'm as Irish as they come."

He sounded more like Oklahoma to me, but I didn't care. I said, "Where's Blarney Castle?"

"Castle?"

"Yeah. That's where the Blarney Stone is. Blarney Castle."

Lenny laughed. "Maybe it is in Ireland, but not in this movie. This is Gober Studios, remember. Our Blarney Stone is in the woods."

It figured. Gober wasn't going to spring for a castle, not if he figured nobody in the audience would miss it.

"Fine," I said "Let's go to the woods."

To get there, we had to go down the village street and through the flock of sheep that was grazing just beyond. The village was mostly false fronts, and it was usually a western town. Take away the fake trees and the painted grass, change the fronts a little, and it would be a western town again.

The sheep herd was fairly small, all in keeping with Gober's economics. One of the sheep bleated as I came along. Probably thought he smelled a friend.

We got to the woods pretty quickly. It wasn't much of a woods, but at least there were some trees. I don't know much about trees, but I thought I could identify a few oaks, some cottonwoods, and maybe even a eucalyptus. It didn't matter whether these trees were native to Ireland or not. This same wooded area had served as England in Robin Hood's day, Texas in the time of the Texas Rangers, and even a Florida swamp. Gober figured that the audience's knowledge of trees was about equal to mine.

Just inside the trees was a big rock. The amazing thing about it was that it was real. It just happened to be there, and it was too big to move. It had been seen in many a western.

"There's the Blarney Stone," Mike said, as if I couldn't have figured it out for myself.

Lenny ran ahead of us and looked behind the rock. He sang out, "He's here," and bent down.

When Mike and I got there, Lenny was straddling Fitzgerald, slapping his face and yelling at him. Fitzgerald wasn't much bigger than a good-sized doll.

"Wake up! Come on, you lazy bum! You're gonna cost me my job."

Fitzgerald just lay there beside the rock. His little green hat was lying beside him, and a leaf of the giant shamrock was clutched in his hand, as if someone had placed it there. The rest of the shamrock was lying on Fitzgerald's stomach. A bottle of Old Skullbanger lay nearby. It figured.

Mike ran over to Lenny on his short little legs and grabbed Lenny's arm.

"Stop it!" Mike said. "Don't you have any respect?"

Lenny looked surprised. "For a drunk? Hell, no."

By that time I'd had a pretty good look at Fitzgerald's face, and also the side of his head. I could tell he wasn't drunk.

"Get up, Lenny," I said.

"You're not the boss around here," Lenny said.

"You want to call Mr. Gober and check on that?"

Lenny thought about that, but not for long. He stood up and moved away from Fitzgerald, and I knelt down to feel for a pulse. There wasn't one, of course. There was blood under Fitzgerald's head, and he was already turning cold. I stood up and took off my hat.

"He's dead," I said.

"Yeah," O'Shea said, giving Lenny a look. "Like I tried to tell you."

3

THE ONE THING YOU don't do if you work for Gober Studios is call the cops. Not until you have to, that is. First you figure out how you're going to keep the studio from getting any bad publicity. Which in this case was most likely impossible. All I could do was delay things for a while.

"It's easy to see what happened here," I said, putting my hat back on. "Jerry was rehearsing a scene, a dance on the Blarney Stone, maybe, and he fell off. He hit his head on the stone, and that's what killed him."

O'Shea said, "Baloney."

"Call Doc Sloane in about an hour," I told Jorkens. "I'm sure he knows someone on the cops who can stall things for an hour or two."

O'Shea said, "Baloney." This time he said it in a much louder voice, however.

"Don't worry," I told him. "The fall is just the story we'll give out for the press until I find out what really happened."

"Baloney," O'Shea said. He was like a broken record. "The press will never hear what really happened, and neither will anyone else."

"Calm down," Jorkens told him. "Ferrell's okay. He handles jobs for Gober all the time. He'll do the right thing. You and I will keep mum."

O'Shea opened his mouth as if to say *baloney* again, but he didn't. He just shut his mouth and looked at me.

"Trust me," I said, giving him my sincere look.

"Baloney," he said.

AFTER I GOT RID of them, I looked things over more closely. There was no blood on the rock, but there was blood on the whiskey bottle, which was about half full. The blood pretty much ruled out a fall, unless Fitzgerald had fallen on the bottle, which was highly unlikely, no matter how drunk he might have been. Even if he had fallen on the bottle, it wouldn't have killed him. He'd been hit pretty hard.

The grass around the body was disturbed as if there'd been a scuffle. So all I had to do was find out who'd been doing the scuffling. Then I'd know who'd swung the bottle, which I didn't touch. I figured there were bound to be fingerprints on it. That would be the clincher, but fingerprints were for the cops to find.

And then they'd have to find a match. If matching prints were on file, that would make it easy for them, but they'd have to find a suspect to match them with. That was my job.

If the prints weren't on file, things would be a lot tougher. Fingerprinting a movie star who has a high-powered lawyer isn't an easy task. Of course, it was always possible that no stars were involved. Maybe Jerry Fitzgerald had been killed by a member of the crew.

I doubted it, however. The cops and I were never that lucky.

I looked at the hat again. It was lying right beside the body. The brim was crushed where the bottle had hit it.

I looked around for a few minutes longer, hoping I might see the pot of gold. It wasn't there, but something glittered at the edge of the stone. I bent down and had a look. It was a gold foil package with the words "Sold for the prevention of disease only" stamped on it. Well, well. I picked it up by the edges and put it in my pocket. Then I walked back to the fake village to see if I could find Mike.

I LOCATED THE LEPRECHAUN along with a few of his pals in the building that served as the saloon in the studio's westerns. Take off the top, get rid of the bat-wing doors, put up a few shrubs, add a new thatched roof, and *voilá!* you had an Irish pub.

I called O'Shea outside and asked if he'd kept quiet about Fitzgerald.

"Sure. But half that bunch already knew. They were with me when I found the body. God knows who they've told."

It figured. "Kendall? Swan? Cooperworth? They all know?"

"Probably not. They don't talk to us much. We're not pretty enough for them."

"How about the Singing Shamrocks?"

O'Shea looked at the dirt street. My detecting instincts detected that I was on to something.

"Sure, and the Irish love to tell a lie," I said. "But now 'tis not the time for one."

"That was awful," O'Shea said, looking up. "Probably the worst Irish accent I've ever heard."

"But it came from the heart."

"Yeah."

"About the Singing Shamrocks," I said.

"Jerry liked the women," O'Shea said. "Even the big ones. Maybe especially the big ones."

"So he liked the Shamrocks?"

O'Shea got a feisty look on his face. "Nothing wrong with that, is there? Or do you have something against midgets?"

"Nothing wrong with a little romance as far as I'm concerned, as long as it's confined to members of the same species. Was it a problem for anyone else?"

O'Shea clammed up again. I looked at him and waited. Finally, he said, "Kendall."

"Kendall?"

"Kendall liked Brenda, too. He told Jerry that if he bothered her again, he'd kill him."

Ah-ha. The old detecting instincts had been right on the money.

"Brenda's one of the Shamrocks, I take it," I said.

"Their names are Brenda, Betty, and Beryl. Or so they tell me. I don't believe it for a minute."

"I believe your name is Michael O'Shea."

"Baloney."

"Yeah. Anything else you want to tell me?"

"Cooperworth."

"Cooperworth?"

"He was after Betty."

"I thought you said that Jerry liked Brenda."

O'Shea gave a leprechaun shrug.

"I told you he liked women. Brenda and Betty are women, and they didn't give us the brush-off like the big stars of the picture did."

"Right. So that's it?"

"Jorkens."

"Jorkens?"

"Have you noticed the echo around here?"

"Never mind the cracks," I said. "What about Jorkens?"

"He was after Beryl."

"And so was Jerry?"

"Like I told you."

I thought it over for a second. "What about Karen Swan? She's a real looker. Wasn't anyone after her?"

"You don't know about her?"

"No."

"She doesn't like guys. She prefers other women."

"Oh," I said. "Was she after any of the Shamrocks?"

"Sure," O'Shea said.

"Which one?"

"All of them."

"Damn," I said, not that I cared who or what Karen Swan liked. I'd just rounded up a guy who preferred sheep, after all. I just hoped nobody from *Inside Secrets* found out about Swan. That would be another job I'd have to handle.

"What about that pot of gold you mentioned?" I asked.

"It's gone. Jerry was the one who carried it around. He told me it was real."

"This is a movie set," I said. "Nothing's real. Except that rock out there, and the trees." I looked down at the green stain on my shoes. "The grass isn't even really green."

O'Shea shook his head stubbornly.

"All I know is what Jerry told me. 'Pure gold.' That's what he said."

Hollywood people, I thought. In some ways they were shrewd, but in others they were like children. They spend their whole lives with illusions. Not that I'm much different. I've dealt with a cockatoo that posed as a parrot and a dog that posed as a wolf that turned out to be . . . well, you get the idea. It's no wonder that as the days go by it gets harder and harder for Hollywood people to tell the difference between the illusions and what is real. Maybe that's why we're sometimes so easy to fool. Maybe that's why I work so hard at not being fooled.

4

I HAD TO CALL Gober and get him to come to the set. He wasn't happy about it, but he came. It took all his powers of persuasion and a number of threats about paychecks and people "never working in this town again" to get everyone I wanted to see rounded up together in the pub. No one was happy to be there, but at least some of them were honest.

"Sure, I said I'd kill him," Jackson Kendall told me. "But I didn't. I don't mind that somebody beat me to it, though, if you want to know the truth."

Kendall was one of those guys who looked even better in person than on the screen, where he looked pretty darn good. And his voice was deep and rich and powerful, just the way it sounded when he sang. He was shorter than he looked on screen, though. Probably not over five feet and six inches tall. Even at that, he towered over O'Shea.

"I told him to stay away from Brenda," Kendall went on. "I didn't like the way the little bastard would run up to her and bump into her all the time."

Brenda and the other two Singing Shamrocks were seated at a nearby table. They were all buxom women wearing Irish country dresses, and they all had glossy red hair, creamy complexions, and green eyes. What their real hair color might have been was anybody's guess.

Brenda was the one who was blushing. I figured the blush might have been genuine, but I didn't know the reason for it. Kendall was ready to explain, however.

"You know how short Fitzgerald was," he said, as if he were a giant among men himself. "Where do you think he'd strike Brenda when he bumped into her?"

I got it then, and Brenda blushed a bit more brightly.

"Sure and he did the same thing to Betty," Basil Cooperworth said in his phony Irish accent, which I had to admit was a lot better than mine. Cooperworth looked the part of a priest wearing his clerical collar and a pair of little half-glasses. He didn't sound like a priest when he talked about Fitzgerald, however.

"I told him to stay away from Betty or I'd break his scrawny little neck," he said, losing the accent.

It was Betty's turn to blush, but she didn't bother. She said, "He played the same game with Beryl. Isn't that right?"

Beryl didn't blush either. She just nodded, while Lenny Jorkens looked at her fondly.

"Which one of you did he lure out to the Blarney Stone today?" I asked.

"Goddamnit, Ferrell, what are you trying to do here?"

That was Mr. Gober, of course. I'd tried to get him to leave, but after walking all the way to the back lot, he wasn't going anywhere until things were settled satisfactorily. Having someone practically accuse one of his prized singers of killing Fitzgerald didn't fit his definition of "satisfactorily."

Lenny Jorkens didn't like it any better than Gober did.

"You'd better watch what you say, Ferrell," he said, an ugly twist to his mouth.

I thought about the way he'd slapped a dead man's face. There was a lot of hate in a person who'd do something like that. But I didn't think he'd killed Jerry Fitzgerald.

"Yes," Beryl said. She was the prettiest of the Shamrocks, and her alto voice was nice and low. "You should be careful of what you say, Mr. Ferrell. There are laws about libel and slander, you know."

"Tell that to the people at *Inside Secrets*," I said. "If they get wind of this mess, they'll make my little accusations sound like a bedtime story."

Gober turned red when I mentioned the magazine. He looked around the room as if some sleazy reporter might be lurking in a dark corner.

"That's all your accusations are," Kendall said. "A bedtime story. You can't prove a thing."

"Probably not. But the police might be able to. You know what I'd like?"

Nobody said a word. I guess they weren't interested. I'd thought Mr. Gober might help me out, but he just sat there, still red-faced, staring at me as if he thought I'd lost my mind.

Maybe I had. I said, "Since nobody wants to guess, I'll tell you what I'd like. I'd like to hear the Shamrocks sing a song."

"Faith and begorra," Cooperworth said. "The man's turned daft."

The accent was just as good as before, but it irritated me more this time.

"I'm not asking much," I said. "Maybe just part of a song."

"Why should we?" Betty wanted to know.

"Because Mr. Gober would appreciate it," I said, hoping he'd back me up this time.

And he did. Maybe he remembered all those other times I'd saved the studio. Or maybe he just wanted to get things over with. The reason didn't matter, as long as he did it.

"Sing him a song," he said. "What could it hurt?"

The Shamrock Sisters looked at each other. Beryl nodded, and they stood up.

"Over there would be fine," I said, pointing to a cleared area in front of the bar.

They walked over and stood side by side. Brenda was a bit taller than the other two, while Betty was on the stocky side. But they were all very attractive. I could see why Fitzgerald had liked them.

"Any requests?" Betty asked.

"Do your hit," I said.

Betty hummed a note, and they launched into a lively *a capella* version of "You Can Kiss the Blarney Stone, but You Can't Kiss Me."

They swayed in time to the music, and their skirts billowed out with their movements. I looked down at their shoes. They were black, but I could see the stains from the painted grass on them. Or at least I could see the stains on Beryl's and Brenda's shoes. There were no stains on Betty's.

That was interesting, because nearly everyone had walked on the grass that day, and they'd be walking on it again. Why bother to clean the shoes?

When the song was over, everyone applauded, and I took an empty glass over to Betty and handed it to her.

"That was great," I said. "I'd like to buy you a drink."

"There's no real liquor in here, Ferrell," Lenny said. "It's all just weak tea."

There was a general laugh at my stupidity. I joined in, and Betty put the glass down on the bar.

"I guess that's it, then," I said. "Thanks for the song."

Everyone seemed to think I was completely nuts, but they didn't ask questions. They just left. Except for Mr. Gober.

"Goddamnit, Ferrell," he said, "what the hell was all that about?"

"It's about this," I said, and I pulled the prophylactic out of my pocket.

"Jesus Christ!" Gober said, looking all around. "Put that away! What are you, anyway? Some kind of pervert?"

"That's always a possibility," I admitted. "But this isn't mine. I found it near Fitzgerald's body."

"In the woods? That's where you usually find things like that."

I didn't ask him how he knew. I said, "I think it was Fitzgerald's. He probably had it in his little pot of gold, the one he kept telling people was real. My idea is that he about halfway convinced Betty that he was telling the truth about the gold and got her to go out to the woods with him to have a little drink and take a look at his treasure. When they got to the Blarney Stone, she asked to see the gold, and this is what Fitzgerald pulled out of the pot. That's when she clobbered him with the bottle. She took the gold. She probably still hoped it was real. But she missed this."

"Knowing that damned lying Fitzgerald," Gober said, "I can see how that might have happened the way you say. But how do you know it was Betty who was with him?"

"I knew it had to be one of the Shamrocks," I said. "Before he died, Fitzgerald pulled the fake clover out of his hat and clutched one of the leaves in his hand."

"How do you know that, for God's sake?"

"When he was hit by the bottle, it dented the brim of his hat. He was hit so hard that the blow should have knocked the hat away from him. But it was lying right beside him. I think he pulled it over to him and grabbed the shamrock to leave a clue about his killer."

Gober nodded as if he might believe me, but he wasn't entirely convinced.

"If it happened that way," he said, "which I'm not sure it did, why single out Betty?"

"Her shoes."

"Shoes?"

I saw what O'Shea meant about the echo.

"Her shoes didn't have any green paint on them. From the grass. She'd wiped it all off. She wasn't thinking clearly, I guess, and she must have believed the paint would give away the fact that she'd been to the woods. But the paint was everywhere. Even you have a little on your shoes."

Gober looked down. "All right. I suppose that's why you wanted them to sing. So you could have a look at the shoes."

"I'd already seen the shoes when she came in. I wanted a reason to congratulate them and get her to hold a glass."

"Fingerprints," Gober said, looking over at the glass that still sat on the bar.

"Right. If the prints on that glass match the ones on the whiskey bottle, the cops will have a pretty good case against Betty. And they'll probably find that she has the pot of gold, too."

"And that's the end of the Singing Shamrocks," Gober said. "The end of the picture, too. Goddamnit, Ferrell, you're supposed to help the studio, not shut it down."

Shutting down the picture wasn't the same thing as shutting down the studio, but there was no need to point that out. Gober already knew it.

"You won't have to shut down the picture," I said.

"The hell you say. What about the Shamrocks?"

"That's easy. Find you someone else who can sing and who looks like Betty. Dye her hair red, and that's that."

"It's not as easy as you make it sound," Gober said.

"Sure it is. This town is full of pretty women who want to be movie stars and singers. You'll find someone."

"Maybe. But what about leprechauns? They aren't as easy to find as singers."

"O'Shea is pretty good. He could carry the part. He even has an Irish name."

Gober nodded. "He does, doesn't he? But the trial and the publicity will be ugly."

"You know what short memories people have. There won't be much publicity if Betty is already replaced by the time she's arrested."

He knew I was right. He said, "When do the cops get here?"

"It won't be long. They may be here already. Dr. Sloane is coming first. He's going to confuse things for a while."

"Come back to the office when you're finished. I'll have another bonus check for you. Then you need to go home. You smell like sheep."

I PUT THE GLASS in a safe place under the bar and went outside to watch Gober walk down the village street. The production obviously hadn't shut down. Jackson Kendall and Karen Swan, along with the whole crew, were at the edge of the village, getting ready to film a scene with the sheep. I could hear the herd's gentle bleating. It didn't do much for me, but then I wasn't Monty Raines. I hoped the hypnotist would be able to help him.

I skirted the shooting area and walked on back to the woods to sit with Jerry Fitzgerald until Dr. Sloane and the police arrived. There was something in my pocket that I needed to return to the scene. And besides, I didn't like the idea of a leprechaun having to wait alone.

THE DUBLIN EYE

Clark Howard

KILKENNY HEARD THE PHONE ring as he was unlocking his office
door. He hurried in to answer it.

"Kilkenny," he said.

"Is this Mr. Royal Kilkenny?" a hesitant female voice asked. The
caller sounded very young. "Mr. Royal Kilkenny, the query man?"

"Yes. How can I help you?"

"Mr. Kilkenny, my name is Darlynn Devalain. I'm the daughter of
Joe Devalain, of Belfast."

An image mushroomed in Kilkenny's mind. Not of Joe Devalain,
but of the woman Joe had married. Of Sharmon. This girl on the
phone was probably Sharmon's daughter.

"How is your dad, then?" Kilkenny asked. "And your mother?"

"My dad's not so good, Mr. Kilkenny," the girl replied, and
Kilkenny, though he had never laid eyes on her, could almost see her
lip quivering as her voice broke. "He's been in a bad accident. An
explosion in his shop. They've got him over at Saint Bartholomew's
Hospital, but it's not known if he'll live or—"

"Did your mother tell you to call me?" Kilkenny asked, frowning. It
had been eighteen years since Sharmon Cavan had picked Joe Devalain
over him, and he had gone off to America to try and forget her.

211

"No, she doesn't even know I'm after calling you," Darlynn Devalain said. "Me dad told me once that he knew you before you went to America. When he heard you'd come back and set up as a query man down in Dublin, he told me you were a man he could always count on. He said if I should ever find myself in serious trouble of any kind to get hold of you and tell you I'm the daughter of Joe Devalain. You'd help me just as if I were your own. So that's why I'm calling, sor. Not for me, but for me dad. He needs somebody to look after his interests. The police, they don't seem to care much about who blew up his shop."

"How badly was he hurt in the explosion?" Kilkenny asked.

"As badly as one can be and still be called alive," the girl said. "Oh, Mr. Kilkenny, he's in terrible shape. Can you come, sor? Please."

The girl's voice reminded Kilkenny of Sharmon. Sharmon, with her deep-rust-colored hair and dancing emerald eyes, the smile that showed crooked teeth that somehow made her even prettier, the wide, wide shoulders, and the strong peasant thighs that even at sixteen could lock a man where she wanted him, for as long as she wanted him there.

"Yes, I'll come," Kilkenny said. "I'll take the train up and meet you at the hospital this evening."

KILKENNY BOUGHT A FIRST-CLASS seat on the *Enterprise Express*, which made the Dublin-Belfast run in two hours and twenty minutes. Dundalk, an hour north of Dublin, was the last stop in the Irish Free State. After Dundalk, the train crossed into Country Armagh, which was part of Northern Ireland.

At Portadown, the first stop in Armagh, British soldiers boarded the coaches and checked all passengers. From Portadown on into Belfast an armed British soldier rode at each end of every coach. Most passengers didn't leave their seats even to go to the lavatory during that leg of the journey.

At Belfast Central the passengers stood for a pat-down baggage search and questioning at a British Army checkpoint in the middle of the station.

"Identification, please," a pink-cheeked, young lieutenant requested. Kilkenny handed over his billfold. "What's your business in Belfast, sir?"

"To see a friend who's in hospital."

"What's the duration of your stay, sir?"

"I don't know. No more than forty-eight hours, I shouldn't expect."

"Your occupation is listed as a 'personal enquiries representative.' What is that, exactly?"

"I'm a private investigator. A detective."

The young officer's expression brightened. "You mean like one of those American private eyes? Like that Magnum bloke?"

"Yes, sort of. Less hectic, though."

The lieutenant frowned. "Not armed, I hope."

"No." Kilkenny wondered why he asked. A sergeant had already patted Kilkenny down and two privates had rummaged through his overnighter.

"Pass through," the officer said, returning Kilkenny's billfold.

Outside the terminal Kilkenny got into a square black taxi. "Saint Bartholomew's Hospital," he said.

The driver glanced at him in the rearview mirror, then looked out the side window at the darkening late-afternoon sky. "That's in the Flats," he said.

"The Flats?"

"Aye. Unity Flats. The Catholic section. I'll take you in, but I can't wait for you or come back to get you. I'm not Catholic, so I can't risk being in the Flats after dark."

"Just drop me at the hospital," Kilkenny said. "That'll be fine."

ON THE WAY THROUGH the city, it started to rain—one of those sudden, blustery rains that seemed to be forever blowing in off the North

Channel and turning the already dreary gray streets a drearier black. Kilkenny hadn't thought to bring a raincoat—it had been so long since he'd been to Belfast he had forgotten how unpredictable the weather could be.

"Bit of a heavy dew out there," he said.

"Aye," the driver replied, turning on the wipers. He made no attempt at further conversation.

Kilkenny wasn't familiar with the section called Unity Flats. He, Joe Devalain, and Sharmon Cavan had grown up in a slum known as Ballymurphy. It was a savagely poor place, worse than anything Kilkenny had seen during his ten years as a New York City policeman. In New York he had worked both Spanish Harlem and the South Bronx, and neither of them was nearly as poor, ugly, or deprived as Ballymurphy. Ballymurphy wasn't the gutter, it was the sewer. Both Kilkenny and Joe Devalain had sworn to Sharmon that they would take her away from the life of poverty in which they had all grown to adolescence.

It had not been Kilkenny that Sharmon picked to do it. "I've decided in favor of Joe," she told Kilkenny one night after they had made love under the back stairs of Sharmon's tenement building.

"I thought you loved *me*," Kilkenny had said.

"I love you both," Sharmon had answered. "Do y'think I'd do this with the two of you if I didn't love you both? It's just that I can't *have* you both, so I must choose, mustn't I? And I've chosen Joe."

"But why? Why him and not me?"

"Lots of reasons," she said lightly. "I like the name Sharmon Devalain better than I like Sharmon Kilkenny. And I think Joe will do better in life than you. He's got a good job at the linen plant— someday he'll probably be a foreman. While you've done nothing at all to better yourself."

"I go to school," Kilkenny protested. "I want to be a policeman, someday—"

"I don't like policemen," she said loftily. "They're a smug lot. Anyway, Joe'll earn lots more when he works his way up to plant foreman than you'll ever earn being a policeman."

Kilkenny had been sick with disappointment. "If it's just the money, maybe I could be something else—"

"It's not just that," she said.

"What else, then?"

"Well, y'see," she replied with a little reluctance, "Joe is—well, *better* at—well, you know—" She sighed impatiently. "He's a bit more of a man, if y'know what I mean."

Kilkenny had thought he would never get over that remark. It left him impotent for six months. Only after leaving Ireland, going to Southampton, boarding a ship for America, and meeting on board a fleshy Czech girl just beginning to feel her new freedom after escaping from behind the Iron Curtain, was he able to function physically as a man again. He had never had a problem since—but he had never forgotten Sharmon's words.

"Here you are," the driver said. "Saint Bartholomew's."

Kilkenny collected his bag and got out. The driver made change for him, glanced up at the waning daylight again, and sped off.

FROM THE FRONT STEPS of the hospital Kilkenny looked around at what he could see of Unity Flats. It was a slum, as Ballymurphy had been, though not quite as stark and dirty. But definitely a ghetto. Sharmon hadn't made it very far with Joe, he thought.

In the hospital lobby, a young nun, wearing the habit of the Ulster Sisters of Charity, consulted a name file and directed Kilkenny to a ward on the third floor. He waited for the lift with several women visitors. The women in the north were not as attractive as the women down south, he noticed. Most of them wore white *T*-necks that clearly outlined their brassieres, wide-legged, baggy slacks or skirts that were too short, no stockings, and shoes with straps that made their ankles look thick. Their hair seemed to be combed and in control only down to their cheeks, then appeared to grow wild on its own, as if it was too much to take care of. They were poor women, clearly. As they grew older, Kilkenny knew, they would all become noble mother figures who would strive to keep their husbands sober, their children God-fearing and Catholic, and their homes decent. They were the silent strength of the poor Northern Irish Catholic household. Kilkenny wondered if Sharmon had become like them.

At the third-floor ward, Kilkenny stepped through double swing-ing doors and looked around. The instant he saw Darlynn Devalain, he knew who she was. She looked nothing at all like Joe, but though he saw only a trace of Sharmon, there was enough so there was no mistaking who she was. Burnt-blonde hair, eyes a little too close together, lips a little crooked, almost mismatched, there was some-thing distinctly urchin about her. That touch of the gutter, Kilkenny thought. It never entirely leaves us.

She was standing just outside a portable screen that kept the last bed on the ward partitioned from the others. She was staring out at nothing as if in a trance. Kilkenny put his bag by the wall and walked down the ward toward her. When he came into her field of vision, it seemed to break her concentration and she watched him as he walked up to her. Their eyes met and held.

"You're Darlynn," he said. "I'm Royal Kilkenny."

She put out her hand. "Thanks for coming." She bobbed her chin at the bed behind the screen. "Me dad's there. What's left of him."

There were a doctor and two nurses on one side of the bed, the nurses just turning away with covered aluminum trays in their hands, walking past Kilkenny on their way out. When they left, Kilkenny had an unobstructed view of the bed. What he saw did not look like a man at all; it looked like a large pillow under a sheet with a head placed above it and several rubber tubes running down to it from jars of liquid hung on racks next to the bed. There was an oxygen mask over part of the face. Kilkenny saw no arms or legs under the sheet and felt his mouth go dry.

"Who are you, please?" the doctor asked, noticing Kilkenny.

"A friend. Up from Dublin. His daughter called me." Kilkenny tried to swallow but could not. "Is he still alive?" he asked. The form did not appear to be breathing.

"Yes. Why or how, I don't know. The explosion totally devastated him. Apparently, he was right on top of whatever detonated. The flash of the explosion blinded him; the noise destroyed his eardrums so that he's now completely deaf; and the hot gases got into his open mouth and burned up his tongue and vocal cords, making him mute. The force of the blast damaged his lungs and shattered his limbs so badly we had to amputate both arms above the elbow and both legs above the knee. So here he lies, unable to see, hear, or speak, unable to breathe without an oxygen mask, and with no arms or legs. But he's alive." He led Kilkenny out to where Darlynn stood. "I've sedated him for the night," he told the girl. "You go home and rest, young lady. That's an order."

Kilkenny took Darlynn by the arm and gently led her out of the ward, picking up his bag on the way. There was a snack shop still open on the ground floor and Kilkenny took her there, found a remote table, and ordered tea.

"How's your mother taking it?" he asked.

Darlynn shrugged. "It's not the end of the world for her. She and Dad haven't got on that great the past few years."

Kilkenny decided not to pursue that topic. "What kind of explosion was it? How'd it happen?"

"We don't know. It's supposedly being investigated by the RUC. But you know how that is."

The RUC was the Royal Ulster Constabulary, Northern Ireland's civilian police force. Like all other civil service in Ireland's British-aligned six northern counties, it was controlled by London and more than 90 percent Protestant.

"They're trying to put the blame on the IRA," Darlynn added.

"Of course." *It would be the natural thing for them to do*, Kilkenny thought. But he knew, as most Irishmen did, that for the IRA to be responsible for every crime attributed to it, the outlaw organization would have to be fifty thousand strong instead of the less than a thousand it actually was. "Was your dad still active in the IRA?" he asked.

Darlynn glanced at him and hesitated a beat before answering. Kilkenny expected as much. He was, despite her father's recommendation, still a stranger to her, and to speak of the IRA to strangers could be dangerous. But something about him apparently prompted her trust.

"No, he hadn't been active for about five years. He still supported the organization financially, as much as he could afford, but he no longer took part in raids or anything like that."

"Had he any trouble with the Orangemen?" Kilkenny asked, referring to the pseudo-Masonic order of Protestants that opposed a united Ireland. Their activities were often as violent as the IRA, though never as well publicized.

"Dad had no trouble with them that I know about," Darlynn said. "Except for his IRA donations, he stayed pretty much out of politics. All he cared about these past few years was that shop of his. He was very proud of that shop."

"What sort of shop?" Kilkenny asked. The last he'd heard, Joe Devalain was still trying to work his way up the ladder at the linen factory.

"It was a linen shop. Tablecloths, napkins, handkerchiefs, a few bedcovers, a small line of curtains. If there was one thing Dad knew, it was cloth. He worked in the linen factory for eighteen years and never got a single promotion, but he learned all there was to know about cloth. Finally, he decided to pack it in. He drew out all his pension benefits and opened the shop. Mum was furious about it, said those benefits were half hers, for her old age as well as his. But Da did it anyway."

"Was that when things started going bad between them?"

"Not really. They'd been at each other off and on for a long time." Darlynn looked down at the tabletop. "Mum's had a boyfriend or two."

"Did you tell your mother you were calling me?" Kilkenny asked.

"I told her after."

"What was her reaction?"

"She got a funny kind of look on her face, like I haven't seen in a long time. When I was a little girl, she used to get a look like that whenever Da would bring her a bouquet of posies. When I mentioned your name, it was like I had done something special for her. Were you and my mother close?"

Kilkenny nodded. "Your mum and dad and me were all three close. Your dad and me were best friends, but we were rivals for your mum, too. Your dad won her. He was too much a match for me."

"He wouldn't be much competition now, would he?" she asked. Suddenly, tears streaked her cheeks.

Kilkenny calmed her down and got her to finish her tea, then walked the two miles home with her because she didn't feel like riding a bus. It had stopped raining and the bleak, poorly lighted streets smelled wet and the air was heavy. Kilkenny's palm sweated from carrying the suitcase. There was something about the way Darlynn's hair bounced in back that reminded him of Sharmon.

Somewhere along the way, he promised the girl he would look into the matter of the explosion that had destroyed everything about her father except his life.

THE DEVALAINS LIVED AS tenants in a little timeworn house that looked like wet newspaper. As Kilkenny and Darlynn got to the door, Sharmon Devalain opened it for them.

"Hello, Roy," she said.

"Hello, Sharmon."

The sight of her reduced him to astonishment. She seemed not to have aged as he had. There were no plump cheeks, no wide hips, nothing even remotely in common with the women he had seen at the lift in the hospital. She didn't look a day over thirty, if that.

"Come in, Roy. I'll make tea."

"We've just had tea, actually. And I've got to go get a room."

"You can stay here. I can sleep with Darlynn. The place isn't much, but it's clean."

"Thanks anyway, but I'd better stay downtown. I told Darlynn I'd try and find out about the explosion."

Sharmon threw her daughter a quick, irritated glance. "She's quick to ask for anything she wants. Even with strangers."

"I don't really feel like a stranger to her. After all, she *is* yours. And Joe's."

"Yes. Well, I'm sure the RUC will appreciate any help you can give them." Her eyes flicked up and down his tall frame. "You're looking well, Roy. Prosperous."

"Hardly that. I make a comfortable living is all. But it's what I want to do."

"Well, you're one of the lucky ones, then. Most people never get what they want out of life. Are you sure about tea? Or staying the night?"

"Yes, thanks. I'll be off. Is there a bus at the corner?"

Sharmon nodded. "Number Five. It'll take you to Great Victoria Street. Will I see you again?"

"Sure," Kilkenny said. "I'll be around."

Only when he was walking down the street did Kilkenny realize that he had not said he was sorry about Joe.

HE GOT A ROOM at the Europa Hotel downtown and spent the night alternating between restless, fitful sleep and sitting on the windowsill, staring out at the night city, remembering.

When the night finally ended and daylight broke over Belfast Lough, when from his hotel window Kilkenny saw smoke rising from the great stacks of Harland and Wolff, the mammoth shipbuilding complex, and when civil servants began hurrying along Howard Street to their jobs in nearby Donegall Square, he showered and shaved and went down for breakfast.

After he ate, he walked over to Oxford Street where the Royal Courts of Justice were located and found that the Royal Ulster Constabulary headquarters were still situated nearby. After telling his business to a receptionist in the lobby, he was sent up to the first floor and shown to the desk of Sergeant Bill O'Marn of the Bomb Investigation section.

"Well, well," O'Marn said, looking at Kilkenny's identification. "A real flesh-and-blood private eye, just like on the telly." He was a handsome man of forty, with great bushy black eyebrows. One of the "Black Irish" that women seemed to find so attractive. He wore a sprig of light green heather on the lapel of his Harris tweed jacket. *Dapper*, Kilkenny thought. "You realize your detective license is no good up here, don't you?" O'Marn asked.

"Certainly," said Kilkenny. "I'm only making inquiry at the request of Mr. Devalain's daughter."

"Who, I believe, is a minor."

"Yes, I believe she is. As I started to say, though, I haven't been retained or anything like that. The girl just wants to know who detonated her father. As I'm sure you do also."

"We already know," O'Marn said. "It was the IRA."

"I see. May I ask *how* you know?"

"The explosion was caused by gelignite. Nobody but the IRA uses gelignite. Every time we raid an IRA headquarters, we confiscate a footlocker full of the stuff."

Kilkenny nodded. "What reason, I wonder, would the IRA have for blowing up Joe Devalain."

"They don't need reasons for what they do," O'Marn scoffed. "They're madmen, the lot of them."

"Are you saying they simply decided to blow up a shop—any shop—and picked Joe Devalain's place randomly?"

"Looks that way to us."

This time Kilkenny shook his head. "I'm sorry, Sergeant O'Marn, but I can't accept that premise. It's always been my understanding that the IRA was much more precise in its operations than that. I thought it only set off bombs in strategic locations where the British Army mustered or patrolled, or where the explosion would produce some subsequent economic impact. I don't see how blowing up a small linen shop is going to do them any good at all."

"Neither do I," O'Marn agreed with an artificial smile. "But then, you and I aren't IRA terrorists, are we?"

"Is the matter still under investigation?" Kilkenny asked, ignoring the sergeant's question.

"Technically, yes."

"But it isn't being worked?"

"I didn't say that, Mr. Kilkenny."

Kilkenny rose. "You didn't have to. I wonder what you'll do about your crime statistics if the IRA ever disbands. Anyway, thanks for your time, Sergeant. Good day."

FROM RUC HEADQUARTERS, KILKENNY rode a bus back out to Unity Flats. On the way he became aware of some of the graffiti that scarred the city. NO POPE HERE! read one. NO QUEEN HERE! countered another. PROVISIONALS FOR FREEDOM, GOD SAVE OUR POPE! was offset by NO SURRENDER, GOD SAVE THE QUEEN! Some city blocks warned: ARMY

KEEP OUT! SOLDIERS ARE BASTARDS! Others proclaimed: ULSTER WILL
FIGHT! The most ominous said simply: INFORMERS BEWARE.

Twice along the way, the bus passed moving Saracens, big six-
wheeled armored vehicles that carried three soldiers and patrolled the
Catholic sections. The great tanks lumbered past children playing on
the sidewalk. They didn't even glance at it, never having known
streets without such patrols.

At Saint Bart's hospital, Kilkenny found Darlynn sitting by her
father's bed, gently stroking the stump of one arm above the bandage.
She looked scrubbed and fresh, like a schoolgirl. Kilkenny drew a
chair around and sat by her.

"When your dad was active in the IRA, did you ever know any of
his contacts?" he asked very quietly.

Darlynn shook her head. "The only time the organization was
ever mentioned was when he and Mum would fight about it. She
claimed it was because he was suspected of being IRA that he never
got promoted at the linen factory. According to her, it's been the IRA
that's kept us in Unity Flats all these years."

"Did you ever know of any meeting places he went to?"

"I'm not sure. There was a pub out on Falls Road—Bushmills', it
was called. I used to find matchboxes from the place when I emptied
the pockets of Da's trousers for the wash. I know after he left the IRA
I never found them again."

While she was talking, Darlynn had unintentionally stopped
stroking her father's mutilated arm. To Kilkenny's surprise, the
reduced figure on the bed began emitting from under the oxygen mask
a pitiful, begging noise. Darlynn resumed stroking at once, and what
was left of Joe Devalain calmed down.

"I don't even know if he's aware of me," Darlynn said.

"I'm sure he is," Kilkenny told her, though he wasn't sure at all.

"I wish there was some way to communicate with him," the girl
said. "Maybe he'd know who did this to him."

Yes, Kilkenny thought, he might. But how did one communicate
with a living soul who could not see, hear, or speak, and had no hands
with which to write or feel or make signals?

"Would you like to come for supper tonight?" Darlynn asked.
"Mum's going out, but I'm a better cook, anyway—at least, Da's always
said I was. It wouldn't be anything fancy, you understand."

"I'm sorry, I'll be busy tonight, Darlynn. I want to make contact with the IRA if I can."

She put her free hand on his knee. "Stop by later, then. Just so I'll know you're all right?"

He promised he would.

As he left the hospital, Kilkenny imagined that his leg felt warm where she had touched him.

BUSHMILLS' WAS NOT UNLIKE a hundred other neighborhood pubs in Belfast. It had a stained-glass window or two, a few secluded nooks, one private booth with frosted glass, and a bar as shiny as a little girl's cheeks on First Holy Communion Day. There was always an accordion player about, and always a stale beer odor in the air. Anyone ordering anything except a pint of stout drawn from the tap got a sidelong glance. All conversation ceased when a stranger entered.

Kilkenny stood in the silence at the end of the bar and ordered his pint. When it came, he paid for it and drank it down in a single, long, continuous swallow. Wiping off the foam with the back of his hand, he then spoke to the bartender in a tone that every man on the premises could hear.

"My name is Royal Kilkenny. I'm a detective down in the Free State, but I grew up here in Belfast, over in Ballymurphy. My father was Doyle Kilkenny. My mother was Faye Quinn Kilkenny. My grandfather on my mother's side was Darcy Quinn, who was Padraic Pearse's man in County Longford and served four years in His Majesty's prison at Wormwood Scrubs for the privilege. I'm up here because a friend of mine named Joe Devalain was blown up in his linen shop three days ago. He's still alive, what there is left of him, but that doesn't include eyes, ears, voice, hands, or feet. The RUC tells me the IRA did it. I don't believe that. But I want to hear it from the mouth of a man who knows for sure. I'm at the Europa Hotel, room 719. I'll be back there within the hour."

As KILKENNY SUSPECTED, IT worked. Two men came for him just after dark, escorted him to a panel truck parked near the hotel, put him in the back, and blindfolded him. The truck was driven for about thirty minutes, on rough streets, making many turns. When finally it stopped, Kilkenny was taken out, led into a building and down some stairs, and finally had his blindfold removed in a small, cluttered room in which a white-haired man sat behind a scarred desk.

"My father was in prison with your grandfather," the white-haired man said. "I'm Michael McGuire."

"It's an honor to meet you, sir," Kilkenny said. Iron Mike McGuire was a legend in Northern Ireland. A third-generation Irish freedom fighter, he was the most-wanted man in the country. There wasn't a child over six in Belfast who didn't know his name, yet fewer than a dozen people had seen his face in nearly a decade.

"I know about Joe Devalain's misfortune," Iron Mike said. "I was saddened to hear of it. Joe was once a loyal soldier fighting for a united Ireland. He left the cause some years back, for reasons of his own, but I understand he continued to contribute money to us, for which we are grateful. There was no ill will when he left us. There never is. A man does what he can, for as long as he can, and that's all we ask. If Joe still had been one of us, actively, we'd right now be after finding out who bombed him. Since he was not, we choose to stay out of it. I can assure you, however, that the IRA had nothing to do with the incident."

Kilkenny nodded. "I see. Well, I thank you for telling me, sir, and for the trouble of bringing me here."

"It's not been that much trouble. I'd be particular, though, if I were you, where I made that little speech you gave in Bushmills'. There's some pubs you'd not've walked out of. Pubs that are patron-ized by the other side."

"I understand," Kilkenny said. "I appreciate the advice. May I ask for a bit more?"

"A man can always ask."

"How would I go about contacting the Orangemen?"

McGuire exchanged a fleeting glance with the two men who had brought Kilkenny. "For what purpose?" he asked.

"The same purpose as my coming here. To see if they were respon-sible. If it was political, what happened to Joe, then I'll let the matter go. But if the Orangemen also disclaim the act, then I've still got work to do."

Pursing his lips, McGuire silently drummed the thick, stubby fingers of one hand on the scarred desktop. "All right," he said after a moment. "I don't believe the Orangemen were involved, but I could be wrong. At any rate, the only Order of Orange faction that is authorized to take lives is the Black Preceptories. It's an internal terrorist group that specializes in kidnapping, torture, and house-burning. It was them that torched the two hundred Catholic homes in Bogside back in '78. The leader of the bunch is Black Jack Longmuir. He works in the shipyards. You can usually find him through the union office." McGuire smiled as cold a smile as Kilkenny had ever seen. "When y'see him, tell him I'm thinking about him. Day and night. Always thinking about him."

With those words, McGuire nodded and Kilkenny was once again blindfolded and led away.

THE UNION OFFICE WAS open around the clock, because Harland and Wolff Shipbuilding was running three shifts. The office was situated in a little corrugated metal building just outside the shipyard entrance. There was no doubt where the union's sympathy and support lay. Immediately inside the door was an Order of Orange flag and a framed rhyme:

> Catholics beware! For your time has come!
> Listen to the dread sound of our Protestant drum!
> In memory of William, we'll hoist up our flag!
> We'll raise the bright orange and burn your green rag!

William was William of Orange, who married the daughter of the last Catholic king of England, James II, then betrayed him, drove him from the throne, and turned Britain into a Protestant country. Five years later the Orange Society was formed in Ireland by the new gentry to whom William had distributed the land. Its

purpose, by its own charter, was to maintain the Protestant consti-
tution of the country. Nearly two hundred years later, it was still trying to do that, although it had since met failure in twenty-six of
Ireland's thirty-two counties. The organization was strongest in
Belfast, where it controlled the trade unions. Nowhere was there a
better example of that strength than at Harland and Wolff, Ulster's
greatest single industrial complex. Of ten thousand employees, only
one hundred were Catholic.

"Might I be of some service, sor?" a bulldog of a man asked
Kilkenny when he entered.

"I was told I might find Jack Longmuir here," Kilkenny said. Several
men in the little office glanced at him, then looked away quickly.

"May I ask what your business is, sor?"

"I'm a detective from Dublin. An old mate of mine was seriously
injured by a bomb in his shop three days ago. I'd like to ask
Mr. Longmuir's advice about how best to go about finding out who did it."

The little bulldog cocked his head. "What makes y'think he'd give
you advice on a matter like that?"

"What makes *you* think he wouldn't?" Kilkenny countered. "Or
are you authorized to speak for him?"

The little man turned red. "I'll see if he's here."

Several minutes later, a young man in coveralls, with metal shav-
ings and dust on his sleeves, came to fetch Kilkenny. Giving him a
visitor's pass, he led Kilkenny past a security gate and into the shipyard. They walked in silence for two hundred yards, then the escort
guided him into a welding hangar where at least thirty men were
working on sections of steel hull. Pointing, he directed Kilkenny up
a metal ladder to a catwalk where a tall man stood with a clipboard
in his hand.

Kilkenny climbed the ladder and moved around the metal catwalk
until he was near enough to speak. But the tall man spoke first.

"I'm Longmuir. What d'you want?"

"Do you know of Joe Devalain?" Kilkenny asked.

Longmuir nodded. He was a cadaverous man with a jaw that was
steel blue from a lifetime of using a straight razor. His eyes looked like
two perfect bullet holes.

"I'd like to find out who did it to him," Kilkenny said. "But only
if it was nonpolitical. If it was a political act, I'll leave it be."

"Why come to me?" Longmuir asked. "I'm a law-abiding British subject. I work, take care of my family, and support the Presbyterian Church and my trade union. I know nothing of bombings and such. Who sent you to me?"

"Michael McGuire."

For just an instant Longmuir's face registered surprise, but he quickly contained it. "Iron Mike, eh?" he said, as if the words were a foul taste in his mouth. "You saw him, did you?"

"Yes. He assured me the IRA wasn't involved in what happened to Joe. He said only you could tell me whether the Black Preceptories did it."

"How does Iron Mike look?" Longmuir asked curiously. "I've not seen even a photograph of him in ten years."

Kilkenny thought for a moment, then said: "He looks old. And tired."

Longmuir grunted softly. "Aye. Like me." He squinted at Kilkenny. "Did he say anything about me?"

"Yes. That he thinks about you a lot."

Longmuir smiled a smile as hateful as McGuire's had been. "I hope he's thinking of me when he draws his last breath." The tall man stared out at nothing for a moment, deep in thought. Then he emitted a quiet sigh. "No one associated with the Order of Orange had anything to do with blowing up your friend," he told Kilkenny. "You'll have to look elsewhere for them that's guilty."

Kilkenny thanked him, and Black Jack Longmuir had him escorted out of the shipyard complex.

IT WASN'T TOO LATE, so Kilkenny rode a bus out to the Devalain house to ask how Joe had fared that day and to question Sharmon and Darlynn, now that a political motive had been eliminated, about who else might have reason to harm Joe. When he got to the house and knocked, no one answered right away. Kilkenny thought they might already have gone to bed. The past few days had to have been very trying for them. Darlynn, especially, looked on the verge of exhaustion.

Kilkenny had just turned to leave when Sharmon opened the door, wearing a housecoat.

"Hello, Roy. Darlynn's not here—she's staying at the hospital all night. Joe's mind seems to be going. He's bucking up and down on the bed, making that pathetic sound he makes, raising havoc. The only thing that seems to calm him is to have Darlynn there, patting him. The doctor says her touch is all he relates to now; he's been reduced to the primitive level, whatever that means. I'd offer you tea, but I'm just out."

She had not stepped away from the doorway or invited him inside.

"Tea's not necessary," Kilkenny said, "But I would like to ask you a few questions."

"I was just ready for bed, Roy. Can we do it tomorrow?" She must have noticed the curious expression that came over his face, because she amended her reply at once. "I suppose we can do it now. It won't take long, will it?"

"Shouldn't."

She led him to the modest parlor with its threadbare sofa, worn rug, and scratched coffee table. She conducted herself very much like a lady, keeping the housecoat well around her, even holding it closed at the throat. Her reserved demeanor brought back Darlynn's words to him: "Mum's had a boyfriend or two." Kilkenny had expected Sharmon to make advances on him first chance she got. Now it appeared she was doing just the opposite.

"I'm sorry Darlynn isn't here," she said. "She'll be sorry she missed you. She fancies you, y'know."

"Nonsense," Kilkenny scoffed. "She's only a girl."

"Look again, Roy. She's older than I was when we first went under the stairs together."

"That was different. I'm sure she only looks on me as an uncle or something." He sat down. "Now then, to business. I've made contact with the IRA and the Black Preceptories. From both quarters I've been assured that there was no involvement in blowing up Joe's shop."

"And you believe them?" Sharmon asked.

Kilkenny nodded. "No reason not to. If either group had done it, there would have been a purpose—the IRA because Joe had betrayed it in some way, the Black Preceps because he was still providing financial support to the IRA or some other unknown reason. Whatever, the bombing would have been to make an example of him. Not to take credit for it would be defeating the purpose of the act. If either group had done it, they'd have claimed it and said why."

"So who d'you think did it, then?"

"That's where I go from here. Who do *you* think might have done it?"

"I haven't a notion."

"Did he have any enemies?"

"Joe? Not likely. You have to *do* something to make enemies. Joe never did anything. Sure, he joined the IRA, but only because a lot of his mates was doing the same. And he ended up quitting that. The only thing he ever done on his own was leaving the linen factory and opening up that silly shop. That was the only independent decision he ever made in his life, and you see how that turned out."

"Was he gambling, d'you know? Could he have been in debt and you not know it?"

Sharmon grunted scornfully. "He didn't have the guts to gamble."

"Do you think there could have been another woman? A jealous husband or a boyfriend?"

She shook her head. "Never."

"Well, *somebody* didn't like him," Kilkenny said. "Can't you think of anybody?"

"Just me," Sharmon answered evenly.

"You?" Kilkenny had known it, but had never expected her to be so candid about it.

"Yes, me." With just a hint of defiance. "And why not? Look around you," she challenged, waving an arm. "This here is what my whole *life* is like. Worn, tattered, musty, colorless. This here is what I gave up my *youth* for, Roy. This here is all I *have*. It's all he's ever given me. Oh yes, I disliked him. And if he'd been poisoned or cut up with a kitchen knife, I'd be your number-one suspect. But I wouldn't know how to make a bomb even if I had the proper stuff."

"No, you wouldn't," Kilkenny said. He thought he heard a noise from the rear of the house—a creaking, as if someone had stepped on an unsteady floorboard. "Could that be Darlynn home?"

"No. She always uses the front. It's probably a loose shutter. Listen, can we finish this another time, Roy? I've a raging headache and really would like to get to bed."

"Sure."

On his way to the front door, Kilkenny noticed an ashtray on one of the tables with something purplish in it. He saw it only for a second, for just as his eyes came to rest on it Sharmon picked it up and emptied it in a wastebasket under the table. "Goodnight then, Roy," she said. "God bless."

"Goodnight, Sharmon."

He did not return her "God Bless" because it had just registered in his mind what the purplish thing in the ashtray was.

Irish heather. Green Irish heather. It turned purple when it died.

KILKENNY WENT TO THE hospital and found Darlynn asleep on a couch in the waiting room. "She was all wore out," the nun in charge of the ward told him. "When her father finally got calmed, we made her come in here and lie down. She was asleep that quick."

"Is he asleep, too?" Kilkenny asked of Joe.

"We never know, do we?" the nun replied quietly. "He doesn't have to close his eyelids to sleep."

Kilkenny went into the ward and stood by Joe's bed. Devalain's form was still, his eyes wide and fixed. "I might know who did this to you, Joe," Kilkenny whispered. "But I must be sure before I do anything."

Stepping to the window at the end of the long room, Kilkenny stared out at the blackness, seeing only his own dim reflection from the night-light next to Joe's bed. *If only I could ask him simple questions he could answer with a nod or a shake of his head*, he thought. But how in bloody hell can you communicate with somebody who can't hear or see? If he had fingers, he could use children's wooden alphabet blocks. Joe could feel the letters.

If, sure, Kilkenny thought with frustration. If he had fingers, if he had eyes. If I could work goddamned miracles, I could read his bleeding mind! He turned from the window and looked at Joe again. Sighing, he walked into the hall, wondering if he should wake Darlynn and take her home. Across the hall, above the door to one of the other rooms, a red light was blinking on and off. One of the patients had pressed the call button to summon a nurse. Kilkenny walked away from it. Then he stopped, turned, and stared at it.

Blink-blink. Blink-blink.

Dot-dash.

Hurrying back into the ward, Kilkenny drew a chair up to Joe's bed and sat down. It had been a long time, thirty years, perhaps too long. Yet if there was a chance . . .

Gently, Kilkenny placed the palm of his hand on Joe's sternum, just below the clavicle. Joe stirred. Kilkenny thought back thirty years. Thought back to the blue neckerchiefs and khaki caps, the gold patches they pinned to their shirts with the letters BSI on them. Boy Scouts International. It was the only youth organization that had ever come into the Ballymurphy slum to help the kids there. The first thing they had learned in the Morse Code class, Kilkenny remembered, was how to do their names.

With his index finger, he began to tap lightly on Joe Devalain's sternum. Dot-dash-dash-dash. That was *J*. Dash-dash-dash. That was *O*. Dot. That was *E*. *J O E.* Joe.

Joe Devalain frowned. Kilkenny began tapping again. He repeated the same letters. *J O E.*

Under the oxygen mask, Joe's lips parted. He began breathing a little faster. He's got it, Kilkenny thought. *He understands it!*

Kilkenny rubbed his hand in a brief circle to indicate he was erasing and starting a new message. He tapped dot-dash-dot for *R*. Dash-dash-dash for *O*. Dash-dot-dash-dash for *Y*. His name. Roy.

Joe's lips parted even more and he forced a guttural sound from his throat. All it sounded like was a long "Aaaggghhh" but it was beautiful to Kilkenny. It meant he had reached Joe Devalain's mind.

Kilkenny began tapping again, slowly, carefully. Making his message as brief and simple as possible. He tapped: Use eyelids. Dot short blink. Dash long blink. Then he waited.

For a brief, terrible instant, he was afraid Joe wasn't going to be able to do it; his lips remained parted, his sightless eyes unblinking. But then the eyelids closed, remained closed, opened, blinked once, closed again and remained closed for a second, and opened. Dash-dot-dash. That was the letter *K*. He was doing it!

Kilkenny watched the eyelids as they closed, opened, blinked. The letters they were making etched in his mind. *K-I-R-R-G*. Then the blinking stopped.

K-I-R-R-G? What the hell did that mean?

Kilkenny took out his pen and tore a sheet of paper from the medical chart hanging on the end of the bed. Turning the paper to its blank side, he wrote down the entire International Code that he and Joe had learned as Boy Scouts. Then he went to work breaking down the blinks Joe had used. The *K* and the *I* were all right, he decided. But the two *R* signals had to be wrong. Unable to quickly decide how they were wrong, he moved on to the *G*. That, in all likelihood, was *M-E*. One of the most common mistakes in Morse was to misread M (dash-dash) and *E* (dot) as *G* (dash-dash-dot). Simply a case of too short a pause between letters, causing the receiver to think it was a single signal.

Kilkenny now had *K-I-R-R-M-E*. Frowning, he scanned the code symbols he had just written. What was similar to *R* (dot-dash-dot)?

Then it hit him. Dot-dash-dot-dot. Two dots at the end instead of one. The letter was *L*. Joe had signaled *K-I-L-L-M-E*.

Kill me.

Kilkenny tapped a new message: No.

Devalain blinked back: Please. Pain. Going crazy.

Kilkenny: No.

Why?

Kilkenny tapped: Darlynn.

Joe shook his head furiously and blinked: Burden.

Kilkenny tapped: Sharmon.

The answer came: Finish me. Please.

Who bomb? Kilkenny wanted to know.

Why?

Pay back.

Again the emphatic shake of the head: Hurt Darlynn.

How?

Sharmon.

She bomb?

No.

How hurt Darlynn?

Sharmon.

Involved?

This time Joe nodded as he blinked: Maybe. No matter. Finish me. No. Who bomb?

Then finish me? Joe asked, blinking a question mark at the end of his signal.

Kilkenny thought about it for several long moments. Then he tapped: Okay.

Joe's next message read: O-M-A-R-N.

Kilkenny nodded to himself. O'Marn. The Bomb Investigation sergeant. Neat. He had access to explosives that had been confiscated from the IRA. He knew how to use them. And he was in a position to bury the case without resolving it.

O'Marn. Yes, Kilkenny had suspected as much when he saw the sprig of dying heather in Sharmon's ashtray. The same kind of sprig O'Marn wore on his lapel. He wondered how O'Marn and Sharmon had met. How long they had been lovers. Sharmon, who didn't like policemen, who had picked Joe over him when he told her he was going to become a policeman.

He wondered exactly how much Sharmon knew about the bombing. Not that it mattered. If she was still seeing O'Marn after what had happened to Joe, that was enough. And Kilkenny was sure she was still seeing him. That noise he had heard earlier from the back of the Devalain house. Along with Sharmon's eagerness to send him on his way. O'Marn had been there, listening.

Another guttural sound from the bed drew Kilkenny's attention back to Joe. He was blinking rapidly, repeating a message over and over. Do it. You promised. Do it. You prom—

Kilkenny put his hand back on Joe's sternum. He tapped: Later.

Darlynn was still deeply asleep on the couch in the waiting room. One of the nuns had covered her with a blanket. Kilkenny quietly opened her purse and took her door key.

IT WAS VERY LATE now, dark and quiet in Unity Flats. He walked the two miles to the Devalain house, passing no one, seeing no one. When he arrived, he let himself in and stood just inside the door. The house was silent. A night-light burned dimly in the hall. Kilkenny moved slowly toward the rear of the house, taking care to stay close to the wall where the floorboards were less likely to creak.

At the door to a bedroom, he saw in the faint glow two naked bodies asleep on the bed. On the doorknob hung a Harris tweed sport coat. Kilkenny moved into the room and over to the single window. It was shut tight and locked.

Slipping back out of the bedroom, he edged along the hall until he found the kitchen. Its window was also shut. Pulling a handker-chief from his pocket, he turned on all the gas jets on the stove.

Before he left, Kilkenny shut the door to Darlynn's small bedroom and the parlor, closing off all the house except the kitchen and the bedroom in which the two lovers slept. Then he let himself back out.

He waited down at the corner, concealed in the dark doorway of a small store, watching the house. No light came on and there was no sign of movement anywhere. Kilkenny gave it an hour. Then he returned to the hospital.

DARLYNN WAS STILL ASLEEP when he put her door key back in her purse. But Joe was wide awake and responded instantly when Kilkenny tapped his first message: Paid back.

Who? Joe blinked.

Kilkenny signaled: O'Marn. Sharmon.

A great, weary sigh escaped Joe's chest, the first sound Kilkenny had heard from him that sounded human. Then he blinked: Now me.

And Kilkenny answered: Yes.

Kilkenny reached over and pinched the tube that was feeding oxygen to Joe Devalain's lungs. As his breathing started to become labored Joe blinked: Darlynn.

With his free hand, Kilkenny responded: Yes.

Joe's throat began to constrict, his face contorting as what was left of his body struggled for oxygen. He had time for only one more mes-sage. God bless, he blinked . . .

Kilkenny sat in the waiting room watching the sleeping Darlynn Devalain until daylight came and the buses began running. Then he woke her and they left the hospital together. On the bus downtown, he told her how her parents had died, but not who killed them. Her mother and O'Marn would be considered suicides. Her father simply had not survived his trauma.

When the bus reached Great Victoria Street, they got off.

"Where are we going?" Darlynn asked.

"First to the hotel to get my things."

"And then?"

"The part of Ireland that's free. Dublin."

Darlynn accompanied him with no further questions.

The Male and Female Hogan

Jon L. Breen

FAIRWAY FLATS WAS ONE of those condominium communities that line the water-guzzling golf courses in the California desert near Palm Springs. The residents would have a nice view of the San Jacinto Mountains as well as the greens and bunkers, Al Hasp reflected as he drove his well-used Mercedes through the gate. A nice place to retire to, unless you hated the desert or hated golf or, like Al Hasp, hated both. Parking in an inconsiderately shade-deprived visitors' area, Al could still hear his partner Norm Carpenter's well-meant but unwelcome instructions playing over in his head: "These people are old, Al. You have to be patient with them. You can't rush them or bully them. They need special handling. Listen to everything they say carefully."

As if Al Hasp, with his years of experience as cop and private investigator, didn't know how to interview all sorts of people, regardless of age, sex, nationality, ethnicity, sexual preference, whatever. But that was Norm, always ready to lecture his partner on everything from theology to his taste in clothes.

Seconds after Al walked up a cactus-lined path and pressed the doorbell of the seventh-hole condo, the door opened and an aged but still lovely face looked up at him cheerfully. It belonged to a small, white-haired, and slightly stooped woman of seventy or eighty. "Mr. Hasp?"

"Yes. Mrs. Hogan? Pleased to meet you. And thanks for agreeing to talk to me."

"Our pleasure. It's not every day we're visited by a private eye. Do you mind that term, by the way?"

"Well, it's not the worst thing I've been called."

She laughed. "Do come in. My husband can't wait to meet you."

Al crossed the threshold from hundred-degree heat into air-conditioned comfort and wondered fleetingly what the Hogans' electric bills must be like. Mrs. Hogan led him through a short hallway lined with old photographs and motion picture lobby cards into a similarly decorated study where a tall, very thin, and militarily straight man of similar age rose from in front of a computer screen to greet him.

"Al Hasp!" The old man gripped his hand firmly. "Grant Hogan. How were my directions?"

"Perfect."

Various social rituals followed. He would be Al; they would be Grant and Marge. Yes, he'd love some iced tea and some freshly baked brownies. The photos and lobby cards were terrific, reminded Al of his boyhood watching western movies at kids' matinees, and was that cowboy bronze in the corner really a Remington? Statistics emerged: Grant was eighty-four and received a hundred jokes a day via e-mail; Marge was eighty-three and had a file of two thousand recipes. While noting to himself that they almost looked those proudly trumpeted ages, the fifty-four-year-old Al truthfully claimed to envy their energy. About fifteen minutes into his visit, the three of them sat in the living room around a glass coffee table supported by what appeared to be moose antlers, and Al was able to broach the reason for his visit.

"You both heard about the death of Clinton Bortner?"

The faces of Grant and Marge turned solemn.

"Wasn't that awful?" said Marge.

"Did they ever find out who did it?" Grant demanded.

"Ah, no, they didn't. Did the police ever come out here to interview you about it?"

"No," said Grant.

"I'm not surprised."

"Should they have?" Marge asked, more intrigued than concerned. "Are we suspects?"

"You're certainly not suspects, and they probably didn't interview you because they figured Bortner was killed in the course of a routine burglary. They decided he surprised some kid looking for drug money, and nothing could get them off that. As an old cop myself, I can't really blame them. The crime happened on a weekend—"

"Why, I thought it happened on a Tuesday," Marge said. "Didn't it happen on a Tuesday?"

"I thought it was a Wednesday myself," Grant said.

"No, we heard about it on a Wednesday, but I thought you told me it happened the day before, on the Tuesday."

"Believe me," Al said, "it happened on a Sunday. There were a lot of visitors at the retirement home where he lived, and it would be easier for a stranger to sneak onto the property. Their drug-crazed youth seems a lot more likely to have bludgeoned Bortner with a fireplace poker than a fellow resident."

"Senior citizens are often underestimated, Al," Grant said with a smile. "Clint went back a long way with some of the people who live there. Through happy times and times that were, well, not so happy. Grievances can fester. You never know."

"I gather Bortner was an old friend of you both. Did you ever visit him in that retirement home?"

"No," said Marge.

"Driving to L.A. is a major expedition for us these days, Al," Grant explained. "We've become homebodies."

"You went to that western memorabilia show quick enough a while back," Marge pointed out.

"Well, that was special."

"I'm told three of Bortner's old cronies from his movie days live in that same retirement home," Al said.

Grant nodded. "Right. And we knew 'em all, didn't we, Mother?"

Marge said, "They were like family in a way."

"According to people at the home," Al said, "two of them seemed to be on good terms with Bortner, spent a lot of time with him, but the third one he never had anything to do with."

"And I guess we know which one that is, don't we?" Grant said, throwing a knowing look his wife's way.

"Emmett Donnelly," Marge said, nodding her head briskly. "They fell out when Clint married his sister Bridget."

"No, Mother, it was after they got married."

"Well, not long after. The next day maybe."

"Bridget's drinking was none of Clint's doing."

"Well, she never drank before she married him. And when she drove her car off that bridge—"

"Clint wasn't there, you know."

"Well, some of us think Clint should have been there. Now, I don't take Emmett's side, but I think Clint had to answer for some of it."

Al could tell this was no new discussion, and the old couple aired their disagreement good-naturedly, not heatedly at all. Al already knew that Bridget Donnelly Bortner had been an alcoholic who died in an accident and that her brother had blamed her husband for driving her to drink. It didn't appeal to him as a motive for a forty-year-delayed murder, but who knew?

"How did two such bitter enemies wind up living in the same retirement home anyway?" Al asked.

"It's just a place old movie people go," Marge said sadly. "Poor souls."

"Aren't we lucky not to be old?" her husband said with a smile.

"There are other places, though," said Al. "That one in Woodland Hills is bigger and better known."

"It was because of Gimp and Terry," Grant said, as if it were obvious. Al knew he was referring to Calvin "Gimp" O'Reilly and Terence O'Neil, two western movie contemporaries of Clinton Bortner. "Those two sons-of-guns have been close buddies all their lives, and they managed to stay friendly with both Clint and Emmett."

Al nodded. "That's what I'm told. O'Reilly and O'Neil always together. Bortner and Donnelly would hang out with them but never at the same time."

Grant chuckled. "I think Gimp and Terry worked on Clint and Emmett separately to come live there, without either knowing about the other one. If they had known, neither of them probably would have gone there. We all went in for practical jokes in the old days."

"I don't think Gimp and Terry would have meant it as a joke, though," Marge said. "They may have thought Clint and Emmett could bury the hatchet after all these years."

"Right you are, Mother. And maybe they could. In each other's skulls."

"I gather you know these three guys well," Al said. "O'Reilly, O'Neil, and Donnelly, I mean. I haven't met them yet. What can you tell me about them? I don't mean personal history so much, but what kind of people are they?"

"We haven't really seen them in years, but they were all good friends," Marge said. "Good men. Not murderers, I don't think."

"We can do better than that for Al, can't we, Mother?" Grant said. "Come on. Let's consider them one by one. We'll do it like one of those word-association tests."

"Okay," Al said. "Start with Donnelly."

"Angry," Marge said. "Always worried about something. And much too serious. But decent."

"Great horseman," Grant offered. "Fearless. Loyal. Little wiry guy. Came back from more serious injuries than any stuntman I can think of, and in later years it started to show. Not much sense of humor."

"Okay," Al said. "How about Gimp O'Reilly?"

"A lot of fun," Marge said. "He liked to put on this dumb cowpoke persona, bad grammar and all, but Gimp was nobody's fool. Kind of wearing to be around for too long at a stretch, I always thought."

Her husband nodded his agreement. "Had to be the center of attention at all times. Knew a lot of jokes. Loved to needle people. Kind of a mean streak with it sometimes."

"That leaves Terry O'Neil," Al said.

"Quiet," Marge said. "Dreamy. Kind of sweet really."

Grant snorted. "Not the horseman he thought he was. Unrealistic about everything really. Might have believed in Santa Claus, the Easter Bunny, and the Tooth Fairy. Oh, and leprechauns. Phony auld sod brogue."

"Oh, you're much too hard on him," Marge scolded.

"Now, Al," Grant said, "walking down memory lane is always fun for us old codgers—"

"Speak for yourself," Marge said lightly.

"—but why are we discussing these old-timers we haven't crossed paths with in years?"

"Bortner's daughter and son-in-law aren't happy with the way the case was handled, so they came to my partner and me. They thought the police were too quick to blame Bortner's death on some anonymous outsider. They thought the detectives should have followed up on some leads they ignored."

"I get it," said Grant. "The younger generation think one of Clint's old movie cronies took that poker to his skull. And you're investigating Clint's murder."

Al raised a hand. "Not really. We need to get that straight. Private investigators do not investigate murders."

"Why, in every book I ever read or movie I ever saw they do," said Marge.

"Right. But in real life it would only get us in trouble."

"Naturally. But then trouble is your business, isn't it?"

Al smiled. "Making money is my business, and I wouldn't make much without my license. Police departments don't take kindly to private operatives looking into murders. No, I'm just trying to find out the meaning of some things Bortner had written in his notebook the day before he died. If the meaning of those notations should turn out to have some bearing on his death, well, we'll consider that a bonus."

Like a witness on the stand, Al was anticipating the next logical question: what did it say in the notebook? But Grant Hogan took a sudden ninety-degree turn.

"Can I take your picture, Al?"

"Huh?"

"I like to take everybody's picture who visits us here. I've always been a photographer. An amateur, mind you."

"But with an artist's eye," Marge said.

"I do my best. Most of what you see on these walls I took myself. Just as a hobby. You had to do something to fill all that time on a movie set between saloon fights and horse falls." Grant got to his feet, more limberly than Al. "Come out back. I have a great idea for a shot."

Moments later, Grant was posing Al standing in the back doorway, with the seventh hole and the San Jacintos behind him.

"Yeah, stand right there. Light's perfect right now. Look like a tough hombre. Won't be hard." Grant went down on one knee and aimed his Canon slightly upward at Al. "That's better. Don't want the damn golf course in the shot. Just you, the doorway, the mountains." He took the picture and rose to his feet with nary a creak. "Great. I love doorway shots. John Ford loved doorway shots, you know. Ever count all the doorway shots in a John Ford picture?"

"Can't say I have, no."

"Ever see *The Searchers*? Full of doorway shots, out of the farmhouse, out of the tipi. I didn't get to work on that one. Wish I had."

Grant led Al back to the living room where Marge was waiting for them. Their iced-tea glasses had been refilled, and more brownies had appeared.

"So did you say Clint kept a notebook?" Marge asked.

"Yes."

"Didn't know he could write," Grant said with a cackle. "Oh, I don't mean to disrespect the dead, but Clint would laugh as much as anybody, believe me. We had a good time with old Clint."

"Mr. Bortner didn't write complete sentences in this notebook," Al said. "It would make my job easier if he had. But his daughter says he was making notes for his memoirs."

Grant snorted. "Hope he could afford a ghostwriter."

"The notebook was full of lists of things from out of his past. Some of the references are obvious, some not."

"Aids to memory," Marge suggested. "They only had to make sense to him."

"Bortner's notebook was lying open on a table in his room when he was found. There were four phrases on that last page, dated the day before. It would be helpful if you tell me what, if anything, they mean to you." Though he remembered all of Bortner's notations, Al took out his own notebook for reference. "The first phrase was 'Back to Ireland.' "

"Clint Bortner wasn't Irish," Marge said.

"But all three of your suspects, if that's what they are, have Irish surnames," Grant Hogan pointed out. "Donnelly, O'Reilly, O'Neil. Not to mention Hogan."

"But we're not suspects," his wife pointed out.

Al smiled. "Right, you're not. Were any of them born in Ireland?"

"No, but they probably had family there," Grant said. "What's your point?"

"I was thinking if O'Neil effected a brogue—"

Grant shook his head. "That didn't make him an Irishman, just an uncured ham. What else did Clint write in his notebook?"

"'The Male and Female Hogan.'"

"Yeah? I guess now we know what brought you to us."

"Well, Bortner's daughter remembers you fondly, and you two were the only male and female Hogans she could think of."

"Melissa was a beautiful child," Marge said. "Haven't seen her since she was, oh, junior high age. I'll bet she's a lovely young woman now."

Though neither young nor lovely had sprung to Al's mind when he met the Bortner daughter, he just said, "Oh, yes."

"Melissa was never really all that interested in her father's movie work," Grant said. "Embarrassed by it, if anything. If she'd paid more attention, she might have saved you a trip down here. Not that we aren't glad to have you, you understand. What else did Clint write?"

"The third phrase was 'The Three Sisters.' Somebody in our office thought that might have been a reference to Bortner's acting career. There's a famous play—"

Grant interrupted with a snort of laughter. "Oh, no! That's rich, that is."

"Why is that funny?"

"When you say Clint Bortner was an actor, that's funny enough. Oh, he made some movies and read some lines, but he got into it the same way most of those guys did, as a stuntman. Not me, mind you. I went to college and was an actor before I started doing stunts. I could do whatever they wanted on a horse, but they valued me more for the way I could read lines. But a guy like Clint, it was the way he handled a horse that kept him working. He looked like a cowboy, hell, he'd *been* a cowboy, so he made himself a career playing ranch hands and villains' henchmen. I don't know if he ever appeared on a stage, but if he did, he wasn't playing in anything by Chekhov. I bet he'd never even heard of Chekhov."

"What was the fourth phrase?" Marge asked.

"It said, 'Told Pappy.'"

"I can't imagine—" Marge began, then broke off when she saw the changed look on her husband's face. "What is it, honey?"

"Hm? Oh, not a thing." Grant turned to Al and said with forced brightness, "Want to see my photo album?"

"Your photo album?" Marge laughed. "You've got a hundred photo albums, my dear, and Al probably hasn't got all day."

"I mean one particular photo album. I can put my hand on it easy. Come on back in the study."

Grant was up from his chair and out the door. Al could only follow.

Hogan closed the door of the study behind them and said softly, "That bastard. I know just what he was up to. Marge doesn't need to know about this. It would just upset her, turn sour a lot of happy memories. You understand?"

Al didn't, but he nodded his head anyway and waited to see what else was coming.

Grant Hogan's photo albums, which filled one small bookcase in the study, looked identical to Al, but Grant was able to find the one he was looking for right away. He leafed through the pages quickly. Al saw shots of horses, rock formations, movie cameras, and vaguely familiar-looking actors fly by until Grant got to the one he wanted, a photo of a man with an eye patch sitting in a director's chair.

"That's the man himself, John Ford. Sometimes known as Pappy. I took this on the set of *Cheyenne Autumn*, not one of his best I'm afraid. Folks said it was his apology to the Indians for the lousy way he'd treated them in his pictures, but he didn't owe an apology to anybody. He always treated Indians with dignity. Well, usually. People always associate Ford with westerns, cavalry, and Indians, but he made all sorts of pictures. And he was an Irishman through and through. Real family name was Feeney. Back in the thirties, he made a great movie out of *The Informer*, the Sean O'Casey play, coaxed and bullied an Academy Award performance out of Victor McLaglen, and you remember how funny McLaglen was as an Irish sergeant in the cavalry movies, don't you?"

"Haven't seen one in a while," Al said, trying to remember if he'd ever seen one.

"Rent 'em. Hell, buy 'em. I think *Fort Apache* was the best one. Now, Marge is partial to *She Wore a Yellow Ribbon*, for the color photography, like Remington's paintings come to life. But my point is, Pappy's heart was in Ireland. That last picture in the cavalry trilogy, *Rio Grande*, he made at Republic so old man Yates would let him take his company to the Emerald Isle and make *The Quiet Man*. Did you ever see *The Quiet Man*?"

"I guess I must have."

"If you don't remember it, you didn't see it. Do yourself a favor. Rent it. Hell, buy it. I usually buy myself. If I rent, Marge gets on me, says I can remember what I had for breakfast on a location shoot in 1945 and can't remember when to take a tape back to the video store. There's something to that."

Al thought Grant's garrulousness was a way to put off discussing something unpleasant. Unless—and this was a less-attractive alternative—the old-timer's mind was starting to cut in and out like a cell phone. When he thought Grant had wound down—don't rush him, Al, whatever you do—Al ventured, "So you think the phrase 'Back to Ireland' might be a reference to John Ford?"

"Yep. No question in my mind."

"John Ford's been dead a long time," Al said, and soon regretted it. It set Grant Hogan off on another round of reminiscences.

"Oh, well, sure, most of 'em have. George O'Brien's gone. Ward Bond's gone. Duke Wayne's gone. Even old Ben Johnson's gone now. Dobe Carey's still around, though. You know, Harry Carey Jr. His dad was Ford's first cowboy star, but they had a professional falling-out and didn't work together for years. Lots of people got on Ford's bad side one time or another, sometimes didn't even know why. The old man was funny that way. Dobe Carey wrote a swell book about his days with Ford. You should read that, Al."

"Yeah, I should. What about those other references in the notebook?"

Grant took to flipping the pages of his album again, stopping at a photo of three tall rock formations in a group. They looked vaguely familiar. "There's your Three Sisters. They're in Monument Valley, on the big Four Corners Navajo reservation, where Ford used to shoot his westerns. Some of the most beautiful scenery in the world, made for a lot of dramatic shots. All of us who worked for Ford on westerns spent a lot of time there. They gave names to all the red-rock buttes and spires, like the Mittens, the Big Indian, the Totem Pole. These three are supposed to look like three nuns. I think just the one on the left really looks like a nun. What do you think?"

"Well, I don't know."

"Depends on the angle you look at 'em from, of course. Anyhow, that's the Three Sisters, and lemme see here." He flipped a few more pages and pointed out a picture of a primitive triangular structure. "There you have the male hogan." He turned a page and pointed to a similar structure, more conical in shape. "And this is the female hogan. They're the traditional Navajo dwellings. Why there's a male one and a female one and where the door goes and who gets to sit where, I won't go into. You could look it up. But that's to show you it's nothing to do with me and Marge. Happy you came to visit, though, don't get me wrong."

Al knew Hogan had something more in mind and hoped he would reveal it in his own good time. Don't rush him, Al, just keep the conversation going. "I guess you worked on a lot of pictures with John Ford, huh?"

"As many as I could. I was one of his regulars. Oh, I had my dry spells when he wouldn't give me any work, just like anybody else, never knew why. When a new Ford picture was about to shoot, I'd go by to see Ford in his office. He'd shoot the breeze for a while, very pleasant, ask me how was Marge, how were the kids, and so forth. I'd never ask him if he had a part for me. That was out. He'd talk a little about the picture he was going to do, and if there was a part for me, he'd say so. If not, well, he wouldn't. All his regulars went through that same ritual. And like I said, you couldn't always know why Ford would give you a job in a whole string of movies, then suddenly never give you any work for years maybe, then start using you again like nothing had happened. It happened to everybody—George O'Brien, Ben Johnson, everybody. Sometimes you could trace it to some particular incident, but sometimes not."

"Was Bortner a Ford regular, too?"

"Yeah, he worked on Ford pictures off and on for years."

"What about Donnelly, O'Reilly, and O'Neil? Were they regulars with Ford?"

"Yep, and of course I'd see them all on other western shoots. Only Ford flick all five of us worked on was *She Wore a Yellow Ribbon*. We were all close in those days. The misunderstandings came later. The picture was shot in Monument Valley, of course. And that's where you'll find the key to your whole mystery."

"You think so?"

"I know so."

"I should go to Monument Valley?"

"Don't take me that literally. But you should talk to those three guys up at the retirement home: Donnelly, O'Reilly, and O'Neil."

"Did one of them kill Bortner?"

Grant Hogan shrugged.

"Do you know who killed Bortner, Grant?"

"I'm not going to make it easy for you," Grant said. "Why should I? But I do have a little story to tell you. Just don't say anything about it to Marge. It'd just upset her."

"Okay."

Grant Hogan talked in a low voice for about five minutes. The story he told Al sounded unlikely, but he seemed to believe it. Then he replaced the album he'd been showing Al and pulled another one from the shelf. "Now one more thing that might interest you."

Grant Hogan turned a few pages and pointed to a photo of a solemn-faced young man in a cowboy hat. "There's the guy that killed Clint Bortner." Grant took the photo out of the album and handed it to Al.

"Are you sure?"

"Oh, you probably can't prove it or anything. Not sure I'd want you to, now that I know what that bastard Bortner pulled on the four of us."

Al turned the picture over. There was no identification of the young cowboy. "But who is this?"

"I'm not making this easy for you," I said. Take it up to L.A. and show it to those three old pals of mine, see what they have to say. When you find out the truth, think about what you want to do next. If anything. Remember he was old, they're all old, and everything will be over soon for everybody. Okay?"

Before Al Hasp left the desert, he was on his cell phone to Norm Carpenter to tell him, "I figured it out."

The Charles King Memorial Retirement Home was called by some of its denizens "Owlhoots' Roost" or "Henchmen's Haven" or

"Just Deserts." Well endowed by an anonymous donor, it accepted the money of those movie old-timers, mostly from the long-lost days of the western, who could afford to pay and quietly subsidized those who couldn't. A building the size of a country hotel, surrounded by meticulously kept gardens, it was more grandly appointed than the Hogans' golf course condo—yes, those certainly were real Remingtons that decorated the spacious public rooms—but just because of what it was, it made Al Hasp feel hemmed in and claustrophobic. The three old men he was facing in a circle of easy chairs wore stern faces that made him no more comfortable. If one of these old faces went with the young one in the photograph, Al couldn't tell which one it was, but he could make a case for any of them. The eyes, the part of the face that provided the most clues over time, were shaded in the photo.

"The investigation's over," Emmett Donnelly said. He was a tiny, spider-like man with a terrible toupee, misshapen arthritic hands, and a way of moving that suggested too many falls off too many horses. "Some kid druggie murdered Clint."

"They've found the kid?" Al asked mildly.

"No, they ain't found the kid," Gimp O'Reilly roared. Though he had walked with a limp since a rodeo accident in his twenties, he was the best physical specimen of the three, big and powerful with a surprisingly unlined face under the ten-gallon hat that never left his head. The strength of his bass voice, able to reach any back row, suggested this cowboy might once have worked on the stage. "But that don't mean the case ain't over. Police don't got the manpower or the political backing to do their jobs, that's it in a nutshell. People get away with murder in this city every day."

"I've been out to the desert to talk to Grant Hogan," Al said.

Terry O'Neil asked, "And Margie? Did you see Margie?" O'Neil was the quietest of the three, round-faced and pudgy, looking more like a retired banker than a poverty-row cowpoke. Now his face had gone from a determined sternness that matched the others to a wistful softening. "She was a darlin' was my Margie. Wasn't she somethin', Gimp?"

"Oh, she was somethin' all right," O'Reilly replied, as always a few decibels louder than anyone else. "But she was never your Margie."

"I won't hear a word against her."

"That was a word in her favor, you horny old sidewinder."

"Jealousy, jealousy," murmured O'Neil in his affected Irish brogue.

"I gather Mrs. Hogan was well-liked," Al commented.

"We all were sweet on her," said O'Reilly, "but only Grant Hogan got her."

"Everybody loved her," Emmett Donnelly said, and the other two nodded.

"And what about Grant Hogan? Did everybody love him, too?"

The three old cowboys looked at each other during a significant pause. Finally, O'Neil said, "He was all right, I suppose. Can't say I loved him."

"He had more education than the rest of us," Donnelly said carefully. "Some thought he was kind of, what's the word, patronizing. He grew up with horses, just like we did, but he'd been to college and he'd read a lot of books and sometimes he seemed to feel superior to others."

"He knew Chekhov," Al said.

Donnelly looked blank. "I don't know him. Either of you guys know a Chekhov?"

"Never mind that," Al said. "I was just thinking out loud. Was Hogan jealous?"

"No reason to be," O'Reilly roared. "Marge never looked at another man. And if she hadda, it'da been somebody higher up the food chain than us dusty cowpokes."

"Nobody should ever marry a cowpoke," Donnelly muttered. "And that includes me."

"Didn't think you wanted to marry a cowpoke, Emmett," O'Reilly said.

"You know damn well what I meant."

"Grant Hogan suggested you fellows might be able to help me out on those three notations in Bortner's notebook," Al said. "His daughter Melissa wants to know what they mean."

"Well, go ahead," O'Reilly said impatiently. "What were they? Nobody mentioned any notebook to us." Clearly, they'd compared notes.

"How about the 'Three Sisters'?"

"Why, I think Clint had three sisters," O'Neil said. "Yes, I believe he did. Now, what were their names?"

"Bortner didn't have sisters," Donnelly said. "It was me had three sisters. At one time. They died one by one. One I can blame on Bortner, I don't mind telling you."

"What about 'Back to Ireland'?"

"That's a laugh," O'Reilly said. "Bortner wasn't Irish."

"Hogan told me a little story when I was down there," Al said. "About the time when you three and he and Bortner all went to Monument Valley to work on John Ford's *She Wore a Yellow Ribbon*."

For a moment, none of the three spoke. Then Donnelly said, "Do you have any idea how many western movies the three of us made, together or separately?"

"True, that is," chimed in O'Reilly, "from Gower Gulch to the soundstages of Fox and MGM. Lots more than we can remember."

"Lots more," O'Neil agreed.

They're making this too easy for me, Al thought. "So your time working with John Ford on a classic film wasn't all that memorable?"

Donnelly shrugged. "Work was work. It all runs together."

"Did you guys do a lot of drinking on movie locations?"

"We did a lot of drinking in those days, yes," O'Neil said, "but not while we were working."

"And the Navajo Reservation was dry back then," O'Reilly said. "Probably still is."

"But wasn't John Ford quite a drinker in his own right?" said Al. "Wouldn't he have had a supply of booze on hand for his own use?"

O'Neil shook his head. "You couldn't drink on a Ford location. That I do remember. Ford didn't drink when he was working, and he didn't allow anybody else to either."

"Did any of you fellows," Al asked casually, "get to go to Ireland with Ford when he made *The Quiet Man?*"

The three looked at each other in the silence that followed. O'Reilly spoke for the group, dropping completely the ignorant cowboy persona. "Not a lot of stunt work in *The Quiet Man*. It was a romance, not a western. We were all basically stuntmen, you see."

"But you all could read lines," Al said. "And Ford took lots of his regulars along. Ken Curtis, the old band singer."

Donnelly snorted. "He was Ford's son-in-law."

"And isn't it true Hogan and the three of you were all having tough times and were badly in need of a job at that time?"

"Hell, that was true at most times," O'Reilly said.

Enough sparring, Al decided. "I'm starting to think all three of you are in this together. Oh, I suppose only one of you swung that poker that cracked Clint Bortner's skull, but you're stonewalling me like a tag team, aren't you? All the times you've been to Monument Valley, how the hell could you not know what the Three Sisters are?"

"You get old, the memory goes," Donnelly said, and the looks he got from his two cronies told him how unconvincing that sounded.

"Here's what happened," Al said. "When *She Wore a Yellow Ribbon* was filming, some members of the cast or crew—I don't know who or how many—were smuggling booze onto the Navajo reservation, hiding the bottles at various strategic locations. Empty bottles were found at a male hogan and a female hogan—and don't tell me you don't know what those are—not far from Goulding's Trading Post, where the Ford unit was headquartered. Other bottles were found around the base of the Three Sisters. Ford was furious that somebody was sneaking drinks and he wasn't able to find out who it was. A few years later, when Ford was about to do *The Quiet Man* in Ireland, all of you were hoping to be a part of it. Besides being desperate for work, you were proud of your Irish heritage. You still had relatives there. You wanted to go. But you weren't chosen, and adding insult to injury, Clint Bortner, who wasn't even Irish, somehow was selected for a small part in the movie. You never knew why you were left out. Then one of you, while visiting Bortner in his apartment, saw his notebook lying on the table, figured out what those four phrases meant, and you realized that he had been the cause of your not getting that trip to Ireland, that he had somehow convinced Ford, whether it was true or not, that you were the ones smuggling liquor into Monument Valley during the shooting of *She Wore a Yellow Ribbon*. You, or one of you, got so angry, you picked up that fireplace poker and brained Bortner with it, then did what you could to make it look like a burglary."

"That's some fancy story," O'Reilly bellowed. "But you can't prove a thing."

"You wouldn't'ta found me in Bortner's room," Donnelly said.

"That's what your friend Hogan said. You were the most logical suspect, a guy who hated Bortner for your sister's death, but you were automatically eliminated from consideration because you wouldn't have been visiting Bortner in his room. That left you other two, O'Neil and O'Reilly."

"You can't prove a thing," O'Reilly said again. "Are you going to try to? You can tell Bortner's daughter Melissa what the notebook means—that's what she hired you for—and let it go at that, can't you? If what you and Hogan have come up with is true, and I'm not saying it is, old Clint Bortner was a poisonous critter who sold out his friends out of pure nastiness. Didn't he deserve to die?"

"Maybe he did. But I'd still like to know the truth."

"I have a question," Emmett Donnelly said. "I'm out of this, but I want to defend my friends here. If somebody murdered Clint Bortner because of what it said in his notebook, wouldn't that person have taken the notebook or at least torn out that page in order to avoid drawing suspicion to himself?"

"Seems like that wasn't necessary, Emmett," O'Neil pointed out.

Al said, "Maybe the killer found out some other way about what Bortner had done. Or maybe he had other grievances against Bortner and this just added to them."

"And which one of us desperate characters supposedly did this?" O'Reilly demanded. "According to our imaginative friend Hogan, I mean."

Al took out the picture of the scowling young cowboy from Hogan's album and passed it across to the three old cowboys. Donnelly looked at it first, gripping it with his gnarled hands and gaping at it. Then he passed it over to O'Neil, whose eyes widened in surprise. O'Reilly got it last and responded with a whoop of laughter.

"And which one of us do you think this is?" O'Reilly demanded.

"I've been trying to figure that out," Al said. "You've all changed over the years, obviously. But you remember what you all used to look like, don't you?"

Donnelly looked at O'Reilly. "What do you think? Could it be?"

"Sure. It was the day after that memorabilia convention Clint Bortner spoke at. Maybe Clint told the story of what he did to us there. Funny to him, a good joke, but very serious to us." O'Reilly poked a finger at the picture. "He was at that convention. He could have stuck around overnight. He could have come here the next day, done the deed, never seen the notebook references. Maybe Bortner wrote 'em *after* he told the story at the convention, to remember them for his memoirs. I never saw him here, but one more old fart could kind of blend into the woodwork."

"But poor Margie," said O'Neil.

"The guy confessed!" Donnelly said.

O'Reilly waved an impatient hand. "Ah, it means nothin'. He could say it's just a joke. He could say he wasn't serious. Still, I'll bet he was."

"What are you all talking about?" Al asked.

"A good joke on you, Mr. Private Eye. He's changed a good bit in fifty-some years, but this is a picture of Grant Hogan."

CELTIC NOIR

Paul Bishop

A

SEE, BOYO, I DON'T much give a frig iffin you're offended.
So, iffin you're being one of them gobshite bastards wots always gettin your knickers in a knot over a little sex and violence then best you be stoppin here.

Surely, aren't I always ready for a fight? But when Kink and Turner smashed open the door to Brigit's flat, I would have shite me shorts iffin I'd been wearing any. I thought it was the Garda at first, but the filth doesn't bother messing with good Catholic girls like Brigit.

I bounced instantly away from Brigit's fat bum—the girl might be named after the saint herself, but isn't she at least three times her size—and groped blindly for the fireplace poker I knew she kept beside the bed.

The flat is a one-room nothing with a thin mattress on the floor where Brigit and I had been doin' the business, so Kink and Turner didn't have far to go once they were through the door. Brigit scrambled away from me and started screaming. I will give her points for taking the time to throw an empty bottle of Guinness at Turner, but it didn't even slow him down.

Kink grabbed for me. The stupid berk must have thought I wouldn't fight knowing he and Turner works for Mandrake.

Unfortunately for him, I couldn't have given a frig iffin he worked for the Pope himself.

As Kink reached for me, I smashed the poker across his wrists, and then swung it back and caught him on the side of the throat. He's a big bastard with muscles on top of muscles, but he still fell to the floor howling like a stuck pig.

Turner backed off, his hands raised in a calming gesture I didn't believe for a second. "What the frig do you want?" I said, whipping the poker back and forth.

"Mandrake wants to see you, shite bucket," Turner said, keeping just out of me range. Kink was still moaning on the floor, and Brigit had turned up the volume of her screeching. She was struggling to cover herself with the bedsheet. That almost made me laugh. The last thing anybody in the room was concerned about was Brigit's udders.

"I've never borrowed from Mandrake."

"This ain't about money. He wants to talk to you."

"He can twirl his arse on a corkscrew."

I swung the poker again and brought it down across Kink's legs just for the sheer pleasure of it.

Brigit's screeching rose another octave to keep pace with Kink's new notes. "Shut up, you stupid slag," I yelled at her. "You're getting on me friggin pip."

When I bent down to snag me jeans off the floor, Turner made his move. And, wasn't I was ready for him to come? I brought the poker up square between his legs, trying to bat his testicles for six. His hands didn't even make it to his goolies. His eyes simply rolled up in his head, and he collapsed like the bag of shite he was.

"What's happening, Decco?" Brigit took a break from her screech-ing. Tears and sweat had run her eye makeup and she looked worse than ever. It made me fancy her again.

"Not to worry, luv," I said, stepping into me jeans and Doc Marten's. I ran a hand over the short black stubble on me head. "They won't touch you when they see I'm gone."

Brigit's eyes widened. "You can't leave me here with them!"

"Watch me," I said. I blew her a kiss, pulled on me leather jacket, and sprinted for the front door.

B

ON THE STREET, I stuck a fag in me gob before nicking an almost new Trident a pair of stupid sods—who shall remain nameless, but you can guess—had trustingly left out.

As I drove, I wondered what Mandrake wanted. Dublin isn't Belfast, but it's still a hard town that don't forgive when you screw up. Mandrake was your man when it came to crime—a mean little willie with ambitions.

At five-foot-six and a massive one hundred forty pounds of tattooed punk, I didn't fit the usual hardman category. Compared to Mandrake, I was a pissant, and I knew it. Mandrake was a right evil bastard, so I had two choices—run like hell, or talk to him.

I cranked the Trident's radio up loud. Me nose twitched. Something was in the air, but I wasn't sure if it was money or aggro. Either way, I was ready for it.

C

AS I STOOD WATCHING Mandrake's wrecking yard, a Garda car rolled by. The twits inside didn't even give me a second look. How that lot ever catch anybody is beyond me. Some of them—like Blake—are right bastards who take no stick from nobody. They're who you gots to worry about. The rest of them couldn't find their arse in the dark with both hands and a torch.

You might think I'm stupid. I ain't. I done loads of them Open University courses on the telly. I ain't stupid. I just ain't like you, and I don't want to be.

I hate effin squares like you—sitting there on your arse reading books. You're boring. I hate boring. Get up, get out, smash somebody's face in. That's what it's all about—a little aggro makes the world go round.

I don't give a shite if you understand me, but I'll give it one shot. Some people likes to drink. Some people likes to smoke. Some idiots like to stick shite in their veins and would swallow anything to get high. Meself? Me, now don't I likes to fight? I likes to feel me fist smash some spotty twat's nose across his face and put the boot in when he goes down. I like to smash me nut into some berk's face and walk away with the blood flowing. Shite that feels good. And isn't that the way of it?

Mandrake ran his business from a beat-up office at the back of his yard. It wasn't high class, but then neither was he. You had to give the bastard the truth of his roots. Corrugated metal fencing ran around the perimeter, and the tops of a couple of cranes could be seen above the fence line along with several stacks of flattened, junked cars.

I made me way around the back of the yard until I found a gap in the corrugated sheeting. There were a couple of big mongrel dogs in the yard who sniffed me out and came running. They were silent and salivating, but I have no fear of dogs and they know it. And aren't dogs almost worse than women when it comes to falling for bad boys?

As the two sleek lumps of fur and teeth charged forward, I extended an arm toward them and lowered it as I bent down. I whistled low through me teeth, and the two dogs suddenly started wagging their tails. They trotted happily behind me through the stacks of junked cars until I could see Mandrake's office.

The noise coming from inside was Mandrake going spare at Kink and Turner. I smiled and waltzed in unannounced, all attitude and cool.

"Wotcher, lads," I said to Turner and Kink. "Mr. Mandrake," I added with a touch of respect.

"You effin toe rag," Turner said.

"Temper," I said with a smug smile, and then kicked him square in the jewels. He went down puking all over himself.

I slid a straight razor out of me jacket sleeve. A sharp flick of the wrist and it whipped open like a switchblade, only deadlier. It was me weapon of choice, and even Kink knew me reputation with it. "Don't even fink about it," I said, pulling him up short on the balls of his feet. "I'll effin gut you from here to your mum's Sunday dinner."

"Put it away, you stupid git." This was from Mandrake. His voice was harsh from too many cigars and too much booze. I flicked the razor closed and disappeared it up me sleeve.

"How did you get past the dogs?" Mandrake asked.

"Nufing to worry about. Right welcoming wasn't they?"

"I don't like smart mouths," Mandrake said.

"And I don't like your effin bully boys disturbing me while I'm getting me end away. Scared piss out of Brigit they did."

Mandrake was a big man, all barrel chest and weightlifters' arms. He wore a flash waistcoat over a black dress shirt done up to the neck. The top button was covered by a diamond stud. "I should have you stuffed in a crusher and sent back to your mother in a soup can."

"Probably," I said, not of a mind to apologize. "Look, Mr. Mandrake. Iffin your messenger boys want to play rough, they shouldn't be surprised when somebody plays rough back." Kink stepped forward, but the razor was back in me hand and he pulled up short again.

"Get him out of here," Mandrake said to Kink with a nod of his head toward Turner. The bigger man hadn't moved since his testicles were introduced to his tonsils. Kink moved slowly away, dragging Turner by the pits.

"Sit down, Decco." Mandrake said me name awkwardly, as if it left a bad taste. "And put that silly razor away."

He wouldn't fink it was silly iffin I slashed him across the face from temple to chin, but I stowed the urge and slipped the cool steel into its familiar dark hole.

"You're like watching a bad movie," Mandrake said. "But I've been told you're useful despite acting like a dog dropping."

I knew the part about money or aggro was coming.

"I've got a job I want you to do," Mandrake said suddenly, as if coming to a decision. He sat down in the big leather chair behind his desk and swiveled back and forth. "I want you to find my daughter."

D

WELL, THAT WAS A bit of a surprise. Hadn't I been in school with Mandrake's daughter—Maureen by name? She was a brain. Knew everything and never seemed to study. Now, though, wasn't she a little punk slut of all things? She was a club raver, one of those I was telling you about wot would swallow anything to get high. The stupid bint was probably passed out in some back room, or colder than concrete on a slab.

There was always something odd about Maureen. Nasty rumor said Mandrake was impotent. Mrs. Mandrake once drunkenly said as much in a local pub. Next day she had a nasty fall, broke her nose, and blacked both eyes.

It kept her quiet for a while, but word was Mrs. Mandrake had recently been a bit loose with her tongue again and had been sent to visit her mother. Interesting, since her mother was dead.

"Where's she got to then?"

"If I knew, I wouldn't need to bother with a piece of shite like you."

I kept me mouth shut. I needed money more than aggro at the moment.

We exchanged stares for a moment before he said, "You take care of this little chore, and maybe I can find some other efforts to put your way."

"Iffin you say so," I said, a bit happier. "When did little Maureen do her Amelia Earhart?"

"She's been gone for three days."

"Is that unusual?" I asked.

"Not particularly," Mandrake said. "I rarely see the little cow these days."

So much for fatherly love. "Where'd you see her last then?"

"Here, in the office."

Mandrake wasn't being exactly forthcoming.

"Is there somefink I'm missing? You tell me you want me to find your kid, but it don't seem like you're burning up your Jockeys to get her back."

"Maureen took something that belongs to me."

"Right, yeah, go on. Wot? Money? Jewelry?"

"A book."

"A book? Now, that doesn't sound like somefink to get yourself knotted about."

Mandrake launched himself across his desk, and didn't he back-hand me so hard he nearly tore me head off? I hit the back wall of the office with a thump and slid down to the floor. The razor gots as far as me hand when Mandrake stepped on me knuckles and ground them into the floor.

I tried to give him a steel toe cap in the back of the knee, but me leverage wasn't right and he took the blow on his thigh. He didn't like it much, but it didn't do no damage. To him that is. He hit me six or four times with a fist as hard as me own skull.

When he was done exercising, he crouched down. There was blood in me mouth, and one of me eyes was down to a slit.

"Friggin' hell," I said.

"Shut up, you five-fingered shite hawk. You do as I tell you, or I'll cut your arsehole open and pull you through backwards. You've got forty-eight hours to find Maureen and get my friggin' book back. After hour forty-nine, nobody will even remember your name. Got it?"

E

THE PHYSICAL DAMAGE MANDRAKE had done me was mostly minor. In the bathroom of an Esso station, I hawked out a wad of blood before splashing water over me face.

The shiny, steel mirror over the basin showed a swollen eye and a bruise the size of a cricket ball. It was nothing time wouldn't solve. The fingers on me right hand, however, still throbbed like soddin' hell. I'd be lucky if I could make a fist, let alone hold me razor. Could be a problem.

As I left the Esso, me nose started twitchin overtime.

Two black Rovers suddenly pulled into the petrol station and dis-gorged a swarm of plainclothes Garda. They were all big and mean, with nasty little truncheons already exposed.

I took to me heels, but a third Rover cut off me escape, and two of the Garda caught up with me from behind. I was taken down to the ground, me already abused face scraping hard.

One of the filthy bastards stamped squarely on me spine before pulling me arms back and shaking me razor out of its hiding place. He knew it was there, so this was no case of mistaken identity.

"You're friggin nicked, mate," he said, as he clamped down on the manacles he'd slipped over me wrists.

"Get off me, you gob stupid berk!" I yelled.

As he hauled me to me feet by me chained wrists, I gave him a back heel in the goolies. He let me go and I took off running, but it was no good. Three steps later, another bastard smacked me in the back of the head with his truncheon and I went down like a ton of coal.

F

I WOKE UP ALONE in a cell. The bracelets had been taken off, but me head throbbed like a miners' brass band playing an off-key melody.

I heard the *look-in* slide open on the cell's metal door. After a few moments, the door itself swung open and a woman walked in wearing a dapper top coat. She had black hair cut short in ragged layers. Trouble. She was the filth. The Irish police. The bloody frigging An Garda Siochana's. Inspector Siobhan Blake took no prisoners, ever.

"Well, Declan," Blake said in a sweet tone. She was the only person who could ever get away with using me real name. "How nice to see you."

I sat up, even though it took a major effort. "Allo, Blakey." I tried a grin. "I'd have come to sees you iffin you'd asked."

It was Blake's turn to smile, but I could see the shark behind it. She wasn't a big lezbo bitch, but she was as hard as they come, and as crooked.

"Of course you would, Declan. But then I wouldn't have had this to hold over your grotty little head." She held up me razor, opening it to let the light from the bare electric bulb flash off the blade. "Carrying an offensive weapon with your record." Blake shook her head sadly. "How many years do you think that's good for? At least two, I'd say."

Me throat felt swollen closed. "Be reasonable, Blakey," I said. "Isn't it only a family heirloom? I'd never think of using it on anyone."

Blake laughed. A full-bodied boomer, it was, but it cut off as quickly as it started, and I knew trouble was coming.

"Don't try to be funny with me, guttersnipe. It's Inspector Blake to you. If I tell you to shite, you ask how much and what color, got it? If you don't, I'll use this heirloom and you'll be air-wanking for the rest of your life."

"Yes, Inspector Blake," I said. I had no doubt Blake could cut me willy off and never bat an eye. She'd get away with it, too. Had half the judges in her pocket and was sleeping with the other half. You didn't piss Blake off.

"That's better, Declan. Much better." Blake undid her coat to show a nice bit of blue sheath dress underneath. It was tight across her full breasts. "Now, you've been a naughty boy, haven't you?" Blake ran her thumb down the edge of me razor. She didn't flinch, but closed her eyes and shuddered slightly. I knew how sharp that blade was. Watching Blake play with it was making me sweat. Suddenly, she flipped the blade closed and stuffed it into her coat pocket.

"Aren't you going to ask me what particular bit of naughtiness I'm interested in?"

"Wasn't I sure you'd tell me?" I was still trying to figure a way out of this alive.

Blake's lips twitched. "How is Mandrake these days?"

Not good.

"Isn't he doin fine?"

"How's his daughter?"

"Maureen?" I was trying to stall. Blake. Mandrake. Not much difference between them.

Blake leaned forward. "Mandrake doesn't have but one effin daughter," she said quietly.

I held me hands out in surrender. "Look, just ask me what you wants to know."

"Where's Maureen?"

"I don't know. She's done a runner, and doesn't Mandrake think I can find her?"

"You?" Blake looked astounded. That stung.

"Yeah, me," I said. "Why not?"

"Because you are nothing more than a pimple on a pig's arse, Declan. An effin' waste of human protoplasm."

I sat on the edge of the metal cell bed and sulked.

"Did Maureen take Mandrake's book?"

"What book?" I asked. "Mandrake is worried about his daughter. She's into the punk scene and he thinks I can find her."

"That's rich," she said. Then she hit me. I hadn't noticed her getting closer, but suddenly her fist was deep in me gut. I found meself retching on the damp stone floor.

Blake crouched on her haunches next to me. "Don't ever lie to me, sunbeam. I'm a human lie detector." She smoothed her hand over me close-cropped scalp. It was a curiously intimate gesture, like a mother touching her son. However, the brass knuckles over her fingers shattered the illusion.

Blake's mouth was close to me ear. "Listen, sunbeam. I know Maureen's got Mandrake's book. She was supposed to bring it to me. Now either she's got a bad case of stupid and had a change of heart, or somebody's changed it for her. Either way, I want that book. Understand?"

"Yes." Even in me condition, her breath on me neck and the breast pushing into me shoulder were getting a rise out of me.

"You may be nothing but a grotty little scrote, but you're my grotty little scrote. Got that? You bring me that book and there's a hundred nicker in it for you. If you don't, I'll bury you and piss on the gravestone."

With that, she stood up, straightened her coat, and walked out of the cell. She left the door open.

Fifteen minutes later, I found the strength and the nerve to follow her.

G

MANDRAKE, HIS DAUGHTER, AND a hundred pounds on offer from the bitch herself Inspector Siobhan Blake. There was something effin weird about the setup, but for a ton in readies I was more than willing to ignore it. There was also a mass of aggro I was due to pay back. The pain of me bruises felt good, but it would feel even better when somebody else was on the receiving end.

I started searching at Copperface Jacks off Saint Stephen's Green. It weren't the most likely spot to find Maureen Mandrake, but word would travel and sooner or later aggro would happen—and aggro would lead me to the stupid slag.

The downstairs bar was packed. There were a few tasty bits about, but nothin that would look at me twice. The beer was lousy and bloody expensive. I downed one pint on the arm from the bartender, and snagged two others from tables when their owners weren't looking. The manager said he'd never even heard of Maureen—liar—and the DJ said he hadn't seen her in a week since selling her some quaaludes.

It was the same story at Buskers in Temple bar (a major quim spot if you pay the lolly to get into their Boomerang club), at the Brazen Head across the river (decent beer, too many tourists, crap music), the Palace Bar (darts, old dozers, and a punk gathering that scares everyone off on weekends), the Bridge (yuppie-crap-punk-wannabees), and McTurkel's (a guaranteed punch-up).

In McTurkle's, however, I spotted Jimmy Riddle, arsehole extraordinaire and purveyor of mayhem. From the boot of his car, he sold me two straight razors. One went up me sleeve, and the other down the side of me left Doc Marten. Armed and happy, it was time to downscale.

At Angels on lower Leeson Street (lap-dancing whores), I was met with blank stares (and wasn't that a good sign word was traveling?), and further down the street at Strings (more lap, less dancing), I was told Maureen was putting it about earlier at Red Box (punks and ravers). Shite, how thick did people think I was? Wasn't this the obvious setup? I certainly hoped so. I'd had enough piss beer to last a month and I needed to hit somebody.

At Red Box, I forced the emergency exit and slipped in. The new Harcourt Street train station was behind me, and inside BiggZ were whamming away on their first set—all attitude and cocaine.

Red Box was a dross bucket of a club knocked through on a cheap refurbish of the old train station. As its name implied, it was a giant square inside, the walls painted red with red strobes strung from the ceiling on unconcealed wires. The stage supporting BiggZ was nothing more than scaffolding, the planking matching the bar on the opposite wall, which had the rough wood supported on ancient beer kegs. And wasn't I less than surprised when Nicky Ryan—all six-foot-six of him—came up behind me?

"Upstairs, you," he yelled over the music, one of his meaty hands grabbing me shoulder. What he makes up for in height, he lacks in brains. Big, but slow. I left the hand there for the moment.

Upstairs, he shoved me into O'Malley's office. Sean O'Malley runs Red Box, but kickbacks to the Bray brothers—Mandrake's biggest competitors.

O'Malley is a little runt, but along with Nicky, he had two other heavies to back his play. I could feel meself getting aroused. This was what I lived for. Me pulse rate went up a notch.

"Decco, me old son," O'Malley said. He threw a dart past me head and into a cork board on the back of the closed door behind me. I didn't flinch. The music from downstairs was only partially muted, so conversation was loud.

"Wot do you want?" I asked.

"It's not me that wants something, now is it, Decco?" He threw another dart, closer to me head this time. I still didn't move. "Aren't you the one wandering all over town looking for something?"

"Somebody."

"Something. Somebody. No difference, since you're going to stop." He threw the third dart.

I exploded with pent-up lust. I snatched the dart out of the air, stomped on Nicky's instep with me Doc Marten's, and smashed me head back into his face. Staying in motion, I threw the dart at the biggest heavy, hitting him in the eye. He went down screeching.

O'Malley and his other goon stood flatfooted in shock staring at their mate. I couldn't have cared less. I elbowed Nicky in the face and then spun around to give him a steel toe to the knee. Two down.

With me razor out of me sleeve and flashing in the overhead light, I took a step and slashed the side of the other goon's face. Three down, and I was on to O'Malley himself. I had the little bastard by the hair with the razor at his throat.

"Right, me old son," I said, throwing his bog Irish back at him. "Where the fook is she?"

"I'll kill you for this, Decco."

I let the razor sink into the flabby skin of his neck. "Last chance. Where the effin hell is she?" With me other hand I wiped me fingers through the blood trickle and held them up for him to see. "See some sense, old son."

His eyes flickered. "Down the hall. The Brays have got her working a room. They think it's funny. If you take her, I might not get you, but they will."

"Won't we all be having fun in hell together then?" I said and smashed his head down onto his desk. It left a dent before it bounced off and he slummed to the floor.

The hallway was a knocking shop. The Brays ran whores on the streets and used the upper floor of Red Box for the mattress action. The Garda knew, but took their readies and stayed away.

I found Maureen in the third room on the right. She was doped up and laying under some sweaty bastard puffing himself out on top of her. I kicked him hard enough to curl him up and then rolled him clear.

Maureen wasn't registering any of this. I hauled her to her feet, grabbed a cotton dress from the floor and pulled it over her head, before half-walking her, half-dragging her out to the street.

The cold air seemed to revive her. "Who the fook are you?"

"Sir effin Lancelot," I said.

"I need a smoke," she said.

"Later." I dragged her to the side of a parked Fiesta and smashed the window with me elbow. I popped the locks and pushed her into the rear seat. I was about to get in and connect the wires under the dash, when another wire was slipped around me throat from behind. It bit into me skin as it pulled tight.

"Gotcha, you fooking weasel," Kink said.

Turner moved into me peripheral vision. The bastards must have been following me the entire time. He smiled and then hit me in the kidneys.

"Where are we going?" Maureen asked, from her unconcerned sprawl on the back seat.

Turner smiled. "Hell," he said.

H

HELL TURNED OUT TO be Mandrake's wrecking yard. I'd been bundled into the passenger seat and the wire around me neck secured to the headrest. Turner had tied me hands with a rough piece of rope and tethered them to the stick shift. He'd then driven while Kink sat in the back giggling and touching Maureen up as he tied her.

I couldn't say I was comfortable, but I was alive and in with a chance. Turner had, of course, relieved me of the razor in me sleeve, but he hadn't even thought to take a gander for the one down the side of me boot.

At the yard, Maureen and I had been left in the car while the two bully boys consulted with Mandrake. We were parked in a wide-open spot, and I figured I knew wot was comin. Apparently, so did Maureen.

"You stupid wanker. Why did you have to stick your face in?"

Now is that gratitude, I ask you?

"You like being humped by one sweaty geezer after another?"

"It beats the alternative."

I would have asked her what was the alternative, but at that moment it became clear. I could see Kink climbing into the driver's seat of a massive crane and crank over the engine. He maneuvered some gears and the huge magnet controlled by the crane began to raise up and swing our way.

"Why don't you just give Mandrake the effin book he's rabbiting on about?" I asked this knowing nobody had mentioned the book since Kink and Turner had grabbed us.

"I don't have his flaming book," Maureen said. It came out high pitched as she had started to pant with fear.

I gave this particular answer some thought. Remembering Maureen's performance in school, I connected the dots. "You gots one of them photogenic memories, don't you? That's why you always gots perfect scores on all the tests in school."

"And aren't you just the little Einstein?"

"You memorized his books, didn't you? Not his wrecking business books—his real business books."

"You're as thick as two planks. Not his business books, his bloody diary. Every filthy thing the bastard ever did."

"Well, shite."

The crane's magnet swayed back and forth above us before dropping down and smashing onto the Fiesta's roof.

"Flippin hell!" I said. "He's your father. Can't you make him stop?"

"He's not me fooking father!" Maureen was screaming. I felt like joining her, but instead I thought rapidly about what she'd just said.

"Your mother was heard blathering on about Mandrake being impotent—"

"And the bastard finally killed her for it."

Stuck to the magnet on its roof, the Fiesta shuddered as the crane lifted it off the ground. The car swung through the air.

"Is she in one of Mandrake's crushed soup cans?" If she was Blake and her Garda thugs could probably still find traces.

"Where else would she be? And isn't he going to put us in the same place?"

"Why go to the Garda with what you memorized from the books?"

"It would have fixed the bastard good." Maureen was straining against the ropes that bound her, yelling to fight her fear and be heard over the noise of the crane. "For hell's sake, he killed me mother."

"But why Blake, the head bitch herself?"

"Because Mandrake killed me father, too. Blake is me half-sister. It was her father, a copper himself wasn't he? He got me mother pregnant while trying to turn her against Mandrake. When Mandrake found out, he had him killed and terrorized me mother into silence. But the years of booze and pressure finally got to her, and she started telling anyone who would listen—including me."

"Why didn't you go straight to Blake?"

"I wanted the bastard to sweat. And then the Brays got a hold of me."

Maureen screamed again as the crane lowered and then dropped the Fiesta into the slot of the crusher. Thick metal walls clanged into both sides of the car. It was time to move.

I scrunched up and wiggled around to where me fingers could draw the second razor out of me boot. I fumbled with it for a second, the wire around me throat cutting deep as I struggled to see what I was doing.

I managed to slice through the rope tethering me hands to the gear shift without fuss, but the wire at me neck proved tougher. It wasn't pretty, and blood flowed, but I finally found some purchase on the wire where it went around the headrest and forced the blade through. The blade was sharp, the wire thin, and I was getting desperate as the sound of the crusher drove me on.

"What are you doing?" Maureen asked. Her eyes were huge as I scrambled past her and into the Fiesta's hatch area.

I lay on me back and kicked out with me Doc Marten's. It took three grunting tries, but eventually the hatch window shattered and showered me with safety glass. I jumped out of the car as the crusher made its first inward motion.

"You can't leave me here!" Maureen screamed when the car began to crease. And where had I heard that line before?

As soon as I popped out of the crusher's bay, Kink spotted me from his position in the crane cab. He shouted and pointed. Turner and Mandrake looked over from where they stood by the crusher's controls. Mandrake jabbed Turner, who stopped the crusher's movement. They wanted me inside, not out.

Mandrake's yard dogs were beside him. He immediately sent them after me and I loved him for it. As the dogs raced toward me, I extended me hand, palm down, and gave a low whistle—or tried to whistle. Me throat was clamped up.

I swallowed hard and tried again. This time sound came out and I lowered me hand as I crouched down. The dogs stopped, confused, wagging their tails slowly and looking back and forth from Mandrake to me.

"Good lads," I said, moving among them and fondling their ears. "Now, get him!" I sent them back racing toward Mandrake.

He saw them coming, disbelief in his eyes. The dogs were only too happy to have a direct command to obey. Mandrake called out to them, but they didn't so much as slow down. He turned and ran. Bad mistake. It turned him into lunch.

That left Kink and Turner. I flashed me blade at them. "Come on, boyos, let's dance." I must have looked crazed with the blood still flowing from me neck.

Neither of the bastards wanted to face me, but Turner was the one in the position to do something about it. With a malicious grin, he threw the switch to start the crusher moving again. He then picked up a discarded wrench and smashed the switch. He and Kink turned to run for the wrecking yard's front gate.

Shite! Turner and Kink or Maureen? Life is one effin decision after another.

The choice was made for me when Siobhan Blake and a clutch of uniformed Garda appeared across the yard entrance. And wasn't it a case of the followers following the followers.

With Mandrake a dog's dinner, and Kink and Turner under wraps. I turned to jump back up on the crusher. And should we praise the saints that Mandrake had been a cheap bastard. The crusher was donkey's years old and slow as me granny getting her leg over.

I ducked in through the hatch and sliced through Maureen's bonds. She scratched out at me with her nails, so I knuckled her in the face before dragging her clear. I dropped her over the side and jumped down next to her. Blake was standing, waiting.

The Fiesta popped and creased as the crusher finally forced it together with a solid crunch.

"And didn't you pull that one a bit fine?" Blake said.

"Where's me hundred nicker?" I asked.

"Where's the book?"

I pointed at Maureen. "Ask your sister."

Blake shot me a look. "You're on dangerous ground, Declan."

I sneered. "While you're at it, have your boffins look through the stacks of crushed cars."

"What for?"

"Wouldn't they be finding something of Mrs. Mandrake? At least enough to take to court."

"You'll get your money." Blake smiled. "You're still a wanker, Decco, but you're my wanker."

Fenian Ram

Simon Clark

John Philip Holland (1840–1914), educated in Limerick, Ireland, emigrated to America in 1873 where he invented the first viable submarine. The U.S. Navy purchased the Holland, *ordered six more, and the age of the submersible warship was born. Legend has it that he built his first submarine as a young man after the unsuccessful Irish uprising of 1867. Little remains of his early work, however, but a few tantalizing sketches . . .*
   —From *Birth of the Submarine*, by Captain E.A. Woolcombe; Curlew Press, 1967

December 5th, 1872

My Darling Kathleen,
   Isn't it a lunatic thing to sit here writing this letter? Isn't it madness to be writing to you to kill time when time is killing me? Isn't it even madder to be writing this when you are only four yours old? And isn't it the ultimate insanity that this letter can never ever reach you?
   But this letter unburdens me. And if, God willing, this should ever find you, you will be a grown woman with a husband and fine sons and daughters of your own, no doubt, and you will be breathing sweet air that

will be all the sweeter because it rides to you over mountains and great plains that are home to men and women who are free. The land and people who I write about now will be strange to you, and perhaps none stranger than I, your own father, one Augustus Nash Lamb. Augustus? Is that really a fine Irish name I hear you ask. No. Not at all, I'd reply. My widowed mother was housekeeper to a Quaker academic in the wild and windy county of Donegal. His was a house that sits as far north in Ireland as you can get without soaking your feet. There I was born (my father's posthumous son), received my rare name, and grew up amid a family of intellectuals. I gained enough learning to be forever a handicap to me and that would make me a stranger to my fellow countrymen.

Later the cancer took my mother, leaving me to return alone to her hometown of Cullenagh on the shores of County Kerry. I had just turned fifteen, a foreigner in my own homeland.

With a chip on my shoulder so big you could have driven a coach-and-four through, I drank away my youth, blacked the eyes of my compatriots in the Cullenagh pubs, womanized, and ruined the reputation of a wealthy widow who lived in the big house of Oisin that stood at the top of Cullenagh Falls. She fled to Dublin. Within months rumors came back like homing pigeons of a newborn child that shared my scowling eyes.

You can't employ a man like me who is eternally angry at the world, so I earned my shilling by setting lines for cod on the scaurs that run out in long fingers of rock from the beach. There, the Atlantic seethes and boils all white around the end of the rocks. A restless anger with no cause that mirrors my own.

Yet even on the darkest of stormy days sometimes a shaft of brilliant golden sunlight will pierce the cloud. Just for a moment or so it's as warm and as bright as summer. So it happened to me. How, I don't know, but I fell in love with your mother. Colleen was a golden-hearted soul with blue eyes, fair hair, and a way that could make me as gentle as the lamb that was my namesake. You were born the year after we married. Another burst of sunlight in my life. But like those short-lived flashes of light on a stormy day my happiness was over before it had seemingly begun. Colleen died of consumption on your second birthday. Once more I was angry at the world and all it held. I knew I had to give you up. At least, thank heaven, you were taken into my sister's family to be brought up as their own.

So, for me, it was a time of turmoil. I returned to my terrible ways, drank the booze like it was milk, blacked eyes, and roamed mountain-tops where I raged at heaven.

I did not like Cullenagh or its people. They did not like me. Yet I continued to circle the town like some dark raven. Not wanting to stay, yet somehow never able to break away. I was a son of that briny soil after all.

A year ago Lord Featherstone doubled the rents of his tenant farmers. Already dirt-poor, they pleaded that he reconsider. Within forty-eight hours the English soldiers had turned out the tenant farmers from their homes. Now families endure the winter in hovels made of sticks on common land. Menfolk are in hiding because Featherstone issued arrest warrants for unpaid rent that will put them in debtor's jail where they'll pick hemp until hell freezes over.

INTO THIS TURBULENT WORLD came one Mr. Holland, a young school-teacher with mild eyes, and a voice that rarely rose above a whisper. He brought with him the *Fenian Ram*. Not a farm animal as you might think but a wee boat that, he told me, would right many a wrong and set Ireland free. You see, he wished to conduct secret sea trials on that remote coast far from prying eyes.

Picture an iron fish with a tail and a long point of a spear for a nose. A big black fish; big enough to house four men in its belly, where panting and running with sweat they work a massive crank. The crank turns a propeller that, in turn, drives the boat through water. On top of this craft is something like a diver's helmet of brass set with little round windows. There, head and shoulders inside this brass dome, stands the captain of the *Fenian Ram*. "Crank faster, lads," he orders. Or: "Slower. Stop. Back crank!" And he steers with a rudder bar that's as long as a broom handle. Insanity again I can hear you say. There I am with three other fellows cranking away like a mad thing until we grunt with sheer effort. Even more insane when I tell you that the iron cylinder can dive under the sea like a whale. But wasn't it a fine, fine occupation for a man like me? Sixpence a day to funnel my dark rage into that crank handle. I didn't have to think; I didn't have to consider my future; or that my beloved daughter would grow up not knowing me. All I had to do was crank, crank, crank. Crank until our breath condensed on the cold iron walls as if that tiny ship were cracking open; crank until my heart beat with all the rhythm of a drum played by a lunatic.

So this was my life. Me, a crew member on this secret ship built by the freedom-fighting schoolmaster. Me, with my back to the world, its woes, its injustices: me, scowling into my metaphorical corner. And so this life would continue, I believed. But this morning everything changed when I found the man in Lord Featherstone's wood.

HE LAY ON HIS back beneath a tree. His arms were above his head, reaching out for the base of the tree as if to claw the bark with his fingernails. Whoever had cut his throat had the skill of a butcher, the cut through the gullet exposing a valley of raw meat that reached the bone at the back of the neck.

A cold wind ran up from the sea, but when I touched the man's face his flesh was somehow colder.

"Augustus Lamb. I knew you were a brawler, but a murderer?" The constable shook his head. "No. But it seems as if I'm mistaken."

I watched the uniformed man looking at me down the length of his rifle.

"It wasn't me, O'Ryan. I've just found the poor devil."

"A murderer always returns to the scene of the crime, doesn't he, Lamb?"

"I'm not the murderer and you know it."

"I do, do I, Lamb? Why's that then, man? You have an alibi?" He held the rifle steady, aiming at my heart. "No. I didn't think so."

"I was—"

"Sleeping the whiskey off in a hayloft. Yes. I don't doubt. After you'd cut this poor wretch's throat."

"It wasn't having his throat slit that killed him."

"Cut himself shaving, did he? Nasty cut, eh? Then what? He tripped over that root while out walking?"

"No."

"Oh, so you do know something then? Come on, man, keep working that tongue of yours. Do you know him?"

"No."

"No, eh?" O'Ryan moved closer to get a better look at the body. "Well, I haven't seen the feller before. Must be a stranger to the town. But he hasn't traveled here recently. His boots look a might too clean to have been walking far in this weather." He jerked his head back at the muddy road. The constable's own boots were smeared with sandy mud that was as pale as whitewash.

"He wasn't walking out last night, either," I added.

"And why do you suppose that?"

"He's not wearing a coat, only shirtsleeves."

"Then someone stole his coat after he was dead. Do you own a blood-stained coat, Lamb?"

"He wasn't wearing a coat when he was outside. His shirtsleeves are rolled up to the elbow. Surely he would have rolled them down before putting on his coat."

"Perhaps," the constable allowed reluctantly. "Now sit yourself down on the ground, Lamb."

"What are you going to do?"

"I'm going to put a chain on you. I don't want you running, do I now? And I don't propose to stand here all day pointing this gun at you."

"Surely you don't think I did this?"

"I'd wager you'd beat a man to death in a bar before long, but I didn't think you'd kill in cold blood."

As he locked the handcuffs to my wrists behind my back I said, "You're going to arrest me?"

"I'll not be charging you yet, but I'll be obtaining a warrant of restraint from Lord Featherstone, then you'll be held in jail pending the magistrate's investigation."

"You're no friend of Featherstone," I told him, angry.

"I'm executing my duty as town constable, Lamb."

"What was in that sack you've got there, O'Ryan?"

"None of your business."

"I know you have sisters living out on the common. Featherstone turned them and their husbands out of their homes. You've been taking them food, haven't you? Featherstone wouldn't thank you for that, would he?"

"You keep that mouth shut of yours, Lamb. I'll break your head into a dozen pieces if you mention that to his Lordship."

"Why should I worry? They'll hang me anyway."

"Maybe."

"I didn't kill this man, O'Ryan."

"Stop lying to me then and tell me what you know."

"I'm not lying, but you can see the man wasn't even killed here."

"How do you know that?"

I nodded at the corpse. "See? He never walked here."

"He flew then, I suppose."

"Look at the soles of his boots. They don't have a fleck of mud on them. They're clean. The man was taken from his house and carried here. Look nearby and you'll find fresh hoofprints from a horse or mule."

"I'd heard you were a clever so-and-so."

"I've never claimed that."

The constable looked at me with knowing eyes. "You can read and write?"

"Yes."

"That sets you apart from nine-tenths of the town, then. Now what does that big brain of yours tell you about the dead man there?"

"He was dead before the killer cut his throat. If he were still alive he'd have bled all over the ground. There's scarcely a drop. If you were to open a vein I'd wager you'd find the blood's already congealed there."

"Then how did he die?"

"There's a little blood in the nose, but no wounds I can see other than the one to the throat—and that was made to disguise the real cause of death."

The constable squatted beside the body that was the color of clay there in the cold morning light. "There is blood in the nose. I daresay there was more on the face but it looks to have been wiped away."

"Are the fingernails torn?"

O'Ryan shot me a surprised look. "Yes," he said, "they are. The knuckles are grazed, too. He fought his attacker before he was overwhelmed."

I shook my head. "No, he *was* fighting to escape, but not from a man."

"You're playing games with me, Lamb. You know what happened, don't you?"

"The man was asphyxiated. That's why there are no marks on his body. A symptom of asphyxiation is bleeding from the nose."

The constable was a man of strong instincts. He knew I hadn't been as free with the truth as I ought. "Speak out, now. Who is this man?"

I sighed. "He's a Frenchie. Guy Drancourt. I worked with him. He and I were crew members on a . . ." I checked myself just in time. "On a fishing smack."

"You're a poor liar, Lamb. I know you're working on the school-teacher's daft little boat. Was he?"

"Yes." I shook my head in surprise. "But you mean to say you know about—"

"Of course I do, man. It's my job to know what goes on round here. I know that Charlie Bibby's been poaching his Lordship's land every night for the past month. He took the herd's stag last night."

My look of bewilderment must have said it all.

The constable explained. "Bibby's been feeding those poor devils living up on the common, my relatives included. I'd be no better than Lucifer himself if I arrested him for that."

"But you must know that the submersible has been built to sink English battleships. Once this thing has been made to work then we'll be building—"

"There you go with your runaway tongue again, Lamb. I don't know any such thing about the schoolteacher's boat being a warship. As far as I'm concerned it's just a harmless bit of eccentricity on Mr. Holland's part. A man's entitled to that. Now." He jerked a thumb at the corpse. "How did that man die—exactly how."

"I don't know."

The constable shot me an angry look. Clearly, he didn't want taking for a fool any longer.

"I swear, O'Ryan. I don't know the exact details of his death. But yes, I do know the man, and when I saw him three days ago he was alive. But my guess is that there has been an accident with the submersible. He was trapped in the vessel and stifled as the air was used up. See, he ripped his hands trying to claw his way out."

"When was the last time you went out on the vessel?"

"Three days ago when I saw Drancourt."

"What have you been doing since then?"

"I've been away to Kilbarron."

"Which is the only place hereabouts that will serve you drink no doubt."

"What are you doing?"

"What does it look like? I'm going to take the chain off you."

"I thought you were putting me in jail?"

"I still might do that. But first you can show me where the school-teacher hides this miracle boat of his."

O'RYAN WAS GOOD TO his word. He took the cuffs from my wrists and we walked side-by-side through the wood to the clifftop. The wind had dropped by this time but the sea still ran a ferocious swell onto the rocks below. Every so often a wave hit the cliff bottom with a mighty thump that sent spray up a hundred feet to wet our faces. And all the time the gray December cloud streamed from those far-flung reaches of the ocean.

At last I voiced what had been on my mind. "There's a detail that's been troubling me, O'Ryan."

"And what's that?"

"Why haven't you reported the murder to the magistrate first before bringing me down here?"

"The corpse is not likely to stroll away, is he?"

"There's more to it than that, isn't there?"

"So you are a shrewd man, Augustus Lamb." He paused for a moment, catching his breath while looking out to sea. "But you're right. If I were to report a killing such as this—a possibly politically motivated murder—the magistrate might suppose then he'd call in the English soldiers to occupy the town until he was convinced otherwise."

"You'll have to report the crime sometime."

"And I will, Lamb. I've decided to file my report tomorrow." He looked at me. "You see, a number of Lord Featherstone's tenants have had more than a belly full of being treated no better than slaves." He walked briskly away, still talking. "A schooner is leaving on the evening tide for America. Officially, it's carrying bales of wool." He gave a shrug that amply conveyed the rest.

"Your sisters will be on there, too."

"Aye, and their husbands. But as there are debtors' warrants on them, they have to leave like thieves in the night. I wish it wasn't so. But there you have it. Their only desire is to live like human beings." He shot me a look. "Your own sister is leaving with her family, too. But you didn't know that?"

"No." I shrugged my shoulders, feeling ice in the pit of my stomach. "But I don't communicate that well round here as you know."

"Aye, you're a black sheep, no doubting that. And you've only yourself to blame, man. Now, is the boat in this cove?"

"The next. Below the old abbey ruin."

"Well, come on then, what's wrong with you, man?"

"My daughter will be on that schooner, too, then."

"Aye, she will. But take heart, Lamb, she'll be away to a better life in America." Those direct eyes on me again. "There's no point mewling about it. You're no good as a father to her now, are you?"

NEWTON, ONE OF MY fellow crewmen, coiled rope on the little jetty. Bobbing beside it was the *Fenian Ram*. Painted Bible black, the craft appeared as a tear-shaped shadow there in the water.

"Keep out of sight while I ask Newton some questions," I told O'Ryan. "If he sees a constable he'll scarper before we get anyway near."

Slipping the rifle from his shoulder, O'Ryan nodded his agreement and ducked behind a line of bushes. I continued down as if nothing were amiss. I walked with my hands in my pockets, kicking stones, whistling a jaunty air. Newton looked up at me as if nothing were amiss, too. For all the world it looked as if he were readying the *Fenian Ram* for another of her sea trials.

"We taking her out, Newton?" I asked.

"Only into the bay," he said, working the rope into a huge, dripping coil.

"But Mr. Holland won't be back until the end of the week, will he?"

"He sent word to test her against the old wreck with the torpedo."

I noticed a pair of strangers watching me from the hut on shore that served as the secret workshop. "Is this new crew?" I asked.

"Mr. Holland said we needed to train more men to sail her." Casually, Newton put the coiled rope over one of the jetty posts. "While you're here," he said, "you can get on board and check the steering gear. Her rudder's seized."

"It looks all right to me."

"It comes and goes. I reckon one of the tiller lines is frayed where it runs over the pulley aft. You go down below and check. I'll shout down and let you know if the rudder's moving freely enough."

"Right you are." I hopped onto the iron back of the boat, raised the hatch, and climbed down into the belly. Inside, there was barely room to stand straight and the entire cabin wasn't much more than fifteen feet from end to end.

Enough light came through the portholes in the dome atop the hull to see the lines running at either side of the cabin back to the steering gear.

"How is it?" Newton called.

"They seem all right to me. Are you sure they're—hey! Wait! What the devil are you doing!"

With a clang Newton slammed the hatch shut. The moment I scrambled back to it, I saw blood smears around the hatch on the iron walls. So this is how they'd finished Drancourt. He'd been tricked down here on some pretext like me. Newton had swung down the hatch and barred it from the other side. Of course the vessel was airtight. Within a few hours the air would have turned foul and the Frenchman would have suffocated. No wounds on the body. No fatal ones anyway. But here were the bloodstains on the hatch where he'd clawed his hands to raw flesh trying to escape. Then he'd been carried away up to Featherstone's wood where his throat had been cut to make it look like the work of some common bandit. But why was Newton doing this? For the last six months we'd stood side-by-side working the crank. And who were those strangers on the beach?

I climbed up to the portholes. There I could see Newton walking along the jetty to meet the two men. They were talking. But what they were saying heaven alone knows, because this iron cylinder was sealed against sound as well as fresh air. There was little doubt now, however, that they'd leave me to choke on my exhaled breath. That might take four or five hours, but they looked patient enough. One took out a pipe and lit it. What struck me then was that all three seemed peculiarly interested in what was happening out at sea.

My view from the porthole in the brass dome wasn't a particularly good one, and for a good few minutes, I couldn't see what they were looking at. But at last I made out smoke, a funnel, then the sea swell lifted the *Fenian Ram* up a good two feet and I saw it.

A British gunboat had steamed into the mouth of the bay. The muzzles of its great cannon gleamed silver. It had all the stealthy might of a monster waiting for its prey to happen by.

When I turned back to the three men, they appeared to be so unperturbed by the presence of the gunboat that they'd taken to sitting on the jetty. Then I identified the reason for this: O'Ryan had that rifle of his aimed at them. I watched as he chained them together. Then he talked to them for upwards of twenty minutes. When he didn't appear to get the kind of answers he was hoping for, he poked the muzzle of the rifle non-too-gently into the side of Newton's neck.

Newton's head bobbed and he had such a look of fear on his face that I wondered if he wouldn't start wailing. Presently, O'Ryan walked down the jetty and I heard the clang of his boots on the boat's hull. In a moment he'd opened the hatch to admit that sweet cold air.

"Newton killed Drancourt," I told the constable as I climbed out. "You can see the bloodstains on the inside of the hatch where the man tried to claw his way out."

"So the man told me. With encouragement." He shrugged the rifle onto his shoulder. "He and his two cronies planned to sell the schoolteacher's little miracle boat here to the English."

"And Mr. Holland would be none the wiser. He won't be back until the end of the week."

"You'll also realize that the Frenchman discovered their intentions, so Newton shut him up in that floating coffin and watched him stifle himself."

"What now?"

"I'll keep these three locked up somewhere quiet for a couple of days, but the problem is that beast." O'Ryan nodded out where the gunboat sat guarding the bay. "The English have been told there's a valuable prize waiting for them somewhere hereabouts. A boat that can swim through water like a fish to sink the biggest battleship? Why, it's going to be worth more than its weight in gold. When these fellers don't deliver, the English are going to come looking for it. What's more, they're going to blockade the approaches to Cullenagh harbor. They'll search every ship in and out to make sure that little boat isn't spirited away."

"They'll stop the schooner tonight?"

O'Ryan nodded. "So they will. And they'll find that half-starved parcel of humanity bound for America. Just what I can do about that I don't know."

"I have an idea," I told him. "But I will need the use of your cuffs."

"THIS IS INSANITY!" NEWTON screamed the words at me. "*Insanity! Do you hear me!*"

"I hear you, Newton. Crank faster."

"No, we'll not do that."

"You've no choice. I'll put this axe through your head if you choose to mutiny now."

"Mutiny! You're insane, Lamb."

"Of course I am. You know that, Newton. I've been mad with anger for years. I've drank like a fish. I've brawled. But now I've the opportunity to redeem myself. You, too."

"No, Lamb. I'm not doing this. You're going to kill us."

But he did do it. And maybe Newton did redeem himself after all. Picture us, my dear Kathleen. I'd chained Newton and one of the strangers to the crank. I took the tiller, and standing there, head and shoulders in the brass dome, I guided the *Fenian Ram* away from her dock and into the bay. The swell had quieted somewhat, yet still it lifted her high onto those glassy mounds then dropped her into the dark hollows of the ocean. The sea slid over her hull leaving only the dome above the surface. With the help of O'Ryan I'd primed the torpedo. The constable is a good-hearted Irishmen, I realized at last. Even with all his blarney about breaking my head.

So there we were, the two men cranking like mad things (the sharp axe a reminder of my orders). Myself steering. At the end of the long pole that juts out from the vessel's nose was the hefty cylinder that contained a hundred fifty pounds of blasting powder. Two hundred yards ahead was the gunboat, sitting at anchor. I knew that in a few hours it would seize the schooner bound for America with its fragile cargo and you, my beautiful clear-eyed daughter.

Moments later, I sang out: "One hundred yards."

So this is the right thing to do, isn't it? If only Mr. Holland could know that his brave little craft can operate as well with a crew of just three.

"Eighty yards."

I looked out through the porthole, the tiller in my hand, the waves rolling the *Fenian Ram* from side to side, spray dashing against the glass, but still she held true to course.

"Fifty yards."

The slumbering leviathan lay at anchor. The guns were turned toward the harbor town ready to blaze at any ship daring to run. I saw the crew standing on decks, waiting for their orders. Still we hadn't been seen. But then, who'd notice this dome little bigger than a stew pot resting in the water, with the black hull of the boat lying invisible beneath the surface?

"Thirty yards and closing."

At that moment the sun pierced the gray winter cloud. An immense wash of radiance enfolded our craft. The sea turned the purest blue; the foam tipping the waves shone whiter than altar cloth. And at that moment it seemed we were sailing toward the gates of paradise.

"Twenty yards."

Mr. Holland had intended that magnets would fix the explosive charge to the side of a ship. Then the *Fenian Ram* would move to a safe distance before detonating the torpedo by a connecting line.

"Ten yards."

There were no magnets in the workshop; those were the items that Mr. Holland was himself collecting in Dublin.

"Five yards."

The torpedo at the end of the spar struck the gunboat below the water line. That was the moment I pulled the firing cord.

For a dozen or more years I carried a furnace of anger in my heart that roared and blazed and seared me from within. Anger that all the drink in Ireland couldn't douse. But at that instant my anger left me. It seemed to me it blazed like a shooting star from my fingertips, along the firing line, along the wooden spar and into the drum of blasting powder. It was my anger that exploded. It was my fury that ripped open the iron monster that would have claimed my daughter. It was my rage—red as blood—that drove the gunboat over onto its side, then down to the bottom of the Atlantic.

It's brighter here on the seabed than I could have thought possible. Sunlight filters down through shifting veils of blue. The sand is rippled and it is the color of gold. Fish move like living diamonds. Light that appears to be the stuff of halos cascades through the portholes. And it is bright enough to see the hairs on the back of my hand. Mr. Holland would be pleased to learn that although his *Fenian Ram* lies deep in the ocean, dragged down by the passing of the gunboat, it is still watertight. The two men here have made their peace with God. I've sat for an hour or more scribbling with this pencil in the ship's log.

But enough is enough, isn't it, Kathleen? I've said my piece. The anger is gone. I am serene. Now I will seal this book inside an oilskin and lay my head down to sleep. I hope I dream of you walking on a beach on the other side of the world. You will have your mother's beautiful eyes, your mother's grace and gentleness. May I dream, dear Lord, that this book is washed upon that other shore; that you find it—and you know that even though I could not be there, I always loved you.

Your loving father,
Augustus Nash Lamb

Authors' Bios

Peter Tremayne is the pseudonym of Peter Berresford Ellis, a Celtic scholar who lives in London, England. He conceived the idea for Sister Fidelma, a seventh-century Celtic lawyer, to demonstrate that women could be legal advocates under the Irish system of law. Sister Fidelma has since appeared in eight novels, the most recent being *The Monk Who Vanished*, and many short stories that have been collected in the anthology *Hemlock at Vespers and other Sister Fidelma Mysteries*. He has also written, under his own name, more than twenty-five books on history, biography, and Irish and Celtic mythology, including *Celtic Women: Women in Celtic Society and Literature* and *Celt and Greek: Celts in the Hellenic World*.

Brendan DuBois is the award-winning author of short stories and novels. His short fiction has appeared in *Playboy*, *Ellery Queen's Mystery Magazine*, *Alfred Hitchcock's Mystery Magazine*, *Mary Higgins Clark Mystery Magazine*, and numerous anthologies. He has received the Shamus Award from the Private Eye Writers of America for one of his short stories and has been nominated three times for an Edgar Allan Poe Award by the Mystery Writers of America. He's also the author of the Lewis Cole mystery series—*Dead Sand*, *Black Tide*, and *Shattered Shell*. His most recent novel, *Resurrection Day*, is a suspense thriller that looks at what might have happened had the Cuban Missile Crisis of 1962 erupted into a nuclear war between the United States and the Soviet Union. This book also recently received the Sidewise Award for best alternative history novel of 1999. He lives in New Hampshire with his wife, Mona.

P. M. Carlson taught psychology and statistics at Cornell University before deciding that mystery writing would be more fun. Carlson's novels have been nominated for the Edgar Award, the Macavity Award, two Anthony Awards, and selection to the *Drood Review of Mystery*'s top ten list. Ten earlier Bridget Mooney stories, including two nominated for the Agatha Christie Award, are collected in *Renowned Be Thy Grave*. She was also the 1992–93 president of Sisters in Crime.

Doug Allyn is an accomplished author whose short fiction regularly graces year's best collections. His work has appeared in *Once Upon a Crime*, *Cat Crimes Through Time*, and *The Year's 25 Finest Criman and Mystery Stories*, volumes 3 and 4. His stories of Tallifer, the wandering minstrel, have appeared in *Ellery Queen's Mystery Magazine* and *Murder Most Scottish*. His story "The Dancing Bear," a Tallifer tale, won the Edgar Award for short fiction for 1995. His other series character is veterinarian Dr. David Westbrook, whose exploits have been collected in the anthology *All Creatures Dark and Dangerous*. Allyn lives with his wife in Montrose, Michigan.

Mary Ryan lives in Dublin, Ireland, and has bought a house near Carcassone, France, where she seeks the peace and quiet to write her novels. Married with two sons, she is a graduate of University College, Dublin, and a qualified lawyer, but has now given up her practice to concentrate on her writing. Published in the United Kingdom, Eire, United States, France, and Germany, her titles include *Glenallen*, *Whispers in the Wind*, *The Seduction of Mrs. Caine*, *The Promise*, *Summer's End*, *Mask of the Night*, and *Song of the Tide*.

Edward D. Hoch is probably the only man in the world who supports himself exclusively by writing short stories. He has appeared in every issue of *Ellery Queen's Mystery Magazine* since the early 1970s and manages to write for several other markets as well. He has probably created more short story series characters than anybody who ever worked in the crime fiction field. And what great characters, too—Michael Vlado, a Gypsy detective; Dr. Sam Hawthorne, a small-town GP of the 1920s who solves impossible crimes while dispensing good health; and, among many others, his outre and bedazzling Simon Ark, who claims, in the proper mood, to be two thousand years old. Locked room, espionage, cozy, hard-boiled, suspense, Ed Hoch has done it all and done it well.

Jane Adams, who lives in Leicestershire, England, is married with a son and daughter. She has a degree in sociology and was once the lead singer in a folk rock band. In 1995, she was nominated for the prestigious John Creasey Award for best new crime writer for her novel *The Greenway*. Her other novels include *Cast the First Stone*, *Bird*, *Fade to Grey*, *Final Frame*, and *The Angel Getaway*. Her works have been published in the United Kingdom and translated in Denmark, Germany, Japan, and France.

Jeremiah Healy's street-smart detective John Francis Cuddy has appeared in several novels, most recently *Invasion of Privacy*. He's also made several appearances in anthologies, including *Legal Briefs*, *Cat Crimes II*, and several of *The Year's 25 Finest Crime and Mystery* volumes. A former president of the Private Eye Writers of America, he has spoken extensively about mystery writing around the world, including at the Smithsonian Institution's Literature series. Recently he was elected president of the International Association of Crime Writers.

Wendi Lee is the author of four novels featuring PI Angela Matelli, the latest being *Deadbeat* and *He Who Dies* . . . . Her westerns include the "Jefferson

Birch" series and *The Overland Trail*. She has published numerous short stories in the western, horror, and mystery genres, and is free-lance editor.

Mat Coward is a British writer of crime, SF, horror, children's, and humorous fiction, whose stories have been broadcast on BBC Radio, and published in numerous anthologies, magazines, e-zines in the UK, U.S., and Europe. According to Ian Rankin, "Mat Coward's stories resemble distilled novels." His first nondistilled novel—a whodunit called *Up and Down*—was published in the USA in 2000. Short stories have recently appeared in *Ellery Queen's Mystery Magazine*, *The World's Finest Crime and Mystery Stories*, *Felonious Felines*, and *Murder Through the Ages*.

Robert J. Randisi has had more than 350 books published since 1982. He has written in the mystery, western, men's adventure, fantasy, historical, and spy genres. He is the author of the Nick Delvecchio series and the Miles Jacoby series, and is the creator and writer of *The Gunsmith* series, a 230-book series for which he writes under the pseudonym of J. R. Roberts. He is the founder and executive director of the Private Eye Writers of America.

Bill Crider won the Anthony Award for his first novel in the Sheriff Dan Rhodes series, *Too Late to Die*. His first novel in the Truman Smith series, *Dead on the Island*, was nominated for a Shamus Award, and a third series features college English professor Carl Burns. His short stories have appeared in numerous anthologies, including past *Cat Crimes II* and *III*, *Celebrity Vampires*, *Once Upon a Crime*, and *Werewolves*. His recent work includes collaborating on a series of cozy mysteries with television personality Willard Scott. The first novel, *Death Under Blue Skies*, was published in 1997, and the second, *Murder in the Mist*, was released in 1999.

The short story is arguably the most demanding of all literary art forms, and few people ever master it. **Clark Howard** is one of the few. While his thirteen novels, including *The Hunter* and *Love's Blood*, are all exciting and rewarding books, his short stories display an even greater number of gifts and talents. His two stories, "Animals" and "Horn Man," are among the best written by anyone of his literary generation. And the amazing fact is that he continues to work at that level. Born in Tennessee, he has also written several true-crime books, including exposés on Alcatraz prison, the infamous Zebra serial killer, and the book *Brothers in Blood*, dealing with a case of murder in Georgia.

Jon L. Breen has written six mystery novels—most recently *Hot Air*—and over seventy short stories; contributes review columns to *Ellery Queen's Mystery Magazine* and *The Armchair Detective*; was shortlisted for the Dagger Awards for his novel *Touch of the Past*; and has won two Edgars, Two Anthonys, a Macavity, and an American Mystery Award for his critical writings.

Paul Bishop divides his time between writing best-selling mystery novels and heading up the Sex Crimes and Major Assault Crimes departments of the Los Angeles Police Department. During his twenty-year tenure, he has worked on a federal task force that coordinated with the L.A. Sheriff's Department, the FBI, CIA, and the Secret Service. Although his main series character is a female homicide detective named Fey Croaker, he also writes about a one-eyed ex-soccer goalie-turned-private-eye. His latest book is a collection of his short fiction entitled *Patterns of Behavior*.

Born in 1956, **Simon Clark** has contributed many stories to anthologies and magazines in the United Kingdom, United States, and to the BBC. His novels have been published in both Great Britain and America, and translations have appeared in Greece, Norway, and Russia. His novels include *Nailed by the Heart*, *Blood Crazy*, *Darker*, *King Blood*, *Vampyrrhic*, and *The Fall*. His latest work, inspired by the late John Wyndham and set to be published in Summer 2001, is entitled *Night of the Triffids*.

COPYRIGHTS AND PERMISSIONS

Printed in the USA
CPSIA information can be obtained
at www.ICGtesting.com
JSHW022211140824
68134JS00018B/991